1. A ROYAL VISIT

Thomas Ley was born in 1599, and so like his great contemporary Oliver Cromwell, he was always one year older than the sixteen hundreds. His home in Cheshire was in the land of cheese and salt—particularly the latter as far as he was concerned—for by trade he was a briner. The industry, through which since early times his town of Nantwich had gained its fame, was the manufacture from brine of white salt; though by this time its prosperity had already declined. In the days of King Henry VIII there had been three hundred workers engaged in the making of salt, and though the seventeenth century saw the beginning of the trend which resulted in its eventual extinction, it was still an important industry upon which the well—being of the second town in Cheshire depended. But salt—making was at this time restricted by the antiquated laws which governed it.

"It's the fault of those Lords of Walling and their hide—bound rules and regulations," Tom's mother often said. "They are taking the bread out of the poor folks' mouths."

It was true that the laws controlling salt manufacture at that time discouraged industry and innovation. Four officers were appointed yearly to regulate the 'walling', as the boiling of salt was called. When it was due the crier made a proclamation, and it was given out which houses were to make salt at that time—this being twelve at the most. Each house had a certain number of boilings allotted during the year and that number could not be exceeded. As the bellman passed the fires were kindled, and from the chosen houses among the veritable forest standing along both banks of the narrow, sluggishly—flowing river, smoke rose above the holes in the thatch which substituted for chimneys.

Thus the day's work began. Twenty six hours made a boiling—two being allowed for the cleaning of pans. Four days' walling made a kindling, at the end of which allotted time the fires were extinguished. Woe betide anyone who continued illegally to boil brine! The Lords of Walling exercised their authority to the full. The miscreant could be fined or have dirt thrown into his salt. In extreme cases he was sentenced to see his house pulled down about his ears.

A great proportion of the workers in the wich houses were women, but it was men who had to draw the salty water from the cold, dark pit. As one of these 'briners' Tom had the most unpleasant job in the industry. Standing near to the river and several yards deep, the spring yielded its never-ending flow of brine to feed the hungry pans. Here the young man drew up the cold water in buckets and poured it into troughs covered with boards, which carried it to the great tanks known as 'ships'. There it was stored for the next walling, whence it was drawn into the wich house to be boiled away for its residual salt.

In winter Tom's occupation was most unenviable; the cold was so intense when cleaning out the pit that the briners had to be dosed with strong drink; but in summer it was tolerable, so on this August day in 1617 the discomforts were forgotten. Nantwich had a royal visitor in the person of King James who expected to see something of the industry for which this part of his kingdom was renowned.

The town was buzzing with excitement long before the king arrived. He had entered the county over Warrington Bridge on his way back from Scotland to London. In Lancashire he had visited Hoghton Tower before stopping again at Lathom House. In both places he had been entertained lavishly. Leisurely royal progresses and hunting expeditions were a characteristic of this former king of Scotland's reign who, since his accession to the English throne, had shown himself in different parts of his new kingdom, expecting a royal reception, much to the discomfort of the gentry, to whom these visits usually meant unaffordable expenses and sometimes even bankruptcy.

From Warrington the royal party descended the vale of the Mersey to Halton and thence to the castle of Rocksavage. This residence overlooked the waters and marshes bordering on the river. An easy ascent led up from the lower meadows; around the house were gardens, orchards and pleasant walks. The king was greeted by Sir Thomas Savage, and having feasted rightroyally in that gentleman's hall, he killed a buck in Halton Park.

Next James went to visit Lady Mary the widow of Sir Hugh Cholmondeley at Vale Royal, the mansion on the site of the Abbey dissolved by King Henry in 1540. Sir Hugh, a distinguished soldier in the reign of the late Queen, had been knighted by her on the eve of the expected Spanish invasion. Here James spent his time enjoying the pleasures of the forest as everywhere else, delighting his stomach at tables loaded with every kind of flesh and fowl imaginable with mutton, beef and pork, pigeons, herons and swans, curlews, quails and partridges, with pasties, pies and tarts, and of course the haunch of venison from the red deer. All these pleased James mightily, inspiring him as he left, to confirm this Vale Royal as "indeed a royal vale".

On Saturday August 23rd, the king paid a visit to Chester, attended by many honourable earls, reverend bishops, worthy knights and gallant courtiers, besides the principal gentry of the shire. He rode in state through the city, being met by the Sherrif and common council mounted on horseback. The trained bands of Chester provided a guard of honour, drawn up outside the Eastgate and lining his route into the city, each company proudly displaying its flag. On a platform hung with green, the Mayor and Aldermen took their places to await the coming of the king.

The Mayor stepped forward and presented him with a cup of gold, delivering the city's sword to his majesty, who of course, graciously returned it. Then James proceeded on horseback to the Cathedral, the civic sword being borne before him by the Mayor and the Sword of Estate by Lord Derby, Chief Chamberlain of the County Palatine. At the cathedral James heard a Latin oration delivered by a scholar of the Free School, then he went up to the choir where a seat had been prepared for him, heard an anthem sung and a prayer said. At a building called the Pentice, abutting on to St. Peter's church, where the Mayor's courts and civic banquets were usually held, the customary sumptuous meal had been made ready for the royal visitor. The banquet over, James returned to his hostess, the "Bold Lady of Cheshire"—a nickname he had gallantly bestowed on her out of gratitude for his excellent entertainment.

The short stay of five hours in the city had cost Chester over two hundred pounds for the cup, banquet, and other expenses. The loyal city had not disgraced itself, but royal patronage was dear at forty pounds an hour, so a collection had to follow to defray the cost of this lavish reception.

11

Now James was to honour the fair town of Nantwich, next in importance after Chester, with the royal presence, this proving to be an overnight stop and not a mere fleeting visit.

At Wich Malbank (by which more dignified name derived from its Norman baronial family, the town was usually known in official documents and proclamations) James stayed at the house of Mr Thomas Wilbraham in the Welsh Row.

Some felt highly honoured that Nantwich, even if only temporarily, should be the centre of a royal court; others were more cynical.

"I doubt that the king's coming will do the likes of us much good," said Tom's mother caustically, as she placed his bread and cheese on the breakfast table. "He takes his bags of gold and his cups, enjoys his grand feasts and the chase, with little thought for the poor folk in this land of his."

Tom looked up, his mug of ale pausing half-way between the table top and his mouth.

"I don't know, mother. They say this king is a very knowing man—his head crammed full of all manner of facts. I've heard tell that he can talk to the hunters with all the knowledge of one of them, listen to a parson's sermon and then recount the heads as if he had composed it himself, and dispute as well as any great scholar in the Latin tongue. Surely you will go to see him, mother; it will be a fair sight by all accounts—the king with his loyal gentry rallied around him, doing honour to our little town."

Tom's mother was not impressed.

"A middle-aged man with spindly legs and a slobbering mouth, a dour Scot who speaks with an accent you could cut with a knife! Now the old Queen!—That would have been a different matter. There was something grand about her which made her subjects warm to her presence."

"How can you say that, mother? You never saw the old Queen, nor have you seen his present Grace either."

"I've heard tell, I've heard tell!" replied his mother. "This king is better known for greeting his subjects with a frown than with a mild salute."

Mrs Ley was not disclosing the source of her information, a disinclination which did not worry Tom, as he was fairly certain that it was old Eli Walsh, who had once served as a retainer at court and had seen both Elizabeth and James at close quarters. It was rare for his mother to reveal the identity of her informants with such a remark as "according to old Eli" or "if I am to believe Master Walsh"; so he expected nothing.

"Begone!" she said, with a suggestion of scorn, "and see your king. If he wants to come back with you, tell him it's not visiting day at the Leys."

Tom laughed as he closed the door on stepping out into the street. It was but a short walk to the salt-works which stood close to the river. There had been a shower of rain and another was threatened, but it had not thinned the crowd. Beam Street was thronged with people as the town turned out to greet Royal James. By the water's edge a group of loyal citizens displayed a home-made flag, another little knot of people, guessed by Tom to be sufferers from scrofula—the king's evil—hoped to be able to press forward, receive James's touch, and be cured.

On the bank of the river a deep pit yawned, measuring several yards from the bank to bottom. Above it stood massive cross-beams, from which dangled ropes and leather buckets. Tom stopped by this pit and removed his outer clothing. The bellman passed; stoking in the chosen wich houses began; barrow-loads of cloven wood were taken from the huge stacks built up close to the salt-houses.

The county was thickly wooded, so timber was still plentiful, though the inroads made into the huge stock available were beginning to show. Already the possibility of burning coal, dug from the shallow pits of Staffordshire, which was used elsewhere, was being considered by those who were alarmed at the prospect of rapidly disappearing forests. But it was known that the foul fog arising from the thatches of wich houses using the black fuel, would offend even the least sensitive nostril, therefore it was easy to dissuade people from such a break with tradition. The advocates of wood-burning were adamant when they

13

spoke of the commodity produced by the rivals. They were usually believed when they said:

"The salt made with coal is nothing so good."

Tom was dissatisfied with his lot as a briner. It was hard work and not well paid, but he was the main breadwinner of the family. His father had been a briner too and had endured it until the plague cut him down in 1604. Only Tom, his mother and a sister were left of the family when the black scourge had passed—except for Grandfer Wyche, who seemingly indestructible, lived mostly by the chimney corner and regaled them with tales of his youth in the days of the Virgin Queen, particularly of the Great Fire which had destroyed much of the town in 1583.

"Aye, it was a wicked day!" the old man would say. "Indiscreet and negligent persons they called them: Aye and drunken sots too! There was a strong wind from the west and soon their kitchen became like Hell's mouth itself. Through the town the fire spread, leaping from house to house. Not one of the buildings in the High Street was spared the ravages of those flames. They travelled down Hospital Street, Pepper Street and Love Lane and put our church in danger. Had not the Lord mercifully made the wind to cease its blowing, even his own house would have been destroyed by those who carried on the work of the devil."

This was because the "indiscreet and negligent persons" had been brewing ale and imbibing excessively in the process. Grandfer Wyche, who had positively no objection to the moderate consumption of ale, strongly denounced such fellows as these.

"Oh, that drunkards would at last learn to be wise!" was his favourite remark. The old man's highly-coloured description of the ferocity of the fire ended with ever-repeated thanks that through God's mercy, although a hundred and fifty houses and many other buildings, including shops, inns, and mills, were destroyed, only two persons died in the fire. Those who heard Grandfer's story always relished the last part most of all: it told of the escape of four great bears kept for baiting by John Seckerston, the ward. These monsters lumbered about the streets, frightening the women who were carrying water so much, that they refused to continue unless men accompanied them with weapons. Grandfer did not intend his story to have anything of comedy in it, but his lurid descriptions inevitably made Tom and his sister laugh.

All this was in the past; since then Nantwich had been rebuilt in its chequered splendour. Time had taken off some of the gloss, but it was still one of the handsomest small towns in the North of England. Down by the river waterworks had been constructed, with a view to checking any future conflagration and avoiding a repeat of such a calamity; a wheel raised the water from the river and along the streets trunks of alder trees with plugholes at intervals served as primitive mains. This waterworks devised by William Sands, made Nantwich the envy of its neighbours in Cheshire.

The new town was worth preserving, and it proudly proclaimed from the facade of a house in High-town the royal patronage received at the time of rebuilding:

"God grante our ryal Queen
In England long to raign
For she hath put her helping hand
To bild this towne again"

It was true—Elizabeth had given liberally, subscribing one thousand pounds to the rebuilding fund, and allowing timber to be cut in the royal forest of Delamere.

Thomas Ley had no doubts about the kind of figure he would like to cut in this fair town of his. He saw himself as a draper, rolling out silks and brocades for the ladies' pleasure, or as a merchant in his counting house, dressed in a fine cloak and breeches instead of drawing up the cold brine from a wretched hole. But this morning he threw off such thoughts as he laid aside his outer clothing. The king was to pass that way. Perhaps his majesty would deign to notice Tom Ley, the humble briner!

His fellow worker, William Masterson, was a strange Puritan soul who lapped up every word of the earnest men of faith. Unlike Tom who had plenty of common sense, though he lacked learning, Will could read and write well, even in the scholar's Latin. He would often stand in an idle moment with his little testament, committing some text

15

to memory. In this book the ways of God were justified to man, and Will could quote from it like any Puritan preacher.

To Tom churchgoing was a duty, to Will it was a pleasure—so long as he considered the preachers godly men. Tom was not an irreligious lad; it came naturally to him to be a dutiful son and a good neighbour. About hell-fire he had his doubts, but to Will it appeared in all its dreadful reality. God views his creatures with eternal love. He wills that men shall be saved, but one must have the grace of inward satisfaction, living in communion with him and making use of the means of grace provided by Christ. Will could feel the pain of the damned at the loss of God's grace and he gave constant and fervent thanks that it was the Lord's will that he should be saved. All good in man is due to God's grace. Every day lost souls, tumbling into a horrible pit, came face to face with Lucifer and Beelzebub, but the Lord would show mercy to those who understood and accepted his word.

No one in Nantwich really knew much about William Masterson's origin. It was generally accepted that he came from the border of Flintshire, and that his father was a gentleman who had broken with his son, threatening to pistol him down if he approached within a hundred yards of the house. It was said too that Will vowed in consequence never more to utter a single word of his ancient native tongue, and had adopted the English surname instead of one in unpronounceable Welsh.

There was some truth in these exaggerated assertions. Will's Welsh ancestry could not be denied, but his family had long been settled in England and no longer spoke the Celtic tongue. His father, though he had quarrelled with his son, had made no such drastic threats. A small landowner, Hugh Masterson had seen to his son's education at Grammar School and Cambridge, but the young man's association with Puritan divines, resulting in his ejection from his first post, had been the cause of a severe breach between father and son. The young man had been Usher in a school at another saltwich, where he had taught the rudiments of Latin grammar to the younger pupils, and had instructed them in the principles of the Christian religion. But falling foul of the churchwardens for his puritanical views, he had come down in the world to his present state.

Nevertheless, the fact that once he had enjoyed a higher status than that of a mere briner, was obvious to all. The result of Will's dismissal was that the elder Masterson had told his son that he would have, henceforth, to make his own way in the world. The supposed change of name was mere fantasy—he had always been Masterson. An English marriage in an earlier generation had removed any necessity to anglicise his surname.

Tom and Will were good friends, but they were as unlike as chalk and cheese. Tom was tall and fair with tousled hair and rough, horny hands, blue-eyed and handsome. Will was dark-haired, rather swarthy and betraying more of his Welsh than his English ancestry. Tom had an open countenance and a hearty laugh, Will an earnest, smouldering look, with skin not fully hardened and muscles only half attuned to the labour of the salt pit.

There was a stir in the crowd; a shout went up; people pressed forward.

"The king is coming!" A horseman spurred up the road, splashing mud on the over-eager spectators. The excitement died down—it was not the king.

The overseer went by.

"Stay strictly at your work. No gawping at the crowds. The king shall see industrious briners, not idle good-for-nothings. Say naught unless you are spoken to, but speak up if His Majesty addresses you—answer his questions but add nothing else."

So it was that Tom, bending over his work and trying his best to avoid taking notice of the cheering crowd, was surprised by the arrival of the king. He was not even aware that His Majesty had approached the pit until he heard a voice behind him.

"That's wet and weary work you have to do there, laddie," said James, graciously acknowledging Tom's respectful greeting.

"An'it please your Majesty, it's all I've ever done. A man becomes hardened to it of necessity when there are hungry mouths to feed."

"So this is the sole brine pit—the supporter of your town," said the king, stepping forward to glance down the dark hole.

"It is our mainstay, your Majesty. We call it the Old Biot and we honour it each year on Ascension Day with song, dance and gay garlands, as the source of our prosperity."

"Indeed?" remarked the king, turning to his host. "You must tell us more about that, Wilbraham."

The gentleman began to apologize for forgetting to inform the king, but James ignored his protestations and addressed Will. "And you, my man, I presume you are a briner too—but not always one," he added perceptively.

Will, who greeted the king a shade less enthusiastically than Tom, hid his true feelings in response to James's query.

"Yes your Grace," he replied "I have seen better days."

The king did not care to ask him what he meant by this statement, but posed another question.

"Tell us young man, since you have something of the air of a scholar. Springs can be productive in two senses—rich in salt content or in the quantity of the brine. What are the qualities of your old Biot?"

"A sixth part of salt and the brine plentiful," replied Will, surprised that the king should show more than a superficial interest— "whereas our neighbours in the Middle-wich have a fourth part, and the brine is thrifty."

The king nodded and turned to Thomas Wilbraham.

"These men must be among the hardiest in our three kingdoms to work here in all weathers."

"Indeed so, your Majesty," replied Wilbraham. "They even descend into the pit on occasion to cleanse it of the salty accretions, but then they are invariably fortified with aqua vitae."

The king looked across at the salt-houses and observed smoke and steam rising above only a few of the roofs. Thomas Wilbraham explained the rules of walling, evolved so that 'the trade be not clogged'.

"Tis strange!" muttered the king. "Tis strange! But one brine-pit and restrictive laws of manufacture!"

"Come here, young man," he called. Tom, who had stood back while the king's host was pointing out the extent of the salt-works, was amusing himself admiring the elegant clothes and dandified airs of the courtiers in James's train. His Majesty turned to an attendant who handed him a small bag from which he drew a glittering coin. "Take this, laddie," he said, handing Tom a golden sovereign. The young man could hardly believe his eyes; he had rarely seen gold before, and had certainly never possessed any. He made a deep bow and expressed a thousand thanks to His Majesty for his graciousness.

"And you, my man," said James, holding another coin between his thumb and fore-finger. Tom glanced at his friend, interested to see how he would react, but Masterson had no intention of risking the stocks, ear-cropping, or some other drastic punishment for disrespect to the King's Grace, so he courteously accepted the gift. The overseer was coming his way; Will immediately placed the coin in a leather purse which he used to carry his wages of four shillings a week, and hurriedly began to haul up another bucket of brine. Tom resumed his work too, and King James and his party were just specks across the wooden bridge, retiring up Welsh Row, before he was able to have a breather. But they had left him a proud man. He had spoken to the King of England—nay, of Great Britain. How many common drawers of brine could say that?

As his friend had expected, Will was unmoved by the day's events. Masterson had no great love for the king's Majesty. This James had inordinate pretensions, claiming himself to be the Vice-Regent of the Almighty with all subordinate powers in the kingdom drawing authority from the monarch's grace.

"A king is not bound to give an account of his actions, and although a good king will frame them according to the law, he is not bound thereto except of his own will and for example-giving to his subjects."

This Will rejected. To him Christ was Lord and all who accepted him were his saints. To him the king did not derive his power from divine election but from earthly sources—a power which had a beginning in the distant past, to be sure, but which had come down to him through the hands of men and not directly from God—a power to be restricted by that admixture of custom and ordinance called "the law", which had an independent existence above the ruler and the ruled. The power of the Tudors had rested on the love and loyalty of their subjects; they had been willing merely to exercise their prerogative; these Stuarts chose to theorize about it and turn it into a political dogma—"The Divine Right of Kings".

"I see you took the king's gift," said Tom as they walked up the High Street to Will's lodging, "for all your fine talk about his great claims to divine right."

"Prudence, my friend," replied Will, "and it will guarantee me a goodly supply of ink, paper, and candles. I doubt that the king would approve of my writings; the irony is that he will unwittingly have paid for them himself."

It was soon clear that Tom's encounter with the king and his acquisition of a truly royal sovereign, was indeed a nine-days wonder and he enjoyed the popularity it brought, but it was some time before he was able to put it to the use he valued most—namely that of impressing Mistress Kate Barton, a young lady whose beauty and vivacity had captivated him. She had Irish blood from some generations back and had inherited the good looks of many women of that race. She was a year older than he was, with shining dark hair, brown eyes, an exceptionally fresh complexion, and a tinkling laugh. She was tall too—only falling short of his own height by an inch or so, with the confident air of someone who knows her capability to attract. How could Tom Ley, the briner, hope to carry off such a prize? He had nothing to recommend himself to her family. Was there anything about him personally which would fascinate her? Her father was a glover with a little workshop in Pepper Street—a genteel trade, so unlike his own crude brining.

Master Barton's thriving business employed several apprentices, and he had a comfortable and spacious house which Tom considered to be the grandest in Nantwich. It was not so fine as he imagined, but of course it held the person of Mistress Kate and that for him was its principal attraction.

Matthew Barton was the son of an innkeeper near Over, about ten miles from Nantwich. He had freely chosen the trade of glover, the hostelry coming into the possession of his elder brother, and had served his apprenticeship with Samuel Brooke of Nantwich. A member of the guild of Glovers and Collarmakers, an aspirant to civic office, he was a capable business man, and his side-lines included a thriving trade in corn and malt as well as an interest in salt-making. Besides the house which Tom so admired, he had another piece of property in the town, occupied at that time by a tenant.

It was all very daunting for Tom. Surely Kate would aim higher than one of his kind. He was uneducated too; he knew that the young lady could read, write and cipher. How could he stand by a wife like that and remain such an ignoramus? Still, his lack of education could be remedied. Will was a scholar and would assist him, but could he ever raise himself above this accursed task of drawing brine?

In the High Street stood the church of Nantwich parish, rising over the roofs and gables of the town. The majestic building of reddish sandstone dated from the fourteenth century, but despite recent renovations there were still many signs of decay in the friable stonework and ancient wood. Though the district had long been officially no more than a chapelry within the Parish of Acton, its church, dependent on a neighbouring abbey until the Dissolution, had assumed almost cathedral-like proportions. Its massive octagonal tower rose up ninety feet, dominating the town and serving as a notable landmark in the gently undulating landscape. It too had been honoured by the illustrious visitor, when Mr Dodd of Shocklach Prebendary of Chester and much else, had added royal chaplain-in-ordinary to his other titles, by preaching to his Majesty's great satisfaction.

Beyond the east end of the church, backing on to some glebe-land, was Tom's house—not an unpleasant little dwelling, suggesting that the Ley family had seen better days. In fact it was the family home of the Wyches, of which they had held the tenancy ever since it was built. Their name, a corruption of Wich, was an ancient one; 13th

Century Richard, made a bishop, was canonised in 1253; a fifteenth century Hugh became Lord Mayor of London. The present Wyches could, however, claim no direct descent from these illustrious gentlemen, but rather from a bastard of the old stock, Harry Wyche, a dissolute man by tradition, whose reputation was best forgotten.

Grandfer, unlike the Leys, had not been employed in the salt works, but had earned his living as a stocking weaver. After the death of her husband in the plague of 1604, a grim year which reduced her family from seven to three, Margery had returned with her remaining children to the old home. It dated from the youth of Grandfather Wyche, over half a century previously, when the heavy hand of Catholic Mary was on the country and the "Old Queen" was the "Young Hope" of the Protestants, imprisoned by her sister in the Tower of London. Granfer's tales of games in the sawyer's pit, "tight-rope" walking along the beams, and being chased away by harassed workmen, were so well-known that the family could repeat them in chorus with the old man as he mumbled away. Still he persisted, seemingly oblivious to the fact that they were such well-told stories.

The house had a single storey and attic rooms. It had been built with a solid brick chimney when many of those of the day were still furnished in the manner of the old Saxons, with a fire in the midst of the house against a hob of clay and a hole in the thatch to let out the smoke, while their oxen sheltered under the same roof. It had escaped the conflagration of 1583 as it stood at the farthest end of the street. Great-Grandfather Wyche had always said that the crucial change of wind had come just as he was adding the "Amen" to his plea for God's mercy. A lesser fire had, however, burned off the thatch some years later, when Great-Grandfather, shooting at a crow in a season of dry weather set it alight with sparks. It had been re-roofed with tiles which, less inflammable than reeds or straw, would be a help in checking the rapid spread of disastrous fires in the crowded town.

As Tom had expected, he was something of a celebrity that evening. Despite her unenthusiastic remarks in the morning supported by the acute observations of Eli Walsh, his mother's attitude had changed. She admitted that she had turned out to cheer the king and had seen His Majesty approach her boy. A poor substitute for the Old Queen, but a crowned head none the less! Tom's sister treated him with awe as if a part of divine majesty had devolved on him, and neighbours came round to see the young man who had actually come face to face with their monarch. Only Grandfer Wyche was unimpressed. He had not moved from the chimney corner that day even for Royal James. He took the coin and turned it over.

"Aye, a pretty piece!" he murmured. "A pretty piece!" Then with half-closed eyes he returned to his slumbers and those memories of his youth in the days of the first Elizabeth.

2. WHITE SALT

Unpleasant as the drawing of brine could be in the cold winter weather, the lot of the waller was little better. The buildings which served as salt-works, with their rough-cast walls, beaten earth floors and open thatch, were unenviable places of work. No plaster would stick in the damp atmosphere, the boards warped, the nails rusted, the draughts whistled through the numerous cracks in walls and woodwork. Scorched by the heat of the fires, chilled by the blasts of cold air from outside, the work-people coughed and spluttered, and only tolerated the unhealthy atmosphere for lack of knowledge of anything better. The labour was not so arduous as the drawing of brine and there was some shelter from the elements, but the boiling-pans, now of lead, later to be replaced by great vessels of iron, needed cleansing, the ever-hungry fires had to be stoked, the dripping salt loaded into baskets for drying.

Six lead pans were ready in each salt-house allotted a walling; the signal was given; the day's work began. The brine came pouring down the wooden gutters to which the wallers added sheep's blood or alternatively that of cows or calves, in the proportion of two quarts to upwards of twenty gallons of brine. The pans were filled; the boiling began.

The glowing fires under the bearers or cross-bars on which the pans stood, were stoked up to bring the liquid quickly to boiling point. A scum rose to the surface and was skimmed off; the boiling continued until half the brine had evaporated. Now the pan was filled again with fresh brine from the ship, and the women added a seemingly strange ingredient—one quart of the whites of eggs beaten into as much brine as before with blood. So this concoction, known simply as the "whites", was boiled sharply and a second scum appeared. This removed, the seething liquid was heated gently, the fires having been abated, and through the clouds of steam, salt became visible. A momentary ebullition as a quarter of a pint of the strongest ale which could be found was thrown in and the addition of "leach brine"—liquid which had run from salt taken up to dry, marked the end of the process before the end-product began to appear. The much-wasted brine began rapidly to crystallise; the workers raked up the solid matter which was now sinking in the pan, using their wooden loots, and when little was left, took up these long, square hoards laden with dripping salt, by the handles, and filled the barrows which were pyramidal wicker baskets of cleft osiers, resembling sugar loaves. The barrow having been filled, the leach-brine was drained off into a trough before the half-dried salt was taken into the hot-house behind the works. Two stone tunnels under the pans carried the heated air into this chamber where the barrows were stacked. From a chimney above it, steam emerged to mingle with the wood-smoke from the fires.

Two hours' boiling wrested the salt from the brine-pans holding forty eight gallons in all making easily enough to fill a barrow and earning the producer the regulated price of one shilling and fourpence. Nothing was wasted; the leach-brine was returned for use in the next process; even the sweepings and cleansings of the wich house were collected and then, blended with the scum which had been brought up by the addition of blood and eggs, it was sold after the walling for a shilling a cart-load, as manure.

The efforts of the salt-makers at Nantwich were not rewarded with a very wholesome condiment. Many people, especially of the upper and middle classes, preferred the imported French salt which was produced by the evaporation of sea water in Bourgneuf Bay on the border of Brittany and Poitou and in the neighbourhood of La Rochelle. However, 'Bay salt' became a generic name for that gained from sea water, and much of it was also of indifferent quality, being mixed with grit and seaweed, heavily polluted, and grey or green in colour. Nevertheless, it was regularly imported in competition with the 'white salt' of the wiches. Even that exhaled a sulphurous stench, and physicians declared it to cause the scorbutic and pulmonary complaints so common at the time. Salt was, however, an exceptionally important commodity, apart from its use on the table, for in the absence of winter feeds, the preserving of meat and fish by salting or smoking was essential. It was also used for curing hides, in the process of glazing pottery, and even for the parboiling of the heads and quarters of executed criminals before displaying them on high.

Thomas was not the only member of his family to be engaged in salt-making, for in the Ley tradition, his sister Alice had become a waller. Unlike Tom, she accepted her lot—at least for the period of her maidenhood. Two years older than her brother, Alice had had a twin, but in the dreadful time of the plague poor Henry had been removed, and her closeness to Tom was a substitute for this broken link. A short while before the king's visit, Alice had suffered an accident—one common enough among the salters; she had been scalded with brine. In the past year there had been two or three serious incidents in the salt-works; one resulted in a fatality when Margaret Evans, an elderly waller, died after a severe scalding. Alice had been luckier, though in lifting a pan for cleansing, the residue had scalded her hand and arm. Though not fatal, the accident had been serious enough to incapacitate her, so at the time of the king's coming she was not present in the salt-works.

This unfortunate occurrence did have some compensation, though it benefited Alice less than Tom. It occasioned a visit from Mistress Kate Barton to enquire about the accident and the progress of the victim's convalescence.

Tom would have been very surprised had he known the strength of Kate's feelings towards him. The manly good looks of the Saxon lad contrasted sharply with her own Celtic beauty. Opposites attracted, and Kate felt herself strongly drawn to Tom. It was true that he was only a briner, but he could rise above labour at the salt-pit. Not that she intended to defy her father; she was quite capable of making him feel that the one she wanted had always been his choice too. Maybe Tom could come into his business or rise in the salt industry. She was certain that some assistance in one of her father's various business undertakings would be welcome, especially as there was no son to take over. Matthew Barton had a significant share in a salt-house. This was common practice; the rights of walling were distributed in all the wiches among a large number of owners; the king, the Earl of Derby, the local gentry and many private individuals had shares; schools, almshouses, and churches, had 'leads'—as the term was—the interest being reckoned by the number of boilings in the lead pans each person or institution was allowed.

The trouble was Tom's pride. He would have to be encouraged to approach her before any parental influence in his favour could be exercised. He would surely think of her as being above his station and a little stimulus from her would be necessary. Her father's stake in the salt-house where Alice worked made the call seem quite natural. Tom's sister was not only surprised at the call but a little overawed. Tom, who arrived home half-way through the visit, was embarrassed, but as usual, Grandfer Wyche kept the conversation going, asking questions about people Kate had never known—some of whom were in fact already dead—and talking of events outside the compass of her knowledge. Tom's encounter with the king did inevitably come into the conversation. Kate had only seen him from a distance.

"Tell me," she said, as Tom accompanied her on the short walk down Hospital Street towards her father's house. "How did the king really strike you? Does he exude majesty?"

"Only lackeys and flattering courtiers could say that," replied Tom. "I had been led to believe something of the sort, but found him just an ordinary gentleman, ungainly in fact and rather comic in his padded clothes, no more richly dressed than some of those around him, not handsome in his person, yet having something pleasant about him."

"Doubtless his golden sovereign shed some of its attraction on the giver," said the young lady with a knowing smile.

"No, not just that," replied Tom. "He did not seem to be enjoying the applause of the throng, and he had a homely way of speaking which set one at ease—despite all his pretensions to divine appointment, against which Will speaks with such fire."

"Your friend sides with the Parliamentarians who would see the king's power reduced," said Kate, who had met Will and found him interesting but enigmatic. Tom's pleasant open nature appealed to her more. She could read him like a book. Behind Will's dark countenance she discerned an honest, serious, but less attractive man, a seeker after the deeper truth and beauty, who could lightly overlook the obvious evidences of it around him.

"He says this king cannot judge a man well and is too much taken up with his worthless favourites, giving them positions of trust," went on Tom. "Mother says much the same too—no doubt the opinion of Eli Walsh, whose words about royalty are never to be disputed."

"Your friend's party welcomed the Protestant alliance with the German Palatinate," observed Kate, referring to the marriage of James's daughter, Elizabeth, to the Elector Frederick, "but they reject the overtures for a Spanish match, fearing that Catholic heirs will undo the Protestant settlement and return us to the days of Bloody Mary. So our king, in trying to set himself on both stools falls between them, as the saying goes. Doubtless Will has strong views concerning this."

Kate was right about Will. The German marriage and the accession of England to a Protestant Union of European Powers had indeed pleased him, while the prospect of a Spanish alliance had caused him sleepless nights and much expenditure of paper, ink and candle.

Tom felt a shudder as he listened to Kate's discourse on European affairs—a shudder at his own ignorance and inadequacy. Her opinions were in fact mainly those of her father who, having no sons, confided his assessment of politics in his daughter. Kate's mother showed little interest, but the girl had a livelier mind and Barton found in her one who would listen attentively to his point of view, occasionally adding some acute comments of her own; but though he liked to discourse on these matters with his daughter and his friends, Kate's father never felt any desire to involve himself—a principle which guided him throughout his life.

They paused by an ancient building—long, low and timber-framed. Once the town's Guildhall, it had been purchased for the purpose of founding a school some fifty years earlier, and it had been enlarged by the addition of a handsome wing or porch on the south side. One inscription, in English, gave the date of erection and the builder's name. "Richard Dale, Free Mason, was Master Carpenter in making this building A. D. 1611". The other inscription, in Latin, honoured the Headmaster, who for nearly half a century had taken charge of the school and had in fact built the extension at his own expense. The substantial pillars of the porch, the carved architraves above, the intricate patterns of the oak timbers around the window, the coats of arms over it, spoke of the loving care lavished on its planning and construction by Master Builder and craftsman.

Tom looked at Kate with ever growing admiration. A bright shaft of sunlight illuminated her, and the blue dress and cloak she wore gave her an almost Madonna-like appearance. His previous contacts with the young lady had been brief. In church, as she knelt in her pew, thoughts which he should have banished in that holy place entered his head. In the streets or on the walk by the river, at the market or some festivity like the blessing of the brine, even a few words of greeting had given him comfort for days. Not long before the visit of the king, a chance encounter had gladdened both their hearts.

In 1283 Edward I, Conqueror of Wales, had granted to the Bishop of Bath and Wells, his Lord Chancellor, who held lands in the Barony of Malbank, a chartered fair to be held on the vigil, the day, and the morrow of the Feast of St. Bartholomew the Apostle. A busy and noisy affair, held first in the churchyard, it had moved out into the streets and common land by the river, when two years later the Statute of Westminster forbade the holding of fairs on hallowed ground. From a simple market it had turned into the great pleasure-fair of the year. To attract buyers, the vendors were accompanied by a crowd of jugglers, 'merry men', and minstrels. There was cock fighting, bull, bear, and badger-baiting, racing, archery, and performing animals. The fairground was often the scene of rowdy behaviour. The doors of the numerous alehouses lining the street to the river—the bane of the Puritans and others concerned about the maintenance of good order— stood wide open, and as the day wore on, drunken brawls became commonplace. In spite of many calls for suppression of the superfluous ones, there were still far more taverns in the town than the population warranted.

Tom and Kate had paid their visits to the fair at an early time, when a bustling but less turbulent atmosphere prevailed. They had met at the end of Beam Street where a bear was chained to a post, pawing the air while dogs snapped around it. Kate turned away in disgust.

"It is an offence against God who made all living creatures to treat dumb animals so wickedly," she said as the crowd roared approval of some mighty attempt by the bear to maim a dog. Tom did not feel quite the same revulsion at this practice; familiarity had hardened him to it. Still he could not disagree. God had given man dominion over animals, but surely he expected him to exercise it with responsibility. It could not be that man should plague beasts or encourage them to attack one another cruelly for mere sport. Kate was much firmer about it.

"Those hardened to this brutality are likely to show less kindness to their fellow men. In the days of the heathen Romans men revelled in cruel sport, watching wild beasts tearing other animals and even human beings to pieces. But we are Christians now and should know better. Do you not think so Master Ley?"

Tom would not have disagreed with Kate for anything. Her indignation had surprised him, but the howling of a dog torn by the bear, the blood dripping from the great animal's side where one of his opponents had bitten him, and the enthusiasm of the spectators as they egged the fighters on, disgusted him. Like Kate he turned away.

"Yet there are enough men and women who derive pleasure from it," he found himself saying, "and not only the common folk. I have heard tell that in a place not much over a dozen miles from here they even preferred that sport to the Word of God."

"Congleton, to its eternal disgrace," said Kate. "Faced with a choice between a new bible for corporate worship and an animal for public baiting, the authorities chose the latter, and now they will go down in history as the 'corporation rare' which sold a bible to buy a bear."

Kate had been whisked away before there had been time for some more intimate conversation. The meeting at the fair had been all too brief; this time he had talked with her for a few more precious moments. Standing in front of the old Grammar School, looking at the retreating figure of the girl, a basket on her arm in which she had carried comforts to Alice, Tom felt he could not let Kate go. A sudden feeling of boldness swelled up in him. Had he not just stood face to face speaking to a king? Had he not received a gift from the royal hand?

It was in a steady but strange voice that he cried out. "Just a moment, Mistress Barton!"

He looked round as if expecting to find someone standing beside him who had been bold enough to call Kate back, hardly daring to believe that the voice had actually come from him. The girl seemed less surprised at Tom's sudden outburst than he was himself. He detected a look of excitement in her eyes as she came up to him, though he had failed to notice other previous intimations of her interest

30

in his person, having hardly dared to search for them there. It gave him hope and emboldened him for his next little speech.

"If the evening is fair, maybe you would care to walk along the Millfields with me tomorrow," he proposed. "I usually like to wander there an hour or two before sunset. I am lacking in company at the moment, and you would be very welcome, Mistress Barton. You cheer me up so."

Tom felt his heart pound as he said these last words. He knew he had expressed himself badly and hoped that Kate would take no offence.

"Why yes, Tom," she replied, smiling at his inexpert way of making the suggestion. "It is an admirable idea. What could be better after a long day confined within the four walls of the house and shop, than a stroll through the cool meadows to see the sun go down. But we ought not to go alone. For propriety's sake someone of advanced years should accompany us. However, we will break with tradition. Bring Alice. She will be very discreet I am sure and, besides, the air will do her good."

The young man could hardly believe his ears. It had come true at last—his dearest wish. Kate turned to go and he surprised both her and himself by blurting out:

"Please wear that dress and cloak again, Mistress Barton. It makes you look like—well like the Holy Mother on the east window in church. Mr Bradwell told us about it. He says it is a heavenly colour. For aught I know that may be true. The sky is blue when we see it through the clouds and Heaven is over the sky they say; but my idea of Heaven, Mistress Barton, is to see you in that dress and cloak with your face and hair shining in the sunlight like crowned saints on the stained glass."

"Now, now, Tom Ley," said Kate reprovingly, though she could by no means be angry at the pretty compliment. "That is an impious thing to say—to compare me with the mother of Our Lord and holy saints. But I will forgive you," she smiled, "and I will be by the mill at seven of the clock. You will not be disappointed."

As he returned home, Tom felt that he was walking on air. He had surprised himself and, beyond all expectations, he had made an appointment to meet the one he so desired. This new confidence, springing from his encounter with the king, was very satisfying, yet had he not said that James looked much the same as any other mortal man? Now here he was making such great play of the possession of a king's gratuity and a few words from His Majesty's mouth. Will would already have spent his sovereign on paper and candles, but he was treating a simple coin as if it were a holy relic. It was foolish to think that the king had spoken to him on account of his own merits. It was just because he happened to be drawing brine when His Majesty wished to see the pit. He would put the money away and not look at it again until there was occasion to spend it. He would buy something for Kate when he had won her; that would be his greatest pleasure—to be able to give her a present which was not cheap and trivial. Yes, he would wrap it up and hide it away until the right time arrived. Bringing it out once more to impress Kate or anyone else would be just vanity. If he wanted to woo her, he would have to do it without the help of a coin hallowed by the kingly touch.

The following evening was fair, so the young people met as appointed. Crossing over the river by the weir, they passed a rather dilapidated corn mill. Tom had liked to go there when a boy and watch the water-wheel turn, hoping that the miller would appear and invite him in to see the millstones grind. More often than not he was lucky as the flour-covered man came out for a breath of fresh air and called to Tom to climb the wooden steps into the dusty interior. It was dark inside, but the miller, a cheery fellow, habitually lightened the gloom by singing some old ballad which Tom barely recognized above the noise of the machinery and the splashing of the water-wheel outside. Nevertheless, he joined in lustily at the miller's invitation, even though their voices rarely achieved unison, the boy usually lagging a few beats behind.

Alice was, indeed, discreet and took her stroll near the mill while Tom and Kate wandered across the meadow. From the long grass a profusion of wild herbs and flowers peeped out. The young couple followed a track, trampled by the feet and rutted by the carts of those coming down to the mill from distant farms. The land rose at first, then gently descended to the water-meadows. Willow trees grew along the bank of the river. The water was at a low level, for there had been little steady rain in the last few weeks. In the distance a wooden bridge spanned the murky stream. On the bank the grass was shorter, and Tom's suggestion that they should sit down and enjoy the cool of the evening was welcomed by the young lady.

"You know I am not lettered, Mistress Kate," said Tom, his feeling of inferiority returning after the burst of boldness. "You and Will make me ashamed of my lack of learning."

"Please drop the "Mistress," dear Tom" said the girl, a little put out by the unnecessary deference of one to whom she wished to draw closer. "I am just your Kate and no great scholar either. I can read and write, it is true, but I much prefer a light romance from the French or Spanish to the heavy dissertations of the frowning divines. Your Will would not approve of my taste—my little fancies like 'The honour and true love of the well-deserving, noble and most valiant knight Sir Paris, and his much admired and amiable princess, the fair Vienna'. It is a romance of Catalan origin written by a man from our town, Master Matthew Mainwaring, who once served in foreign parts as a soldier."

Tom was relieved and cheered by Kate's confession of her taste in literature. No longer feeling that the discussion would be beyond him, he ventured a comment.

"These romances from the French and Spanish are fair to read, I'll warrant, but they are far from the lives of folk like me—and, begging your pardon, Kate, even of you. There is little of the reality of our lives in them—the knights valiant and noble doing mighty deeds, the ladies virtuous and much admired. There is no romance in the brine pit, or even in the glovers shop."

"There you are wrong, Tom;" said Kate, looking straight into his eyes, "there is romance in everything if we can find it. The doings of knights in burnished armour and ladies in silks and satin, seem romantic because, being far from our reality, we only see the glittering side of them. We do not think of the knight, saddle-sore, covered with dust and spattered with blood, his back aching from the long wearing of amour, bruised from the blows received in combat; nor do we see the lady shivering in some uncomfortable, damp, rat-infested tower."

"Yet these are people of the gentry. They have learning. Their feelings are finer than those of common folk."

"On the surface—yes—because they are more articulate, but a common man or woman can burn with a love as great as any of the gentlefolk. Do you not know that, Tom? Do you not believe that at a future date, some such story could be told about a glover's daughter and a brining man?"

The unmistakable meaning of these last words made Tom catch his breath. The sun was going down, the western sky had reddened and the fleecy clouds above them had pink edges. The great red globe of fire was dipping below the distant line of trees on the edge of the wide forest, which stretched mile upon mile across the county. He placed his arm across Kate's shoulders.

"What would they say now in your foreign romances?" he asked in a low voice.

"Oh Tom," said the girl, who felt that she had encouraged him enough. "Be your own man. Speak whatever comes naturally to you."

"Dear, sweet Kate," murmured Tom, throwing off the last of his reserve, "my pet, my honey-lamb."

Then drawing her to him, he kissed her with a passion which would not have disgraced Sir Paris or any other of the courtly lovers.

3. GOD'S PROVIDENCE

A narrow staircase between two shops in the High Street at Nantwich, led up to an attic chamber which was Will Masterson's little world. The house, rebuilt after the Great Fire of 1583 with some of that oak cut by royal permission in the forest of Delamere, comprised a shoemaker's shop at street level, the living quarters of the Master Cobbler and his family above it, and two attic rooms, one of which was occupied by Will.

The tiny room, which even in daylight hours was poorly illuminated through the heavily leaded panes of one small window, presented a scene of disorder to Tom Ley, as on a grey autumn evening some three weeks after his romantic walk with Kate along the river bank, he climbed the staircase to take his first lesson in reading from Will.

His resolution to learn his letters had faded in the days immediately after the meeting, as the first flush of enthusiasm passed, but the news that just as she had expected, Kate's father had proved pliant to her persuasion, revived his interest. Mrs Barton was loath to see her daughter married to a "common briner," but her husband dismissed the objections, telling her not to ape gentility, and reminding her that the fact that the Bartons were so prosperous was due to his own industry and her support.

"The lad will make good yet as sure as my name is Matt Barton. There is plenty of opportunity for him to rise above his present station and I will see that he does."

This promise did not, however, result in any immediate change in Tom's status, but it strengthened his determination to improve his knowledge and deserve any promotion he received. His first approach to Will for assistance received a strangely brusque reply that the former schoolmaster had finished with teaching and had only time for the study of God's word. Tom was disappointed but he did not let this refusal break his friendship. He felt that Will would come round and give him what he wanted and his judgement was correct. A few days later, Masterson said he had changed his mind, and in the way of an apology, declared that he would be pleased to instruct Tom in anything he chose to ask if it lay within his power.

Wary at first of the pitfalls she suspected, Tom's mother was less enthusiastic about the marriage than he would have wished. The prospect of his advancement both matrimonially and at work was tempting, but it was Grandfer Wyche who was largely instrumental in winning her over. As ever Margery respected her father's wisdom. He laid more stress on the young woman's character than the acquisition of any material gain from the marriage, for even at their first meeting, the old man had gained a favourable impression of her.

"A man may be advised to choose honesty before beauty as they told us in the days of my youth," he said admiringly, "but this girl lacks nothing of either to win a young man's heart. Margery, do not be deceived. It is not always true that a fair face hides a fickle heart. Had that been so, I would never have had such happiness with your dear mother."

Despite their close relationship, Tom had never before visited Will's attic room, and the sight of his friend sitting at a rickety table as close to the window as possible in order to catch the light, made him feel momentarily that he was visiting a stranger rather than Will from the brine-pit. A tankard half full of ale, a crust and crumbs of bread and a plate on which a few pieces of cold meat still remained, filled half the table, the other part being covered with leaves of paper, an inkhorn, two leather-bound books, one of which Tom took to be a bible; the other he could not recognise; it was a slim volume in an ancient, tattered binding—certainly not a foreign romance this time. A candleholder and two spare candles added to the clutter on the table; on the floor, close to Will's chair, three or four large volumes were piled up ready to hand. Tom wondered how his friend could ever manage to read through such massive tomes. Under the slope of the roof, stood Will's bed—a mean pallet with a rough blanket. Two stools and a large chest, on which some hastily discarded clothes were lying, were the only other pieces of furniture Will had, but this, on account of the smallness of the room, was more than enough. Masterson was just dipping his quill in the ink when Tom entered the room. He finished his sentence, which lacked only three words; then he looked up.

"Welcome to this famous seat of learning," he said cheerfully. "The High Master will give you his personal attention."

He began to gather together the papers which lay scattered on the table. Tom, to whom the black symbols meant nothing as yet, could not hide his curiosity.

"What is it, Will, that you spend all your time writing?" he asked.

"My journal," replied his friend "but no ordinary diary of trivial events. This will be my commentary on life, an instruction in the ways of Providence which approves or censures actions and brings rewards and punishments. This will be a moral weapon to fight off evil and instruct those into whose hands it falls."

"You speak of judgements," remarked Tom. "For what kinds of offences?"

"For any which offend God, be they insults to him or any of his creatures – for breaking the Sabbath, blaspheming, excessive drinking in alehouses, whoring, the baiting of bulls and bears. The list is long and some examples would serve me better. Listen to this," he said, taking up one of the sheets. "*'There was a remarkable judgment lighted upon a wicked debauched fellow, one Robinson, a bear–ward, who followed that unlawful calling whereby God is dishonoured – especially at such Popish Festivals called Wakes. He was cruelly rent to pieces by a bear, and so died fearfully.'*"

"And again here," he said, pointing to another entry. "*A woman in Chester brazenly going upon the walls to gather plums on the Lord's Day, fell down and broke her neck.*"

His finger travelled down the page.

"*William Symme had his nose bitten off in a drunken quarrel, and later lost one of his eyes.*"

"Five Aldermen of Macclesfield meeting in a tavern, drank excessively of sack and aqua vitae; three of them died next day and the other two were desperately ill."

Masterson looked up at his friend. "Will you hear more?" he asked; but without waiting for Tom's reply, he indicated another passage.

"The wife of Richard Capper ran away from her husband, married another who was married, and having lived with him till his death, married another. The judgment of God befell her in her secret parts, which rotted away and thus she lingered a long time."

"A poor man stole a jerkin off a weaver's shuttle from Richard Bailey. He was followed and accused of theft, but denied it and cursed himself on his knees if he had done it. The Lord struck him suddenly and according to his own execration, and he died presently."

Tom listened in silence. He agreed with Will in condemning most of these practices, but he was not as sure as his friend that Providence always brought retribution to erring mortals. He knew that many villains went unpunished by God or by man. He knew too that Will disapproved of innocent sports, and he had no doubt that there were instances in his diary of men and women both old and young dying after indulging in some harmless pastime on the village green. At this very time the Book of Sports was being prepared which in the following year checked the Puritan attacks on the use of even part of the Sabbath day as a time of recreation. This counterblast against the political influence of the Puritans gained much popular support, but further enraged Will and his fellows.

"And as for our good people's lawful recreation our pleasure like-wise is, that after the end of divine service our good people be not disturbed, letted or discouraged from any lawful recreation such as dancing, archery, leaping or vaulting, nor from having of May Games, Whitsun Ales and Morris dances and the setting–up of maypoles, so that the same may be had in due and convenient time without impediment to Divine Service."

This, the book said, would avoid filthy tipplings and drunkenness and the breeding of idle and discontented people in their alehouses.

Will Masterson would agree that those evils should be suppressed; but not by Sabbath-breaking. Never!

Tom heard his friend go on to read examples of the Hand of Providence—a woman who was drinking had the glass struck from her hand by lightning; a man watching others bowling was struck down by a sudden seizure; but he did not comment, as he had no wish to offend the sensibilities of his friend. He was, however, prompted to ask Will a question.

"All your stories show the wrath of the Almighty visited on sinners. Have you no examples of rewards for the just?"

"God's Providence is to be seen all around us," replied Will. "You must yourself have been blessed by many of His mercies, but here I have listed some which prove the ways of God and His intervention in the affairs of mortal man. It is also my intention to give a true and exact relation of these events in our nation which show the Hand of the Lord upon His people."

"Look you here, Tom," he continued, forgetting that his friend was unable to read. "See, they are all written down. Did we not pray for rain last season and were we not rewarded? Have I not written here how Mistress Venables, a religious gentlewoman, benighted and snowbound, addressed herself to prayer whereupon help came to her presently? Were we not spared in the third year of this reign, when a horrible and bloody plot of malignants would have destroyed not only the king's person but the whole of our Honourable Parliament? Have not the efforts of those who would hand us over to the Papists been thwarted by the failure of the proposed Spanish marriage?"

"Why then was the young Prince Henry, who as Grandfer says would have served us ten times better than this Charles, taken from us by a fever?" countered Tom, "—and the good Sir Raleigh arrested and imprisoned on a weak charge of treason? Did not the plague visit us in the year four and rob me of my father and brothers?"

"You must not question the workings of Divine Providence," replied his friend severely. "As the Apostle says: *'We see yet through a glass darkly'*. There will come a time when the purpose of all of them will be revealed to us."

The discussion ended here and the lesson began, but on the way home, Tom thought deeply on Will's severe Protestantism. Could he be as sure as his friend that he would be counted among the elect and be saved? What about Kate? He could not imagine an existence now or hereafter without her. The sound of a distant roll of thunder and a few large spots of rain as he left Will's lodging caused him to smile. *"The Lord hath his way in the storm"* was a text his friend had quoted on this occasion and several times before. Perhaps he had better hurry home at once ere God sent some dire punishment on a doubting Thomas.

As the weeks went by and his scholarship improved, Tom veered more and more towards Will's puritanical ideas. The former school-master was very persuasive; his fire and enthusiasm were difficult for one in Tom's position as a pupil, to resist. Will was so pleased with his friend's scholastic progress that he could easily have been guilty of the sin of pride in the efficiency of his teaching; but, as usual, he ascribed the constant improvement of his pupil to the mercy of God who had blessed his efforts so signally. In spite of his steady conversion to Will's point of view, Tom had no such reservations, and Masterson would have considered him a sinner had he seen him one evening sitting on the window-seat in the comfortable house by the glover's shop proudly displaying his newly-acquired skill to his lady-love. Kate's father liked to encourage her interest in literature, so after a business visit to Chester he had returned with two volumes.

"The Triumph of Time" by Robert Greene was described on the title page as: *"A pleasant history, wherein is discovered that although by means of sinister Fortune truth may be concealed, yet by Time in spite of Fortune it is most manifestly revealed."*

The other one which interested Tom immensely was entitled: *"The Discovery of the large, rich and beautiful Empire of Guiana with relation of the great and golden city of Manoa, which the Spaniards call El Dorado,"* written by none other than Sir Walter Raleigh. This gentleman, after thirteen long years of imprisonment in the Tower and the constant threat of death, had been sent on a further expedition to find the famed City of Gold in America. The world had opened out and various nations of Europe were sending out explorers to the Western hemisphere, at first regarded as the sole preserve of the

Spaniards and Portuguese. Some of the most exciting adventures of the time were recorded in these books of travel; this one by such a notable explorer and talented writer was among the best.

Kate offered to lend the book to Tom, but seeing that he still found difficulty with the harder words, she volunteered to read a passage to him instead.

"Do so, my dearest," he said, leaning back on the seat with his eyes half-closed while the words of Raleigh and the voice of Kate transported him to strange realms beyond the sea.

"I never saw a more beautiful country," wrote Sir Walter, "nor more lively prospects—hills so raised here and there over the valleys, the river winding into diverse branches, the plains adjoining without bush or stubble, all fair green grass, the ground of hard sand, easy to march on, either for horse or foot; the deer crossing in every path, the birds towards the evening singing on every tree with a thousand several tunes, cranes and herons of white, crimson, and carnation perching on the river's side, the air fresh with a gentle, easterly wind and every stone that we stooped to take up, promised either gold or silver by his complexion."

For a moment after Kate had paused, Tom said nothing. He was still in the Americas, tramping with Sir Walter over strange, uncharted country. Then, as if awakening from a dream, he opened his eyes.

"Can you feel satisfied, Kate," he asked, "never to see one hundredth—nay one thousandth—part of the wonders which God has made for us?"

"Why, Tom," exclaimed Kate, surprised at this revelation. I never knew you had the urge to be an explorer like Drake or Raleigh."

"I don't know that I really have," replied Tom. "It is just a fancy which enters my head when I hear these stories. The dangers are great and I could never leave you, my dearest, but all these marvels men write about—the wide seas, the grim and rocky coasts, the fair, smiling fields and great mountains, seem to beckon and tempt me to go over and admire them, while I am confined to a little patch of Cheshire no more than a stone's throw from our own wich."

"But you must never imagine that these sights would ever tempt me away from you," he hastily repeated, stroking a wisp of hair from her forehead. "Do not be offended by my confession. Not all the gold and silver from Sir Raleigh's Guiana, mined, floated down the Orinoco, and heaped up in front of me, would ever persuade me to desert a true and loving wife."

Tom was not surprised when he arrived at Will's lodging a few days before the Feast of St. George, that, instead of having to climb up to the garret where his friend worked and slept, he was shown into a large room full of people, in the part of the house occupied by the shoemaker, who was a man of Will's persuasion. For two or three days past, his fellow-briner had been more cheerful than usual; Tom had even suspected him of humming a tune which sounded more like one of the country ballads popular at the Annual Wakes, than the Psalm of David normally expected from a serious Puritan. It was not until work was over that he had asked Will to explain his exceptionally good humour.

"Come to my lodging after supper," his friend had said shortly, "and you will learn all you wish to know."

Tom was thankful that there was not long to wait before he could satisfy his curiosity. It was a cause for some wonder to his mother that he should venture forth at such a late hour, particularly in the heavy rain which had been falling all the evening, but she did not question him about it, considering that at the age of nearly nineteen he was old enough to look after himself; consequently she merely gave him some instructions about entering the house quietly and bolting the door, as she and Grandfer would be retiring early.

The excitement blazing in Will Masterson's eyes, which Tom saw as he entered the room, had transformed him once again. There had been Will the briner, at the pit-head in his shirt sleeves, pulling on the ropes with his muscular arms, and Will the scholar, quill in hand, bending over his precious diary. Now it was Will the preacher, with stern face and hand raised to still the murmur in the assembly, pronouncing the words of the second commandment, as the text of a speech that was really a sermon.

"Thou shalt not make unto thyself any graven image," Will was saying as Tom opened the door. Then he repeated it slowly for dramatic effect, the weight of his words and the tone in which they were spoken conveying the awfulness of the sin of any transgressor. "Thou shalt not make unto thyself any graven image."

"Friends," said Will in a resonant voice worthy of any preacher, "you all know that some of our following were apprehended by the misguided constables three short months ago and arraigned by the Attorney General in the Court of Star Chamber, for having in this county broken down and defaced by force of arms and in a riotous manner, seven, ancient crosses made of square stone. These idolatrous stumps erected by our purblind ancestors, before which generations of ignorant worshippers have bent the knee, were rightly smashed by the true servants of God, who with their hammers, chains and crowbars wrecked these dumb and dark images which hold the mind in thrall.

"Know you not, blind magistrates that we are forbidden to worship even the true God by idols. The Jews in their wisdom forbade the making of any images. Hence the very standards carried by their Roman conquerors were an abomination to them. Set up in a holy place they were an offence to God. But we do not only reject the signs and symbols of foreign powers or strange heathen gods. Our own true Christian religion requires no such likenesses; the commandment forbids them. They are a denial, my friends, of the truth of the Word, for an image teaches lies. Does it not suggest to us that God is confined in a body, like men, whereas we know that He is an infinite spirit. We read in the Book of Habakkuk, chapter two, verse eighteen 'Woe unto him that saith to the wood, "Awake!" to the dumb stone "Arise, it shall teach!" Behold it is laid over with gold and silver and there is no breath at all in the midst of it'.

"Brothers, think of the Word not of the form of God. Not even in your fancies should you make an image of Him. The power of faith must govern our worship. Let not imagination play a part! Know too, that God is a jealous God. He will punish the idol worshippers and visit the sins on their children into the third and fourth generations if they keep up the false worship they received as a tradition from their fathers, but He will show mercy to his faithful worshippers. Thousands upon thousands in generations to come will receive his mercies if they keep his commandments. Those to whom earnest prayer and preaching and solemn attention to God's Word come before obeisance to mute idols, will rejoice in the blessings the Lord will shower on them.

"My friends, you know too that God in his infinite mercy sent wisdom to the judges of the Court of Star Chamber before whom our brethren in Christ bore witness to their faith, and they were promptly acquitted. Now they have returned to us ready to carry on the work which they so successfully began.

"These images with their painted coats and colours, darken the light of our churches and obscure the brightness of the Gospel. Stone pillars stand in our graveyards and market places like the great statue set up by King Nebuchadnezzar on the plain of Dura, to which at the sound of the cornet, flute and harp, and all kinds of music, the heathen in their folly fell down and paid homage. In the township of Sandbach, but eleven miles from here, two of these abominations stand mocking the faithful in the market place. Rally round, all you who are of our persuasion—you who would see these idols laid low. In three days' time it will be the Feast of St. George. That is the day on which the town of Sandbach, after a thousand years of ignorant worship, will finally be cleansed of these objects of Popish superstition."

There was a murmur of approval in the room when Will ended his speech. After such godly words clapping would have been unseemly, but there was no doubt about the unanimity among those present— with the exception of Tom who had not yet decided on the attitude he should take. Another man, who was unknown to him, stood up and all present bent their heads.

As the lengthy prayers continued, Tom began to wonder if the crosses Will wished to break were really so evil. He had never seen them although they were so close to his home. From Kate he had heard the story of their erection long ago when the old Saxons ruled in the land. She had often accompanied her father on journeys he made to market, for other business purposes, or to visit relatives. They had called on an uncle who lived somewhere beyond Sandbach and she had come back with a pretty story which appealed to her sense of the romantic.

Long ago, Peada, the son of Penda King of Mercia, fell in love with the daughter of Oswy, King of Northumbria, a follower of the true faith who had conquered his father's realm. Oswy would not allow a marriage unless Peada agreed to become a Christian and the young man concurred. Accordingly, he set off on a journey to Northumbria to bring back his bride, Sandbach being a resting place on his return. To mark the baptism of Peada and his Christian marriage, these Saxon men put up two fine crosses in the market place, on which strange scrolls and writings were graven, and quaint pictures of the life of Christ.

He could not believe in his heart that these carvings were so wicked. It would be a far more sinful act to destroy the work of the Saxon craftsmen who had laboured so long to make something of beauty. How would Will feel if the works of his pen were taken and burned by strange hands? What of that once heathen prince rejoicing at having embraced the true faith to gain the princess he desired, who put up this memorial to his joy so that it would be remembered by generations to come? It would be an insult to him to destroy these crosses—almost as bad as trampling on a Christian's grave. He decided that he would not go. But how was he to tell Will? His respect for his friend and tutor prevented him from saying it outright.

The opportunity to avoid this dilemma came when, on the following day, he visited Kate. There was no work for some days at the brine-pit. All the ships of the houses due for walling had been filled, and improvements were being made to the Old Biot, the sides of which were being strengthened and the approaches levelled. Kate's father was planning a business journey to Chester and she had approached him about the possibility of allowing Tom to accompany them.

"Surely one who aspires to become a merchant will need some knowledge of what is before him. He has made great efforts to improve himself and is almost a scholar now," she added with a little exaggeration. I know he will serve a statutory period learning the merchant's trade; that he accepts willingly. The daughter of the house marrying her father's apprentice is quite a common occurrence, but in this case the romance has begun before the young man enters your business. Tom will learn all you have to teach him and I am sure, dear father, he will serve you well."

Kate looked earnestly at Matthew who never could resist the power of those bright, brown eyes.

"Tell me one thing," she said, "and set my mind at rest. Has your reluctance stemmed from the fact that not only merchants' sons-in-law usually come from a higher class than Tom's, but also his apprentices?"

"No, no," said Barton hastily. "I do not object on that account. If I have shown any reluctance at all, it was merely to judge the strength of your determination. When you marry he will be my son. People put their own children to their trades without ceremony. So be it! I can assure you, too, that I have sufficient influence to silence any criticisms from wherever they may come. Tom's family is a good one; they have fallen on hard times, but it is a good one. We only need to go back a generation or two to discover that."

Kate did not know anything very remarkable about Tom's ancestry, but she was glad that her father believed it—and if he believed it he would prove it.

Barton was explaining. First the Wyches:

"Landowners in the past—deprived of their inheritance by the misfortune of an ancestor."

Then the Leys;

"Related to men of the cloth and substantial yeoman farmers."

There was some truth in this latter assertion, as the Reverend John Ley, a well-known clergyman with puritanical leanings could be claimed as a kinsman.

These revelations—true or false—pleased Kate, and she gave a sigh of relief.

"Then it is settled," she said. "You promised to advance him when you gave us your blessing, so let him come on this journey with us. I know he wants to see something of places outside his own neighbourhood. We cannot take him on an expedition of discovery to El Dorado. Chester on a Feast Day is the best that we can offer."

46

Barton nodded his approval. He was glad of this opportunity to get to know the lad and enjoy a little male company. So it was arranged; Tom was able to excuse himself to Will, who to his surprise accepted the explanation without question.

Although he had no pretensions to horsemanship, Master Ley could sit astride and manage a mount which was of a docile nature, and Barton provided two well-groomed, handsome animals for the men, the superior one of which he rode himself. Sometimes Kate rode on a pillion seat, but on this occasion she followed her father riding her own little white mare.

The road was of an average surface for the first four or five miles: rutted, but being on higher ground, free from mud and pools. The morning was clear; a nip in the air made a warm cloak a necessity, but there was no sign of any rain to turn the road into a slippery quagmire. There were unusually few travellers on the road which was a highway between two important towns; only an occasional farm cart, pulled by patient oxen, rumbled along the road, and had to be passed carefully by travellers to avoid stumbling in the channels carved out by the massive wheels of previous traffic. On descending to lower ground Tom was dismayed to see before them a broad stream flowing across the road. He had heard that many of these fords could not be passed without hazard and he was surprised to see Barton's horse plunge unhesitatingly into the water. Kate looked back at Tom as he stopped short of the stream. His horse, as yet unaccustomed to his hand on the rein, reared up.

"Come on!" called the young lady. "Marvel will not let you down."

Tom joked as he splashed through the water.

"Little use I would be as an explorer in foreign parts, if I cannot take my horse through an English ford."

Here the land had been cleared; and for some distance on each side of the road it was enclosed and farmed. The county had been steadily deforested in recent years, but a huge stretch of woodland still covered the greater part of Cheshire—a county teeming with deer, hares, rabbits, foxes, otters, and rich in birds such as pheasants, moorhens, partridges, pigeons, woodcocks, plovers, teals and all kinds of smaller varieties. Tom had never been far beyond the margin of the forest of Acton. The sight of mile upon mile of woodland stretching away into the distance, until the lines of trees became a blur on the horizon or a dense, dark, seemingly impenetrable mass, made him think of the immensity of God's work. To the left of the road, high on a rocky eminence, stood the ancient castle of a crusader knight, with its great round towers and strong curtain wall daring the invader to attack it.

As they came down a gentle slope before the town of Tarporley, they gradually overtook a long line of pack animals. The three horses quickly passed by the slowly moving train and were greeted by a big, gruff, hulking man, with a broad-brimmed hat well down on his forehead and his coat splashed with mud, who was walking beside the sumpter horses, goading them on with a stick over a difficult patch of road. Tom looked at the loads the animals were carrying.

"Salt from the wich," said the man without waiting to be asked about the contents of the panniers. "Too heavily laden, if you ask me. Those who load up the poor beasts should have to pass these infernal fords and contend with this clammy clay."

Tom had never really thought about the salt being carried away far over the county. He had watched the pack trains leaving Nantwich, and for him that had been the end of the matter. Perhaps this was part of a shipment going to Ireland or somewhere else beyond the sea. It pleased him to think that he had played a part in producing it.

By the time they reached Tarporley, where they were to stop for luncheon, the young man had become saddle-sore. A rest was welcome and Mr Barton did not hesitate to order the best of everything, as it was his custom not to stint himself while travelling. He seemed in no hurry to resume his journey after a leisurely meal, a glass of French white wine and a pipe of tobacco in the inn parlour, some special pleading by Kate being necessary to persuade him to remount. It was essential to reach Chester well before sundown and there were at least ten more miles to cover. Leading the way, Barton turned his horse from the high-road soon after leaving the village.

"We should cut at least two miles off the journey," he insisted, as Kate queried the wisdom of departing from the usual route. "These byways can hardly be in any worse condition than the stretch of road I travelled from here to Chester last time I came this way. By making a detour some of the most devilish potholes can be avoided."

Kate bowed to her father's superior knowledge and for a time his opinion was justified. It was Tom who first espied some figures riding out of a dark wood a short distance away to the right. They were also three in number, but the only significant thing he could discern was that they were wearing long, black cloaks and had bulky packages strapped on to their horses.

"Highwaymen!" called Mr Barton. "Ride on steadily."

He drew from his saddle-holster two pistols, one of which he raised up with a defiant gesture in full view of the highwaymen. He discharged it into the air which caused the men to stop and confer. Barton rode on, Tom keeping as close as possible to the elder man's horse.

"Hold on tight, Kate and you get in front, my lad," he cried, spurring on his horse.

Neither the inexperienced Tom, who could not coax his mount into anything much more than a trot, nor his two companions though more mature in equestrianism, could manage enough speed to outdistance their pursuers. Tom obeyed Mr Barton's instructions then he spoke a quick, but earnest prayer which was almost immediately answered, as several labourers working in the fields, having heard the sound of a pistol, came in sight in the nick of time. With his additional troops mustered at the side of the road, Barton decided to risk another shot to scare off the bandits, and fired the other pistol in their direction. Tom thought it odd that the highwaymen had never offered to fire at them, but he was thankful for it. The ball plunged harmlessly into the field, for in truth they were out of range; the shot would not have been sufficient to scare them away, but the sight of the workmen "armed" with scythes, rakes and pitchforks, was enough to put them to flight.

"I shall have to tell Will to put this in his diary," said Tom as they rode on to rejoin the main road. "It is as good a proof of God's Providence as any of those he read out to me."

There was no other incident before they reached Chester, but the sight of the gibbet on a low hill at Boughton, a mile or so from their destination, filled Tom and Kate with horror, and even the hardened Mr Barton could scarcely forbear to shudder as they passed below the gallows tree. He had seen many such sights on his travels, but this was a particularly unpleasant one. A malefactor hung there in chains, and by his condition he appeared to have been suspended for a long time in that place—a warning of dreadful retribution which was in store for highwaymen and their like. The flesh, picked by crows, was shrunken on the bones, and the iron casing clanked and creaked in an eerie fashion as it swung to and fro in the wind. Long after they had descended from the hill and were almost in the land of the living, the mournful sound of the dead man in his iron overcoat reached them. The imaginative Kate said it was as if the voice of the robber was protesting his innocence and pleading for mercy. Mr Barton pooh-poohed this as a piece of fantastic nonsense with the grim remark that he was looking forward to seeing the three men who attempted to rob them, hanging in the same place next time he passed that way.

Once out of sight and earshot of the hideous gallows, they passed quickly through the straggling suburbs of Chester to the old, red, sandstone walls which encompassed the city, and entered by the great Eastgate long before the sun went down beyond the River Dee.

4. ST. GEORGE'S DAY

The ancient city of Chester was a completely new world to Tom. The timber buildings huddled together inside the walls, exceeded by far in number though not in excellence, those of his home-town. The narrowness of the side streets, the height of the buildings nodding across to one another, shut out much of the light, and the channels were obnoxious with refuse and ashes. Close to the Eastgate a large pool or cesspit had become too great an offence even for the city dwellers hardened to such unpleasantness, and not long before, they had petitioned the mayor for its immediate removal. The main thoroughfares were, however, broad and well paved, the houses being raised on pillars with covered sidewalks above, and warehouses at street level. These were the famed rows which distinguished Chester from most other places.

Tom admired these walks and thought them convenient and a security from the sun and weather, but in Mr Barton opinion they made the city look old and ugly, "darkening the streets and hindering the light of the houses." From the vantage point of one of these elevated walks, Tom, Kate and her father, viewed a strange sight. The steeple of St. Peter's in the centre of the city was a lofty stage to which diverse people from mountebanks to clergymen had climbed on festive days to perform a public spectacle.

Cheers went up as a strangely-clad man ascended to the very top of the tower, using extravagant gestures to attract the attention of the crowd; there, after fixing the flag of St. George to a bar of iron which supported the weather-vane, he sounded a drum, shot off a musket and flourished a bright sword. Kate gasped as he then stood on his hands with his feet in the air, while fireworks crackled and spluttered at ground level. Tom applauded this dangerous feat, but Barton remained impassive. He had seen it done before, and insisted that it had never been so expertly performed as at the grand St George's Day parade in

1610, when honour was paid to the late High and Mighty Prince Henry, then Prince of Wales, Duke of Cornwall, and—the title most relevant in this city—Earl of Chester.

Following this display, the onlookers were delighted by the appearance of two Greenmen, their clothing embroidered and decorated with ivy leaves, having black, shaggy hair, and wearing garlands of the same foliage. These club-swinging characters were followed by an artificial dragon, and the legend was acted out as the fearsome beast was shown pursuing savages, entering its den, casting fire, slain, bleeding and staggering. Hard on its heels came the popular figure of St George wearing a helmet and carrying a shield, a squire leading his horse, with three others in his train and a drum sounding as he marched triumphantly through the city.

Other characters followed. "Fame" came on horseback, trumpet in hand, pronouncing an oration. "Mercury" appeared, artificially winged, descending from Heaven in a cloud. "Chester" was represented mounted on a fine horse, followed by minions carrying the arms of St George and the king. "Peace" was there and "Plenty" too, making speeches; the latter was appropriately wearing a wreath of wheat ears on her head and a garland of the same athwart her body, and she strewed grains of corn abroad among the multitude as she passed.

Grim characters were also presented—"Hatred" with a wreath of snakes about her head, and another with hands, face, and arms besmeared with blood. "Love" drove away "Hatred" and then along with "Joy" marshalled the succeeding sport of the day.

Finally, the procession and crowds together, led by the Mayor and Aldermen arrayed in scarlet robes, betook themselves to the Roodee, a fine, spacious piece of ground between the city walls and the river, a detachment of halberdiers and musketeers marching with them. The ships, barques, and pinnaces in the port of Chester displayed the arms of St George on their main-tops and discharged volleys of shot. Bells, which had been carried in the procession, were presented to the Mayor.

A proclamation was made to bring horses to run for the bells and a double race was run to the delight of the spectators. Foot races followed; prizes were given; speeches were made and wreaths were placed on the heads of the victors.

None of Mr Barton's party followed the crowds to the Roodee. Matthew wearied the others with his disparaging remarks about the spectacle they had just enjoyed and his constant comparisons with the triumph in honour of Prince Henry. Soon, however, he had a business acquaintance to meet, and he left the young persons to occupy themselves for the rest of the afternoon.

Tom was anxious to walk along "Caesar's Walls," as he called them, though Kate insisted that much less of them than he imagined, was truly Roman. Still, it was a sure novelty to view the city from above, and standing on the elevated walk over the old Eastgate, he could think of himself as a soldier of the twentieth Legion marching off on some expedition to quell the troublesome tribesmen of the North, or returning from Hadrian's Wall to Deva, full of honours, after establishing the Pax Romana in the wild extremity of the great Empire.

"I have heard that one can make a complete circuit of these walls," said Kate—"nearly two miles until we are here again. Despite the ravages of time and invaders, they still guard the heart of the city."

The couple began to walk slowly along the parapeted pavement. Though once completely enclosed, the city had now burst its seams and spilled out into green fields. Large and small houses were jumbled up together in the compass of the great sandstone circle. Gardens with trees and bushes, vegetable plots haphazardly planted, untidy waste land, ruined buildings, pools, middens and ditches, presented sights usually invisible from street level, which would have been better not seen at all. Within the walls there were patches of void ground and even cornfields in some places, which surprised Tom, who had not expected any agriculture inside the boundaries of the city.

There were grander sights to be seen. Inside the city and hard by the wall, stood the cathedral—once the Abbey of St Werburgh—its squat, undramatic towertop nevertheless higher than their own vantage point.

Here and there where the land fell away, bastions projected from the fortifications—daunting strongpoints set there to discourage any Welsh or English attacker. The most important of these strongholds

53

dominating the defences, was the castle of Chester, a time-worn fortress standing at the top of a moderate incline which descended from its cluster of towers to the waters of the Dee.

By the riverside, crowds swarmed on to the wide green meadow. The ships, riding at anchor flying the colours of St George made Tom think once more of foreign parts. Since Roman times, Chester had been a port of no mean size, the Dee being navigable for quite large vessels until the silting up of the river caused it to diminish. By King Richard II's time the chronicles spoke of shifting sands, and in the sixteenth century a partial remedy for this evil was attempted. A new quay was erected on the Wirral shore about eight miles from the city, at which large ships then prevented by treacherous sands from reaching Chester, were able to dock in safety. Efforts were also made to improve the harbour below the walls and at one time rubbish collected by cleansing the city had been transported to the riverside to make a bank to enlarge the Roodee; but larger ships could no longer come into the city and its days as a port were numbered. The trouble was, so it was said, that "the ground or bottom of the creek was altogether of a loose, light, skittering sand, which upon any powerful gust of wind or current of water, gave way like drifts of snow, and so it was that these mighty heaps of sand were brought by fierce and strong winds up into the narrow creek from which there was no return, neither wind nor water being able to recoil it."

Kate led Tom to the massive edifice of reddish stone which they had admired from the wall. A closer inspection showed the decaying condition of the masonry-stones hollowed out by the weathering of ages, pinnacles perforated the fine edges of the carvings long worn off. The lofty, cool interior had an atmosphere of holy calm.

Kneeling in the painted chapel with its coloured glass and the statues which he had heard so strenuously denounced as idolatrous and Papist, their existence mocking the piety of a true Christian, Tom's thoughts returned to that evening in the shoemaker's shop not more than a few days earlier. He had come thus far with Will, believing that his friend's biblical knowledge had made him wiser than Tom Ley could ever hope to be, but now they were at the parting of the ways. He could not accept the destruction of something which generated only holy thoughts in him and reinforced his belief in the truth of the Word—the blessed life and sacrifice of our Saviour, the piety and martyrdom of the saints. The peace and quiet in the chapel soothed him in contrast to the frenzied fervour of his friend's preaching.

A shudder came over him as he thought of Will urging on his zealous friends to destroy Peada's crosses—perhaps at that very moment. Almost as if they were advancing towards the altar in front of him, he seemed to see the swinging hammers, and hear them crash on the stout stone, with Will standing in front pointing an accusing finger at the hated monuments. Would God bless or censure this action? Will had spoken of divine interventions. A premonition came upon him that they would be punished for it. Yes, there was Will, lying bleeding and insensible before the stones and stumps of the shattered crosses! He looked up at Kate; she noticed the troubled expression on his face.

"Do not worry, dearest," she said when he explained the cause of his anxiety. "Will has much faith in Divine Providence. Surely the Lord will bless and keep safe one whose trust in him is so strong."

They returned to the walls. Tom leaned over the parapet.

"Kate," he said, without turning his head to see her reaction to his request, "may I come to your room tonight?"

The young man's confidence that he had succeeded in winning Kate was waning. There was still no betrothal or marriage in sight, nor had there been any marked improvement in his status. This visit to Chester, made on the pretext of him learning something of the trade he would eventually take over, had done nothing for him. Barton had gone off alone to meet his business associates, and had not once taken Tom into his confidence. Very pleasant it was, inasmuch as it allowed him more time with Kate, but it did not bode well for the future. He had a feeling that her father was less enthusiastic about the match than he had been at first and the dread that he might still withdraw his permission was always present. His love for Kate, once transformed from a desire to win her to a joy in success, was becoming a feeling of having to hold on desperately to the dearest thing he possessed.

"Tom dear," said Kate gently, placing her hand on his arm as it rested on the wall. "Do look at me. You need not be ashamed."

He turned his head and saw a light in her eyes which he had scarcely hoped for. It was an acceptance; he knew it at once. The walls were deserted though it was by no means a late hour. All the world and his wife had gone to see the celebrations on the Roodee. A lone pedlar, carrying two large baskets, came into sight round the bend a hundred yards away. He stopped some distance from the couple, put down his loads and changed hands, before descending the steps by the Eastgate, and disappeared from sight. Tom drew Kate to him, kissed her forehead and cheeks and then her mouth gently.

"It is a risky business," he said, as if regretting that he had made the suggestion. "Do you not fear your father's wrath?"

"He will not beat me or disown me, but it would be well if we were assured that he does not come to know of it. Though seldom guilty of drunkenness, he is a good trencherman and wine bibber, taking more than a 'little for his stomach's sake'. As you must already realise he always contrives to enjoy himself to the full when he makes these journeys. Drink induces sleep, and if we wait until he retires we should be quite safe until morning."

The inn where they were staying could only supply two rooms, so Tom had to share with Mr Barton, but with the bed curtains drawn, and Kate's father under the influence of good French wine, it was hardly likely that his absence would be noticed. Tom kissed Kate again, and laid his hand on her breast to feel her beating heart.

"Love demands nearness," he whispered, "and tonight we will be closer than ever. If I were asked why I love you, I could only say: 'You are my Kate; you are beautiful; you are gentle and kind.' Others are so too, I know; yet their beauty does not dazzle me, nor the kindness of their natures tempt me. I feel that God in his great book wrote your name opposite mine, in letters which can never be erased."

Mr Barton was long in the inn parlour that evening and Tom despaired at ever being able to join Kate. The babble of conversation and gusts of laughter which wafted up from below, suggested that there was a full, merry company present, and it gave Tom hope that his prospective father-in-law would be well plied with wine before retiring. At last, soon after the watchman beneath the window had called out the midnight hour, the bedroom door swung open and the creaking floorboards announced the arrival of Mr Barton, as he shuffled with unsteady steps across their well-worn surface.

A single, guttering candle stood on a small table by Kate's bed. She laid aside the book she had been reading by its flickering light, and smiled at Tom as he appeared. He thought he had never seen anything or anyone so beautiful. Her long ringlets fell down to her shoulders like a dark shimmering cascade against the whiteness of her pillow and nightgown. The far corners of the room were shrouded in darkness, the only light the feeble, unsteady gleam of the candle flame. The closeness of her embrace, the softness of her skin, the perfume of her hair, the sweetness of her whispers, filled him with ecstasy. A sudden draught blew out the almost spent candle, which had shortened itself to half its length since his arrival. Tom rose and struck a light. The pale flame illuminated Kate's face. Her cheeks were flushed, her hair disordered, but just as beautiful in its confusion. A tiny tear of happiness showed in the corner of one of her eyes.

"May God grant me a son," she said in an unnaturally low voice. "Father would forgive me anything for that."

Tom leaned towards her, and said touchingly: "A little girl, another you, is all my heart's desire."

"A girl I—"said Kate wonderingly. "Then truly you do not believe that 'women are a necessary evil, a deadly fascination, and a painted ill'. But if you want it so, I'll beg the Lord to send 'another me', as you so sweetly put it."

"Lynette!" she said, with sudden inspiration, looking at the title of the romance which lay open by her bed.

"Lynette! There you have a name with a sound of music and poetry in it to grace a little girl."

5. DUMB AND DARK IMAGES

It is a happy man who never doubts the rightness of his actions—
who can see God's clear light leading him on the narrow path through
the dark valley of life. Will Masterson embraced that perfect faith
which removes all fears and doubts, but as he was ready to admit, it
had not always been so. With typical Puritan exaggeration, he
described himself as "one who lived in and loved darkness, a grievous
sinner and hater of light", who despite his former rejection of
godliness, had been raised from the depths and taught submission to
the will of his Maker. Haunted and tormented in a whirlwind of
questioning and doubts, he had wrestled long with his thoughts, had
struggled hard against disbelief and temptation, emerging at last
triumphant. The strength of his Calvinistic creed was that it related all
human life to God—God supreme, revealed in Christ. Confession of
sin, repentance, belief in salvation—the perfect gift of God—had
brought him at the age of twenty eight to an iron certainty, and had
raised him from the dark vale of despair to the exaltation of one who
has "found Christ".

This state of religious assurance possessed him, as in the early
morning light, while Tom lay still abed in Chester dreaming of his
Madonna-like Kate, Will led a band of the faithful—smaller than had
been expected, but sufficiently large to accomplish their purpose—on
the road to Sandbach, bent on destruction. Will marched in front
leading the singing of a psalm. John Shenton, the blacksmith, his
experience with the hammer much valued, brought up the rear pulling
a handcart laden with hammers, but the going was good and the day
promised to be fine.

Eleven miles was no great distance for unencumbered marchers,
and the only difficulty they encountered was at one ford where the
handcart had to be unloaded before crossing and reloaded with its
assorted tools and weapons on the other side. Two horsemen rode by,
one ambling in the direction of Nantwich, the other spurring his horse

past them towards Sandbach. Realizing that the inhabitants would be forewarned, Will urged on his men to cover the last four miles as soon as possible. Some beggars passed, the men with their long staves striding along, the women trying to lead on a crowd of ragged children in some sort of order, but they gave Will's party a wide berth, as if fearing they might be pressed into service by the psalm-singing Puritans.

At the last milestone before Sandbach, Will Masterson called a final halt while he gave out detailed instructions for the demolition of the crosses. Clubs were issued in case of an attack by the enraged citizens. The blacksmith had brought a musket and another fellow had a rusty sword, but Will would not allow these lethal weapons; he gave strict orders that even the clubs should only he used in self-defence. The musket and sword were returned to the handcart, which was left at the milestone in charge of Shenton's son, the youngest member of the party, a boy of fourteen, while the grim-faced Puritans with instruments of destruction on their shoulders and determination in their hearts, silently entered the little town.

The market place was deserted when Will stood up, and pointing at the crosses with an accusing finger, denounced them, in a voice which rang round the square as if the very stones were to hear and understand his accusation. Scarcely had he finished speaking when the doors of houses surrounding the market place opened and equally determined and similarly armed men advanced on the Puritans. A group placed themselves between Will and the crosses.

"Stand aside!" he thundered. "Do not think we are ignorant persons like those who throw down crosses to find mythical pots of gold beneath them. We do the work of God and man in destroying these objects of superstition. The Lord forbids such dumb and dark images in his holy scriptures, and the King's learned judges but a short time ago acquitted our brethren who broke such crosses in sundry places in Cheshire and were arraigned for it before the High Court of Star Chamber. Stand aside, I say for as Gideon laid low the altar of his father and cut down the grove that was by it, I have sworn that these idols shall remain no longer an abomination in the eyes of the godly."

"Canting Puritans!" called out an equally stern voice from behind the line of townsmen defending their heritage, and a figure in cassock and surplice stepped forward.

"Blasphemous sons of Satan, do not dare to lay your hands on these holy crosses which have stood in this place for nigh on a thousand years as witnesses to the piety of our ancestors—those humble craftsmen who dedicated the excellence of their talents to the glory of God, those holy priests who blessed them and their labours. Can you not see that it would be a vile crime to tear down the work of their hands—a blasphemous act to smite with your cruel hammers the likeness of our Saviour? You speak of Gideon, but this is no heathen altar. We love the Word as you do, but we know that the Word was made Flesh and dwelt among us. For us Christ was made Man and with his sacrifice brought us salvation—so as a man we see him here—living, crucified, risen from the dead. Nor do we bow the knee to any Roman bishop, you erring Puritans. Never call us Papists—we abhor that name as you do. Go your ways in peace and do not trouble us again."

The parson raised his hand as if to call down the fire of heaven on these sons of Belial, but his action made no more impression on Will than his words had done before. Thrusting him roughly aside, he gave a signal for the onslaught on the crosses, but the push the parson had received, insignificant as it would have been on level ground, caused him to fall from the steps of the cross on to the cobbles, where he lay stretched out for a moment as if a bolt from Heaven had struck him down. Enraged that his parson should have been so roughly treated by the leader of these threatening intruders, a burly townsman sprang forward and dealt Will a mighty blow with the stout club he was carrying, knocking him to the ground where he lay insensible with blood flowing from a deep gash in his head.

The worsened situation could well have resulted in a pitched battle, had not the parson risen and forbidden any more violence from the inhabitants. He protested that he was a Man of Peace and that God himself would punish, without there being any need for his people to sin by laying violent hands on fellow men, but in truth Will's was the stronger and more determined party, and discretion was the better part of valour.

Many of the townsfolk had not turned out to face the Puritans, some already melted away convinced by Will's assertion that he and his followers were acting legally; others realising the strength of feeling shown by the iconoclasts, had no desire to be caught up in an affray with such zealous fanatics. Even if they drove them off, armed with such precedents, they would most probably return with reinforcements, so the inevitability of the destruction of their crosses stared them in the face. Thus they had to stand and watch as the Puritans with mocking words began their orgy of destruction.

Will saw nothing of the deed he had provoked. Carried away to the first milestone, he was placed on the handcart and pushed for two miles along the road towards Nantwich. Near the village of Wheelock, Richard Sandham, a noted Puritan, would give him shelter, and it was to this man's house that the still insensible Will, bleeding through his hastily tied bandages, was carried.

Sandham's wife had some skill in herbal medicine, so it was in her care that the leader of the iconoclasts was left, while his Christian soldiers with their hammers and crowbars brought the hated monuments to the ground. The honour of the first blows went to the blacksmith, whose tremendous strokes of the heavy hammer crashed six times against the stone, unyielding as yet. As the blows rang round the square, cheers from the Puritans and groans from the townsfolk mingled with the noise of the hammer. Others joined in and the crashing of metal on stone sent sparks and splinters flying, but still the cross stood firm.

"Ropes and chains!" ordered Shenton, so these were fastened to both crosses. Hammers and crowbars went to work again; then with a long pull and a strong pull, the loosened part of the larger cross came crashing down upon the steps.

"Its neighbour!" shouted the blacksmith and the iconoclasts belaboured the smaller monument almost in a frenzy, until it too collapsed into a pile of rubble.

"Your Dagon is fallen down!" shouted Becket the cobbler, Will's landlord, as they went to work with crowbars wrenching off pieces of the broken stone.

"Crows pull down crosses and daws must set them up again," punned Becket, whereupon the rest of his party burst into mocking laughter. Now this self-appointed leader stood on the steps of the smaller cross, the stump of which was still fixed in its socket, and raising his hands in imitation of Will's style, he praised the Lord whose image he had just laid low.

"Blessed be the Lord God of Israel from everlasting to everlasting, and let all the people say: 'Amen.' Praise the Lord."

It was no great surprise to Tom on his return to Nantwich to find his friend absent and to hear of his misfortune on the cross-breaking expedition, his premonition in Chester Cathedral having warned him to expect something of the sort. Nevertheless, his concern for Will led him to persuade Mr Barton to lend him a horse, and in the company of the blacksmith, he rode to Wheelock.

He found his friend resting in the parlour of a plainly furnished but substantial farm house, his wound freshly bandaged by Mrs Sandham and his fever lowered by her expert use of herbs. Will was noticeably chastened by the fact that not only the crosses but he himself had been laid low. His detailed account of the march to Sandbach was followed by a dramatic description of the destruction of the monuments, the outline of which he had heard from his fellows, the rest being supplied by his own vivid imagination. He had little to say about his brush with the parson and the wound he had received in consequence, except to insist that all servants of the Lord must be prepared to suffer for their beliefs.

Tom listened in silence and Will noticed his lack of enthusiasm.

"Do you not rejoice with me," he asked, "that these objects of superstition have been broken and their pieces scattered?"

"No, Will, I cannot," replied Tom honestly. "Your knowledge of God's Word is greater than mine—you have all the biblical texts on the tip of your tongue—but I cannot reconcile the destruction of these holy works with true religion. My conscience forbade me to march with you and your deed can give me no pleasure. I can only rejoice that my friend feels satisfaction in the belief that he has been an instrument of God, and that serves to make him well again. Permit me my conscience, Will, and I will allow yours."

Masterson extended his hand to his friend, pleased that Tom had confessed the original reason for his absence from among the soldiers of the Lord. He had realised almost at once that his persuasion had not been fully effective and had suspected that the journey to Chester had been contrived to provide an excuse for his absence. He valued their friendship and was not going to let this break it up. There was always hope that Tom would at some future date come round to acceptance of the truth as he himself saw it.

Shenton had gone to the kitchen to refresh himself, and Mrs Sandham brought some cold beef and ale into the parlour. Will filled Tom's tankard and passed it over to his friend.

"Tom," he said confidentially, "I have a mind to marry."

"Marry?" repeated Tom. He had never thought of his friend as a marrying man. "Whom have you in mind?"

"Your sister, Alice," returned Masterson, "Do you think she would look kindly on me?"

Tom could hardly believe his ears. He would have been little more surprised if Will had said he wished to marry the Infanta of Spain.

"I am sure Alice will have no objection if you pay court to her. She has always admired your intellect. She is a chaste and kind girl and would even excuse your part in the destruction of the crosses with its adventurous appeal; but I feel that mother would find it disagreeable; she has no strong feelings about Puritanism or High Church ceremonies, but the idea of a son-in-law who goes off belabouring church windows with a walking stick, or inciting a crowd to smite ancient crosses and gets a broken pate in the bargain, would not appeal to her. Grandfer, too, whose memories go right back to the beginning of Puritanism, has few good words for those who wish to take away all the things of beauty in our churches."

Will smiled reassuringly. "Do not fear that I will offend your mother and grandfather. Perhaps the Lord sent this hurt to show me that there is a better way than acts of violence. Can we not rather change the hearts of men by the purity and power of the Word and make them see the sinfulness of their disobedience to God's commandments? Then they will neglect and finally dismantle these objects of superstition of their own accord."

After parting from his friend, Tom had intended to return immediately to Nantwich, but on coming out into the open road;

63

curiosity overtook him and he turned his horse in the direction of Sandbach. Shenton had no desire to reappear where he would be recognized as one of the iconoclasts, so Tom rode alone. There had been a market that day, held around the remains of the crosses, but by the time Tom arrived, the stalls were being dismantled. More than once as he rode round the square, he received black looks from the townsfolk, who fearing that some further irruption would disturb the peace of the town, denied their usual civil welcome even to passing and seemingly innocent strangers.

The stump of the once smaller cross, now considered by the Puritans to pose no further threat to true worship, stood taller than its broken neighbour. Some stones still littered the cobbles, three large sections lay piled up at the foot of the major cross. One piece had found a home as a step for a cottage opposite, the rest must no doubt have been carried away.

To Tom it was a pitiful sight—almost as if a living being had been maimed. A man made straight for him across the square; Tom felt uncomfortable, fearing that the stranger was about to challenge or reproach him, presuming him to have had a part in the sad business.

But he spoke mildly. Tom had the impression that he expected some reward for his advice.

"Pieces there for the taking, young master, if you can carry them away. A bit of useful building stone! The gentry got more than their fair share, but I managed to find a lump or two—just what I needed to finish the wall of my well. I am just repairing it, you see, when I hear this tremendous crash. I come out and lo! there are stones all over the place—just like the manna the Bible says fell from Heaven. So I pick up a few and load them on my little handcart, and now my well is as good as new."

Without replying, Tom turned away in disgust. So much for venerating these 'objects of superstition'. To this man they were just useful building stone, to others time-honoured decorations for their parks and gardens.

He was glad that Will had dedicated himself to gentler methods of persuasion. This change in tactics was more likely to recommend him to mother and Grandfer, and Tom was flattered by the idea of having

Will Masterson as his brother-in-law. He would make it his business to see that Alice accepted him. She had always spoken well of him, though by no stretch of the imagination could he believe that it would be a love match to compare with his passion for Kate. His sister was anxious to leave the drudgery of the salt-house, which would also tell in favour of Will's proposal. His brining days were likely to be drawing to a close and that was a further favourable point. The school at Walbury needed a master; Will was a likely candidate to fill the vacancy, for now the parish had a parson with puritanical leanings. His friend had often spoken of Mr Malbon, for whom he had the same kind of respect as Tom had for him. It would be necessary for Will to conform outwardly to the tenets of the established church to obtain this post, but he felt sure that with Mr Malbon's support any puritanical indiscretions on his part would be condoned. His betrothal and marriage to Kate and Alice's union with Will, could mean that at last blissful days were ahead for the Ley family. God's Providence and a true-life romance!

As Tom had expected, Alice received Will's interest in her with enthusiasm, and her mother was not at all averse to the match, especially when she heard of the resolution her prospective son-in-law made to Tom. She would lose another wage, to be sure, but she could resume her father's trade of stocking weaving. Grandfer had a little money and a frame of the type invented by William Lee in 1589. Tom promised, too, that he would give her any assistance which proved necessary. He would not be far away from her, and though it was scarcely possible for Margery to visualise him as a prosperous merchant, she knew her boy was talented enough to rise in the world. When he did so he would not forget his mother. She was glad for Alice's sake too; the girl was over twenty, at an age when she should already have a new family around her; by her age Margery had already borne two children.

Tom's sister could by no means be described as a beauty. Her grey eyes, corn-coloured hair and pale skin, roughened by the salty air of the wich house, the small, stubby hands hardened by constant use of rake and broom, made her a typical Ley, unlike Tom who derived his good looks from the Wyches, a family well-known in the town for its handsome offspring. She was much shorter than Kate, though this was to her advantage, as she did not exceed the moderate height of her husband-to-be. In spite of her plainness Alice was of a modest, uncomplaining temperament, and one could easily see her as the obedient wife of a masterful Puritan 'paterfamilias'.

Perhaps it was this lack of outward beauty which attracted Will— "fair women a snare for young men". Certainly he had spoken on these lines not long before, and Tom had taken his words to mean that he was little interested in marriage. Will's perception could penetrate the outward shell. In his religion it was the inner beauty of the Word he sought, not the outward show, so in choosing his life's partner golden glitter did not dazzle him, and he recognised the beauty of the soul. Tom considered himself fortunate among men that in Kate he had found both.

On his return from Wheelock, Masterson was a regular visitor to the Ley's house. The courting settle, on which generations of Wyches and Alice's father had spent sweet hours, was placed at his disposal. No one quite knew how long this grand piece of oak had been in the family's possession. Grandfer said it was since the days of King Richard the Crookback, and he embroidered the tale with some superfluous details. His great Grandfather had made it himself; it was "on the very day when the tyrant fell at Bosworth Field and young Henry Richmond found his crown hanging on a thorn bush" that his ancestor had driven in the last nail. Margery maintained it was later. She had heard from her mother that at the very time when Queen Anne was languishing in the Tower awaiting her cruel fate, the old settle had been "bought from a great man's house". Whatever its origin, it was an ancient piece of furniture, and it had long been a tradition among the Wyches and the Leys, that a kiss on the courting settle was necessary to ensure a happy and fruitful marriage. Will thought this a frivolous though harmless superstition, but nevertheless, to avoid offending the family, he complied.

There was little romance in Will's proposal, though beneath his stern exterior he was a compassionate and affectionate man. Though he seldom betrayed the fact, he had a strong, brotherly feeling for Tom and it had not even been impaired by the younger man's avoidance of participation in the destruction of the crosses and his subsequent confession. To Will this marriage was an opportunity for close union with another—two souls indissolubly bound together in Christ—a companionable, respectable, holy relationship, without grossness or

66

jealousy—-an opportunity to instruct an almost virgin mind and to pass on his knowledge of God's word with daily prayers and homilies to a family which would grow up in a household dedicated to the service of the Lord.

A few days after Will had done his duty on the courting settle, Tom heard to his immense satisfaction that Mr Barton had at last decided not only to give formal consent to the marriage, but to find a place for his son-in-law and probable heir in the business enterprises he controlled. The date was fixed. Tom was in the seventh heaven of happiness when he considered that before Michaelmas, he would be joined for life to his darling Kate.

6.   THE CHESHIRE PROPHET

Even the discomforts of wind and rain, the hazard of the rough Cheshire roads among the worst in the country and the danger of becoming a victim of highway robbery, did not take away Matthew Barton's zest for travel. He loved nothing better, whenever time allowed, than to sit astride his horse and jog along the highway, making frequent and lengthy stops at country inns to refresh himself. He could have produced a gazetteer of the hostelries in Cheshire and even to some extent in neighbouring counties. He knew the bug-infested "penny-hedge inns" and the "good ordinaries". He could make his way without hesitation to "a neat and excellent place", where one could dine on chicken, plover, sturgeon, tarts, mince pies, and jellies for eighteen pence, and drink aqua vitae and French wine like a civilized man instead of swilling ale. In his younger days Barton had travelled well beyond the borders of his native county, even as far as London, which he had described as "a place full of high buildings, foul streets, and many sweaty bodies".

Kate did not share her father's passion for sitting long hours on a horse, though she welcomed an occasional change of scene and liked to please her father by accompanying him; but Tom's new enthusiasm for travel made him an ideal substitute for her on Mr Barton's journeys. Matthew was pleased to have him as a companion, especially as he found his future son-in-law's respect for his knowledge of the highways and byways very flattering.

One such journey was made to visit Matthew's brother, the innkeeper, near Over. Dating from the fourteenth century, the *Swan Inn* stood hard by the bank of the River Weaver, its well-worn timbers leaning so far towards the water that it seemed on the point of taking off at any moment and turning itself into a real swan. It boasted a crudely painted sign instead of merely having a pole bearing a bunch of evergreens, which was often used to identify a minor hostelry. A fading, scrawny bird floated past the pinnacled façade of a gentleman's residence, along a waterway almost indistinguishable from the grass of its bank.

The inside of the inn was low and depressing, the beams dangerous to a man of above average height, but the rooms were clean, gleams of copper and brass shone from the nooks and chimney breasts, the floors were freshly sanded and the tables scrubbed. The landlord greeted Matthew warmly, some months having passed since they last met, and he eyed with curiosity the strange choice his brother had made for his eldest daughter's hand. His wife, however, was a jolly, bustling, little woman and her friendliness to Tom soon made up for the landlord's cool reception.

The long ride had given them good appetites, so it was fortunate that Mrs Barton's fare excelled that in any of the other places Tom had visited. He told the landlady so.

"I wouldn't be surprised to hear that travellers come miles out of their way to eat at this inn," he said, this compliment convincing Mrs Barton that he was a young man of taste who deserved some pampering.

"Aye to be sure they do," she replied, "and not only that, but the parson of Weaver—a bachelor man, he is—often rides all the way over here to eat his Sunday lunch, though there be three other inns on the road where he could stop. He says that if his housekeeper could cook like I do, he'd publish the banns and marry her without delay."

The brothers began to exchange news. Henry Barton had heard all about the destruction of the ancient crosses—even down to the eventual fate of the pieces. He did not approve of these violent acts, although on the whole he was inclined towards Puritanism. He had some news of his own to tell.

Farmer Crowton's ploughboy, the idiot Nixon, who fell into trances and ran about prophesying, was to go up to London at the invitation of the king himself. Mr Cholmondeley had told his Majesty about the lad, and James's curiosity had been aroused to see this strange prodigy. Some of the prophecies he had uttered were merely of Cestrian importance, others were predictions of national and even international events.

Henry Barton brought out a piece of paper on which he had recorded a few of these utterances related to him by one who was actually present when Nixon fell into a trance. It was an unattractive document in crabbed handwriting, creased, and bearing a grease mark in one corner, as if it had been written on the kitchen table. Matthew read out slowly:

"*If a favourite of the king shall be slain, the master's neck shall be cleft in twain*'. Now what do you think of that?" he asked; then he answered his own question: "If the Duke of Buckingham shall be slain—there's a sure choice for that title—then King James shall be beheaded. How could that possibly come about? Buckingham might fall to some assassin—or perhaps some other favourite of whom we know nothing as yet—but who under Heaven would chop off the head of our King?"

"His mother was executed," Henry reminded him.

"Aye, but that was ordered by another monarch—our late Queen. Who rules now in these islands or elsewhere and would execute our king? I would not baulk at '*slain*'—kings have suffered that fate before,—but '*his neck shall be cleft in twain*'. That can only mean execution by the public hangman."

"Read on," said his brother. "There is more."

"'*The Men of the North shall sell precious blood—yea their own blood—and a Man from the East shall bring his lord to the tribunal.*' This just confirms my belief that the prophet talks nonsense. As I see it, he implies that our king will be sold by Scots—those '*Men from the North of his own blood*'—brought to a tribunal by some mythical '*Man from the East*' and suffer decapitation. Listen to this! The prophet speaks in riddles. '*When an oak tree shall be softer than men's hearts, then look for better times, but they be but beginning.*'

"This too: '*The departure of a great man's soul shall trouble a river hard by and overthrow trees, houses and estates.*' '*Men and horses shall walk upon the water, but trouble is preparing for the kings, and the great yellow fruit shall come over to this country and flourish.*'

"So here we have the history of our times! Buckingham or some other favourite shall be slain, the king tried and sent to the block; a great man shall die in a storm, and a foreign army will invade England. How an oak tree and a great yellow fruit come into the story is beyond me. What a farrago of nonsense!"

"Perhaps these prophecies about a king do not refer to his present majesty at all," ventured Tom—"the Prince of Wales perhaps, or some foreign ruler—or is there perhaps some juggling with the word 'master'? I must admit I'm ignorant, but tell me Mr Barton, what is so remarkable about these sayings? Perhaps he just made them up. We do not know yet if there is any truth in them—and are we going to find out in our lifetimes? How far ahead do his predictions stretch?"

These matters would become clearer within a ring of smoke. Matthew Barton agreed that some proof of the prophet's ability should be shown so he began filling his pipe from his brother's tobacco box, a practice which Henry good-naturedly always permitted.

"I heard of a Frenchman once, who in the last century foretold events as far ahead as 1999. He was on safe ground there, to be sure. The worms will have had their way with all of us long before then. Have some of Nixon's other prophecies been fulfilled? Before I believe in this soothsayer, I'll have to be shown that something he said has come to pass."

His brother seemed a little offended, as if he himself had some responsibility for the veracity of the prophetic statements.

"I would not scoff and cry 'Liar!' Some of his sayings have already been proved. It seems that the first time he showed any wonderful powers was while he was driving one of his brother's oxen. He used the goad with great cruelty, and the man guiding the plough threatened to tell his master. Nixon replied that it did not matter as in three days the ox would no longer belong to his brother—and this came to be true—for as he had foretold, the beast was taken in payment of heriot by the Lord of the Manor. Then again he promised an heir to the Cholmondeleys when an eagle should sit atop their house at Vale Royal. Sure enough, a bird perched on the great bow window and could not be scared away until the babe was born—a healthy son, just as Nixon had promised. He said too that black birds should sit on Headless Cross and there should be a great battle, a wall of Mr

Chomondeley's should fall, which if it fell a certain way would indicate that the Church would flourish. There were many other things too which I cannot call to mind. Oh yes! He said that the Lord of Oulton would be hanged at his own door."

"Has that come true?" asked Tom rather incredulously.

"In a way—yes. A fatal accident befell the gentleman at the gates of his park, when his horse threw him and he was dragged along with one foot in the stirrup.

Another thing—our prophet rarely speaks. Only when he is in a trance are his words full of meaning. For the rest of the time he babbles only gibberish—some strange, heathen language understood by nobody. You and I, brother, could make claims because we have read and talked about them. This man is illiterate and an idiot, yet in his oracles he speaks as if with certain knowledge. Tell me if you can, where does it come from?"

"I know what I'll do," he said brightly. "I'll take you to see the dreamer myself."

The way to Nixon's cottage was over the river, which they crossed by a plank bridge, and along a narrow path towards an isolated farm. It was a muddy way through fields of young corn and hedged-in meadows. The land was still partly wooded, copses straggled along the borders of the cultivated land, offshoots of a larger wood, itself just a projection from the great Delamere Forest.

After clambering over several stiles, they came in sight of a ramshackle cottage standing on a rise. If the *Swan Inn* was decrepit, this was a positive ruin. Wattle showed between the beams, and the thatch needed patching. Hens pecked their way in and out of the vegetable patch and scratched in the dust round the dunghill by the back door; ducks waddled out of a dirty pond in front of the cottage, and from a sty, closer to the house than one would expect for comfort, porcine grunts could be heard. In the gloomy interior of this miserable dwelling, the three men found the prophet huddled in a corner, tearing lumps off a loaf of bread, dipping them into a dish of gravy and overstuffing his mouth. His mother welcomed the visitors after a fashion, but from Nixon they heard nothing but grunts, little different from those uttered by the swine; he spoke only in unintelligible monosyllables.

"Is he always so surly?" asked Matthew Barton, surprised at this unsociable behaviour.

"He's difficult," said the mother. "He doesn't say much except when he is in one of his trances—and then we can't stop him—neither coaxing nor blows will bring him out again. He doesn't like work either. We always had to beat him to get him out of doors. Farmer Crowton says he taught him nothing except to lead his oxen in a straight line and hold his goad correctly. The children hate him and he hates them. They come around and tease him, and that puts him in a bad humour like he is today."

Nixon picked up a large bone and began gnawing off the meat. Tom could see him better now. He had a great head which he suddenly raised to look in the direction of the visitors, and goggly eyes which stared vacantly beyond the three men as if he were unaware of their presence.

"He'll have to smarten himself up before he goes to the king," said Matthew Barton, looking with evident disgust at the prophet's unshaven chin and dark matted hair. Nixon's mother agreed.

"He's a wayward lad," she said. "If I tell him to do something he snarls at me like a bad-tempered dog. Mr Cholmondeley will have to take him in hand. He always obeys him. That kind gentleman gave him a sovereign for some new clothes, and another one for me. I got the suit for him, but he refused to put it on and just sits around in that old jacket and breeches."

Tom found Nixon's appearance disturbing and was tiring of the unedifying spectacle of watching him stuff himself with meat and drink. He nudged Mr Barton, who understood his meaning.

"Thank you Mistress Nixon. I hope your boy is well rewarded by the King."

He turned to go and lifted the door latch. The two brothers were already outside the cottage, and Tom was about to close the door, when suddenly a loud, clear voice from the corner intoned in perfect English:

"Men shall fall from a high place and suffer no hurt, but children yet unborn shall bewail their falling. I see men and women, spotted like beasts and their nearest and dearest friends affrighted at them. I see towns on fire and innocent blood shed."

He pointed a finger dramatically at Tom.

"Thy happiness shall be broken," he declared, "and thou shalt find no peace until thou comest to the great melting mountain."

The prophet sank back and resumed his supper, grunting as before as if nothing had happened. Matthew Barton uttered a few petty oaths which would have made a true Puritan blanch; the look of embarrassment and disappointment on his brother's face changed to one of satisfaction that he had not brought them to the seer in vain. Tom felt depressed by this prophet of doom and gloom. All this about birds, fruit, great melting mountains, and falling from high places! What did it mean? From whom did this man receive his power? From God or the devil? He had been taught that sinners are punished by God's hand even in this world, and the good are rewarded with bountiful mercies.

"By my faith, he was worse today than I've seen him before," said Henry Barton, as they returned across the fields to the *Swan*. He is loath to go to London, you know. I suppose that's what made him so sullen. They say he foretold his own death. He ran around Over, shouting: "I'll be clemmed if I go! I'll be clemmed!—and that in a place of plenty! Everyone laughed at the idea of starving in the king's palace, which only enraged him more. Then mocking children ran after him until he grabbed a big stick and chased them away."

Tom did not dare to tell Will about his encounter with the prophet, but he confided in Kate. She comforted him. "Man's life is but short," she said. "Let us not permit the dark cloud of these foreboding words to blot out the sunshine of our happiness. We are all in the hands of our Heavenly Father; contentment will come if we trust in Him. Pray with me, Tom, and say to the Lord in all humility: "Thy will be done.""

7. THE BLACK SCOURGE

On the thirtieth day of August in the year of grace 1631, a proclamation of Robert Cholmondeley, Lord of the Manor, was read to the inhabitants of Wich Malbank by John Offley, his deputy steward, who accompanied by the bailiffs, came into open market when it was at its height. Thomas Venables, Bailiff of the Court Leet, made a solemn "Oyez! Oyez!" and John Offley proceeded to read out the proclamation which Venables repeated in an "audible and public voice." It was read for the second time in the High Town, then it was nailed to a post where it stood for four or five hours.

This simple sheet of paper bore the dreaded news that the plague had been raging in many parts of the country—in London, Yorkshire and Lancashire, especially in Preston, where it had been reported that the town had been almost depopulated and corn was rotting on the ground for want of reapers. It was also in Shrewsbury, Wrexham, and many other parts of Wales and the Borders, but thus far Cheshire had been preserved. Public fasts were kept; prayers were said each day that the county of Cheshire should be spared this fearful visitation. The Bartholomew Fair was due to take place in eleven days' time; the crowds which would accompany the vendors from distant parts of the county and beyond its confines, could not be permitted to bring the black scourge of the plague to Nantwich.

The bailiff's voice rang out across the square and the local men and women, elevated in the proclamation to the position of citizens of Wich Malbank, listened attentively to hear the worst.

"Forasmuch as it is feared that some parts of the county of Chester as well as diverse places in the shires and towns adjoining, are already infected with this disease…"

Tom who was standing in the crowd shivered with horror. The 'public voice' went on:

"...To the end that all means may be used to prevent the danger of infection from the town of Wich Malbank and places adjacent, which the great concourse of people to the said fair may be likely to endanger, it is therefore thought fit in His Majesty's name, to command, appoint, and give notice to all manner of persons, foreigners, strangers and others that live in or near to any place infected, that they abstain to come into the said town for the space of five days..."

This was the Year Four all over again. "May God preserve Kate and my little children," murmured Tom.

The crier was elaborating on the prohibition of trade.

"...For the space of five days to wit the fair day and four days next after, no clothier, draper, upholsterer, brazier, pewterer, pedlar, or other chapman shall send or convey any manner of wares or merchandise to the said fair from any place or places before prohibited.

God save the King and the Lord Viscount Cholmondeley!" he concluded with a flourish.

Tom was only a small child in that dreadful 'Year Four', but he had dim memories of crying bitterly because he was forbidden to see his father, of the long hours of confinement to the house, of the grim cart of death rattling along on the cobbles outside, and the mournful pealing of the great bell announcing another victim. The plague had been very hot that year in London and many other towns and cities. On July 29th, it was brought from Chester to Nantwich, and in the space of six months the town's market trade had been spoiled, it had been abandoned by its more wealthy inhabitants, and over four hundred of the townsfolk had been carried off by the dread contagion. There had been outbreaks in the intervening years, though none was so severe; now the threat of mass sickness was very real once more.

Tom's old family had been decimated by that former visitation. How could he let his new family be exposed to the same dreadful danger? His life with Kate had been filled with bliss for above twelve years; his visit to her room in Chester did not result in her immediate conception, nor was his wish for a baby girl granted at once. Sadness there had been too, for the first children of the marriage, both boys, had died in infancy. Then Tom's 'heart's desire', duly named Lynette, was born, a pretty child, who promised from birth to fulfil his desire for 'the very image of her mother'.

His education now matched that of Kate and Mr Barton and he had not even any qualms about taking on Will in a discussion about the burning topics of the day. Mr Barton was pleased with his son-in-law's participation in many of his undertakings, frequently saying to anyone willing to listen, that his assessment of the young man had been entirely correct, for he had found a husband for his daughter who had an excellent head for business. Of course the statement was not quite accurate, for it was Kate who had chosen her own husband, but Matthew had acquiesced; he was content and liked to praise himself for his perspicacious judgement, so for several years his relationship with the only one he could call his son, remained very close.

The tenancy of Barton's other house became vacant, whereupon Tom and Kate received a comfortable, spacious bow-windowed residence with some fine panelling and decorative plaster ceilings, looking out over a pretty garden to green fields and the river beyond.

In 1625 Tom's situation changed to some extent, for Barton had been widowed when his wife died producing a male heir, who rapidly followed his mother. In that year he married again, this second union being blessed with a healthy son. Apart from the solace of his new wife, Barton considered his other two daughters, Frances and Mary to be in need of a second mother to guide them through girlhood into womanhood. For Tom it did, however, mean that he was no longer the sole pride and joy of his father-in-law and even the birth of a lusty grandson, Richard, did not restore him to full favour.

The inauspicious sayings of the prophet Robert Nixon were not forgotten. There were other portents too. In the month of November 1618, in the same year as Tom's marriage, the prophecies he had uttered were reinforced. In the eastern heavens there appeared a comet—a blazing star which filled everyone who beheld it with dread forebodings of God's judgement for sin—portents foretelling the coming of dire happenings—pestilence, famine, a change in the kingdom. It had often been the case in the past, as was known to any reader of the histories, and the threat that its coming posed spread panic among certain classes.

Tom watched as the comet appeared brightly in the night sky—a silent wanderer across the great void above. He had dim recollections of having seen a comet once before; he was a boy of eight whose grandfather had taken him to the highest rise he could find in this lowland county to let his eyes sweep across the night sky and view this messenger of fate. Tom had not felt himself threatened by this apparition as a child, nor did it make him tremble as a man. A bright star could bring good news too. Did it not once herald the coming of the Saviour of the World? He too was a wanderer in time—and maybe someday in space.

He looked down into the bright eyes of his loving wife standing beside him. The comet was a lone traveller, but he had his companion at his side. He imagined for a moment this long-tailed star had come out to greet Tom Ley, and congratulate him on his marital bliss. In his optimistic mood of the moment he could not think of this second appearance as a dire warning of anything, but a bright sign, marking the beginning of a long period of happiness.

There was, however, one event in that year which had given him cause for deep thought. It happened in faraway Bohemia, a land of which young Tom knew nothing other than that it existed somewhere in the outer regions of the Empire. But this ignorance did not prevent him from thinking of the words of the prophet, when Matthew Barton related a happening which though it had an element of comedy in it, was the prelude to an awesome tragedy.

"Men shall fall from a great height." Yes, yes, he remembered the words exactly.

"'Tis passing strange," he said, "passing strange that a country idiot should have known so much."

The Holy Roman Emperor Matthias was childless, and knowing that he was nearing his end, desired to secure the succession for his cousin Ferdinand of Styria, who having an heir, was likely to keep the family dominions intact thus continuing Habsburg supremacy in the Empire. The crowns of Bohemia and Hungary were elective but these were duly promised to the devout Catholic Ferdinand. The Protestant nobles, realizing the danger of this Jesuit-dominated succession, protested without success to Matthias, then resolving on force, entered the Hradschin Castle at Prague, seized the Emperor's deputies

Martinitz and Slavata together with their secretary, and flung all three of them with mocking words from a high window.

"Jesus, Maria! Help!" screamed Martinitz as he was thrust bodily over the sill and descended straight down by the castle wall into the courtyard below to what appeared to be certain death. As Slavata and the secretary followed him, one of the rebels jeered:

"We'll see if your Mary can help you!"

A second later the mocking changed to amazement:

"By God, his Mary has helped!" exclaimed the scoffer, as the victims of the Protestant anger were dragged to safety. By great fortune, they had landed on the soft surface of a dunghill seventy feet below the window and none had suffered much hurt.

This Bohemian Revolution sparked off by the ignominious defenestration of the Emperor's deputies, assumed the proportions of a full-scale war. The rebels invited Fredrick of the Palatinate, whose wife Elizabeth was the King of England's daughter, to assume the crown—a Protestant king in opposition to the Catholic Ferdinand— and James I, unwilling to be drawn into a war in distant Bohemia, refused to act even though his own daughter and the ex-king Frederick, their forces defeated at the Battle of the White Mountain, were fugitives from the victorious Catholic powers. Only when the pursuing armies of the Emperor were carrying the war into Frederick's hereditary lands on the Rhine, did James agree to some half-hearted intervention.

Tom checked the date of the clairvoyant's pronouncement. The words had been spoken exactly ten days before the event. *"Children yet unborn shall bewail their falling."* That certainly meant that this act of violence would be a 'casus belli'. Had all of this special significance for him? He doubted it, but other words had been spoken which Tom chose deliberately to ignore.

Another flash of memory returned in 1629. James I had been dead for four years, but Buckingham was still the favourite and Chief Minister of his son, Charles, who allowed him a free rein in foreign and domestic matters. This Duke's unsuccessful policies at home, and ill-fated expeditions to aid the Protestants in Europe earned him widespread unpopularity, and even at one stage impeachment, only averted by the King's dissolution of Parliament. In 1629, his career was ended by John Felton, a former naval lieutenant with grievances of his own, who stabbed the hated nobleman to death at Portsmouth while he was preparing a second expedition to help the Huguenots besieged by the French king's forces at La Rochelle.

"If a favourite of the king shall be slain, his Master's neck shall be cleft in twain."

Was the death of this Buckingham the fulfilment of the prophecy? Clever predictions indeed! But not the worries of a young man blessed with a lovely wife and two fine children, once a briner, now a man of business, with ambition to rise even above the status of a merchant, well-known and respected in his own locality, which he had once considered to be the summit of his ambition.

Thus Tom came to the crisis of his life. The advance of the plague in 1631 was merciless. Even before the proclamation had been made forbidding access to the fair, he had considered the possibility of sending his wife and family away to the country. When he mentioned it to Kate, she was adamant that she should stay by his side, but reports began to come in thick and fast and at length, anxious for the safety of the children, she relented.

"If you leave it too long, dearest, you will be stopped by watchers and warders," said Tom persuasively. "If only for the children's sake, I pray you seek some safer refuge."

In the country, near the confines of the Great Forest, a cousin of the Bartons dwelt on an isolated farm. Kate's father thought his son-in-law's insistence on evacuating his family unnecessary panic, but he agreed to the plan, and it was arranged that Kate and the children would stay the night at the Swan Inn, and then travel on to Cousin Wright's home on the following day.

The house, once filled with life and beauty, was cold and dark to Tom on the evening of their departure. He had been parted from his family before, when on business trips or with Matthew visiting the scattered Bartons and others he knew in and around Cheshire, but this was quite a different matter. He had supped and slept at strange inns in towns full of unknown people, but then he was away from home.

There he would not expect to hear the pretty prattle of Lynette, the babyish cries of little Richard, or the soft voice and musical laugh of his beloved Kate. They belonged to the bow-windowed house in Nantwich, as did the sights which delighted him so; his wife, her ringlets bobbing, humming a little air as she moved among the roses, lilies, snapdragons and honeysuckle of the flower garden, or busied herself cutting the sweet smelling herbs to set among the blooms in the house, Lynette toddling beside her mother, happily making herself a posy and baby Richard, kicking and gurgling in his cradle. The house was still the one he knew, but these sights and sounds had gone.

Tom sat before the glowing embers of a small fire over which his supper had been cooked. For a moment he doubted the wisdom of his action. Should he not simply have put his trust in God to deliver him from this peril? Why was he trying to improve Providence? He lit a candle and climbed the dark stairs to an equally lonely bedroom. Life without Kate! Was it life at all?

The journey to the Swan Inn was uneventful, but Kate was surprised at the unexpectedly cool reception she received from her uncle and aunt, who were of the same opinion as her father that leaving Nantwich had been premature—and they told her so—ignoring the fact that, had she delayed the authorities would quite probably have prevented her from leaving. Henry Barton promised that he would escort his niece and her children to Cousin Wright's himself, so he sent Kate's servant back to Nantwich, but on the following day he disappointed her with the excuse that he could not spare the time. The inn was still open which made Kate nervous. Travellers bring diseases, so a stay in this place would be jumping out of the frying pan into the fire. The third day came and Uncle Henry was nowhere to be seen when Kate came downstairs—only Aunt Bessie.

"He's in his room—feeling less than his usual self—has complained of a headache and dizziness when he tries to rise. He only managed to stagger a few steps, then he said it was like on a ship at sea."

This sounded ominous, but Aunt Bessie tried to make light of it.

"There is a saying that tanners and inn servants are immune to the pestilence," she declared. "Let's hope it's true for innkeepers as well—"

She stopped. Kate's face was deadly white; a shiver of fright ran down her spine. Even the dangers of the road paled in face of this horror.

"Do not tarry, dear," said Aunt Bessie kindly, dropping all pretence in an instant that Henry's malaise was not too serious. "Take the little ones, and either go back to Nantwich or on to Cousin Wright's. I've seen the plague before. I remember the year sixteen four and you, too, will recall how it struck us in 'twenty five'. The Lord's hand is upon us. Did not great storms scarcely a month ago, disturb the purity of our air with terrible thunder and lightning and a strange kind of hail? After the storm comes the pestilence. Why must I have such a stubborn husband? He would keep this inn open, putting profit before safety. Leave at once, Katy. I can spare John to go with you.

Kate made all speed to pack her saddlebags; the servant, a sullen youth of barely seventeen, was given his instructions and the children were brought down—Richard sleeping, Lynette skipping along as if starting out on some adventure. As she rode across the river and headed her horse towards Cousin Wright's, the last glimpse of the Swan Inn was of Aunt Bessie with a lump of chalk scrawling 'INN CLOSED' across the front door, too late to prevent the entrance of the pestilence, but in hope that this quarantine would check it.

The way towards the Wrights' house became rougher and narrower, not a proper road, nor even a track. Kate began to feel weary; a dull, thumping headache oppressed her; the children could go no further. Barton's servant eyed her suspiciously. He made her uneasy—she had a feeling that he was only looking for a suitable opportunity to leave her to her own devices.

"How far to Cousin Wright's?" asked Kate, as they came out on to a better stretch of road.

"Seven or eight miles," was the gruff reply, but Kate knew that he meant 'long miles', which in these parts were a third above the statute mile fixed in the days of Queen Elizabeth. Her depressed feeling, unremitting headache and the onset of fever, made her suggest that they should stop at a spring where she could refresh herself with cool water. The gnawing fear that the pestilence had already struck, grew upon her. She could hardly rise to remount and staggered towards her horse. Little Lynette, attracted by the profusion of wild flowers growing in the long grass at the side of the road, had run off towards them. Turning to catch her, Kate heard a sudden thudding of horses' hoofs and to her horror saw Barton's servant speeding away.

"For the sake of God!" she cried in an agonized voice. "Do not leave me here. Have pity on me and my poor, defenceless children!" Kate's voice rose to a piercing shriek, but the terrified servant galloped off without even turning his head towards the distressed woman.

There was no point in crying or delaying. He was gone and was unlikely to return. Kate made a sling for baby Richard and lifted Lynette on to the pillion. The horse went on at a trot. Eight long miles to Cousin Wright's! Her weakness was growing and almost caused her to faint from the horse. A shower of rain began to fall, but Kate hardly noticed it. By this time she had no idea how far she had gone or where exactly she was heading, and she just held a slack rein, letting the horse amble on.

From the hollow below, came a wisp of smoke; a tiny house stood on the edge of the forest in an indentation, which meant that the dwelling was surrounded on three sides by trees. They rose up sharply behind the cottage, and from a distance appeared to be growing from the roof. Kate's eyes were half glazed, but with great effort she pulled on the rein and directed her horse across the field to this haven. A long path led to a neat, little house with all the available surrounding space given over to the growing of vegetables. A dark figure at the window bore witness to the fact that her approach had been observed, and Kate had not reached the front door before it opened and a woman well into middle age, dressed in dark blue or black, emerged to greet her.

Kate felt too weak to dismount.

"Bless you, young lady, you look mighty sick and weary," she said comfortingly, "and the two mites to care for."

She lifted Lynette from the horse, but the child would not take the strange hand and clung to her mother.

"Give me the baby. I'm used to little ones—had none of my own, but I brought many an infant into this world and comforted the mothers."

Kate swayed. The woman placed baby Richard in a large basket which stood near the door.

"Why, dearie," she said, supporting the sick woman, "come inside. I have something to cool your poor head and make you feel better."

"Dear God, protect my little children," cried Kate in a husky voice. "Tom! Tom! Where are you?"

She looked wildly around inside the cottage.

"Don't ever leave me, dearest heart. Let me not die here, so far from the one I love! Tom!" she cried again, as if recognizing someone, and she stretched out her arms in an embrace which only encompassed thin air.

She tottered a few steps and was checked in her fall by the old woman who had just drawn back the curtain which screened off a corner of the room. She made Kate as comfortable as possible on her own rough bed and rambled on aloud after the fashion of one who lives alone, as she busied herself attending to her patient.

"Poor little lamb," she said soothingly. "Meg Broomhall knows what to do. The plague and I are old enemies, but I have found out the secrets which he has not surrendered to the leeches and apothecaries."

She cackled as she began undressing Kate to look for the tokens—the dark patches and painful buboes—which were signs of the relentless advance of the disease.

"Don't worry, pretty one. I'll catch him by the tail and fling him out of doors. Old Meg will not let this black scourge get the better of her. She'll soon have you fit enough to see your Tom again."

Kate heard nothing of the woman's chatter, for she had lapsed into unconsciousness.

Even before the official solemn thanksgiving for the turning away of God's hand, for the deliverance of the county and Wich Malbank in particular from the scourge of the plague, Tom sought news of his family. The ravages in neighbouring counties were abating, and it seemed reasonable to assume that there would be no outbreak in the neighbourhood. Tom was annoyed that he had put his wife and infant children to the trouble of making a tiresome journey, when they would have been just as secure at home. To reassure himself that they were safe and well, he wrote a long letter to Kate which he entrusted to Francis Miles, one of his servants, a reliable youth who could be expected to find Cousin Wright's house and return without delay. Miles did exactly that, and was back in Nantwich within twenty four hours, but he brought news which struck Tom with terror. Kate had never arrived at Cousin Wright's, and the surprised relative had no knowledge of her whereabouts.

Tom saddled a horse and rode off without ceremony, relying on Miles to inform his father-in-law. It was already afternoon, so he rode hard in the direction of the Swan Inn in order to be there before nightfall. He had not given instructions to Miles to visit Kate's uncle and aunt, as he had naturally assumed that his wife would have reached her destination at Cousin Wright's. She had certainly come as far as the Swan, for had not her father's servant returned from Over soon after her arrival?

As he approached the inn from the road which crosses the county from North to South, he sensed something different about the place. On coming nearer he observed that it was closed. Weeds had taken root between the cobble stones, the windows of the public rooms were boarded up, and the door still bore the faint outline of "INN CLOSED" written in chalk by Mistress Barton, but partly washed off by the rain.

Tom banged vigorously on the front door and rattled the bolts, but no response was forthcoming, nor was there any reply to his calls of "Uncle Henry!" At last another door at the back of the house opened and a female figure emerged; she advanced slowly down the yard, not the cheery, bustling Aunt Bessie who had been so pleased to hear his flattering words about the excellence of the food she served, but a haggard, careworn, little woman, who approached him nervously like a child expecting to be admonished for some fault.

"Where is Uncle Henry?" asked Tom. "Why is the inn closed?"

"God saw fit to visit us with the plague," she replied despondently. "Henry was taken away; now I am left with no one to help me. They won't even come near the Swan since they found out how he died. Trade's ruined and I'll have to tramp the roads as a beggar woman."

Tom tried to console her with the observation that people would come back as soon as the danger had finally receded, but Aunt Bessie stubbornly refused to accept his reasoning. She wailed on until Tom cut her short:

"And Kate—the children? Where are they?" he stammered out, fearing the words which would be a dagger to his heart.

"Gone. They left as soon as Henry took to his bed—on to Cousin Wright's, I assume. I sent John with them, but the villain never returned."

Even though he had long suspected the truth, Tom felt inexpressible horror at the mention of Henry Barton's death. He had tried so hard to protect his family, but in his zeal he had exposed his loved ones to the very danger he had been so anxious to avoid. Though it meant a short reprieve, Tom could not rejoice that Kate had made a timely departure from the inn, for he knew they had never reached their final destination. Somewhere between the Swan and Cousin Wright's his dear wife and children had disappeared or died.

"This John! Where can I find him?" he asked in a tone so sharp that it startled Aunt Bessie.

His appearance had changed drastically too, he seemed to have aged ten years in a moment. She stopped her lamentations at once.

"I suppose he's gone back to Eastham where his parents live. Shaw's the family name. And tell him he needn't come round here again unless he wants to feel the weight of my broomstick."

Leaving Kate and her children alone troubled Shaw's conscience a little, and to appease it he had in fact turned his horse's head back in her direction, while secretly hoping that he would be unable to find her. This proved to be the case, and not wishing to return to the inn, which he knew to be infected, he had made his way to the family home at Eastham. He did not dare to tell his father and mother that there was a plague victim at the inn, nor did he mention his desertion of Kate, only saying that Mr Barton had unjustly dismissed him for some trivial offence—much to the displeasure of his parents who had prided themselves on having found a comfortable place for him.

Shaw was a youth constantly beset with fears. There was fear of his father's grim rage and his master's rod, fear of God's terrible anger against sinners wallowing in iniquity, fear of storms with great streaks of lightning and pelting hail, and fear of the plague with its dreadful swellings and raging fever. He even entertained fears of things much less likely to happen—of earthquakes, or the end of the world and its last trumpet. Thus the approach of a stranger, whom he believed to be an agent of retribution, struck him with terror. There was no safe place to hide in a one-roomed cottage with a ramshackle barn and shed. He considered flight for a moment, but realizing that a man on a horse would catch him long before he reached the forest; he decided against it and shrank into the farthest and darkest corner of the house when Tom Ley knocked on the door.

After hearing the complaint against his son, the elder Shaw, who knew the lad's ways, hauled him cringing out of the corner and with plentiful cuffs wrung out of him a confession of his lamentable failure to carry out his duty. Leaving the youth to the tender mercies of his father, Tom hastened to the spot which had been described to him—not that there was any indication of the way Kate had taken, but at least it was a starting point in what was to prove a protracted investigation.

The vicar of Weaver, James Minshull, the bachelor man who had enjoyed Mistress Barton's Sunday luncheons so much, was very scrupulous about the accuracy of all the entries made in his parish register. His clerk dutifully recorded each baptism and burial with proper details of date, name and trade or profession duly entered, as for instance:

"1629 ffeb 12.Eliz dau. John Moyle, brewer, killed by a wagon."

Some of the more unusual points were added when necessary: *"drowned in a well", "choked with bread and butter", "slain with the stroke of an axe", "strangled by his own hand"*, or *"killed by the fall of a tree in a sawpit."*

Even the words *"died of the plague"* were appended, a practice not followed by all the parish clerks, who thought it would cause panic; they would be cut off from other villages and local trade would be ruined.

It was thus with much regret that the Reverend Minshull was unable to have exact details entered of the two persons he was called upon to give a Christian burial namely a young mother and child who had patently succumbed to an attack of the pestilence. The sexton of the parish had been awakened early one morning by a rumbling of cart wheels outside his cottage. He had hurried downstairs in his night shirt, pistol in hand, to find the moon shining on a deserted scene, and in the shadow by his step, a bulky shape lay, which proved to be the bodies of a woman and child wrapped in the same blanket. Enclosed, the sexton found a small canvas bag containing some jewellery and a pair of fine gloves, proving that the person who had left the corpses on the doorstep had kept their identities secret for fear of being marked as carriers of the plague, and not for any nefarious reason. A quick interment was necessary, and the obsequies completed, the entry in the register was duly made;

"1631 Aug. 20: Mother and child, died of the plague."

So it had to remain, for even when the danger of further outbreaks of the epidemic had receded, no clues were forthcoming as to the identity of the victims until the arrival of Thomas Ley.

Not only was the Reverend Minshull scrupulous about the entries in his parish register, but he prepared his Sunday sermons with painstaking exactitude. The danger of plague having been lifted, Minshull was to give thanks to the Almighty, and he would preach on a text from Psalm 91:

"I will say of the Lord, He is my refuge and my fortress; my God; in Him will I trust."

Mr Minshull had prayed hard for the turning away of the *"pestilence that walketh in darkness"*, and his little flock had prayed earnestly with him. He had almost doubted when he looked on the face of Kate, pale and serene in death after such a woeful end, with the little babe pressed close to her breast, but to him this chilling sight had been sent as a warning of what was in store for those of little faith. He redoubled his efforts to convince his congregation that only by holding fast to their faith, could they avert a catastrophe.

"A thousand shall fall at thy side, and ten thousand at thy right hand," insisted Minshull, applying a quotation which sounded hyperbolical in this case. Then after a suitable dramatic pause; *"But it shall not come nigh thee. Because thou hast made the Lord which is my refuge, even the most High, thy habitation, there shall no evil befall thee, neither shall any plague come near thy dwelling."*

Master Minshull was scarcely older in years than Tom Ley, but the weight of cares he bore for his parishioners had given him the air of a much more mature man. Beneath his clerical garb and somewhat stern exterior, beat the heart of one who could show plentiful sympathy for human frailties—no pedant or fanatic—but a man of kindly humour and moderation. His failure to marry had been a sin of omission, rather than a deliberate act of celibacy, a state of affairs which several young ladies of the parish would have been only too pleased to remedy.

As soon as Tom entered Minshull's study and stated his business, the vicar's expression changed from one of satisfaction at having achieved a resounding peroration to his sermon, to one of nervous anticipation and then ineffable sadness at the bad news he would have to impart to the young man standing before him. He was ashamed that he had not shown enough pity for the poor mother and child—that he had thought of these innocents, lying plague-marked, wrapped in a blanket, as a sign or warning from God and not as a piece of human misery. Now he had before him the distraught husband, searching for the lost ones, hoping against hope to find them safe and well.

Tom had not finished explaining the purpose of his visit, before Minshull went to a small drawer and took out the canvas bag.

"I am sorry—truly I am. This is all I have for you. You can touch them," he said, hurriedly. "They have been warmed and cleansed with vinegar."

There was little of value in the bag. Kate had not thought it wise to go on a journey wearing much jewellery. The fancy gloves which the bag had also contained, had been buried with her; but Tom knew the rings, one of which he had bought with King James's golden sovereign—a token of their love which she always kept with her. He stared at them, lying in the palm of his hand, and spoke in a hollow voice.

"The children! My pretty chicks? Were they taken too?"

The vicar's expression changed again on hearing the word 'children', this time to one of surprise.

"Children? There was only a baby boy."

For a moment Tom's deadened senses quickened.

"Lynette—my little girl?" he said in a choking voice. His chest heaved. Mr Minshull laid his hand on his visitor's arm and led him to a chair.

"Oh God! God!" cried Tom, breaking down. "Why didst thou forsake me in my hour of need?"

The vicar reproved him gently. Whilst he had sympathy with the bereaved man, he could not let this pass.

"You must not call on God like that, my friend. Rather ask him for strength to bear this grievous loss. Give thanks that you yourself escaped from the plague. Pray to him that your child, Lynette, still lives, for truly I buried no little girl. Who among us can question the wisdom of the Almighty? Seek the Lord and his strength; seek his face evermore."

Tom raised his head; his cheeks stained with tears, and looked into the vicar's eyes.

"Reverend Sir," he said; his voice unnaturally calm now. "How can he who has not felt the glory of human love, understand this loss? You say I must not question the wisdom of the Lord: *'He giveth and he taketh away'*. He gives us the capacity to love and takes away the object of our affections so soon. Once before, I was told that I must not question Divine Providence. Then I was in doubt. Now I am in rebellion."

"Rebel not Friend," the vicar said; "rather let us pray. Kneel with me and ask the Lord to give you strength. Ask him to direct the search for your little girl and bring it to a happy conclusion."

Tom prayed with the vicar, but he could not banish the black thoughts which filled his mind. His ride back home began at a fast and furious pace more appropriate to a cavalry charge or at the Palio of Sienna. He spurred on the poor beast recklessly, earning the curses of passers-by as his horse's flying hoofs sprayed them with mud and water from the cart ruts. Fortunately for Hunter's wellbeing and his own safety, a heavy downpour made him slacken his pace, but he still rode on at a quick trot, oblivious of the water cascading down from the brim of his hat and soaking through his cloak and doublet, wetting him to the skin.

He had returned to enlist the help of his father-in-law to find Lynette. Barton blamed Tom to some extent for the catastrophe and though he respected his son-in-law's great grief and never reproached him openly, relations between the two men became strained.

Kate had been her father's special pet before the coming of his new family, and Lynette had won a place in his heart by bringing back memories of the childhood of her mother, so using his local knowledge and his contacts in different parts of the county, he cooperated with Tom in his frantic efforts to track down the person or persons who had abducted his infant daughter or concealed the truth of her death.

His wife was gone beyond all doubt, and Tom's search for Lynette came to an end soon after he received a long, sympathetic letter from Mr Minshull. The parson of a neighbouring parish, subsequent to enquiries made by the Vicar of Weaver, had reported the sad but all too commonplace story of a chapman and his family who had succumbed to the plague. Unable to enter the market towns due to watch and ward restrictions, they had camped near to his village expecting to resume their travels when the danger passed. Unfortunately they had contracted the sickness they had hoped to avoid, and all four of them had died. Among them was a young girl unknown to those who had previously made contact with the pedlar, and in every point of the description which the reverend gentleman

91

had given, she matched that of Lynette. It was a bitter blow, but even after such a shattering discovery, Tom continued his search for nigh on two weeks, until with hope taken away, enthusiasm waned, and at last he and his father-in-law despairing that any further clues would be forthcoming, had to accept the belief as final that little Lynette was either dead or had disappeared without trace from the face of Cheshire.

8. SOLDIER IN GOD'S CAUSE

The year of our Lord 1620 saw the birth of English journalism, when a tiny newspaper of one sheet only was published in Amsterdam. Two years earlier the Dutch had begun to issue the first papers of weekly news, and a large English colony existed in Holland of merchants permanently resident or passing through, including many extreme Puritan views who wished to separate from the Anglican Church. Thus there was a market for a newspaper in a country where political interference was least likely to hamper its publication.

The success of the venture led to its introduction into England and weekly issues of these small news sheets appeared, dealing with foreign affairs. The Thirty Years War was now raging on the Continent, so *"The Weekly News from Italie, Germanie, Hungaria, Bohemia, the Palatinate, France and Low Countries"*, gave those thirsting for information the latest news of the battles, marches and sieges, as well as some of the more intimate, unpleasant stories of this brutally fought war.

The king fulminated against these newssheets, eying foreign news with suspicion and determined that home reports should not be printed. They were banned in theory, but continued to circulate until 1632 when an ordinance of the Court of Star Chamber forbade their publication.

Tom was an avid reader of these leaflets, which received the name of "Corantos", meaning something which circulates (with news). He had a group of friends who met from time to time at the Crown Inn, where the reports were discussed over wine and tobacco. This was a great improvement on the old haphazard way of hearing news from pedlars and other travellers, when it had often become deliberately elaborated or merely distorted by inaccurate reporting.

One evening in the summer of 1631, the news under discussion was the most tragic event of the whole German war. The city of Magdeburg, a key city by the River Elbe, defended for Protestantism, against the Emperor's army under the command of John Tzerclaes Tilly and his Lieutenant-General Pappenheim, had fallen. The circumstances of its capture were so horrendous that they sent a shock wave round the whole of Europe. The most brutal and bloody massacre since the days of Genghis Khan had befallen Magdeburg, whose name signified "The Maiden City". Over the chief gate, stood a wooden statue of a young girl with a wreath of innocence in her hand, posing the question "Who will take it?" Once a Catholic bishopric, its churches and cathedral had been seized by the Protestants and were ruled by an administrator, but the Catholic Emperor appointed his son to the see and his generals were given orders to enforce his will on these recalcitrant people.

Gustavus Adolphus of Sweden who had replaced Christian of Denmark as champion of the Protestants, promised arms and men, so the Administrator of Magdeburg, re-entered the city on August 4th and declared he would defend it against all comers with the help of Gustavus, which was given great prominence by Protestant pamphleteers.

Then Tilly joined his subordinate, Pappenheim, and the two generals pressed home the siege of Magdeburg. All eyes were on Gustavus who had landed his troops in North Germany, but he was unable to reach the city on account of the indecision shown by the Electors of Brandenburg and Saxony who hesitated to join him. The king had hoped that they would hold out for two months until he could force the wavering princes into an alliance. But that was not to be. On May 20th the lines broke at the Maiden City and the storm burst upon it.

Tom had to make an effort to keep control of himself when he came to this part of the narrative. The burghers, fearing the massacre and plunder which would follow conquest by force, begged their general to make terms but he refused. Then fiery Pappenheim, without consulting Tilly, led his troops in an early morning surprise attack; the fortifications were overrun, and the Imperial troops ran riot in the city. The streets were scoured with artillery; the citizens sought shelter in their houses to await their fate, as the Walloons and Croats burst in with unrestrained fury.

Soon all the gates were open to the streams of Imperial cavalry and infantry and a nightmare of rape and murder of the most ghastly kind spread through the whole city. *"Neither the innocence of childhood, nor the helplessness of old age, neither youth nor sex, neither rank nor beauty, could abate the rage of the victors"*. The Imperial army was completely out of control; whether by accident or design flames sprang up everywhere, until Magdeburg, once one of the finest cities in Germany, had been turned into a raging inferno. In less than twelve hours, the whole place, except for two churches and a few houses on the outskirts, was reduced to a heap of ashes.

Tilly's troops, driven out by heat and acrid smoke from the conflagration, returned to ransack the cellars where the citizens had hidden away their valuables. The food, which had been above ground, had for the most part been consumed, but the barrels of wine remained in the cellars to console the plundering soldiers who for two days rampaged about in the smouldering ruins.

Of the city's thirty thousand inhabitants, barely five thousand had survived when the fire died down. The richer ones who remained alive could ransom themselves, but many women and some of the men were taken away by the victors. Fearing that plague would strike his army, Tilly ordered the thousands of bodies poisoning the air to be thrown into the River Elbe, thus to be carried swiftly away from the city and left to the predators and carrion crows.

A Te Deum was sung in the great church, once more the cathedral of a Catholic bishopric, to celebrate this tarnished victory. Cannons were fired and the General announced that the city of Magdeburg would henceforth be known as Marienburg.

In a ditch, hard by the main gate, lay the half-burnt and battered statue of the Magdeburg Maiden, toppled from her pedestal above the entrance to the city, not wooed and won gallantly and honourably, but violently raped by a cruel suitor.

There was silence in the room when Tom had finished reading the harrowing account of Magdeburg's fate to the company. Most of the men were visibly moved and there were tears in the corners of some eyes. There was much denunciation of the inhuman Pappenheim, the "godless" minions of the fanatical Ferdinand, slave to the Jesuits. Some even voiced criticism of Gustavus for his failure to move, and more of them turned on the Electors whose lack of cooperation with the Swedish king had left threatened Magdeburg to the mercy of Tilly's army.

Tom did not join in the vehement religious tirades, but he was highly angered by the inhumanity of which he had read, and the weakness of those who had failed to prevent it. He felt sure that it was not the Catholicism of the Emperor's men which had made them cruel barbarians, but he had no doubt they ought to pay for their crimes. Swift retribution should follow; it was not good enough to wait for the hereafter. Such unbelievable cruelty must be punished—if not by God, then by man.

"Were I still single, I would go to fight," he declared to Kate as she sat brushing her shining, dark hair and listening to his graphic account of this latest news.

"I would not be fighting for Protestantism, but for mankind, for verily this was a crime against humanity."

Kate's tender heart was touched by the gruesome tale of fire and slaughter.

"Poor innocents!" she cried. "Poor little children! How they must have suffered!"

"Dearest," said Tom, "it does not bear thinking about. How could I bear to see you ravished and my lovely children brutally pierced by a Croat's spear?" He soothed his wife with tender words.

"Do not let these cruelties upset you, precious one. Come, let us think happier thoughts and trust that God will preserve us, here in England, from the barbarous acts we have heard described tonight. "

For a few weeks, Tom could not banish the horror of the siege of Magdeburg from his mind, until the coming of the plague, the flight to the country, and the terrible catastrophe in his own family, almost subdued it. His full sense of desolation at the loss of Kate did not come upon him immediately; the frantic search for Lynette occupying his waking hours but in the time when sleep should have eased the pain, the blackness of the night was matched by the blackness of his mind. Kate, with whom he should have spent another twenty or more happy years, was outside his world. The divines could only speak of God's all-embracing love and of union with Christ. He wanted reassurance from them. This Heaven of theirs would have to hold his Kate in it.

As the search for Lynette became ever more hopeless, the sorrow he felt in his waking hours increased. Every beam and every stone in Nantwich spoke of Kate. He hardly dared to wander past the mill or cross the little bridge, afraid of the memories which would come back to him—sweet memories in themselves, but bringing such pain in the knowledge that he would never see his dear one in this world again.

He reproached himself bitterly that Kate had died, abandoned by the one who was dearest to her heart. No, not abandoned! Sacrificed by him, for his faith had been too weak in the hour of trial. He should have kept his family by his side and trusted in God's power to preserve them. His little Lynette—"another you, all my heart's desire"—as he had spoken of her to Kate on that wonderful evening in Chester. She too was gone, abducted by tinkers, or dead and buried in some strange place. A sweet, spring flower cut off before it had had a chance to blossom! It made no sense to him.

With these sorrows weighing on his mind, Tom found it difficult to concentrate on his work, and his already strained relations with Barton worsened. Kate's father, saddened as he was by the loss of his favourite daughter and two grandchildren, had come to accept the hard facts of life. His son-in-law's nature was different; he could not rise so easily above these great sorrows. Barton, the realist, did not hesitate to contrast their views. In his age, man's existence was precarious and short; every family had these tragedies, but life must go on. Tom found this callous and turned his back on his father-in-law, but though he could not understand his attitude, Barton pitied him and could not take offence.

At last Tom decided to make a clean break with the past, to leave the Wich where he had been brought up and had spent his happy years with Kate, and seek his fortune in places free from reminders of his life with her. There, if he could not forget his sorrow, at least he could come to terms with it.

One evening he went to meet his friends at the Crown Inn—the first time he had done so since the death of his wife. The news was good for the Protestant cause. Tilly had invaded Saxony and the Electors had been driven to declare for Sweden.

The allied armies of Gustavus and the Saxons had crushed the Imperialists, first at Breitenfeld and then on the Lech, and the Emperor's old general had been killed. The Swedish king had blazed his way through Southern Germany into the Catholic bishoprics, taking the great cities of Frankfurt, Munich, and Nuremberg, wiping out the Spanish garrisons, winning over German princes, recruiting men to swell his army everywhere he went. All this served to bring back to Tom the tragedy of Magdeburg which had been overshadowed by his personal woes. He saw again the wooden figure over the town gate, now with the form and features of his beloved Kate; then the same figure, charred and fallen, lying in a ditch.

He made up his mind there and then that he would seek his fortune as a soldier in the service of humanity. In that whirlpool of activity he could find a cure for his sickness if he stayed alive. If not, unless he had been grossly deceived, the way would be open to a Heaven which held his Kate.

Mister Barton was not at all pleased to hear of Tom's plan. He had begun to find his son-in-law almost indispensable in his business which had grown considerably in the latter years.

"To me it is madness," began his advice. "Going to the German wars like some disgruntled serving man or runaway apprentice! Why throw away your chances of rising further in the mercantile world to join in the quarrels of these German princes? They take no bread from our mouths, nor do they make us one mite richer. The Emperor may oppress his princelings; they may cry out against his intolerance. Let the Swedish king defend them; he stands to gain power from victory, but Thomas Ley's reward will be negligible. Magdeburg fell and it was a heinous crime, but your going will change nothing."

Tom protested that as a good Protestant and humanitarian he must play his part. If everyone shared his father-in-law's view, then surely nothing would be changed.

"Your real reason for going is plain," insisted Barton. "The Kate you loved has gone for ever. Though you took exception to my words before, I am not as hard as you might think. I mourned her for a decent interval, but believe me, Tom, there is no return from love lavished on the dead. Stay here, son, and take yourself another wife, like I have done. You are young and strong; you will raise a second family.

Tom was deaf to these and all Barton's other pleas, but at last he wrung out of the older man a blessing on his venture.

Tom's mother took much the same view as Mr Barton, though without actually suggesting that he should marry again. Granfer Wyche had already gone to join his ancestors, or he would have sent the young man off with some stirring story which reflected his own martial ambitions.

It only remained for Master Ley to wind up his affairs in Nantwich and to perform two other duties. One was to send a letter of thanks and some gold to the Reverend Minshull who had given him so much assistance in his long search for Lynette. He recommended that the money should be distributed to the poor of the parish, particularly to families which had suffered from the plague. The second duty was to pay a farewell visit to his sister Alice and his friend of long standing, now his brother-in-law.

Will expressed surprise at Tom's decision, but he approved of his support for Protestantism. With plentiful reference to biblical texts, he held forth on the coming downfall of these new Amalekites and Midianites, and then took him into the church where the parson prayed over him for upwards of half an hour.

Their parting was emotional. Following her husband's lead, Alice called him a "soldier in God's just cause", "champion of the Queen of Bohemia" and a "Protestant hero", as she kissed him on the cheek. Will grasped his friend's hands:

"O Lord God to whom all vengeance belongeth, show thyself! Lord, how long shall the wicked triumph? Go, brother, and God be with you. For the Lord will not cast off his people, neither will he forsake his inheritance!"

At first Tom had no definite plan in mind as to how he would go about seeking service in the Swedish army, except that the best policy would be to go to London where he would no doubt be able to contact agents looking for possible recruits. So he purchased Mercury, a silver-grey stallion, recommended to him as a reliable and swift animal, and taking a hundred and fifty pounds, two pistols, a sword and a saddlebag crammed with necessities for the long journey, he set off expecting to reach the capital in six or seven days if no mishap occurred. The going was better than he had experienced in Cheshire, so he covered about twenty miles on the first day and a similar distance on the second.

At Lichfield, while at supper, he was joined by a party of travellers who were on their way to Cambridge, and though it was not his destination, he was glad to accompany them for as long as possible. It was a jolly band, consisting of students, merchants, a cleric and a number of other people who did not reveal their identities. To Tom's satisfaction, they passed the time like the pilgrims of old in the "Canterbury Tales", laughing, joking and telling stories. It was the right company to take his mind off his troubles. For safety's sake it was the sensible thing to do, for the counties north of London were notoriously infested with highwaymen.

Time with this entertaining band of companions passed quickly, but soon after leaving Peterborough they parted and Tom rode on alone, covering the greatest distance he travelled in any one day— almost forty miles.

The sun had set when he arrived in Royston, a small Hertfordshire town noted for its royal residence, once the favourite hunting lodge of King James, still used to a somewhat lesser extent by his son Charles, when Royal Royston became the centre of a busy and fashionable court at the Palace in Kneesworth Street.

Tom, who had been on the road since a very early hour and had eaten bread and cheese out of his haversack instead of stopping for luncheon, was glad to find an excellent hostelry, the "Bull Inn", at the top of the High Street, which had sheltered travellers for over a hundred years. He hoped to meet a new companion here—one who would guide him through the Home Counties to the capital. Fortune smiled on him for once, though not exactly in the way he had expected.

He had finished his meal—excellent by any standard—and with his legs stretched out, he sat in the parlour enjoying his tobacco—a habit which he had acquired from the example of his father-in-law to whom the old clay pipe was a constant source of solace. The evening being chilly, the landlord had a good fire burning. A man drew up closer to the blaze and spoke to Tom, who was contentedly puffing away while warming his toes. He was an old soldier who had served in 1620 under Sir Horace Vere. The ageing James, while not approving full-scale intervention in the continental wars, had allowed English volunteers to be equipped by a national subscription. These two thousand two hundred willing recruits were excellent soldiers and acquitted themselves well at the defence of Heidelberg and Mannheim, but they were too few and made little impression.

The old soldier, who introduced himself as Edward Baines, spoke with pride of his former comrades, most of whom had found a resting place in German soil.

"Those men," he said, "were the salt of the earth, the gallantest in outward presence and in fighting spirit, second to none who for many ages have appeared at home or abroad. All volunteers! Not like the rabble we sent in Twenty Five to Count Mansfeld—a poor, undisciplined rascally lot, so ill-provided that most of them died before they arrived in Germany, and the plundering, pot-swilling crew who survived, hardly knew one end of a musket from the other, doing little more execution with pikes than they would have done if the Count had armed them with meat skewers.

"So it was too with the rabble who went to Cadiz. Lame, impotent, unfit men, they were, pressed into service, undisciplined, untrained and unarmed. Many of the officers were courtiers, ignorant of military matters; muskets were found to be defective; food was bad and there was plenty of drink. Result: chaos and beastliness! They proved rather a danger to their own men and killed more of them than they did of the enemy."

The man had a scar on his right cheek which went up to just below his eye. He saw Tom looking at it.

"See!" he said eagerly. "My tokens of honour!" He rolled up his sleeve to show his arm which bore more scars.

101

"They took a musket ball out of me, too," he said pointing to his thigh, but to Tom's relief he did not offer to show him the mark.

"My fighting days are over. I am forty one and not so sound in limb as I was. A soldier has his bad times, but if his commanders are good, it's the life for a true man. With some generals it's always promises instead of pay, then the men run riot. This King Gustavus, with his Swedes, Scots, and Germans will keep them under his thumb so long as he sees them properly paid and fed. Without that, not even the strictest regime of flogging and hanging will discipline an army."

"A man cannot fight with an empty belly and the wind whistling through his tattered cloak, I'll grant you," said Tom. "But surely there is something more. You yourself, what made you embark on that service? Were you fighting for the Protestant ideal, the Bohemian Queen of Hearts, or just for your warm cloak, bread and cheese, and the hope of plunder?"

Baines had his answer ready at once,

"The Protestant cause? No! Luther, Calvin, and the Bishop of Rome! Their people all talk as if they were the only ones to have been granted God's ear. It's all the same to me; I'd duck at the altar if I had to, just as soon as I'd applaud a Puritan preacher thundering against churchyard crosses. The Queen of Bohemia? Perhaps. I'm an incurable romantic. The bread and cheese? By my faith, I didn't go for that! There was always plenty of good, red meat in the Baines household. The truth is I'm a proper fighting cock; I am a terror to see when my blood is up. New places and high adventure—that's what I crave for. What about you, Friend? I take you for a man of mettle. Don't you ever want to break out and live dangerously?"

Tom confided his intentions in him and Baines had a suggestion to make.

"There's no need to go on another forty miles to London," he said, "a couple of leagues away, over the heath, is the house of Sir John Faulkner. He's a gentleman, but no great lord, which makes him easier to approach.

"His ancestor, old Sir John, did some service to King Henry I forget which one and so Harry had him kneel on the spot and dubbed him knight. He was granted some monastic lands and well he prospered, but after his death the Sir Johns went into decline. The present one—the heirs were all given the same Christian name—has ambitions as a soldier. 'Our kingdom has been too long at peace,' he says. 'Our old commanders are worn out and few have been bred in their places, for the knowledge of war, and almost the thought of it, is extinguished. Peace has led us to think that by mere possession of men and ships our kingdom is safe, as if soldiers were born not made.'

"So he plans to take a troop of horse to join the King of Sweden's army. Go over to Ashley and speak to him. If he likes you, there's your passage to Germany. He's a good reputation in these parts. Though I am no cavalryman, I'd learn to ride and fight as a trooper for the honour of serving under him, were I but ten years younger."

Tom took Baines's advice, and next morning clattered over the cobbles down the High Street, quickly leaving the "royal place" with its cluster of half-timbered houses and flint stone church, for an invigorating ride in the direction of the market town of Hitchin. A high stretch of humpy, windswept, flower-covered heath afforded a wide view over open country which sloped away steeply at first, descended to cornfields and woodland, then gradually gave way to the drearier landscape of the fens. Squat towers and needle-like spires of country churches were discernible here and there. A dozen miles away to the northeast, lay the University city of Cambridge, and beyond that the cathedral of Ely, its tower visible on a clear day from a distance of thirty miles.

Tom had no inclination to linger over the scenery, but made his way straight to Ashley and the home of Sir John Faulkner.

A driveway flanked by trees led through a small park to the hall—an Elizabethan timber-framed structure extended to the front in red brick, which despite its comparative newness, had already mellowed and presented a pleasing effect. Tom's good suit of clothes, his feathered hat, his well-groomed hair of medium length—neither foppish nor definitely Puritan—his neatly trimmed pointed beard and small moustache, but more importantly the confident bearing he had acquired since his entry into his father-in-law's business, gained him admittance.

Sir John Faulkner sat in his plain, high-backed chair, his hands resting on the arms, a pet dog at his feet, listening patiently to his unexpected visitor's story. He had the features of a typical country gentleman, his hair and beard cut in a similar style to Tom's. His expression was kindly, but Tom judged him to be a man whom it would not be easy to deceive; he would have to be frank with him.

"First things first," said Sir John, when Tom had finished. "From what or whom are you running? I can see that you are a man of some education, and from your speech not of these parts. Yet you come to me with a request to take you to Germany as a soldier of fortune. Before I say any more, I want your word that you have done nothing illegal. I will not countenance any runaways from the law."

"I assure you," replied Tom, "on my word of honour, that I am running away from no living being—only memories. I am, and was ever, an honest, law-abiding citizen who in changed circumstances would seek his fortune in foreign parts. I do not pretend to be a gentleman, but if you will accept a merchant's word of honour I give it with all my heart."

Sir John's face betrayed evident pleasure at this affirmation. So it was a family tragedy which had driven this man from his home. Tom was reassured, but he thought it wise to lay stress on his Protestantism, and so he continued.

"Our brethren of the Reformed Faith in Germany have suffered cruel repression, but now they have found a worthy champion in Gustavus. I would support his cause to avenge the crime of Magdeburg and other bestialities of the Imperialists. I would not fight to force a man to change his religion, but I will fight to defend our faith and to end this war between those who should be brothers. Then, perhaps, I can find peace within myself."

"Well spoken!" said Faulkner, rising and clapping Tom on the shoulder. "I will take no man who does not know the principles for which he fights. This continental war is our opportunity to put something right which has long been amiss. The danger, above all, is that a people not used to war believes that no enemy dares to venture upon it. To defend our country and our faith we need soldiers, cavalry as well as infantry, and the country is so deficient in good horsemen that it is a question whether or not the whole Kingdom could make two thousand good horse that might equal two thousand French. Our volunteers go to serve in foreign wars—in the Dutch and now in the Swedish forces—but as foot with the pike and musket, and not in the cavalry. The English troops of horse in the army of the Hollanders have disappeared for lack of recruits. The king should recommend the exercise of horsemanship to the Universities of Oxford and Cambridge. There the young gentlemen could practise on their mounts at home instead of having to go to foreign parts to learn this dexterity. Then, too, it should be a duty imposed on the nobility and high officers of state to keep a certain number of horses fit for military purposes, for that aspect too has been woefully neglected. Not only are our men unfit for cavalry service, but there has been a decay in the breeding of horses. Those however, are matters to be taken up by our masters and even if accepted, they would not bear fruit until sometime in the future. For the present, I and a number of likeminded gentlemen are to raise a body of horse and join the army of Gustavus. This troop will be in an honourable position, for although the infantry is a polyglot army with only a nucleus of Swedes, the rest being made up of Germans, Scots, some English, and mercenaries from other nations, his artillerymen and cavalry are mainly his own subjects—Swedes, Finns, and Laplanders, with only a sprinkling, of foreigners—who have joined him as we will be doing to learn his new tactics. But more of that later!"

There was a pause. Tom waited, hoping for acceptance, but a little overawed by Sir John's knowledge of the soldier's trade which he would have to learn. Faulkner sized him up.

"How old are you?" he asked.

"Twenty nine," replied Tom, subtracting a few years in case Sir John thought him too old for such an undertaking.

"A cavalryman's life is hard service for one unused to labour—in the saddle all day, sometimes on short rations. Have you any skill with the sword or pistol?"

"I can acquit myself well enough with either," replied Tom, "and as to the privations I may have to suffer, never fear for me. Before I was a merchant, I worked as a briner in the salt pit. We were said to be among the hardiest men in the Three Kingdoms—and that I had from King James's own mouth."

Faulkner laughed.

"So the old king saw you on one of his royal progresses, did he? He spent much of his time hunting near here. Folk in Royston complained that it was expensive having the king around so often, but at least it had the good effect of preserving the district from poachers."

Tom was accepted and the troop assembled. Horses' hoofs thudded daily across the heath, swords clashed on swords, brawny arms flourished poleaxes, and the park resounded to the noise of sham fights. Sir John had acquired the theory of Gustavus's innovations in warfare. Briefly, the Swedish king drew his riders up in small squares, little moveable fortresses, with plenty of room to skirmish, instead of the great crowded columns of his opponents. Between them, small detachments of musketeers were placed for the protection of the horsemen, as a musket ball carried further than a pistol shot. The musketeers, too, were trained to fire in a novel way. No longer did one rank fire at a time then march to the rear—or two ranks at a time, as had been done in the Swedish service. Gustavus trained the whole body to give a "salvee" of simultaneous fire, the first rank kneeling, the second stooping forward, and the third standing upright firing over the shoulders of the second. The great crack of thunder and the hail of lead, poured at once into the ranks of the enemy, struck more terror into them than intermittent salvoes. The musketeers, in turn were covered by pikemen and could advance before the latter, fire their weapons and then retire to reload. The cavalry, too, was drawn up differently. Gustavus arrayed his Horse three deep instead of six deep; he taught them to reserve their fire as they charged at the gallop instead of a trot, then after discharging their pistols, to set about the enemy with their swords and charge home.

Tom found these exercises and war games exhilarating, and gradually his black depression lifted, leaving only an aching sadness which was banished in the hurly-burly of activity. The aptitude he showed for cavalry training, his education which was superior to most of the others, and his pleasant personality, led Faulkner to appoint him a corporal of horse. The comradeship of his fellow troopers, the excitement of travelling to the coast, the novelty of a passage across the grey ocean to serve this crusader king of Sweden and avenge wrongs done to his Protestant brothers, gave him a fresh aim in life. Disillusionment would come, but on that memorable day in the summer of 1632, when the mercifully unruffled waters of the North

Sea splashed against the sides of the crowded vessel, Tom's sense of purpose was firm. The activity of his body had brought a new calmness to his mind. Truly God had directed him to make a mark in this service.

9. LYNETTE

"Thou shalt not suffer a witch to live," says the Book of Exodus. "Thou shalt not suffer a witch to live," thundered the prosecutor at the trial of Margaret Broomhall, arraigned at Chester Assizes on a charge of consorting with Satan.

Though the fanaticism of the witch-hunters in Queen Elizabeth's day and the determination of King James in the earlier part of his reign to stamp out the practice of the black arts had moderated in later years, the popular fear of witchcraft, malice against unpopular persons and the occurrence of strange, lingering death caused such charges to be made. Formerly only an ecclesiastical offence, witchcraft became a civil crime in 1542. This was elaborated in Elizabeth's reign and made even stricter by King James in 1604. Each witch was believed to have a "familiar" in the shape of a small animal, and a search was made on the body of the accused for a mark where it fed on her blood. The witch was generally thought to be ugly.

"Every old woman with a wrinkled face, a furred brow, a hairy lip, a gobber tooth, a squeaking voice, a squint eye, or a scolding tongue", could be accused of being a witch, but in fact many were younger and more handsome; some were even men. The casting of spells did not need to be accomplished by sticking pins into an image of the victim; the malicious mumblings of some old crone were sufficient for a charge to be brought if something untoward happened to the supposed victim of the curses. The devil in league with the witch had caused by his malevolent power, in some cases death or sickness to the person bewitched; in others, loss of crops or livestock.

This particular case which came up before a learned judge and a jury mainly composed of small landowners, was based on slender evidence. Only common marks could be found on the alleged witch's body—none of which could reasonably be declared a third nipple at which the familiar fed, or the devil's sucking place. Nor could any animal be positively identified as a familiar. Nevertheless, sufficient evidence was concocted for her to be brought to trial. The accused, who though advancing in years, did not conform to the common belief in the ugliness of witches, was accused of casting a spell on a pedlar. This unfortunate man, while enjoying a drink in the only hostelry at Rushbury not far from the city, had a sudden seizure and lost the power of speech. A "Cunning Man" who practised white magic, was called in, and he declared the pedlar to be bewitched. His "investigation" on which the villagers placed great reliance, led them to a cottage far outside the village and close to the Great Forest.

Old Meg Broomhall, whom everyone believed to live alone in this secluded place, had long been considered a cunning woman or white witch. Older people in the village spoke of having consulted her when something was lost or stolen and of obtaining remedies from her in cases of sickness. Recently, however, she had completely withdrawn from society, never appearing in the market as formerly, and discouraged callers, who found only bolted doors to greet them. She admitted that a pedlar had knocked at the time in question and that she had told him to leave her in peace as she did not require anything from him, but denied having uttered any curses.

When however the investigators entered her house to search for the familiar, a strange thing came to light; no cat, toad, or other small animal was discovered, but Meg was found not to be alone as everyone had imagined, but to have the company of a pretty, little dark-haired girl of about five years of age.

The questioning was long and severe; torture was not applied as, unknown to the common law, it was a royal prerogative in England, but the almost equally unpleasant process of "watching" was carried out. This meant that the victim was kept awake for twenty four hours or more to see if the familiar would come to her. Though none appeared and Meg would not admit that she had practised witchcraft, a strange confession was wrung out of the old woman.

The child was the daughter of a stranger, who passing through two years earlier, had been stricken by the plague. Meg had comforted her, and using secret but Christian arts, had attempted to cure her. The lady had been one of her failures, hence together with her baby boy she had succumbed to the disease. Meg had enlisted the help of a woodcutter, and not daring to enter Rushbury, she had taken the corpses of mother and child on a cart by night to the village of Weaver, where they had left them outside the sexton's door. She swore that she had not murdered or robbed the woman and had only concealed the place of the deaths in order to avoid the consequences of admitting contact with the plague. She had returned all the valuables the woman had in her possession, but had taken such a fancy to the little girl and her winning ways, that she had kept her as a companion. Before she died, the lady had declared herself to be Mistress Kate Ley from Wich Malbank, and she had called the little girl Lynette. That was all that she could tell, and Meg Broomhall threw herself on the mercy of the court.

The vicar of Weaver testified that the woman and child had indeed died of the plague, the sexton confirming that their arrival at his front door was exactly as the court had been told. The deaths had been entered in the parish register of Weaver and the valuables checked by Thomas Ley, had all been returned just as Meg had declared in her statement.

The charge of witchcraft, like that of murder, failed; nor was there any evidence of robbery. At the most Meg Broomhall could be described as a cunning woman, which had been general knowledge for a long time. The concealment of the child, Lynette, was, however, incontrovertible, and for this lesser offence, motivated only by love, she was sentenced to one year's imprisonment.

Will Masterson's marriage was in one sense highly successful, for his wife proved eminently receptive to his puritanical ideas. A Low-church Protestant from the start, her fervour after a few years of marriage became almost equal to her husband's evangelism, though its strictness was tempered to some extent by Alice's womanly nature. In another respect the marriage had been a failure, for Masterson's wish for a family had not been gratified. Will found this a matter for intense mortification, but he never abandoned hope that God would at last send him a child.

"Do we not read in Holy Scripture how Abraham, who believed his Sarah barren, was blessed with a son, even when she had passed the age of child-bearing?"

To some it would have seemed that the Lord was deaf to his long prayers and humiliations, but as the years passed by, Will continued to believe that they would be answered in God's own time.

Mr Minshull himself brought the joyful news to Nantwich that Tom's little daughter had been found. Margery Ley wept with a mixture of joy and sorrow.

"Foolish, foolish boy!" she said. "Rushing off to the German war! If only he had tarried a little longer. Another year here and he would have lost nothing. That war would have waited for him. It's been going on at least ten years and is hardly likely to end this year or next. But he was always like that— as soon as he decided on something it was done. Such a sweet, darling butter-fly. Just like her mother—and now, maybe Tom will never see his little girl again."

Lynette stood shyly apart, bewildered by this forgotten grand-mother's tears. She had been dressed in new clothes by Mr Minshull's housekeeper, for although she had been well-fed and treated with kindness by the old woman, Meg had been unable to supply her with decent clothes, and the dress she was wearing when discovered, was patched and tattered.

Mr Barton was less demonstrative, and his wife, rather jealous of Lynette's prettiness, made only a show of fuss in order not to be thought callous. All parties agreed on an ideal solution to the problem. Barton had enough with his own family and Margery Ley considered herself too old to be responsible for the upbringing of a young girl. As everyone knew, Will and his wife were pining for a child; the possibility of Alice emulating Abraham's Sarah did not occur to them; so it was unanimously agreed to ask the childless couple to act as foster-parents.

Will was at evening prayers when Mr Minshull arrived to bring him the news. The calm atmosphere of the place pleased the vicar. He felt responsible for the little child after having helped her father in his long search. He had been entrusted by the authorities with the task of returning her to those who loved her and he felt sure that this godly home would be the right place for Lynette.

"Found?" interrupted Will incredulously as Mr Minshull began his story. "My brother's little daughter found!"

So the supposed confirmation of Lynette's death which had ended Tom's long, fruitless search had been false!

"Where is she then?" he asked.

"With her grandmother Ley at Nantwich, but a suggestion has been made that she should come to live here if you are willing to take her. I know you are a godly man, reputed well both as a schoolmaster and a Christian. I know, too, that you loved your wife's brother both as a friend and a kinsman. Dear Sir, can you find it in your heart to take this little girl?"

Will walked to the door and called his wife. Alice hurried in, puzzled by the summons. She had thought the parson to be one of her husband's Puritan friends, and had not expected to be called in or consulted.

"This reverend gentleman has brought us wonderful news. Our little niece, Lynette, has been found and we are asked to give her shelter and bring her up as our own child—at least until Tom returns—when it will be his responsibility to decide her future."

Alice's face shone with pleasure. At that moment she looked really pretty. She did not even need to give her verbal approval—it showed in her eyes. Will spoke for both of them.

"Nothing could give us greater pleasure, Minister," he said. He raised his hands and his eyes.

"Blessed be the name of the Lord from this time forth and for evermore. He maketh the barren woman to keep house and be a joyful mother to her children. All thanks be to him!"

Will could well afford to bring up Lynette in the style which Tom would have wished. His father had relented at the last moment and had left his erring Puritan son sufficient money to enable him to enjoy a better standard of living than the average schoolmaster of the day. His comfortable house stood just across the river from the church, the smaller dwelling adjoining the school in the churchyard being occupied by the usher. His home was far from the simple lodging he had once inhabited at the house of the shoemaker, but as befitted a Puritan, there was no ostentation. Though the air of a scholar still pervaded the place, a woman's touch was also evident, even in Will's inner sanctum where he received Mr Minshull. He was a conscientious schoolmaster whose Latin and Greek were better than most of the teachers in minor grammar schools. He achieved good discipline in his classes, although he did not share the almost universal belief in the efficacy of the birch as an aid to learning.

"I am sure that the application of the rod can greatly discourage a boy from learning," he said. "Rather should a pupil be encouraged to give of his best to a Master he loves and respects. This extreme whipping breeds such a dislike of learning, that the children think themselves happy to be set any menial or unpleasant task by their parents which will keep them from school."

He used reproofs, loss of place in the form, and curtailed play for those guilty of minor offences. Nevertheless, this did not prevent him from dealing harshly with those who showed no respect for God's commandments—fighting, robbing orchards, and above all, using filthy or blasphemous words were severely punished. His pupils knew this and respected him for it, so there were few occasions on which it was necessary.

This lack of flogging appeared to some outsiders as a lack of discipline which more than once brought Will into conflict with a parent.

"Qui parcit virgae odit filium—he who spares the rod hates his son," quoted the irate Doctor Pennington, to whose belief in the medicine of the rod, Will replied tersely;

"Nullum medicamentum est idem omnibus"—the physician having to agree that in his field too, the remedies he applied would not be the same in every case.

In his home too, Will ruled with a firm but kindly hand. One of the few occasions on which he severely rebuked Alice was over the birching of a young serving girl who had committed a venial offence which he would have corrected with a reproof rather than the rod.

His religious beliefs were just as firm, but he was more careful not to clash openly with authority. There were no more excesses like the cross-breaking expedition to Sandbach, only a steadfast determination to study God's word, keep his commandments, and spread the light to those around him. His school day was a long one. He rose ere the sexton of the parish had tolled the bell at six o'clock and devoted the time to prayer and study before taking his first classes at seven. This was an hour earlier than some schools in the neighbourhood, but Will was determined not to let anyone accuse him of sloth. In the winter, when school started at eight, he allowed himself a mere half-hour longer in bed. The prayers which preceded and ended the school day developed into what almost amounted to a full-scale service; the pupils were catechized rigorously; attendance at church was strictly observed.

Will looked forward to the time when those of his persuasion would separate from the Anglicans and form their own congregations. For the present he had to content himself with the Established Church, but under Mr Malbon, the parish was as far on the road to more enlightened worship as he could expect. The King had no intention of allowing this dissent to grow. There were signs that the High Church Anglican orthodoxy would reassert itself. Then there would undoubtedly be a clash between Charles and a considerable body of his people.

There were indications, too, of a quarrel based on reasons other than differences in theology. Charles believed that good government was founded on true religion and that the church alone could teach that. He was an unshakeable Anglican, but his Queen was a Catholic; were there not signs that his high church sympathies led to an extension of favours to Papists? Charles had been brought up to believe firmly in Divine Right.

"Parliaments," he said, "are altogether in my power for the calling, sitting and dissolving. Therefore, as I find the fruits of them to be good or evil, they are to continue or not to be."

Parliament had not yet reached the stage of claiming supreme sovereignty; but it denied the king the right to take any action which he alone considered necessary. The theory of the "sacred, fundamental laws of the kingdom" was used to justify this attitude—laws based on the "acquired wisdom of previous ages to which king and commoners were subject alike".

On the practical level the Parliamentarians resisted the king over the administration of justice, arbitrary imprisonment, and the raising of

114

forced loans or irregular taxes. In 1629 Charles dissolved Parliament and the eleven years of his personal rule commenced.

There was no doubt on which side Will would come down in a struggle between King and Parliament. He envied his brother-in-law, who had cast his lot with the Protestants in Germany, and felt pride that his education of the adolescent briner had borne fruit at last, ignoring the fact that it was Tom's desperation after the loss of his family, rather than any religious fervour, which had sent him hurrying to the Continent to fight with Gustavus. For this reason, too, he knew he had to care for Tom's child and ensure that she was brought up a good Christian of the true faith. He shuddered to think that, but for the blessed intervention of the Almighty, one of his own family by marriage might have fallen into the hands of Papists or unbelievers.

Both Will and Alice were charmed by Lynette whom they had not seen since she was a baby. They could not repeat often enough: "the very image of her mother"—the same dark hair and eyes, the rosy complexion—just as Tom had wished. She had recovered her confidence and spirits while staying with her grandmother and prattled on about Auntie Meg and the hut by the forest, but seemed to have little recollection of the tragedy which had brought her there. Alice wanted the child to call her mother, but Will did not approve of the deception.

"Tom may return," he said. "We would not wish him to think that we had tried to usurp his position with his daughter. So it was agreed that they should be Uncle and Aunt to Lynette, as they really were.

Would Tom ever return? Will and Alice loved their brother dearly and could not wish him any harm, but as time went on and the child won their hearts, they both cherished a secret hope that somehow God would show a way whereby they could see their dear Tom again and keep the pretty little maiden they had grown to love so much.

10. AT WAR IN HIGH GERMANY

It was a November day in 1632 which saw Tom's baptism of fire. Reading of martial exploits or the privations suffered in sieges, practising, with his comrades on the heath, marching through ravaged countryside, skirmishing in villages—none of that had brought home to him the horror of battle. Nothing had equalled the cacophony of musket and cannon fire, the shouts of "Gott mit uns!" or "Jesus Maria", the howling of "Sa! Sa! Sa!" from the charging Croats. It had been a terrible experience which would be etched on the memory for ever—yet one which had hardened him to withstand future horrors.

To begin with there had been the dreadful suspense of waiting on that plain near Leipzig. Dark was the sky, pierced only by pale starlight; darker still was the tension in every breast. As bobbing torches like so many glow-worms showed where the King of Sweden and the imperial general, Wallenstein, marshalled their forces, threw up their earthworks and planted their cannon, it became almost unbearable. What would the morning bring? Would Gustavus or Wallenstein prove to be the greater general? What was in store for Thomas Ley—was it glory or death?

With light came reassurance. The mist which had conspired with darkness to shroud the battlefield began to clear. A king rode majestic-ally along the ranks—a King called the Lion of the North. The massed voices of the Protestants swelled into a song of praise. The sound of Martin Luther's great hymn "Ein feste Burg ist unser Gott" rose to Heaven—a mighty declaration of faith which drowned the chanting of the Catholic priests in the opposing camp and brought back confidence to Tom. He knew he would be doing the Lord's work on this day near Leipzig, away from the fair fields of home, away from loving friends and relations, but still under God's protection.

Then came the storm—infantry at push of pike, others with muskets primed to give the devastating salves of fire perfected by

116

Gustavus—the mist swirling round, hiding then revealing, then hiding the target again. The long line of imperial soldiers concealed in that ditch! The crackle of muskets, the hail of bullets cutting down his friends. The first blood he drew—driving his sword into the entrails of a musketeer who had shot a comrade!

The roar of cannon! Seven of them right behind the musketeers! The piteous shrieks of horses, the moans of dying men—a hellish chaos of sound. And his own commander toppled from his horse though mercifully unhurt. "Gott mit uns!" Tom cried as he rallied his troop. "Gott mit uns!" came the response as the standard bearer raised their blue and white banner aloft.

The enemy was in difficulties. Count Pappenheim and the reserves were hurrying towards the field; in the meantime the gap had to be stopped. Miserable bands of camp followers with soldiers in front had served this purpose until it became too hot for them when they followed their natural instincts and fled. The imperial artillery was taken. Hopes were high for the Swedes. Victory and the establishment of a Protestant Union with the Golden King at its head! Calamity followed. Gustavus, spurning danger, rode to the relief of his threatened left wing. Shot and pierced by spears, the Lion of the North breathed his last breath on German soil. Tom was beside him almost to the end, until the grey bank of fog gathered him in. Then, alas a riderless horse emerged from the gloom and the cry went up "The King has fallen!"

A blinding flash from behind the imperial lines! The powder magazine had gone up. Grenades, bombs, pieces of wagons and men were blown in all directions. But the enemy rallied nonetheless. Pappenheim and the reserves were back. Pappenheim fighting to the last, unable to decide the day for his side, followed his arch foe to a soldier's death. But Tom saw little of the final battle. One moment he was riding towards the enemy, his courage firm and his eyes clear. Then he was lying half dazed by a dying man on the blood-soaked ground. God be praised! No bones were broken. He was ready to fight again. But fighting was no longer needed. The Swedes held the field. Nine thousand men lay dead and many more were wounded. The imperialists had lost their guns, their baggage and their powder. Prisoners had been taken but in this hard-fought battle, they were few. Fog thickened by smoke from burning Lützen, closed in again to end a truly bloody day.

Before the battle Tom had listened to a preacher hark back once more to the destruction of Magdeburg—calling faithful Protestants to take up the sword and punish those transgressors to defend all godly men from the violent power of their enemies, to preserve the German land from spoil and rapine. He ended his exhortation with the words already so familiar to most of his hearers.

"And when they cry for quarter, meet them with the answer, 'Aye, Magdeburg quarter ye shall have!' Tell them, that as you cut them down."

Magdeburg quarter had been given and received; the tumult had ceased. A victory had been won. But for what? Had it been worth the sacrifice?

The following year was for Tom Ley one of constant movement and ceaseless activity. Though he was involved in no great battle, his physical endurance was taxed to the limit by the marches and counter-marches, his mental strain increased by the horrors he had to witness. Sometimes in moments of less stress, a picture of his old hometown would flash upon him, especially his parting sight of it when he stood by the brine pit on the very spot where King James had given him a sovereign, and he thought of that golden day. Such was the beginning and the end of a story! A royal gift had emboldened him to speak of his love for Kate, but cruel Fate decreed that his happiness should be broken. He had been promised a renewal of that contentment. But when and where? The future still appeared dark to him.

Tom already knew something about the geography of Germany. He had a picture in his mind of walled towns and formidable castles with pointed turrets, soaring high above the burgher's houses, and of great Gothic cathedrals. He had imagined a land of industrious peasants farming the great northern plain; and of wine-growers whose vineyards clung to the sides of that long, deep cleft in the earth through which the mighty Rhine flowed northwards to the sea. He had heard, too, of the rich life in the German cities—the craftsmen, the merchants and the bankers of towns like Cologne and Mainz, Nuremberg and Augsburg.

But this Germany, through which he rode and fought, was a different land. Some of the districts were comparatively untouched, even after fourteen years of war; others had been completely devastated before the Swedes under Bernard and Horn arrived. The death of King Gustavus had seen a breakdown of discipline in the Swedish Army. He had sometimes licensed his men to plunder, and when the king gave his consent it was ruthlessly carried out. To destroy the resources of Maximilian of Bavaria, he had burned and pillaged the dukedom systematically, end to end. Now the new generals were far less able to control the polyglot army, swelled by the recruitment of more mercenaries to replace the fallen, and the Swedes left a trail of destruction wherever they went.

Tom's first flush of enthusiasm gave way to harsh disillusionment. No longer could he hear the ranting against the godless Imperialists with equanimity. He had seen men of his own army reeling about drunk, forcing helpless girls, driving old men and women from their homes, putting houses to the torch. He had seen spreading trees bearing their shameful fruit—the men and women hanging from their branches; he had seen lines of soldiers standing in front of firing squads; he had seen countryside stripped bare, crops trampled down, peasants plundered by Imperialists and Swedes alike, left to starve in their miserable hovels, burghers robbed of their life's savings and their cherished possessions; he had seen churches desecrated and convents sacked. Misery upon misery! He had seen it all.

To make matters worse, plague ravaged town and country taking off men and women in their thousands, with famine following in its wake. The huge armies with their hordes of camp-followers, greater in numbers than the fighting men, were a breeding ground for disease. Again Tom faced death from this black pestilence; again he was spared, though he saw many of his comrades succumb.

Some heartening news reached his army in February 1634. Their great opponent, Wallenstein, the Duke of Friedland, was dead. Suspected of planning to desert to the Protestants and judged guilty of treason, he had been murdered by conspirators who had the support of Vienna. He had been succeeded by the Emperor's son, the young King Ferdinand of Hungary, as nominal commander-in-chief, with the genial but incompetent Matthias Gallas appointed to be his chief field commander.

In the autumn of 1633, the troops of Gustavus Horn, one of the two main Swedish armies in the field, were campaigning at the head of the Rhine Valley to secure it against attack by Spanish or Austrian power. The key fortress of Breisach, on a steep eminence above the swiftly flowing river guarded the higher waters of the Rhine. From it the traffic along the waterway could be controlled; thus to the Swedes, its capture would mean that the transportation of a Spanish army overland to join the Emperors forces, would be rendered almost impossible. So Breisach had to hold out against Horn's close blockade at all costs which it valiantly did until relief came.

After Lützen, Tom's troop had been placed under the Swedish marshal, a man from the king's own school, whom he would have liked to see as Generalissimo. If Lützen was a baptism of fire for the Englishman, it was on these campaigns that he really proved himself as a soldier—on raiding parties, acting independently, and when Sir John, wounded and unable to take command, handed over to his lieutenant, the third son of a Hertfordshire gentleman. Then it was Tom who supported the officer rather than the other way round—a fact noticed and commended, which marked him out for promotion in the eyes of his captain. Even the growing feeling of cynicism did not impair Tom's fighting spirit. He had imposed this task on himself. He would fight with the Swedes, the leaders of a new Protestant League of Heilbronn based on Gustavus's idea of the 'Corpus Evangelicorum'. But he would fight for the reputation of the men of his own country and his beloved commander, Sir John Faulkner, so long as they were together, so that no man might scoff and call the Englishman a coward.

Now he was fighting with more care for self-preservation. That feeling of desperation had gone completely. God would guide him through this struggle, and some day he would return to happy times and quiet pursuits.

Late one damp, chilly afternoon in the rapidly gathering twilight, his troop rode into Mühlbach, dignified with the name of market village, but to Tom it seemed little more than a huddle of thatched houses round a small church and a mill on the stream. The valley was narrow here, the hills on each side low and only partly covered with trees. All along the route a scene of desolation met his eye. Much of the corn in the fields had been trampled down by cavalry or laid low by the weather and it rotted on the stalk where it had fallen. The vineyards had been ridden through, a tangled mass of shrivelled vines and poles presented a scene of utter desolation. Mühlbach itself was no better; some of the houses had been burned; most were empty, the villagers having fled. The trees in the orchards had been hacked down for firewood; the vegetable gardens had been stripped bare; the stalls and pens were empty of livestock.

The buildings at the far end of the village were in better shape. None of them had been burned out, though all appeared to be deserted. The door of one of these cottages, rather better in outward appearance than its neighbours, was standing open. As he rode up, Tom could hear a strange sound coming from the interior—a mixture of crying and talking—not rising or falling in pitch, but carrying on in an incessant murmur.

He dismounted, and stooping to avoid knocking his head on the low lintel, entered a large room which made up the ground floor of the cottage. It was dark inside, the light from the small window at the back being cut off by the shadow of some trees.

If there were any rooms above this spacious domestic area he could not tell, for he saw no ladder or steps leading to an attic. Several people were lying around the room, apparently dead, but one was certainly alive—a boy of about fourteen from whom the crying-talking sound was coming. On seeing Tom enter, he shrank into a corner.

"Nicht furchten!" said Tom. "Ich Freund."

Despite this assurance the boy dared not venture out—not even when the Englishman advanced and offered his hand —but only screamed more loudly, so Tom did not persist. Leaving the lad shivering with fright in the corner, he looked round the room. He could appreciate the reason for the boy's terror. Two men lay on the floor, a woman on the bed. The remains of a fire smouldered in the hearth; close by lay a pile of wood and beanstalks. Tom stirred the fire and threw on some branches.

"Nein! Nein!" shrieked the boy. "Bitte nicht! Gnade! Gnade!" and then continued in a torrent of German which Tom did not understand, though it was plain that he was begging for mercy.

Having previously witnessed a dreadful scene, he believed that this latest intruder would treat him as brutally as those who had burst in before. It was easy to visualize what had happened. Imperialist soldiers had ransacked the place and killed all the occupants except this boy, who, spared either by accident or design, had been terrified

121

out of his wits. Tom could not be sure how he survived, as his German failed him, but he noticed a large mark on the lad's head—not a sword cut, but a bruise which he could have received as a result of being knocked unconscious with the butt of a musket. Some blood had clotted on his fair hair, his face was deadly pale, his eyes staring with fright.

But gradually as Tom spoke gently and reassuringly, the boy calmed down and his wailing turned into intermittent sobs and whimpers. Corporal Ley called in two of his troopers and ordered them to take out the dead and bury them in the garden. They lifted up the first man. Tom saw his face.

"God!" he cried in horror. "What have they done to him?"

His eyebrows had been burned off, and over his forehead ran a deep sear. His hands, too, had marks as if a hot iron had been applied, and some of the fingers had been hacked off. Tom could understand better why the boy was so afraid of the fire. The marauders had tortured the man, presumably to make him disclose the hiding place of some of his goods.

The troopers lifted up the man and carried him and his elder son round to the back of the house. Tom covered up the woman who had obviously been ravished before being killed, until his men could come back to bury her. He took a piece of bread from his knapsack.

"Komm, essen!" he said.

The boy, who had stopped whimpering and was staring at Tom—surprised that he was supervising the removal of the bodies—came warily forward.

"Gut, Brot!" said the Englishman. "Komm, essen!"

The boy snatched the coarse, rye, half-loaf, tore off a piece and ate it greedily. Tom produced a piece of bacon.

"Sieh! Schwein!" he said, unable to think of the proper German word, pointing instead to the thick, fatty chunk which he had cut from his ration, but had not found time to eat on the long day's march. The boy who understood well enough, gave him a look of gratitude—the first time his expression had changed from one of utmost misery.

"Mutter? Vater?" asked Tom, pointing to where the bodies had lain.

"Ja," replied the boy resorting to simplified German. "Bruder auch. Schwester hin. Soldaten nehmen Schwester."

So it seemed that the plunderers had fallen on the poor family, raped the mother and killed her, tortured and murdered the father and abducted the sister to use at their pleasure.

"Du allein?" asked the Englishman putting his arm on the boy's shoulder. He would have to make an instant decision. He could not leave him here; the village was almost deserted. There was no headman, no priest, no young person to be seen. Only a few sullen, ancients, too weak to start out on a hazardous flight, remained in the dark corners of their cottages. On the edge of the village bodies lay in a shattered orchard where the plunderers had met resistance from the enraged peasants; bullet marks and blood stains on the churchyard wall showed that a firing squad had been at work. The boy would starve here or wander off into the forest to die at the hands of a raiding party or common bandits. There was only one humane solution.

"Ich dich nehmen," he said. He could not think of the word for servant. "Mich helfen. Essen, trinken—gut! Komm! Du Soldat."

He placed his helmet on the boy's head. It looked quite comical as it came right down to his ears. He lifted up the front, peeped out, and at last he smiled. Then he stood up.

"Ich komme mit dir, Schwede. Ich Diener, du Meister!"

"Nicht Schweden," said Tom as he mounted his horse and lifted him up in front of him, "England".

"England?" repeated the boy, turning his head towards his new master. "England gut."

Tom appreciated this generalized praise for his nation, and his heart was lighter as the troop marched out of the village, for he had found a new friend.

The boy, who introduced himself as Georg, was very useful; he proved his worth looking after Tom's equipment, dealing with sutlers, and most of all as company for him. He was quite a presentable lad when he had been smartened up and provided with some new clothes. He was short for a thirteen-year old German boy and decidedly thin, but not lacking in strength and endurance. He had a quick sense of humour and a way of speaking which some people might have taken for undue familiarity, but Tom was rarely offended; he was only too pleased to have the comradeship offered by the boy.

Since he had entered the Swedish service, there had been periods of activity in battles and sieges when there had been no time to brood on the past, but on long marches or lonely night watches, the sad remembrance of the dreadful day when he first realized that his dear wife and children had gone for ever, returned to trouble his heart. George—Tom insisted that he should add the English 'e' to his name—went some way to filling the gap left by that loss. He looked very much like Tom with his fair hair and blue eyes, so much so that they were often taken for father and son. The boy soon picked up enough English to converse quite freely and Tom's knowledge of German improved, so at first their conversations were carried on in a quaint mixture of the two languages.

Tom soon discovered that George was not an ignorant peasant lad as he had at first imagined, but had even mastered the rudiments of Latin, and his education compared favourably with that of a pupil at the Grammar School in his home town, Nantwich. George later explained that, though his father was a poor man, he had cherished the hope that one of his sons would study for the church. The parish priest assured him that it was even possible for the son of a quarryman to gain admission and advancement, and he supported Konrad Waldheim's ambition.

Thus George received the basic education to prepare him for eventual entry into a seminary at Freiburg. The boy was an apt pupil, though he had no fixed idea of going into the church. Even at the tender age of thirteen he weighed up the pros and cons. It had been thrust upon him, but it was a gentler calling than hewing stones in his Lord's quarries. Would he ever be a holy man like Father Jacob? Perhaps it was not God's will that he should become a priest and he would be shown another way in which he could serve him.

At first Tom found the idea of having such a well-educated servant awkward, but George did not seem to mind. Tom was so much older—a soldier and a leader, soon promoted to cornet of horse. What was more he had saved him from almost certain death. In any case, the informality of their relationship as master and servant soon made the equality of education irrelevant.

On July 12th 1634, Marshal Horn and Bernard of Saxe-Weimar met at the South German city of Augsburg. Between them they had twenty thousand men, and having united their forces, they marched for the Bohemian border. They stormed and captured the town of Landshut, but then lost Regensburg, so they swung round and marched after Ferdinand, King of Hungary, who was leading the Austrian army in an effort to link up with his cousin, another Ferdinand, the Cardinal-Infant of Spain. This young man was more at home wearing a helmet than a biretta. Brother to the King of Spain, he had studied war and statecraft, before being appointed Governor of the Netherlands. Now having laid aside his priestly robes and sacred chalice in favour of full armour and a marshal's baton, he appeared on the German scene at the head of a Spanish army of experienced troops.

The King of Hungary crossed the Danube on August 16th, and the Cardinal-Infant's force swelled his ranks to thirty three thousand. A small Swedish garrison was trapped in the ancient town of Nördlingen by this army; the task of Bernard and Horn's twenty five thousand men was to dislodge the Austrians and Spaniards, for they could on no account let Nördlingen fall. The loss of another town would be a political, if not a military disaster. The King of Hungary was steadily bombarding the garrison. Time was certainly not on the Swedes' side.

The battle exploded in fury early on the morning of September 6th. Strong points on the wooded hills round the town were won and lost; the Spanish infantry in the centre, fighting with professional skill, countered the Swedish hail of shot by kneeling down when it was apparent that the enemy would loose off a volley at them, and rising to return the fire before they had time to reload. On the plain in front of the city, the Swedes delivered charge after charge against the Spanish lines, yet failed to break through. Each assault was delivered with increasing determination to succeed, but it was not to be.

After seven hours of furious combat, Horn retired across the valley to entrench himself. The Swedes were divided, and triumphant cries of "Viva Espana!" rang through the air as the Spanish cavalry thundered down on Bernard's spent troops driving them from the field. Unable to check the rout, Horn's men were carried along with them; thus the whole army was scattered and virtually annihilated.

Tom Ley had fought throughout the battle like a man possessed, if not to win, at least to survive. He saw Sir John Faulkner fall, shattered by musket balls; his friends dropped from the saddles one by one, arms hacked off, legs and cheeks laid open by sword slashes, there to be trampled down by their own squadrons or finished off by the enemy. Yet his guardian angel permitted him hardly a scratch; it seemed that he would be the only member of his troop alive at the end of a battle which was turning into a massacre. Then his luck broke.

It was on the seventh or perhaps the eighth charge against the imperial lines—Tom had lost count. How many more times would they have to wheel round and hurl themselves against the Spaniards? Five? Six? Seven?—or until they dropped exhausted from their mounts? No! For Tom it was the last effort. Through all the noise of battle he seemed to hear that one crack of a musket which was meant for him. A searing pain ran through his body; he heard a great swishing sound, then all was silent.

The Swedish army had been utterly crushed. More than half of the magnificent regiments and squadrons of Gustavus were dead; Marshal Horn was taken; four thousand other prisoners were being invited to turn their coats; the rest had been scattered to the winds.

The Three Ferdinands—Emperor, King and Cardinal, had triumphed, and the Catholic star was in the ascendancy. But this war had become endemic. Power politics were taking over from religion as the leitmotiv of the conflict and the German tragedy would drag on for many more years.

11. STRUGGLE FOR SURVIVAL

Barely three miles as the crow flies from the battlefield of Nördlingen, on the road to Donauwörth, and the south, stood a little chapel of ease by the wayside, a place of worship for remote parishioners or a stop for travellers seeking spiritual refreshment.

In normal times, this pleasant little building at the foot of a wooded hill, with its cool flagged interior, its painted statue of the Virgin, a stoup for holy water, and a narrow stone bench round the wall, was a place to induce holy thoughts and set the traveller on his journey with renewed confidence.

It was in this little building that Tom Ley recovered consciousness. He was lying on a stone floor, but yet it seemed that someone had tried to make him comfortable. A makeshift pillow was under his head; a cloak had been thrown over him. He tried to raise his head but could see little at first. As his eyes became accustomed to the gloom, he realized that he was in a church—yet it was different. A great pile of straw lay near his right side; an indeterminate shape could be seen beside a small fire which glowed in front of him. He tried to raise himself further, but excruciating pain in his right shoulder made him fall back.

He remembered now how he had been struck down in the battle and recollected something of jogging along on a horse's back, each jog caused by the animal's passage over the uneven ground giving him such pain that it seemed to tear his body apart. He looked up again, this time towards the entrance. The door had been torn off its hinges and lay on the floor. Starlit sky and the outline of the trees which came down close to the chapel, was all he could see. The place appeared to be deserted. He could hear a low sound inside the room, almost like breathing. From outside, eerie, distant noises came across on the breeze which sighed gently through the trees—the same grim sounds he had heard at Lützen—only then much nearer. He imagined he could distinguish the last desperate cries of wounded men and horses left on the battlefield, the rumble of wheels, and the tramp of living animals in the army of the victors. There were no sounds of revelry from the imperial camp. The celebrations of victory were long over. Dawn was coming—he could see that through a gap in the wall which had once been a window—but the entrance was still dark, shaded as it was by the woods in front. Why had they brought him here, wounded, to die alone, a prey to corpse robbers or bandits?

Suddenly, from the half-light outside, a familiar figure emerged, stooping, carrying something heavy in one hand. Once again Tom fell back, then the figure was at his side, towering giant-like above him as he lay on the floor. "Master Tom! I bring water."

"George! It is you," said the wounded man feebly. "You found me."

"Yes master— after long search. I find you and bring you here."

"All alone?" asked Tom, incredulously.

"Horse help," replied the boy, and despite his pain Tom smiled faintly at his friend's quaint recognition of the horse's services.

"He too!" went on George, pointing to the huddled shape on the other side of the fire, which Tom had not recognised as a sleeping human form.

"He take out musket ball and stop blood. Kaiser's soldier—but good man. I wake him now."

So he had been rescued by his little servant and an imperial soldier who was sleeping wrapped in his cloak. His guardian angel had not deserted him after all.

The Austrian stirred even before George had shaken him, and he rose to his feet. His tattered uniform with blood on the sleeves, showed that he too had not come out of the battle unscathed. He looked down at Tom with a calm and friendly expression. Was it just one of sympathy for a wounded enemy, or satisfaction at the success of his surgical skill?

128

"Es geht mir schon besser," said Tom, reassuringly. The Austrian did not reply, but turned round and spoke to George.

"He say we must move now you are better. Peasants come or Kaiser's soldiers—both bad for us. We hide somewhere else."

It had now become light and Tom could see how badly the chapel had been desecrated. The image of the Virgin still stood, but the eyes were missing as if someone had gouged them out with the point of a dagger—which probably was the case. The place was filthy; Tom suspected that animals as well as men had used it as a resting place.

He gritted his teeth as his companions helped him to his feet. The Austrian thrust two pistols into his belt and took Tom's arm round his shoulders.

"Leopold Brunner," he said, introducing himself, but he volunteered no further information. Though Tom felt too weak to walk, he did not protest as they led him to the door. Outside the chapel, two horses were tethered to trees. They were poor specimens—dragoons nags, not cavalry horses, which were good enough for mounted infantry. These beasts had been captured by the resourceful George while his master lay sleeping on the chapel floor.

"I cannot ride. I am too weak," protested Tom. "Take me back into the chapel."

"Master, wait! The cart comes," replied George, cheerfully, and to Tom's surprise, round a bend in the track which wound through the wood, came a third horse drawing a small farm cart. He was astounded at this development, but relieved to be able to lie in the cart as even a short period of standing had made him feel giddy.

"I take your thalers and bring peasant's cart while you sleep," said George, spreading a blanket over Tom. "We find a better place to hide until the army goes."

Leopold and George mounted the dragoons' horses and the cart moved off, first through the wood and then along a dusty country road. Tom felt much more comfortable than he had done in the chapel; the throbbing pain in his left shoulder had eased; he laid the right hand, across which he had received a sword cut, on his chest. The jogging of

129

the cart did not trouble him much, the quantity of straw underneath cushioning him against the jolts.

He saw little of the landscape they were passing, his view being confined first of all to the tops of trees and a patch of blue sky, and then, when they came out of the wood, to a wider expanse of the heavens, with some white clouds drifting across it. The sun irritated him in the open as he lay on his back, so he asked for something to shade his eyes. Leopold took off the feathered hat which gave him rather a dashing appearance and George placed it on Tom's head, tipping it over his eyes to give him some protection from the bright light. After about an hour's driving, the cart rattled to a stop in front of a house very similar to the one at Mühlbach where Tom had found George. It was a little further out of the village than the Waldheim's cottage had been, but in all other respects it was its twin.

As they helped Tom out of the cart, he could see the yellow thatch of the cottages and the little white spire of a church in their midst, about half a mile down the road. The fugitives had decided to tell the farmers who sheltered them on the way, that they all belonged to the Catholic army, and having been separated from their regiments in the heat of battle, they wished to rest and recover from wounds before re-joining the main body or some imperial garrison. But in the first case it was unnecessary. The peasant farmer had been well paid, and though plainly worshipping as a Catholic, he had not much time for either party.

"Danes or Swedes, Austrians or Spaniards!" he said. "It is all the same to me. A Catholic with a rosary in one hand and a drawn sword in the other, or a Protestant with a bible in his pocket and a pistol in his belt! We suffer just the same."

Food was not in such short supply here as it was in Mühlbach. The Swedes had passed through, hurrying to make contact with the Imperialists at Nördlingen, but to the great relief of the inhabitants of the village, there had been little time for plundering. The peasants in Bavaria, as in most parts of Germany, knew the fearful meaning of that word, for during an earlier incursion, this village and the surrounding countryside had been thoroughly pillaged. So they had made their preparations to resist if the number of marauders was not too great for them, but fortunately on this occasion their ancient pistols, pitchforks and billhooks had not been used.

The farmer provided them with a plain but substantial meal and led them to the loft. Tom managed with some difficulty to ascend the rickety ladder, and once in the loft he laid himself thankfully down on a pile of clean straw which the farmer's wife had spread out for him. Leo removed his breastplate and jacket, re-bandaged his own arm, then came across to Tom and bound his shoulder and hand with the touch of one who had had much experience of attending to his comrades' wounds. The clean linen bandages felt pleasant after the soaked rags which had not been changed since the bullet had been probed and removed. Tom raised his good arm when Leopold had finished, and extended it to the Austrian.

"Danke vielmals Freund," he said. Leopold's face did not betray much emotion. He looked down at Tom from beneath his bushy eye-brows, then turned and spoke to George.

"He say he had to help wounded man— even enemy. He tell me all men should be brothers."

"All the same he deserves my thanks— and you too, brave boy. Except for you, I should be lying stiff and cold at Nördlingen instead of recovering here."

"No need for thanks from you, Master Tom," said George. "You took me in your army and are good to me. I must thank you."

For several days Tom and Leopold remained confined to the attic. George went out on foraging expeditions or just to see the lie of the land, making his reports to Tom like an experienced soldier. It was here that Ley heard for the first time the outcome of the battle—the fine Swedish army, the pride of King Gustavus destroyed; survivors trickling into garrisons hardly sufficient to make up a few regiments; the turncoats bribed or threatened into taking service with those they had been trying to kill; the noble Marshal Horn captured; Bernard of Saxe-Weimar a fugitive on a dragoon's nag; Sir John and most of his friends mown down in those murderous attacks on the Spanish lines.

What was left of the army would be an unknown force to him—he had little desire to return. It would not be desertion to fail to re-join an army which had virtually ceased to exist. Yet how could he reach his home again? There were hundreds of miles to travel, through strange and dangerous country, and a sea crossing to make. Ah, home!—green fields, timbered houses, the time-honoured mellow, sandstone church, the sluggish, winding river—even the smoking, steaming salt-houses and the deep, dark, brine-pit! His service in this war had exorcised the ghosts of the past, but should he succeed in returning home, would he be able to pick up the threads of his old life again?

Tom had always been hardy and he soon recovered his strength. The wound healed cleanly—a tribute to Leopold's skill, but Tom doubted that he would be much use with his sword arm for some time. Still, he had no intention of returning to service; he would only need it in case of attack by other fugitives or bandits. He decided that in these circumstances it would be better to rely on a pistol. He had lost his own, but Leopold supplied him with one of the two he carried.

He was intrigued by this Leopold. Why was he hiding out here when his army had been victorious? The Austrian said little, but Tom did not judge him to be of a taciturn nature, as he conversed quite freely with George. It was more likely that his own lack of fluency discouraged the Austrian. That could be remedied by more practice and he begged George to ask Leopold to speak directly to him more often, explaining that he could understand German well enough without an interpreter, if it was spoken slowly.

Brunner was quite a handsome man when the powder and grime of battle had been washed off him. His reddish-brown hair was longer than Tom's; his eyes of a blue so pale that it was almost grey, were thoughtful and expressive. He had a mature look, and Tom imagined him to be only five or six years younger than he was; but when in fact he did discover his true age, he found the Austrian to be ten years his junior.

After several days of inactivity, Tom began to feel restless. There was nothing to do except to wait. He had no books, not much conversation and no exercise. The mid-September weather was deteriorating and heavy rain would soon turn the roads and tracks into quagmires, making travelling difficult—sometimes even impossible. He pointed out to George that he was now fit enough to leave and reminded him of the dangers of delay. The boy went into conference with Leopold, returning with welcome news.

"He says we should go tomorrow. The army has moved on."

Brunner came over and confirmed this statement.

"But is there any place to go?" asked Tom with a sigh of resignation. "The whole land is in flames."

It was George who supplied the answer.

"He says his home is at peace. It is a beautiful place with great high mountains. The salt lands are there—he tells me all about it."

Salt! The great mountains! A strange feeling came over Tom—a distant memory. He could not feel more at home than in a land where salt was made.

"Thy happiness shall be broken, and thou shalt find no peace until thou comest to the great melting mountain."

The long-forgotten words of the half-witted prophet, Nixon, spoken so long before, suddenly rose up from a dark corner of his mind. He had scorned this saying and for nearly seventeen years he had forgotten it. Now it returned to him word perfect, just as if it had been spoken yesterday.

"Yes," he said to his friends. "We will go."

Tom was puzzled as to why this Austrian soldier should have chosen to help him. There were thousands of wounded lying on that field, from his own side as well as the enemy. George told a remarkable story of his own presence of mind and determination which shone through his modest relation of the events. When the battle had died down and his master did not return, he went out on the bloody field of Nördlingen to search for him. Amid this spectacle of horror he frantically turned over the heaps of bodies, some quite dead, some twitching, some horribly mutilated, others still conscious and calling for water. He did not have to search the whole battlefield; from survivors who had reached the camp, he learned that Tom's cavalry had retreated with Marshal Horn, and had been caught up in the whirlwind panic of Bernard's flight. Evening was coming on and dreaded shapes were moving around the fallen—those sinister birds of prey, the robbers who took their pickings from the dead and from the living unfortunate enough to be left lying on the field.

133

Down a bank where the ground was rough and broken, stood a tall figure by one of the hillocks. He was distinguishable as a cavalry soldier, wearing a plumed hat with a white band—the imperial field sign. He stood staring at just one of the thousands of bodies which lay on that field of woe. Then he knelt down beside it to say a prayer over a dead comrade. George, who was busy dragging out one whom he believed to be Tom, suddenly looked up to see a grim shape in a long brown cloak, wearing military boots and the hat of an erstwhile officer, creeping up on the unsuspecting man. With a cry of "Ho there!" to the Imperialist, George picked up the nearest weapon he could find—a broken pikestaff—and flung himself on the would-be murderer jabbing him with the sharp spear, thus causing him to turn away from his intended victim. The Austrian scrambled to his feet and drawing his sword, dispatched the villain with a single thrust. The man crumpled to the ground, and lay on a pile of the dead he had been robbing—one further victim of the Battle of Nördlingen.

This was the beginning of a partnership, their first task being to search for Tom. At last they found him, lying apart from the others, fully stretched out on the six feet of German earth which could easily have been his deathbed. It was not difficult to secure horses. Tom was laid across one of them and taken to the chapel of ease. The rest he knew.

With the help of George he also pieced together the story of Leopold's service in the Imperial army. He understood that on his way to the University of Heidelberg, he and a friend had rested at an inn in Augsburg, where they had been partly cajoled and partly impressed into Wallenstein's army. From the first, Leopold had thought of desertion, but the Duke's tolerance to Catholic and Protestant alike and his superior organisation had persuaded him to stay. Wallenstein, held to be inferior to Gustavus in the art of entrenchment, was held to be above him in providing for his troops. His requisitions of corn, flesh, wine, bread and beer, were equally divided among the regiments and shared out in the established proportions to officers and men. Even luxuries—butter, almonds, hazel nuts, salted fish, vinegar, oil and tobacco, were provided whenever possible.

Educated as a Lutheran, Wallenstein later became a professing though not devout Catholic, who did not impose any religious test on his followers. He resisted the Edict of Restitution, issued by the Emperor to restore Protestant possessions to the Catholics, and this had been a cause of his dismissal from his first command in 1630. After the murder of the great general, which Leopold deplored, he was not anxious to serve under the Ferdinands, fighting in the cause of a Jesuit-dominated Emperor in the company of fanatical Spaniards. He was not a true Austrian; his homeland was in the Empire but not in the Archduchy. His lord was the Prince Archbishop of Salzburg who had kept his realm out of the conflict. As thoughts of home grew stronger, feelings of loyalty declined in proportion.

Tom was curious as to Leopold's own religion. He assumed him to be a Catholic, but saw no outward manifestations of the faith, such as crossing himself, telling his beads or giving especial reverence to wayside shrines. Nor did he show any signs of hostility towards Tom, whom he knew full well to be a Protestant. It eventually became clear that Leopold's family had once been Lutheran, but faced with the choice of dispossession and persecution in a Catholic province, they had chosen to conform. Nevertheless, Brunner's Protestant sympathies remained, not as a fanatical adherent, but as one who, having experienced both faiths, saw tolerance of the differences between Christians as the only true road ahead.

Though he had been of superior rank during his service, Tom felt himself to be on the same footing as Brunner, but with George it was a different matter. For some time he had been embarrassed by the boy's habit of calling him "master". They were no longer in the army, and the relationship of servant and master had disappeared. In spite of George's youth, he felt sure he should be given equal standing.

That evening he performed a little ceremony.

"You are no longer my servant George," he said. "You are my valued friend. Henceforth we will be two adventurers, Tom Ley and George Waldheim," and he playfully gave him a box on the ear which he believed was a custom practised by the ancient Romans when freeing a slave.

Leopold corrected Tom, remarking that they were now three bold cavaliers. George was happy, for he felt that he had stepped up in an instant from boyhood to equality with grown men.

The travellers decided to leave very early on the following morning; it was barely light when they rode out on to the rough path leading through the woods and along the valleys towards the frontier of the Prince-Archbishop's lands. Night travel was fraught with danger and could only be risked in an emergency. At first there were no signs of fugitives from either army, but close to the village of Blindheim, they came upon the scene of a struggle between peasants and plundering Swedes—or were they Imperialists? The fight had taken place in a field of trampled corn under which the bodies of soldiers and civilians still lay poisoning the air. The three friends avoided the larger towns and villages. Sometimes a column of smoke and distant cries warned them off; in other cases the fear of plague, which had followed in the wake of the fighting, kept them out of walled cities.

Tom had expected some difficulty in riding so soon after suffering a serious wound, but he held the reins well and kept up with his companions. They had purchased good horses in place of the nags on which they had escaped from the battlefield. The animals were fresh, and not being unduly pressed, they were a pleasure to ride. The fresh air and mild exercise was a relief after several days of confinement to the farmhouse; it was what was needed to revive Tom in body and spirit. The distance they had to travel was about one hundred and fifty miles, so at the leisurely pace which they set themselves, it took about ten days to reach their goal. They stayed at inns when they deemed it safe; otherwise they camped in the open. Again George did most of the foraging; his age and accent were least likely to cause suspicion that the travellers were former members of the hated army which had devastated their lands, on whom the country folk, when they caught them outnumbered or defenceless, took a not entirely indefensible revenge.

The recent surges of the plague across the country had contributed almost as much to the hostility of the peasants in this region as the war itself. In many places there were hardly any inhabitants left to welcome them to a village; in others they were greeted in a surly fashion, and sometimes the frightened people were unwilling to admit them at all. Even George's ready tongue and Tom's plentiful supply of silver groschen were not always persuasive enough; but the boy's persistence and the local knowledge of the Salzburger eventually surmounted these difficulties, and guided by Leopold, they passed by devious and sometimes perilous ways, out of the lands of the Elector of Bavaria and into the realm of the Prince-Archbishop.

Feeling safer now, the friends were using the main road. By the last milestone before a small village which, said Leopold, stood on the border dividing the lands of the Elector and the Archbishop, they stopped for a well-earned rest. At last they were beyond the battle area—at least the armies had not yet reached this southern part of the Reich.

Tom sat on the milestone while Leo rested on the grass and George stood tightening the straps of his saddle. Thoughts of his home and relations in Cheshire were never far from the Englishman's mind. When aroused by high political and religious motives, passions could run high. Would such passages of arms as he had witnessed in Germany, be repeated there? He could not bear the thought of such savagery as he had seen during the last two years, descending on the peaceful meadows and quiet towns of his own dear land.

"God preserve our England," he said, looking back at the strife-torn land which he fervently hoped he had now placed behind him. "God help my poor country if it should ever come to this."

12. THE PROMISED HAVEN

The early 17th Century was one of the high points in the history of Salzburg. Ruled by its Prince-Archbishops, the city had in 1634, been thus far spared the horrors of the war which had been going on for seventeen years. Fearing the approach of the Swedes, the ruling Archbishop, Paris Lodron, had refortified the town, strengthening its walls and towers and building defences on the Mönchsberg and Kapuzinerberg which rose up on either side of the River Salzach. Like his predecessor, Markus Sitticus, he had a passion for building. The old Gothic cathedral, damaged by fire in 1598, had been demolished to make way for one in late Renaissance style to rival the churches of Italy. A new Residence in the city, a summer palace at Hellbrunn with an extensive leisure garden, the castle Mirabell and a University, were all erected in the reigns of these two Archbishops.

It was a dismal autumn day when Tom arrived; the mountain tops were clad in a mantle of white cloud; a fine drizzle fell on the city. Leopold told him that they had missed the Feast of St. Rupert by a mere four days. It was he who had brought Christianity to the area and had founded the Abbey of St. Peter, the forerunner of the new cathedral in which his remains were still kept. Thus in memory of this patron of Salzburg, the twenty-fourth of September was kept as a holiday.

"I hope God sent them better weather in honour of the saint," said Tom, as in the gathering gloom the three travellers passed through the gates of the city.

He looked up at the old, grey fortress, crowning an eminence and the hills flanking the Salzach, topped with new fortifications.

He had to express his admiration.

"A mighty task for a would-be conqueror."

Leopold nodded.

"We are prepared, but hope and pray they will not come."

Behind the walls, a maze of narrow streets opened out into a wide square, at one end of which stood the cathedral—fourteen years in the building, completed and consecrated with great ceremony by the Archbishop, seven years before Tom's visit. There it stood with its Italianate facade and massive dome, so different from the pre-Renaissance churches he had seen so often on his travels. He had, naturally, not thought much about church or town architecture during his campaign through Germany, but now that the war was over for him, he had time for such speculations.

The inn was better than most of those at which he had rested on his journey from Nördlingen. Leopold led them down a narrow side street across which one could almost shake hands with a neighbour, to the renowned *Zum Weissen Lamm*, an excellent hostelry, where the meat was tender and liberally served, the beer the best Tom had ever tasted, the fire bright on a damp, chilly evening, the beds comfortable and warm, and the service friendly. Tom believed that his father-in-law would have placed this house very near the top of his list of inns.

Leopold was pleased to renew his acquaintance with a buxom, vivacious serving girl whom he had previously known—older by four years than at the time of his last visit, but still readily available. That evening Tom and George saw little of their friend who retired to a secluded corner with Luise. Later, as Tom carried his candle up the dark, stone stairway and passed Leopold's room, the sounds he heard could not be mistaken for a devout Herr Brunner at his evening prayers.

Tom had to admit that he was pining for female company. Since his wife's death, his only experience of women had been the soldiers' wives and the blowsy camp followers, whores, and rough ignorant peasant girls who by choice or compulsion marched with the army. He abhorred any such relationships; he could not think of one of these lying in Kate's place. Nor did he consider availing himself of girls such as Luise—a cut above the camp followers, but well beneath him. Still, the thoughts of a soft voice reading aloud in the dim light of evening, a musical laugh, the touch of soft skin and moist lips or strands of glossy hair, thrilled him with their possibilities. To be loved and to love as he had adored his Kate! How he had missed that passion which had been replaced, first by anguish and despair, then by an aching emptiness.

Leopold often spoke of his sister, Amalia, but Tom gained the impression that she was an immature child, romping about, pigtails flying, sitting legs astride on the garden wall, or climbing up trees to tease her brother from their spreading branches. He was only vaguely interested in this girlish Amalia; and besides, Leopold's tales, entertaining as they were, reminded him all too strongly of the tragic loss of Lynette.

On the following morning Tom rose early, but even while he was still abed, the drone of voices, the clatter of wheels, the tramp of horses, penetrated into his darkened chamber. On opening the shutters, he could see that there had been a complete change in the weather. Little sunlight could reach this alley, but he observed above the roof opposite, that the morning sky was blue.

On emerging from the warren of streets on the left bank of the Salzach, he took in the full beauty of the scene. Warm sunlight streamed down on the damp city. Steep, snow-capped mountains such as he had never imagined, rose up on all sides. Who could ever reach the summits of such forbidding giants? What mysteries would the intrepid climber uncover? What wonders would he see?

The streets were even busier than he had imagined; pack horses, donkeys and mules, carts and carriages, streamed along the winding street; country folk in peasant costumes pushed and jostled against him on their way to the market square. Even while Tom had slept, buying and selling had been in full swing. He had risen expecting an early departure for the nearby town of Hallein where Leopold's home was, but his friend suggested that after four years away, a few days would make very little difference. It was clear that the thought of a few more nights in bed with Luise was keeping him in Salzburg. Tom had to accept it, and to him it was really of little consequence. He was fascinated to see a busy city untouched as yet by either war or pestilence.

He took this opportunity to buy a new suit of fashionable clothes. His breeches and boots were still the same as he had worn at the battle of Nördlingen, though George had found him a shirt, a jacket and a peasant's cloak to replace the blood-stained and torn ones. He could certainly have provided himself with a more presentable wardrobe, but he shunned robbing the dead and only obtained replacements by purchase or bargaining—illogical perhaps, for he needed them more than the corpses—but, nevertheless, it was against his principles.

As it was, he felt like a scarecrow or a vagabond in this cosmopolitan place, and to avoid being taken for a fugitive or a country yokel, he sought out a reputable tailor as soon as he heard that their departure for Hallein would be delayed—George's country clothes would gain him little respect in Salzburg, and having enough money for both, Tom provided his young friend with an outfit such as that worn by a boy of fifteen or sixteen who came from a family of some standing. The tailor, a wizened little man, scenting Tom's thalers, fussed about him recommending this and that as the last word in fashion; but he did his job well, and when Master Thomas Ley finally emerged with a black velvet cloak slung over his shoulders setting off his dark red doublet and breeches, he was better dressed than he had ever been at home, not ostentatiously but with good taste, from his broad brimmed hat and wide lace collar, to his spurred boots with their turned down tops. His status as a man of some importance thus assured, he felt confident to explore the city.

Since he had first met Leopold on the field of Nördlingen, Tom had found his accent difficult; here in Salzburg he heard this quaint speech on every hand. He made valiant attempts to master it, talking to anyone who would listen to him, and with the help of George, he learned much about the strange wonderland to which he had come. Some of the stories he heard were confused with old superstitious legends, but from each tale a kernel of truth emerged, which gave him a desire to learn more.

Leopold, when he could be seen, spoke of the ancient Romans who had come up from sun-baked Italy to fortify these parts, of Saint Rupert and the Irish priest, Bishop Virgil, who built the first cathedral. Others told him of strange, wild people who had lived there before the Romans came—barbarians with long, flowing moustaches, living in a land of witches and dragons, who wore strange, winged helmets and bronze collars which were still sometimes dug from the ground. People said they were white-skinned men with yellow or reddish-brown hair who fought great battles against those of small stature and

141

dark complexion. In some stories gods descended from the skies to join in the fray, at the end of which the fair men were scattered to the four winds. All this mixed with tales of gnomes and goblins who lived in the great dark salt-caves. Leopold, who had read Caesar and Tacitus, knew them to have been Gallic people, and he gave Tom a brief history of the pre-Roman era; this removed the supernatural from the stories, but reduced their spell to a much lower level.

Brunner's appearances at *Zum Weissen Lamm* were brief which made Tom suspect that Luise was not the only centre of attraction his friend had in Salzburg. He was itching to move on again and tried tactfully to bring Leopold to a decision. At last he received his consent.

"It's a good day's journey," Brunner said—"all of twenty miles. We will leave at seven o'clock."

Next morning the last stage of the journey from Nördlingen began, as Tom, George and Leopold rode alongside the course of the River Salzach. It was a deeply slashed valley with streams tumbling down from glaciers and over great waterfalls on mountain faces cut with gorges. Tom found this positively frightening at first, but he soon came to appreciate its beauty. He had no time to bother about Celts and Romans; the scenery occupied half his thoughts, the other half being taken up by speculations about Leopold's home and family.

It was not until he reached Salzburg that he had learned about the elder Brunner's profession. Chancing to meet Leopold in the old Getreidegasse, which runs parallel to the Salzach, he walked along with him for company. In an even narrower lane, leading off the street, they entered an apothecary's shop, and although he did not fully understand their conversation, he detected an affinity between Leopold and the master druggist, which suggested to him that they followed the same calling. When they emerged from the low beamed shop, he asked his friend outright: "Are you an apothecary?"

"No, not I," replied Brunner in a rather scornful tone. "But I could have been. My father is a Master Medicine Maker, but I elected to study law—or rather shall I say—I chose to go to where law is studied."

"And the difference?" asked Tom.

"The difference?" replied Brunner. "My English friend does not know about the University—a little jurisprudence, a few duels, a lot of wenching and many glasses of captured sunlight! By Our Lady, that's a sight better than pounding away with mortar and pestle among the rows of glass jars in a dull, dark apothecary's shop."

"Or a dusty lawyer's chambers?"

"A little jurisprudence was mentioned," replied his companion gaily. "After the University! Who knows?"

"And your father? Did he not want another man of medicine in the family?"

"Oh, but there's always Rupert—dear pestlepounding Rupert—honest as the day is long, but quite, quite dull. Now little Amalia, that's a different case. You'll like Amalia, Tom," he said confidentially, putting his arm on his friend's shoulders. "She's such fun."

All three men had rested well at Salzburg, Tom had almost fully recovered his riding ability and the road which led down through the Tauern Mountains into Carinthia—an old Roman way—was firm enough in spite of earlier rain. The weather was changeable, low clouds drifted across the valley, but the rain did not last long, and as they approached Hallein the sun peeped out once more from the clouds. Now that Tom had a better understanding of the language, Leopold seemed to open out more. To the Englishman he appeared quite a different person. He pointed to the great mountains and told him of the masses of salt rock they concealed. Tom spoke of the saline springs and recalled his brining days, which surprised Leopold who had thought of him, by his education and bearing, as always having been in a superior class.

Hallein! The salt towns here often had the syllable "Hall" as part of their name, or they were sometimes simply called that. Tom learned that it was similar to the ending "wich" in his own salt district of Cheshire.

The River Salzach hurried on its way through Hallein which clung to a steep hillside. On an island in the river the old familiar salt-houses were clustered—so like the wich-houses of Nantwich yet so different in their astonishing surroundings—a great lump of mountain with a

143

tree-covered base and a ragged top dominating the town. But this forbidding giant was a melting mountain of salt, clay, and gypsum, generously spewing out its brine from the dissolved rock, which the conduit, here known as the "Soleleitung", carried down to the island to be boiled for its saline content.

It was a cheering sign. Here was the prophet's "great, melting mountain", which had teased his brain so long ago.

Tom wondered what Leopold's family would think of a son who brought home two men who were to them complete strangers, expecting them to be accepted as guests. He feared that they would not be able to rely on their hospitality for long. He still had some money, but what would happen when the supply dried up? Would this trail ever lead him back to England?

They dismounted and led their horses up the steep, cobbled street lined with tall houses, their massive bases sloping outward until Leopold stopped in front of a high wall, its monotony broken only by a green gate.

"The shop is closed now," he said. "We can go in through the garden."

This was quite extensive, being completely surrounded by a wall—a true apothecary's garden with healing herbs in profusion and gay flowers along the borders. A track by the side of the wall led to a stable block. Tom was the last to enter and the clang of the gate as he stepped into the garden had a finality about it. He felt that he was shutting off the past once and for all before entering into a new life.

Leopold threw open the stable door in the manner of a soldier expecting to find a hostile party inside. There was plenty of room for the horses, but no groom in sight, nor did anyone respond to the young master's shout. So he tethered the horses himself, and the task completed, he indicated a path through the tall plants, leading to the back entrance.

"The House of Brunner!" he said proudly. "The finest apothecary's house in the Archbishopric of Salzburg!"

Above the entrance, under a pillared gallery, were the initials *J.B.* and the date *1502*. Apparently, before the building had been converted into a shop by Leopold's grandfather, this had been the main portal. Tom was about to enter, when the sound of deft fingers plucking the strings of a lute reached him from above. Then a girl's voice, well rounded, with no hint of shrillness, broke into a flowing melody which the lute player was accompanying. Tom looked up above the doorway to ascertain the source of these magical sounds. Leopold, insensitive to the charm of the singer and the harmony of the lute, smiled at his friend's continued interest in a date stone and a plain wall.

"Come," he said, beckoning to him. "Upstairs!"

A passage led up a well-worn staircase which ascended to the first floor where the rooms of the family were situated. The steps carried on to another storey, presumably the home of servants and apprentices. The singer broke off in the middle of a line, bringing Tom back to earth. The door at the top of the steps opened, and a young man of about twenty years, still holding the lute in his hand, faced them on the threshold. A lively dog, the like of which Tom had never seen before, with a long body and short crooked legs, began barking and rushing around the visitors' feet.

"Leo!" cried the young man, throwing his arms round his brother before laying down the lute. Tom took the instrument which was poking in his face, and laid it on the table.

"Leo!" was all Rupert could find to say. The girl singer, who had been sitting by the window, threw down her embroidery with little ceremony and rushed across the room to greet her brother, while Tom and George still stood unnoticed in the background. Disentangling himself from their embraces, Leopold took the arms of his friends.

"Leo, Tom and George," he said, "three brave soldiers of fortune home from the wars! And here—Amalia and Rupert, Brunners from the crowns of their heads to the soles of their feet!"

"A friend's brother is a brother to me," said Tom, greeting Rupert, and then turning to Amalia, he raised and kissed her hand.

Leo's stories of the wild tomboy were incredibly out-of-date. Gone were the flying braids; in their stead delicate, fair ringlets framed a small, round face of striking beauty, and a string of amber beads circled a white neck. Her cheeks were flushed with pleasure at seeing her brother again and her light blue eyes sparkled. Two dainty feet in white slippers peeped out from below a gown of reddish gold. Who could not respond to such charm? Certainly Tom, starved of love, could not avoid being smitten by this Amalia. She could hardly be more than eighteen years old, and he was thirty five, but from the moment he set eyes on her, he never doubted that she was the only one who could replace his lost Kate.

The excitement of the reunion brought the elder Leopold and Frau Brunner hurrying in to embrace their son. Tom felt himself an intruder at this sentimental moment, so he and George drifted over to the other side of the room. He opened the casement and looked down over the neatly laid out garden. A large chestnut tree grew close to the stable wall. So this was the scene of Leopold's anecdotes! He smiled at the thought of how he had been innocently deceived by his friend into believing Amalia to be an immature girl.

The land sloped away above the garden wall, so the upper storeys, as well as the roofs of houses were visible. Over all rose the precipitous slopes of the salt mountain which to him linked the old and the new—his hometown, Nantwich, with its brine pit and salt houses, to this long-sought haven he had found in faraway Salzburg.

Tom turned round to see the family welcome still going on. A number of other people had come in—he did not know whether they were of the household, relations, or neighbours, and in the babble of conversation he found his German failing him.

The family's guests were being neglected, so Amalia broke off from the welcoming party to come across to them. She had some spiced wine brought in, and sat down beside Tom on the seat she had chosen before in order to follow better the intricacies of her embroidery. Leopold having left the room to renew some other acquaintanceships, Herr and Frau Brunner made up for their former excusable lack of courtesy by greeting their guests warmly. Amalia tried to resume her needlework, but the light was fading and she soon laid it aside. Tom leaned back in his chair. He felt quite at home in this pleasant room with its old-fashioned, painted furniture, the rich Turkey carpet on the table, and the heating stove, a giant in its class, in the corner. A servant brought in a candelabra which he placed in the centre of the table. The excitement of the return had died down and calm reigned once more in the Brunner household.

At supper time that evening the family heard of Leopold, the bold soldier. All of his exploits were not for the gentler ears of his mother and sister; nor were the excesses of his comrades; but the young man acted as his own censor. He strictly avoided the worst stories of torture and rape, of peasants being roasted alive, having their thumbs thrust into the barrels of pistols or cords twisted round their foreheads until their eyes started out. Nor did he dwell on the wolves and hungry dogs feeding on unburied bodies in the streets and fields, or Swedes trying to outdo their opponents in barbarity by forcing urine down their victim's throats, demanding that they drink to the Swedish Alliance. These he saved for his circle of male companions.

One story, which since it was of the highest importance, all were allowed to hear, concerned the death of Wallenstein. Tom had never heard the full details of the murder, and Leopold considerately stopped now and again to explain something he thought his friend had missed. He had been in the Duke's army, quartered at Pilsen in Bohemia, where exaggerated stories had gone around of Wallenstein's megalomania. It was believed that he would make himself King of Bohemia, create a rival Emperor subservient to him and distribute the German states to his friends. Doubting his sanity, many of the officers went over to the opposition. Then proclamations were posted commanding the army to take no orders from Wallenstein, but to obey only those of General Gallas.

"I was in the camp when the news broke," he said, "dicing over a drum. A great shout went up that a traitor had met his doom. At the castle of Eger his loyal officers had been slaughtered and the assassins had invaded the Duke's apartment in the house where he lodged. His captains had been surprised and murdered at dinner; Wallenstein was killed in his own bedroom.

'Are you the villain who would deliver the Emperor's people to the enemy and tear the crown from his Majesty's brow?' cried the English captain Devereux. 'Now you will die!' and he drove his halberd into Wallenstein's breast."

At this point Leopold was dramatizing the scene for the shocked ladies, the rather amused Tom and George, and the phlegmatic elder Leopold.

"Then they rolled him in a carpet, dragged him down the steps, and put him on display. His murdered captains, too, demonstrated only too well that now the age of Wallenstein was over; Ferdinand and his captains were in charge."

"Did the Emperor actually order the deed?" asked Tom.

"They acted independently, but Ferdinand willed it, approved of it when it had been accomplished, and rewarded the assassins well. I bewailed Wallenstein's fall. If his plans had succeeded, maybe peace would have come to Germany, but his negotiations for the cessation of the struggle were not supported in Vienna and his approaches to the enemy were interpreted as treachery and desertion.

But I could not go along with some of my friends who would have risen in arms to avenge him. There was a meeting in the churchyard near the camp. Some officers tried to whip up the men's anger with fiery speeches, but I refused to go. It was a good thing too; the ringleaders were arrested; the mutiny was broken. He had the qualities of a great leader, that Wallenstein, both as a soldier and a politician, but pride and ambition were his downfall. His noble traits were not matched by the qualities of a good man. Mutiny for Wallenstein, and a dead Wallenstein at that! No, meine Lieben; I deplored his murder but I followed the flag until the best opportunity came to leave the service altogether."

He looked across the table at Tom.

"You, my friend, were there when Gustav Adolf died at Lützen. I saw the fall of Wallenstein close at hand. We have both witnessed the exit of a great leader from our Teutonic drama. So henceforth the stage is left to lesser men, which I fear will be all the worse for Germany."

"May I ask you, Fraulein Amalia," said Tom after supper, hoping that he would not embarrass the girl, "the name of the beautiful song you were singing when I came up?"

Amalia blushed.

"In truth I know not whence it came. It is a song of long ago, sung by the troubadours. It tells of the joy of spring, the beauty of the garden, the love in the heart; but then sadness creeps in, for surely winter will come when all withers and dies."

Tom observed Amalia as she spoke. He was wont to look into the speaker's face as an aid to better understanding. In this case it was a pleasure. Her red lips parted to reveal a row of perfect teeth. So beautiful, yet so unlike Kate whom he had thought to be the pinnacle of feminine charm. He found her speaking voice as pleasant as her singing. He liked to hear the soft, South German accent, especially when spoken by a woman—so preferable to the harsh, guttural speech of Northern parts.

"A sad song," he said, "yet beautifully sung."

"Ah, but you never heard the last verse. I broke off as your footsteps sounded on the stairs. Then comes the spring once more and with it new life. All that has withered shoots up and blooms anew."

Tom felt a sharp pang at the appropriateness of the little song. His own life was being renewed in the presence of this lovely girl.

"Please sing it once more, Fraulein Amalia," he begged. The girl protested that Rupert had gone and that she had no accompanist, but the earnest look in Tom's eyes persuaded her. She took the lute herself and began to pluck the strings—not as expertly as her brother, yet producing a passable accompaniment. Then, in her dulcet tones she began the bittersweet song of life and love. Though he could not recognize all the words as Amalia sang them, the message was perfectly clear. Listening to this girl, her voice rising and falling in beautiful cadences, Tom knew that at last he had found his Promised Haven.

13. LUKE BLACKSHAW

Sixteen forty one! The Ulster massacres! What dread visions these words conjured up in the Protestant mind for many years to come! The greatest and most barbarous slaughter that ever the sun beheld! A hundred thousand—nay, two hundred thousand—men, women, and children, plundered, tortured, burnt alive, thrown into bogs to drown, even crucified, women raped, children spitted on knives as their parents watched! No horror was too great for the Protestant pamphleteers. The shock and anger at the sack of Magdeburg paled against this welter of anti-Irish, anti-Catholic propaganda. Of course there was more than a little truth in the stories; there had been a brutal massacre; but in the popular mind the events had been exaggerated ten and twenty fold. It is probable that as many as fifteen thousand people perished in those dread October days, which was mass murder terrible enough to need no exaggeration.

Ireland had been ruled by the Earl of Strafford, once a Parliament man, now the King's trusted minister. He was accused by Parliament of treason against the "fundamental laws of England"— a new concept—for planning to bring over an Irish Army to set the king up as a tyrant. The charge of treason was legally weak, but the ancient custom was used which allowed Parliament to pass a Bill of Attainder. Thus he was sentenced and beheaded on Tower Hill. Charles, after promising that not a hair of his minister's head should be harmed, gave way to the people and Parliament which was now in the ascendancy, and assented to the bill.

"A favourite of the king shall be slain"—another of his trusted ministers had gone, this time with the king's consent, but the master's head was still on his shoulders. The king's personal rule had lasted eleven years—a time of religious oppression and oppressive taxes. Matthew Barton had protested against Ship Money, but had paid up in the end; William Masterson was concerned at the persecution of the elect by Archbishop Laud—the imprisonments, the humiliations, the

150

fining, the mutilations. He had denounced them in his diary but he had made no active protest.

The king, trapped in his attempts to impose religious conformity in Scotland and to counter rebellion in Ireland, was forced to raise new taxes, so a recall of Parliament was necessary. The MP's, conscious of their power, drew up the "Grand Remonstrance" in which they listed the evils of Charles's rule. An army was dispatched to Dublin and Parliament hoped to keep control of it, but the king felt he must resist that demand if royal authority was to be maintained.

Among the ministers attached to this army was Chaplain Blackshaw. Young Luke earned the approval of the most ardent Puritans. A former pupil of Will Masterson's, his home was close to the city of Chester, but his father decided that he should attend school at Walbury on account of Will's far-reaching reputation as a learned, godly and humane schoolmaster. A star pupil in classical studies, he could compose so well in the Latin language that it was said his prose style was hardly distinguishable from a genuine passage of Cicero. At University he exceeded the achievements of his fellow undergraduates in Greek; his knowledge of the Humanists and his biblical scholarship eventually equalled and in some fields even surpassed that of his former tutor. Will took great pains with Luke Blackshaw. He felt that this serious, conscientious pupil would make a name for himself, but he had another purpose in mind. From the very beginning, he considered Luke a suitable husband for Lynette.

He was eight years older than the girl, but that was of no account. Will treated her exactly as his own daughter, and what better match could one desire for his offspring than a godly young man like Luke Blackshaw?

Years had come and gone since Tom's departure; his little, toddling infant daughter had grown into a tall, dark-haired girl, with a rosy complexion and hazel eyes like her mother, but having inherited many of the appealing ways which reminded Will of his friend Tom. At the age of thirteen she had such a mature appearance that it did not seem incongruous to be thinking of a suitable match, and a union with Luke could hardly be bettered. Blackshaw's father was a freeholder of some substance. Luke had taken a University degree and ordination. Either he would succeed to a living or an appointment as a schoolmaster, provided of course that he did not choose to marry before Lynette reached a suitable age.

Will had not neglected to instruct Lynette. Alice had no book-learning, but he insisted that she gave her brother's daughter the correct grooming in womanly duties and deportment. He himself saw to her more formal education. He had no plans to turn Lynette into a scholar, but he hoped that she would acquire sufficient knowledge to feel at home in the house of the learned Luke.

Lynette had great respect for the young man, but she found his aspect forbidding. He was handsome enough in a severe kind of way, with dark-brown hair, a prominent but straight nose, arched eyebrows, a small moustache, and a resolute clean-shaven chin. His spare, muscular frame looked as if it would be more at home in following the athletic pursuits of fencing, boxing, or cudgels than standing in the pulpit or bending over the scholar's desk. The fact was that he was just as proficient in these physical activities as in the academic field, though his desire to practise them had been subordinated to study. He hated Laud's High Church ceremonies, but he had never been heard to urge the wanton destruction of works of art when advocating the purification of worship.

It would have been an exaggeration to say that passion was kindled in Luke for this girl of thirteen. He had always thought of Lynette as a pretty child, lively and intelligent, sometimes even pert, yet suddenly subdued when aware of his presence—a show of awe which he found very flattering. He was one of only two boys, and had been treated almost as her own child by his much older sister, Jane; but his romantic experience of the opposite sex was practically non-existent, having been confined in the main to sharing the emotions of Helen, Penelope and Diana of old, or in his Cambridge days the appealing heroines of Will Shakespeare's dramas—a fact which later he rarely admitted. Nevertheless, there would surely come a time when he would wish to marry and raise a Christian family. A union with such godly people as Will and Alice, through Lynette, would please him intellectually and spiritually. She had the promise of growing into a beautiful woman and had been brought up on true Christian principles, with the example of a Puritan father and mother to guide her. Thus she would eventually take her place with ease as mistress of his household.

So Luke readily agreed when Will suggested that the girl's hand should be his. An unofficial betrothal—just a statement of intent—should be followed by a formal ceremony in about two years' time, possibly on Lynette's fifteenth birthday. Blackshaw broke the news that he had volunteered to serve as a chaplain in the newly-raised Army being sent to quell the Catholic rising in Ireland. This accorded well with Will's plans, and it was agreed that on Luke's return a formal announcement should be made.

It fell to Alice's lot to break the news to Lynette. The girl was in her chamber preparing for bed; a single rush light standing on a chest close to the bed gave enough illumination for the girl to undress and lie down between the sheets; but her aunt brought another light, and in the yellow candle flame, her expression seemed graver than usual. Lynette was not surprised when Alice said in a business-like way:

"Make yourself comfortable, dear. I have something to tell you."

Lynette hopped into bed. Had Tom been present, tears would have come to his eyes at the memory of that wonderful night in Chester when he had gone to Kate's bedroom. The girl looked so like her mother—younger of course—but the white nightgown, the candle throwing flickering shadows across the room, the leather-bound book lying by the bed, the dark hair, the sparkling eyes! They would surely have brought back a very poignant memory of the night when he first lay beside her mother.

"Have you ever thought of the day when you will no longer be able to live here?" began Alice. "Your uncle is growing old, as I am too, and we must provide you with a secure future before we die. Your father went away long ago, believing you dead, and God in his mercy sent you to us as an answer to our prayers. We love you dearly, Lynette, and it would be a bitter blow to lose you completely, but a match with one we know and respect would be no loss; it would set our minds at rest to see you promised now, even though the ceremony will not take place for a few years yet."

Lynette began to look agitated as she realised the meaning of her aunt's words.

"Is there someone to whom you would have me betrothed?"

"Yes, there is," replied Alice kindly; "a man who will have some standing as a clergyman. You know him, he is Luke Blackshaw—a worthy man of God who will love and cherish you as a Christian gentleman should."

"Oh, mother!" said Lynette—she sometimes used this word when making a special plea. "Not Luke Blackshaw! I do not love him. He frightens me."

Alice looked scornfully down at Lynette.

"You are not expected to love him now," she replied. "You will learn to do that when you are married. As to being frightened of him, that is pure nonsense. No kinder or more considerate man breathes in this county of ours."

"I believe you when you say that he would show kindness to me, mother, but why does he always look so stern—just as if he were about to call down God's fire from Heaven? When I marry I want a handsome man, whose heart will speak to me as soon as he sees me, who will woo me with pretty speeches and sweep me away in a great storm of love, then catch me up and whirl me on to a land of beauty and happiness."

"What fanciful nonsense you speak, girl," said Alice, surprised at the fecundity of Lynette's imagery. "I cannot conceive where you get such ideas—unless—"

She picked up the book which lay on the chest. It was one of Kate's bright romances given to his granddaughter some time ago by Matthew Barton along with a few other books and some trinkets from Thomas Ley's house.

"I see," said Alice, taking the book. "Henceforth you will confine your reading to those improving works which your uncle has prescribed for you."

Lynette objected that it had been her mother's book—one of her favourites, Grandpapa had said; but Alice ignored her protests.

"You can drive these silly thoughts right out of your mind. Your uncle has decided that you are to marry Luke Blackshaw, and marry him you will. God has called him to service in Ireland as an Army Chaplain, but when he returns in one or two years' time, the betrothal will be arranged."

Tears began to flow from Lynette's eyes and she buried her head in her pillow. Alice's annoyance was increased rather than mollified by this expression of grief.

"Next Friday, Mr Blackshaw visits us, and you will be polite and respectful to him. You will treat him as one who has agreed to give you his protection when we are no longer able to do so, who will love and cherish you as a wife. Otherwise you will feel the weight of your uncle's displeasure if not his rod."

Lynette raised her head. Tears still coursed down her cheeks.

"What must I say to him?" she asked weakly.

"You must answer him clearly and intelligently and try to divert him with your conversation. Mr Blackshaw is a man of earnest disposition, but once he is stimulated, it proves fascinating to be in his company. I know you are young, Lynette—barely fourteen—but you are my brother's daughter, and both he and his Kate were people of wit and perception. They would have seen the wisdom in this betrothal, as you must too."

"Is my father really dead?" asked Lynette rather piteously. "I wish he had not gone off to fight for the King of Sweden. I do not believe that he would have delivered me up to this long-faced Mr Blackshaw."

"I will not have this insolence!" replied Alice, very sharply. "As far as we know your father still lives, but his long absence suggests the possibility that he may have fallen in one of those barbarous battles in the Empire. Unless he returns, you will continue to be in our care and you must obey the commandment: *'Honour thy father and thy mother'*, accepting Uncle Will and me as your parents."

"We do love you, dear," she continued, softening her tone. She brushed some of the tears from Lynette's eyes.

"We could not want you, the only child of our home, to be unhappy. Lie back now and sleep. You will find Mr Blackshaw a perfect gentleman who will turn into a perfect husband. I am sure that you will learn to love him in the end."

Lynette's first meeting with Mr Blackshaw after this new relationship with him had been established was not a great success, and the chaplain went away without having risen much in the girl's estimation. He still seemed stiff and unapproachable, and it was only the inevitability of bending to her uncle's will, which made her attempt to draw closer to this unattractive man. Blackshaw could find little to say to a girl of thirteen. He could not talk to her as if she were a mere child, and yet what did she know of Armenians and Separatists, the Et Cetera Oath or the Grand Remonstrance? Nor could he meet her on common ground in a discourse about classical literature.

Although he had such contempt for her intellectual capacities, he looked at Lynette with growing interest. She was strikingly pretty. Strange that he had only just become aware of how beautifully she was developing. He could scarcely believe that she had not yet reached her fourteenth birthday; she was more like a girl of eighteen. He felt a shock as he found himself admiring her physical adornments and he brought himself back to the main consideration. She would without doubt turn into a very worthy wife. The possibility that any other could emerge from this ideal household, never entered Blackshaw's head. "*A virtuous woman is a crown to her husband,*" says the Book of Proverbs. "*Who can find a virtuous woman? For her price is far above rubies.*"

"Do you like gardens, Mr Blackshaw?" asked Lynette to make conversation. "I regret that it is such a cold, grey day; otherwise we could take a stroll down to the little stone seat. Uncle Will agreed to have part of the vegetable garden given over to flowers, and we planted some apples and quinces by the wall too. I do so love flowers. I would have the whole house full of them, but my aunt grumbles and says the garden is the place for useful plants. Which are your favourite blooms, Mr Blackshaw?"

The chaplain had not given the question of preferring one flower to another any thought. He considered for a moment.

"The lily, I suppose," he replied. "Our Lord speaks in glowing terms of it: *'Consider the lilies of the field—even Solomon in all his glory was not arrayed like one of these.'*"

Lynette could hardly keep her face straight as he pompously quoted the Scriptures.

"He would have to bring the Bible into it," she said to herself. "How could he go away without letting me know the measure of his holiness?" She laughed inwardly. "Such a wicked thought, but how true!"

Mr Blackshaw volunteered nothing more about flowers, so Lynette tried another theme.

"I have no doubt that you admire Will Shakespeare's plays," she said, smiling winsomely at the embarrassed minister. "I read some from a book of my mother's, but now I have been forbidden to study anything which Uncle Will has not determined for me."

"Very wise," said Blackshaw. "There are corrupting influences in this secular literature, not meet for the eyes or ears of a young girl." He coughed discreetly. "Yes, I had some slight acquaintance with the drama in my College days, but now I have no time for these follies and fripperies."

"But Mr Blackshaw," protested Lynette. "Will Shakespeare was a great man. I should dearly love to see one of his plays performed. Gallant braggarts, fair maidens, fine heroes, captains and kings, booted heroines striding about playing, the manly part! And all the grand show! Cannons firing behind the scenes, music playing and the people applauding! It must be a wonderful sight!"

Blackshaw looked disapprovingly at Lynette. Here was a task—a challenge to subdue these ungodly wishes. That this young girl, looking so demure, clad in russet brown and white, should harbour such desires!

"No, no!" he cried in alarm. "The theatre is a place of sin, the players a coarse, ruffianly crew. This tawdry, worldly show does not compare with the simple, glorious truth of God's word. Read and study the Scriptures and the works of holy men. Receive your pleasure from the outpouring of heavenly grace."

He took the girl's hand.

"I leave soon for Ireland," he said, "to do God's work there. When I return our betrothal will be formally announced. I will stand by you, my dear, and be your guide and mentor. Trust and follow me and happiness will attend on you."

14. CALL TO ARMS

By mid1642 the march of England towards civil war could no longer be halted. Enraged at the king's attempt to arrest five of their members during a sitting of the House for "alienating the king's subjects and raising tumults", the Commons prepared ordinances calling on all to back their cause, to muster the militia, to bring in horses, plate and arms. And so war came. The king raised his standard at Nottingham, a city which he considered strategically favourable for the expected help from the Netherlands and the recruits he hoped to raise in the neighbouring loyal counties. It was not an impressive ceremony, performed in a heavy rainstorm; later in the week the flag was blown down—an evil omen many said—but it was Charles's call to arms. To counter the ordinances of Parliament, he issued Commissions of Array to enlist men for his campaign, proclaiming the Commons traitors and rebels, but as yet few recruits joined his colours.

A Puritan schoolmaster was a likely prey for the unruly soldiers of Lord Grandison, who gathering troops in the northwest Midlands for the king had taken over the town of Nantwich and had sent his men out across the countryside, officially to gather in all the arms they could find. But weapons were not the only booty they collected. Money, plate, linen, clothes, writings, meat, drink, horses and mares—all these came into the category of what they considered lawful plunder. In Cheshire the rival factions had striven for the past few months, there as elsewhere, to gain the first advantage.

The Parliamentarian, Sir William Brereton, tried to stir up the city of Chester for his party. It was a vain hope in such a loyal place. A fracas ensued when he caused a drum to be beaten in the streets to enlist recruits for Parliament. The drum was guarded by halberdiers and when the constables attempted to arrest the men, they were resisted and forced to retire. The common bell was rung and the citizens of Chester rushed out to see what was the matter. The Mayor of the city stepped up to one of the men, and wresting a broadsword from another, cut the first man's drum into pieces. Sir William, saved from the wrath of the crowd by the Mayor, appeared before the magistrates, but he was discharged.

Checked at Chester, he tried his luck at Nantwich, and demanded the men of neighbouring hundreds to come furnished with arms, matches, powder and bullets to a muster on the heath just outside the town. At the same time the King's party came close to them and advanced until they faced Sir William's men. They almost came to blows, but at this early stage of the war they were loath to fight, and after the intervention of some local gentlemen of quality, Sir William withdrew and tried another salt-town—Northwich, in the valley of the Weaver—where he assembled the nucleus of an army, though it numbered only a few hundred men.

Lord Grandison's invasion was far more serious. This nobleman, a nephew of the famous—or infamous—Duke of Buckingham, was on his way to join the king who was collecting together all available forces in the Midlands. Charles had just visited Stafford and Chester, where he had received the usual ceremonial welcome, but not as much gold as he had wished, nor the city magazine and the trained bands, which they maintained would have left the city "naked and exposed to the hazard of what dangers might befall them in troublesome times."

Will Masterson was in Nantwich when the Cavaliers arrived. It was not entirely unexpected, for a rumour had gone around that the Commissioners of Array had met together secretly at a house in the forest of Delamere where they took an oath to plunder and disarm the town of Wich Malbank. They had asked for the assistance of Grandison and he had hurried from Shropshire to meet them. It was late morning when a horseman arrived post-haste at the Crown Inn bringing the news that Grandison had been sighted with upwards of a thousand horsemen troopers and dragoons. In the Long Room of the hostelry, the leading townsmen met to discuss how they should receive these Cavaliers. Mr Clutton spoke up first:

"There should be no talk of parley," he said emphatically, banging his fist on the table. "This king who would tax us at his pleasure, deny the privileges of his Great Council of Parliament, and force Romish practices on us in our churches, sends his army here to bend us to his will. Let us take up arms at once to defend the freedom of the gospel and the fundamental laws of the land. I shall order the townsmen in my company to fire as soon as these Cavaliers come within range and to refuse any offers to treat with them."

Henry Fletcher, a little man of jovial appearance with a wide mouth and twinkling eyes, was less enthusiastic about resistance.

"What chance have we, Master Clutton, against Lord Grandison's cavalry? What can a few men, unfamiliar with musket and pike drill, do in an unwalled town with only chains to draw across the streetends? They will not hold up a thousand Cavaliers for long and will only serve to kindle their wrath. It would be a far better thing to throw ourselves on their mercy."

This speech made Clutton even angrier.

"That is craven talk, Master Fletcher," he stormed. "A far better course to throw ourselves on their mercy! Before even a shot is fired! If that is so, why did we take up this quarrel at all? There are stout hearts among our men, which will make up for their deficiencies in training; they will prevent the subjection of our town, and if, as it is reported, Lord Grandison is on his way to join the king, they will hold up his progress and weaken the royal army."

There were murmurs of approval, but more of dissent. After speeches both for and against resistance had been heard, a vote was taken which went decisively in favour of negotiation. Will, who was in the inn parlour, saw the gentlemen coming through to carry out the majority decision. He stopped Clutton whom he knew well.

"Is it peace or war?" he asked.

"We treat," replied Clutton, using the word with obvious distaste. "I am for fighting."

Will nodded. He knew enough of Clutton's fiery personality to guess the part he would take.

"I am not against resistance on principle," he said; "but in this case I would come down on the side of negotiation. This town is woefully unprepared. The King is at Shrewsbury, but thirty miles away, and could bring up a large force which we could not resist. What are a few muskets and rusty pikes to us? Parley with Grandison and gain the best terms you can; then prepare the town to withstand further attack."

Clutton did not seem fully convinced, but he raised no further objections and hurried away. Will walked to the townend which led out on to the common. A short distance away, across the open heath, the lines of horsemen could be seen drawn up in battle array. Fletcher and two others who had chosen to treat with Lord Grandison, rode briskly out. A short parley ensued and the men returned, smiles all over their faces, their confidence in the willingness of the Cavaliers to grant acceptable terms seemingly justified. The Lords Grandison and Cholmondeley had agreed on their honour that no man should be hurt, nor any arms or goods taken. They desired only that the weapons should be laid up in the church or some other convenient place until they heard further from the King. The chain was drawn aside and the horsemen rode in. Will stepped out of the way as a troop entered with shouts of triumph, sweeping aside all in their path. Cavalrymen and dragoons dismounted and entered the houses; the townspeople, who had been brought out by curiosity into the street, scattered to protect their homes and possessions—mostly in vain.

Finding the street crowded, further troops rode through the back gardens, trampling down vegetable plots and flower borders, blocking up all ways out of the town to prevent escape. A proclamation was read out stating that all arms must be brought in; the Cavalier leaders set up their headquarters in the Town Square; all arms brought in were stacked in the churchyard. Other goods—plate in particular, to supply silver for the King's mint—were sorted and entered as lawful booty. Other plunder, which could not by the greatest stretch of imagination be classed as military supplies, was however, appropriated by the looting squadrons which rode out into the countryside to rob houses great and small where there was anything worth the taking. The bridge across the Weaver was guarded; even the furthest of exists would be blocked to Will before he had time to reach them, so he resolved to make a detour of a few miles to a place where the river could be forded without attracting any attention. Of course he knew the country better than these Cavaliers, and he would outwit them. Hurrying back to the Crown stables, he saw a party of Cavaliers approaching, and he was just in time to lead away his horse before the "enemy" commandeered the rest.

"So much for the word of honour of milords Grandison and Cholmondeley!" said Will to himself as he saw the Cavaliers burst in. He quickly mounted his horse and forced his way through the crowded streets past the brine-pit and salt-houses, intending to follow the course of the river until he reached the ford. There was another bridge just ahead, but that would probably be guarded, so he decided to risk descending the bank and entering the water, though it was by no means the ideal place. Suddenly he saw three or four Cavaliers, spurring across the field behind him.

"Hold there! Master Puritan!" cried one of them, imperiously, recognizing Will's persuasion by his sober habit. "Hold! I say. We would have a word with you."

Masterson protested his need to depart urgently, but the soldiers insisted that he should accompany them to the town, back to his starting point. He was taken to the Crown Inn where his captors led him into a long room, lately the scene of the discussion by the leading townsmen when the question of resistance or non-resistance to the King's forces had been in the balance. Now the very men who had taken part in that debate were, like Will Masterson, being held as prisoners "in His Majesty's name"—among them Mr Clutton who had spoken so loudly and eloquently for fighting.

An elegant Cavalier colonel with long, curled hair and a haughty look, sat behind an oaken table across which were spread documents, an ink horn and a generous supply of pens.

He looked up at Will, surveying him from top to toe with a contemptuous sneer on his face.

"Your name?" he asked, sharply; but this was only a formality; he knew his prisoner well enough.

"William Masterson," replied the Puritan patiently.

"I know you for what you are, Schoolmaster of Walbury," replied the colonel. "You are a disloyal pedagogue and a pretended divine. I have heard of your denunciations of His Majesty's rule, your ranting speeches which you choose to call 'sermons', and your support for the traitorous parliamentary rebels."

Will protested that he made no claim to being a clergyman—only an honest schoolmaster; he admitted that he had expounded the Word of God to friends, but averred that he had made no disparaging remarks about King Charles in these discourses, his references having been solely to biblical monarchs; he wished to know on whose testimony the colonel was basing these allegations. He would like to confront that person and challenge him to show evidence that he, Will Masterson, had ever urged anyone to commit rebellion or treason.

The Cavalier was in no mood to listen to these assertions. He cut Will's defence of his conduct short.

"Nevertheless, Schoolmaster, I know you for what you are. You will be confined here until our departure, and a fine will be levied on you, the sum to be determined by my Lords Grandison and Cholmondeley. Take him away!"

Will's period of confinement in the Crown Inn was not unpleasant, but his main worry was for the safety of Alice and Lynette. Now that they had his name on their list, he felt sure that his house would be plundered. The company of the other gentlemen was a diversion, but as each day passed, exaggerated fears of finding his house a smoking ruin and his wife and niece abducted, tormented him.

From Thursday until the following Monday, the robbery went on. Will's confinement was not very close, and he and the other gentlemen received messages via the servants that all the great houses had been ransacked. Sometimes the plundering was carried out in an orderly fashion. At Crewe Hall, for instance, the intruders entered the empty house to find all the arms stacked on the table ready for removal; in other cases the Cavaliers demanded politely in the name of King Charles what they required and duly received it. Sometimes, however, violence was done. At a house just outside Nantwich, a man slow to deliver a musket was shot in the hand and shoulder.

On Monday morning Will soon became aware that the Cavaliers were moving on. He had been threatened with a fine, but nobody had mentioned it again. Could it be that in the confusion they had forgotten to punish him? The captives had been only loosely guarded; now even those who had been set to watch them had melted away. As soon as he realized that he was no longer a prisoner, he hastened to the stable. To his great surprise and relief, his own horse was still there, though most of the others stabled with it had disappeared.

"Perhaps they scorned to ride a 'canting Puritan's nag,'" he said, "in case some of those 'disloyal sentiments' have rubbed off on the horse."

His heart pounded as heavily as the animal's hooves when he rode the few miles to Walbury expecting the worst. From afar it seemed that there had been no change; as he rode down the long slope and approached the sleepy little village no smoking ruins were in sight, only the old church and the school hard by—the hub of his life—and the pleasant, half-timbered house which sheltered his dear ones. All looked the same as when he had ridden to Nantwich on the previous Wednesday to confer with his counterpart Mr John Dolman at the school in Churchyardside, to exchange views and books with him, as he did periodically with several of the local schoolmasters.

Lynette was the first to notice the approach of her foster-father, and she frantically rushed into the house to bring out Alice, who came out with her eyes red from weeping tears of sorrow, to welcome her husband home with tears of joy. Neither Lynette nor her aunt could wait for Will to arrive and they ran up the road towards him. Will bent down from the saddle and kissed Lynette, who, younger and sprightlier than her aunt, had outstripped her; then he dismounted and comforted his wife whose tears of joy did not cease flowing even when she had her husband in her embrace.

Alice had believed a rumour which had spoken of a fierce battle at Nantwich with many casualties and she had feared the worst; now she was so glad to see Will again that she forgot to tell him of the raiding Cavaliers, until, on entering his home, he found the place stripped bare. Even Lynette's dresses and other articles, seemingly useless to the plunderers, had been taken; the explanation was simple; the Cavaliers had held a market in a neighbouring town and had gone on their way with their pockets full of jingling coins instead of having their saddlebags stuffed with superfluous goods.

Will, relieved that his loved ones were unharmed, accepted the loss of worldly possessions stoically, especially as his treasured diary had not been touched.

"These trials are sent to test us," he said. "Like Job, the Righteous, who suffered undeserved calamities much greater than these, we must learn to bear them with patience."

Lord Grandison joined the King at Shrewsbury, as did the Earl of Forth, formerly an officer in the Swedish army. Welsh levies were assembled and the southward march began. The Earl of Lindsey, nominally commander-in-chief under the King, clashed with Rupert, the second son of Frederick, Elector Palatine, who had come over from the Continent to serve his uncle. Schooled in the German war, he was considerably more modern in military outlook than his superior, and the quarrel about tactics ended when Lindsey threw down his baton and declared that if he were not fit to be a general, he would die as a colonel at the head of his regiment.

Six thousand infantry and three thousand cavalry made up the royal army; the Cavaliers, gaily dressed and well-armed, proudly wearing their red sashes, the infantry swelled with rustic recruits, armed with scythes and billhooks. "To London!" was the cry. At Bridgenorth the King was greeted by prolonged ringing of church bells. "To London!" shouted the Cavaliers above the joyful peals. Recruits poured in to join the loyal forces. By the time Charles reached Wolverhampton, his army numbered over thirteen thousand.

Meanwhile the Earl of Essex, in command of a large Parliamentarian force, had marched across from Worcester to Warwick to intercept the King.

"For King and Parliament!" cried these orange-sashed men, for they were fighting not to depose or humiliate him, but to deliver their "poor, beloved monarch from traitors who had misled him and clouded his fine understanding and rendered him as if it were a beloved parent fallen insane"—so ran the proclamation. Ballads were sung on both sides; a Parliamentarian song, *The King's Great Counsel*", listed all the misdeeds of the monarch—the corporal punishments, the billeting, the taxes, the exactions—succinctly giving all possible reasons for supporting Parliament. The Cavaliers, in their turn, mocked the pretence of the Roundheads to serve the King by opposing him.

While the Earl of Essex was at Kineton, a village between Banbury and Stratford-upon-Avon, the King's cavalry by a rapid march in the dark, reached the escarpment of Edgehill, where it drew up, blocking the way between the Parliamentarian army and the main road to Oxford and London. High up on this ridge, with a panoramic view of pasture and ploughlands beneath them, the King's army was in battle array with infantry in the centre and cavalry on the wings. The army of Parliament, in a disadvantageous position below, was roughly equal in numbers to the royal forces, each side having twelve or thirteen thousand men. Charles's standard, borne by Sir Edmund Verney, flapped in the breeze on that bright, cold October morning in front of the King's redcoated footguards. Charles rode along the lines, addressing his men with words of encouragement:

"Your King is both your cause, your quarrel and your captain," he said. "Come life or death, your King will bear you company and ever keep this field, this place, and this day's service in his grateful remembrance."

After both sides had exchanged cannon fire, the royal cavalry attacked. Down the hill charged Rupert's horsemen, tearing through the Parliamentarian lines, scattering their foes and driving many of them through their own reserves in great confusion. After them went the young German prince and his horsemen, until they were deflected by Parliamentary soldiers coming up with ordnance.

Meanwhile all was not going well with the King's forces on the battlefield. The centre was bare of defence on one side as Rupert's cavalry pursued the Roundheads far off the field and fell to plundering their camp at Kineton. One party of Parliamentary horse had drawn off when the initial Royalist charge was made, and making their way up the hill under cover of the hedges, they fell upon the Royalist centre. The King's standard was captured; Sir Edmund Verney its bearer was killed. Lord Lindsey fell as he had predicted. Only the reappearance of Rupert and the oncoming night, saved the Royalists from defeat. Now it was the King's turn to attack, but it was October and early darkness put an end to an indecisive action. Both sides camped on the field, unwilling to allow the other to claim the victory by remaining in sole possession. For Essex it was a symbolic action, as he was preparing to depart for Warwick and leave the way to Parliamentarian London open to the King.

The night was bitter; a piercing north wind blew; the ground was white with frost. Under the stars, men huddled round fires of brushwood, thorns, and broken pikestaffs; freezing cold added to the agonies of the wounded. Some of the luckier ones who had come out unscathed, still wearing breastplates and their cloaks drawn tightly around them, stamped about all night to counteract the biting cold of a cruel autumn; others jostled for a place as close as possible to the flames .

By one of the larger blazes, newly fuelled with braches from the shattered hedges, stood a captain—a thickset man with heavy features and a prominent nose, his complexion marred by a few warts. He had laid aside his headpiece and the light from the fire illuminated an already ruddy face. He spoke in a slow but determined way. His companion, a colonel, bore a strong resemblance to him, though the lines of his face were less heavily drawn. It was clear that these two country gentlemen-in-arms were related. The first man was speaking with emphasis:

"Your troopers," he was saying, "are most of them old decayed serving men and tapsters and such kind of fellows, and their troopers are gentlemen's sons, younger sons and persons of quality. Do you think that the spirits of such base and mean fellows will ever be able to encounter gentlemen that have honour and courage and resolution in them?"

The other man looked searchingly at his cousin.

"It would be a good notion to match them, Oliver, if it could be executed. Can you bring us such men who have a spirit in them that will do something in this work? Can you equal the Cavalier gentleman's honour, courage, and resolution?"

"Yes, John, I can match them with men of religion. They are of greater understanding than the common soldier, and therefore will be more apprehensive of the importance and consequence of this war. He that takes the felicity of the Church and State to be his end, esteems it above life, and therefore will the sooner lay down his life for it. These men of parts and understanding know that flying is the surest way to death, and that standing to it is the likeliest way to escape, there being many usually that fall in flight for one that falls in valiant fight. And the choice of these religious men will avoid those disorders, mutinous plunderings and grievances of the country of which the debased in armies are commonly guilty. Believe me, John, I had rather have a plain, russet-coated captain that knows what he fights for and loves what he knows, than that which you call a gentleman and is nothing else. It would be well that men of honour and birth should enter these employments, but if they do not appear, the work must go on—better plain men than none."

"I say again—a good notion, Oliver. We must pray steadfastly for success in this recruitment."

Another officer, a man of commanding appearance, about the same age as Oliver, robustly built, with regular features quite unlike those of the two other gentlemen, approached the fire.

"Pardon me, captain," he said, "but your conversation interests me. The idea that one battle would decide the war has been banished for ever on this bloody day. We know now that we must fight a bitter struggle—for how long we cannot tell. In such a war your way is the only one for us. The views you expressed take me back many years to my worthy colonel, Sir John Faulkner, who fell at Nördlingen—a sad loss, for he was a man whose ideas were the forerunners of your own. He would have none but godly men in his service, even though they fought among mercenaries—only men who understood the cause and the quarrel, and he trained them in all the arts of war, never sparing himself until they became a credit to the army of the King of Sweden."

"You served under the great Gustavus?" said Oliver with interest.

"At Lützen—I was near him when he fell—then for nigh on two years I campaigned with Marshal Horn in the Upper Rhineland and at Nördlingen."

The stranger drew closer to the blaze to warm himself. In the distance, a red glow showed where Kineton, fired by Prince Rupert, continued to burn, but the soldiers chilled to the bone on this night watch drew no warmth from it. A soldier, who had gathered a few handfuls of green wood, stoked his commander's fire, hoping thereby to gain some comfort from the flames. Oliver extended his hand to Tom.

"Well met, Captain," he said. "I shall be pleased to exchange views with one whose knowledge of the tactics and discipline of the Golden King's army rests on more than a reading of the *'Swedish Intelligencer'*".

He turned to introduce his companion to the newcomer. In spite of the fact that he was higher in rank, Oliver's cousin had taken a secondary role.

"My kinsman, John Hampden, Parliamentarian and Colonel of the Greencoats. My name is Cromwell—Oliver Cromwell—Member for Cambridge and captain of the sixty seventh troop of horse in this army."

"Thomas Ley," replied the stranger, accepting Cromwell's handshake and saluting Colonel Hampden respectfully. "A merchant in better times, a soldier in these troubled days. Thomas Ley, captain of horse in the regiment of my late colonel's son, Sir Ralph Faulkner, serving like you, for King and Parliament."

15. THE RETURN

Seven years and a thousand miles separate the Thomas Ley seeking his Promised Haven in the saltlands of Austria, from the Captain of Horse in conversation with Cromwell and Hampden on the field of Edgehill. Seven years of happiness in a new home, which came only to an end when Tom, hearing of the approaching war in England, knew that he, a soldier trained and experienced in the Swedish school, could not stand aside while his own fair country was ablaze and men were taking sides dictated by their consciences. Then too, though the mountain scenery was unsurpassable and the beautifully situated city of Salzburg was finer than anything he had known at home, he increasingly thought of his earlier days at Nantwich and longed to see the familiar scenes and homely faces at least once again before he died. At first he had tried to shut off all these past memories which always ended with recalled tragedy—the loss of his wife and children—but gradually his homesickness conquered this feeling and it would have brought him home earlier, had not his happiness with Amalia been just as complete as that which he had experienced with Kate. He came, he saw, he conquered. Just as on that first evening, when he listened to her sweet voice singing the old melody, plaintively at first, then full of hope, his heart had gone out to the girl; she too had known that she must receive and cherish it like a precious treasure. Tom's interesting, good-humoured nature and handsome, manly appearance—a man from a far land, speaking so strangely, yet always finding something lovable to say—threw down her maidenly defences when he laid the first proofs of affection on her lips. The elder Brunner was not averse to the marriage and offered a generous dowry. The only problem was conformity in religion. For Amalia Tom would do anything. She was his religion and he hers. She and her people had had to conform too. Together they would keep their purity of heart whatever might outwardly appear.

In business Tom was as successful as in love. For a while he tarried in Hallein, but his money was not inexhaustible and he had no

171

intention of being dependent on another father-in-law to establish him in business. Then a remarkable piece of good fortune came his way, which Tom, hardly daring to hope that God would continue to shower him with such favours, could only ascribe to Divine intervention. He fell in with a group of English merchants who were exploring the area searching for new markets. The decline in trade and industry in war-torn Germany as the conflict dragged on year after year, was a bonus to others, and encouraged them to strike out into new fields. The sixteen thirties saw a general expansion of English trade after the decline in the twenties—in Europe as well as with far continents. The North Western coast of Europe from the River Somme to the frontiers of Denmark was the preserve of the Company of Merchant Adventurers, while the Eastlands Company forced a monopoly in the Baltic, the Muscovy Company in Russia, and the Levant Company in the Eastern Mediterranean. Attempts to force France and Spain into a monopoly were unsuccessful, so only Western Europe and the corresponding part of the Mediterranean Sea remained open for free trade. There were, of course, interlopers in Holland and the Levant, but in general the divisions held. Leghorn on the Western coast of Italy was for English merchants the "Amsterdam of the South", and it was from there that the representatives, whom Tom met, had originated. The main export from England was still textiles to Northwest Europe, especially Hamburg. Cargoes of a lighter type of cloth—the "new draperies"—were often despatched to the Mediterranean, as were metalwares, including iron guns, lead, tin, and pewter.

This expansion of trade led to organisational problems. The established London merchant could no longer accompany the cargoes to foreign parts or entrust them to the care of an apprentice, but the employment of experienced commission agents overseas was necessitated. Sometimes a junior partner in the firm was stationed abroad to deal with the niceties of buying and selling in a strange country. These agents had to have a shrewd acquaintance with the local markets, to know when and where to sell, to gauge prices and to have some knowledge of one or two European languages.

Tom's experience of marketing salt and other goods whilst working with his first father-in-law stood him in good stead. His employment necessitated some travelling in South Germany and even to Italy, so a knowledge of German was indispensable. This he had; and furthermore he acquainted himself with enough Italian not to be outwitted by a bargaining Genoese or Venetian merchant.

Fortune smiled on George as well as on his friend. As soon as they had settled down in Salzburg, Tom saw to the young man's education. It was, of course, necessary that he should study the learned languages if he were to enter any of the professions, which his obvious talents demanded. He had acquired English rapidly and the classics did not present his quick mind with much more difficulty. Tom and his father-in-law agreed that the new University of Salzburg would be the natural place for him to study, so George spent his years of formal education there. More interesting to him than rhetoric, logic and grammar, was the practice of medicine; the shop in which his patron, Apothecary Brunner, was the master, held delights for him unrivalled in the long halls and study rooms of the University. All the time he could spare from his classical studies was devoted to the task of familiarizing himself with the apothecary's and the physician's business. George did not, however, neglect his University work and graduated with marked success.

The elder Leopold Brunner was a devoted Paracelsian. The Swiss physician had once made his home in neighbouring Carinthia, and when accused of necromancy, he fled from Basel and took refuge in Salzburg where he died. His successful, if experimental, application of mineral medicines, his defence of the doctrine of signatures, whereby we recognize the powers and virtues of herbs in healing intuitively according to the appearance of the plant itself—heart shaped leaves as a cardiac tonic, kidney shapes good for the renal system, spotted leaves to cure acne, flame-coloured flowers to soothe inflammation—and so on. These were the foundations of Brunner's remedies which he passed on to his apt pupil, George. This strange Theophrastus Bombastus, this Swiss von Hohenheim, wandered about curing the sick and increasing his knowledge of medicine by learning from midwives, gypsies, nomads, brigands and people of all classes who could contribute to his understanding. The astrological significance of plants in healing, also defended by Paracelsus, did not escape Apothecary Brunner. The great man had gone as far as stating that astrological conditions rule the application of cures. Beneficial at one time, a medicine may be harmful at another, depending on the influence of the planets. Herbs come under zodiacal or planetary influences as we do, and so a like herb should relieve afflictions in each part of the body. Brunner following his renowned predecessor, practised surgery—then the stepchild of healing, long considered cruder than medical treatment, but now developing into a skilled

173

profession due to the work of Paracelsus and Paré. George was happy in the world of healing. Like his friend Tom, he had found his niche.

The sixteen forties began with disturbing news. There was no sign of an end to the internecine strife in Germany. Parliament was storming at the king in England. Rebels were carrying murder and destruction across Ireland; Charles was denying his Parliament's privileges, musters and preparations for a struggle which would divide the country, set subject against master and brother against brother in a welter of blood and tears. Tom looked round his comfortable home on the first floor of a tall house overlooking the Salzach. He would have to leave all this—his books, his pictures, the comfort of his family, and enter into the thick of the fight once more to defend his beliefs. There was no doubt as to which side he would take. Last time he had volunteered to defend the Protestant cause against what he thought to be the repression and brutality of the Imperialists; but then his enthusiasm had been kindled against a background of despair at his own personal losses. Now he would have to go in the full bloom of his happiness.

Amalia! How would she take it? His two children Mariana and Karl! None of them had ever known hardship and tragedy. On the evening when he finally came to his decision, he broke the news gently to his wife. He was close on twenty years older than Amalia, but that had never clouded his relationship with her. In his company she matured quickly and took over the household duties with quiet competence. He had loved Kate passionately and she had never tried in any way to usurp or challenge his natural position as head of the family, but probably because of her superior station and education when he had first wooed her, a certain feeling of inferiority had never left him, even when by his industry and study he had raised himself up to be her equal. No quarrels, no bitterness, had resulted from this, but throughout his first married life, Tom had felt a need to prove and maintain his position, even though it was not being challenged. With Amalia it was different. From the start he was the leading partner, but he had no desire to browbeat his wife and force her into the humble position of one dependent on his every whim and favour; he was too devoted to her for that. Together they were friends in love, living in matrimony because that was the only life they wanted; two complementary beings, not striving, to take on any role which did not fall naturally to them.

Amalia said nothing at first when Tom had finished laying his intention before her. In the semidarkness of a room illuminated only by a few candles, he could not determine by the expression on her face how she was taking it. Then she spoke.

"Dear Tom," she declared in her low, melodious voice, "you must do what you believe to be your duty. If it must be, I know that God and all the saints will protect you."

"Liebchen," said Tom coming closer and looking earnestly into his wife's calm blue-grey eyes. I cannot drag you and the little ones around with me like common camp followers, but yet I would not have you stay here. I must find a place in England where I can leave you in safety while I am campaigning. Our business has been profitable and my wealth, though it falls well short of a great fortune, exceeds that of a successful tradesman or small town merchant; so you will be well provided for. This is my wish, but I will not command you, dearest one, to follow me and leave your beautiful mountain home for the flatter fields of England, to be among people whose language you find strange, to mix with those of a strict Protestant persuasion who abhor a Catholic almost as much as Beelzebub. My conscience tells me to fight for the liberties of Parliament and people, against a king who would deny them, so my fellows will be those of the lower church party— The Presbyterians and the Separatists—godly men, but fiercely sectarian. Yet I would have you come. What do you say, dearest Amalchen?"

Amalia laid her hand on his.

"Oh, Tom," she said. "How could you think that those considerations would make me pause? Water meadows or mountain pastures—English, Celtic or Teutonic speech—they are things of such little consequence when weighed against the pleasure of being with you. What does it matter how we say our prayers?—"Vater unser" or "Our Father"—God knows when we speak to him, and the belief in our hearts remains the same. You told me once of someone in the Bible who spoke these beautiful words—so beautiful that I thought them worth committing to memory. *'Whither thou goest I will go, and where thou lodgest I will lodge; thy people shall be my people and thy God, my God.'"*

Tom kissed his wife and stroked her hair gently. He pressed her close to him. There was nothing more he needed to say. The journey could begin.

There was, however, one more consideration and that was George. The two men had been together so long and had grown so attached to one another that the idea of what would probably be a permanent parting, could not be countenanced. He had grown from an undernourished boy of below average height, into a tall, very presentable young man.

When Tom broached the subject, he was immediately fired with enthusiasm at the prospect of accompanying his friend to England and serving with him in the Army of Parliament. Though he had gained much knowledge of Latin, rhetoric and philosophy since his arrival in Salzburg, it was his mastery of the apothecary surgeon's trade on which he prided himself most. His dedication to the cure of bodies, was as earnest as Preacher Blackshaw's zeal for the care of souls. He had no attachments in Salzburg which would hold him there, nothing to draw him back to the Rhineland; there was only Thomas Ley, his friend, who was returning to England. He would accompany him and show the English the skill of a German apothecary surgeon.

Events were moving fast and time could not be spared for longdrawn out preparations, so Tom quickly wound up his affairs and took a ship from Leghorn. A smiling sun and a fair wind welcomed the Ley family to the Mediterranean Sea. To Mariana who was six years old, and Karl who was four, even the strange rolling of the ship could not dampen the excitement of seeing the wide expanse of heavens and the great sheet of water stretching out and out, till somewhere in the misty distance it met the sky—a dim line far, far away. How would it be, where Heaven and Earth met? Was England there—the land where Vati had lived as a little boy?

To Amalia this sea travel was hardly less wonderful; the splashing of waves on the sides of the ship as she cut through the water, the foaming wake behind her, the creaking masts, the flapping sails, the strange cries of the swarthy, foreign sailors, fascinated the young woman, who had never seen the sea before; such was the pleasure created by the novelty of the journey, that it lasted even to Marseilles and beyond.

Progress to that port was good, but then a contrary wind held them up for a while, and new experiences awaited them in the sultry atmosphere of the French city. When at last a pleasant breeze swelled their sails once more, and the hot, enervating weather in Marseilles was behind them, the anticipation of the family rose. Though Tom had told them that it would be many days before England was sighted, each glimpse of a strip of coast caused shouts of excitement from the children; though Amalia was wiser, she too had become so eager to see her husband's homeland that she could hardly restrain her pleasure at the thought of this new adventure—even though Tom was going to war and, for a time at least, they would have to be parted.

Soon the Balearic Isles were lost in the haze; the coast of Spain was a faint line, the not so distant Africa, mysterious and foreboding. Before they reached the narrow straits through which they had to pass into the wider, lonelier ocean, the distant sighting of a ship approaching from the African coast filled Tom with apprehension. He had not wished to alarm his family, but each night he had prayed earnestly for a safe passage free from the Barbary pirates, the scourge of these times, whose depredations along Western European coasts struck terror into the inhabitants of the seaboard in every country from Iceland to Spain and Italy.

The *"Esperance"* was swift; it was an armed merchantman which Tom had chosen with care, hoping that it would outdistance any pursuer. When he could no longer conceal the danger from Amalia, she took it calmly; the children, oblivious of the peril, thought it high excitement, as away over the gently heaving waters of the Mediterranean, another ship came into view—mast, topsails and the hull;

"A Spanish frigate no doubt," said Tom.

Little puffs of smoke but only the faintest sound reached them from the drama across the water. More puffs and the pirate was partially dismasted. The two shapes closed up, but they were shrinking fast as the *"Esperance"* hastened towards the open ocean. At last only one form could be distinguished—a mere speck—then nothing.

"God be praised!" cried Tom, as the ships disappeared from sight; he remembered thankfully that from the day of his escape from the highwaymen on the road to Chester, so long before, right up to this very journey, he had never in all his travels by land and sea, fallen victim to robbers or pirates.

The Leys passed out into the ocean without further incident, but the favourable weather in the Mediterranean did not hold, and by the time they reached the English Channel, Karl and Mariana were complaining that Vati's home was "oh so far away!" and Amalia was asserting that she could imagine nothing more heavenly than the feel of firm earth under her feet—English or otherwise.

Only George was unaffected, and cheerfully told the suffering Leys on the waters of Biscay how lucky they were to have an apothecary on board, to whom a case of 'mal de mer' was a trifling indisposition, which he could whisk away in less than no time with something from his magic box. Though his optimism irritated them a little, the medicine he produced from his cabinet, and the smiling face of the physician, worked wonders which Tom described as nothing short of miraculous; but as the cures coincided with the subsidence of the storm, and the trusty *"Esperance"* returned from rolling on the billows to an even keel, perhaps it was not so marvellous after all.

The white cliffs and green sward of the Kentish coast cheered them in passing; then the port of London, with its high-masted ships anchored along the busy wharves, welcomed the weary travellers to England. The atmosphere in the capital was highly charged. King Charles was in the provinces raising men. King Pym reigned here in Parliament. Along the streets the city regiments marched out to exercise and be reviewed in the fields just beyond the confines of London. People congregated discussing the reputed movements of the King in Yorkshire, the latest divisions in Parliament, or just complaining about the evil times. Preachers harangued the crowds with fiery sermons in St. Paul's Churchyard, urging men to take up arms for the Lord. "God with us!" echoed from the walls of the venerable pile. Parliament issued appeals for money and plate; powder and arms were stored up in safe places.

For a few days, Tom and his family lodged in the Blue Boar Inn at Holborn on the outskirts of the city. Amalia and the children all found the crowded atmosphere of London oppressive. They were unused to the jostling crowds in a city far greater than their own Salzburg. The alleys between the closely packed houses seemed narrower, the stenches, the noise and the smoke more repulsive, the feeling of unimportance among the milling masses stronger in a city full of people speaking an unfamiliar language. Nonetheless they found much in London that was interesting. They stood before the old, grey Tower down by the water, holding its dark secrets, the guardian of London since the days of William the Norman; they gazed up at the medieval cathedral, which crowned a hill in the heart of Lud's town; they shuddered at the sight of the rickety bridge with its line of shops, spanning the busy Thames, its top bristling like a hedgehog with sharp spikes spitting the heads of some who defied the law; in Westminster they saw the Parliament house where John Pym and his fellows defied the King and the Palace of Whitehall which Royal Charles had left for safer parts of his Kingdom.

Tom thought that his best policy would be to ride to Royston and visit Sir John Faulkner's Hall at Ashley. There would be a son who would most certainly be taking up the Parliamentary cause. He hoped to find a patron at Royston, and he was not disappointed.

Sir Ralph Faulkner had broken the tradition of a Sir John ruling at the Hall, his elder brother who bore that name, having died at an early age. The baronet listened to Tom's story without once interrupting him. He was overjoyed to meet someone who had not only served under his father, but had stood by Sir John's side when he fell at Nördlingen. A few of his troopers had drifted back, but most had fallen or, having been captured, they had gone over to the Imperialists. Sir Ralph had not met anyone before who had been able to tell him so much about his father's campaign in Germany. Tom, who was closer to his colonel than most of the others, could describe lucidly to his son Faulkner's conduct in the war; moreover he could discuss the views of his commander, frequently expressed to him in the periods between engagements.

Sir Ralph confirmed that he, like his father had done, was training cavalry to take part in the inevitable conflict, and he offered Tom a captaincy in exchange for the benefit of his experience in continental warfare. His intensive training under Sir John and the two years he had spent serving in the Swedish army, put Tom streets ahead of Sir

179

Ralph's raw recruits, even after an interval of seven years away from soldiering. The baronet himself, commissioned as a colonel by Parliament, bowed to his advice, and his efficiency earned him universal respect.

Faulkner was kind enough to offer shelter to Tom's wife and children, so that his right-hand man should have no domestic worries whilst campaigning. Amalia and the children found the atmosphere of Ashley Hall most congenial; they loved the fresh air on the breezy heath or in the extensive grounds, the animals in the Home Farm, and the spacious rooms which they could explore on rainy days. Only the absence of husband and father cast a shadow over this idyllic country life.

Tom did not dwell on his work in Salzburg in conversation with Sir Ralph, or his temporary conformity to the old religion. He was a Protestant Parliamentarian officer giving up a profitable living in foreign parts to further a just cause; his wife, free from the chains of repression, was at liberty to practise the reformed religion which her family had once accepted. Nor was George forgotten. Faulkner promised to use his influence to secure for the skilful young man a post as a regimental surgeon.

The standard was raised; the troop was trained; and so on that fair October morning they rode out with the Trained Bands to join the Lord General Essex, now in possession of Worcester. Captain Ley proudly showed off his professionalism to his new colonel; George, the Apothecary surgeon, marched with them, anxious to practise his medical and surgical skills to save the lives of many as he had once saved that of one. In a way of triumph, with people lining the highways and shouting "Hosanna!" they bore the orange colours of Parliament, displaying the familiar motto "God with us" emblazoned on the standard. They marched along Watling Street, the military road of the ancient Romans, and there were no better turned out men in the whole army of Parliament. As they passed by, some went out from their houses to give them cheer, but others remained indoors on their knees praying fervently for the success of their cause. Onward towards the Midlands they advanced, confident in the ability of their leader and the justice of their cause.

"With such a general and such men," they said, "we shall make short work of the King and his supporters."

But Thomas Ley and George Waldheim knew how it had been before. Those troops of the Elector Frederick going out to defend themselves against the Catholic Emperor! The men of Tilly marching to oust the Winter King! Could they have imagined that their country would still be a vast cockpit of the Nations over two decades later? All the illusions we have at the beginning of a conflict—so brave and honourable! How they are banished as war debases our feelings and actions!

Thus Edgehill was fought—Englishman against Englishman; and at the end of that bitter day of tumult and carnage, thousands lay dead under the stars. Neither side had gained a decisive victory. The war went on.

PART TWO: FROM WAR TO PEACE

1642 - 1651

"I have heard the king has his crown by divine right, but we the people have a divine right too."
Sir Robert Howard.

16. CROMWELL AND FAIRFAX

"It hath pleased God to bring off Sir Thomas Fairfax's cavalry over the river from Hull" began Cromwell's letter of 28th September 1643, when the two future Lord Generals joined forces for a campaign in Lincolnshire.

Two such different men, these Lord Generals-to-be! Sir Thomas, the son of Ferdinando, second Baron Fairfax was a strong, silent man, chivalrous, and of a mild disposition. But in battle he threw off his natural reserve, became full of fire and energy, and was so transformed that, as a contemporary put it, "no man durst speak to him." Like an avenging angel, he displayed his personal valour to the point of recklessness, earning himself great respect from the men under his command. Dark to the point of being nicknamed "Black Tom", he cut a striking figure on his white horse. He had seen previous military service, both in the Netherlands and against the Scots in the short campaign of 1640, and did not lack the scars to testify to it. Since the beginning of this war he had fought with his father in his native Yorkshire, but defeated at Adwalton Moor, Lord Fairfax was besieged in Hull, and thought his son's cavalry would be better employed in conjunction with the Earl of Manchester's forces over the Humber.

Oliver Cromwell, twelve years Fairfax's senior, now a colonel under Manchester, matched the ability of the Yorkshireman as a leader of cavalry, but his direct vigorous speech, his forceful personality, his plain but striking features, his alternating moods of tenderness and fierce anger, his fervent Puritanism, were in sharp contrast to the characteristics of Sir Thomas.

Unschooled in the practice of war, Oliver had gained his knowledge of modern tactics from such books as *"The Swedish Intelligencer"* and *"The Swedish Soldier"*. He had a natural aptitude

185

for military matters which developed into real genius, and he took up the art of war at the stage reached under Gustavus, using the moral stimulus and, on occasions, even the very words of the great Protestant champion.

At this time, when the great Royalist advances which would have won the war for Charles had been checked, and much of the fighting was in disjointed campaigns between the forces raised by gentlemen in each county, the cooperation of Fairfax and Cromwell under Lord Manchester, gave Parliament one of its first victories of note at Winceby. The psalm-singing Roundhead cavalry attacked fiercely, justifying the intensive training they had received from Cromwell, and they drove the Cavaliers from the field even before the infantry had time to come up and join in the fray. Oliver himself, unhorsed and close to death under the hooves of charging horses, managed to avoid that catastrophe and received "a poor mount at a soldier's hands". He survived, and that had more significance for the cause than any fruits of the victory at Winceby.

Tom Ley's troop was in the van with Cromwell. He had soon accustomed himself to the renewed physical activity as a captain of horse, and his old wounds did not trouble him. His respect for the piety and efficiency of Cromwell grew as he came more into contact with him, but his opinion of Lord Manchester was low, the "sweet, meek man" having little talent as a military commander. He would have preferred to serve in his own county—to defend his native town and the smiling countryside around it. The further north he moved and the nearer he came to Cheshire, the more his impatience grew to see his home again and to play his part in its defence. His chance came when Fairfax was recalled from the East Midlands to march against the Army from Ireland. These soldiers had been inactive since a truce called the Cessation had been signed by Charles's Lord Deputy Ormonde with the rebels, to end the organised conflict. Though this did not put an end to sporadic Irish raids, it was the King's reply to the alliance of the English puritans with their Scottish brethren. Thus, simultaneously, armies were advancing southwards from Scotland and across the Irish Sea. Sixteen vessels gave the Parliamentarian navy the slip and carried two thousand five hundred seasoned soldiers over to Wales. Charles had wanted to use men of the Catholic Confederacy in Ireland, but there had been revulsion against it, even in the Royalist camp, so these reinforcements were government troops, mostly English and Protestant. Nevertheless they met irrational hostility from many, who regarded them as Papists, native Irish, and perpetrators of the Great Massacre.

Sweeping through North Wales, the Anglo-Irish army reached Chester, driving Sir William Brereton, the Parliamentary commander, before them. Despite any prejudice felt against Ireland and the Irish, the army was welcomed at first by the people of Chester, who were relieved that the pressure which the Roundheads had been exerting on their city would be relaxed. The men were poorly clad and shod, provisions were short; some of these necessities were supplied by the local people. The Mayor sent through all the wards to get wearing apparel for them—suits, doublets, breeches, shirts, shoes, stockings, and hats. The district round about Chester was scoured and clothing was sent into the city. But, remembering the outgoing of this same army only a few years earlier, the people of Chester were anxious to rid themselves of their potentially troublesome guests. So they offered city plate to the value of one hundred pounds to the chief commander if he would remove his troops from the city. This general was John Byron, newly raised to the peerage, who had fought for the King in battles at Edgehill, Roundway Down, and Newbury. The choleric, vainglorious lord had only been appointed to this command because Lord Deputy Ormonde could not be spared in Ireland. He became, for a time, the terror of the Parliamentary army. The puritan, John Vicars, writing in *"God's Ark"*, his chronicle of the war, described him variously as a "bloody bragadocio", "that pretended lord", and a "Turkish commander."

The weaker forces of Sir William Brereton were scattered at Middlewich and all the strongpoints fell to Byron's army—until he was stopped before the gates of Nantwich.

Captain Ley heard of the approach of the Scots and the arrival of the Anglo-Irish army while in winter quarters near Gainsborough. Though he did not know that his birthplace was already under close siege he could not suppress the urge to join in the fight in his own locality. Sir Thomas Fairfax was to withdraw from the East to stem the Royalist tide in Cheshire and Wales. This was Tom's chance. He went immediately to Sir Ralph Faulkner with the request that he be transferred to Sir Thomas's force. His colonel was loth to lose Tom who had proved an excellent commander.

187

"Your men are the backbone of my regiment," he said, "the only ones I have, who, come what may, will stand and do execution. Not even Oliver's own regiment put up a braver show at Winceby Fight."

This praise made Tom feel ashamed to be pressing for his release; especially as such personal kindnesses had been shown to him by Sir Ralph and his father.

"Do not think that I lack appreciation of the favours you have shown me, Sir Ralph," he said. "I would rather continue to serve under you than in any other regiment, but I am sure that you too would feel the urge to defend your own county of Hertfordshire if it were threatened by an army with a reputation as bad as that of Byron's men. I do not believe, as it has been reported, that they are four thousand bloody Papists thirsting to begin another barbarous Irish Massacre in Cheshire, but though the severity of this invasion will probably not approach that of the events in Ulster, my service at home and abroad has taught that matters often get out of hand when passions run high. I will be happier when I can draw my sword in defence of my parental home and the people I love who are still there."

Sir Ralph spoke sympathetically in reply.

"You are right, Tom," he said. "A soldier can fight well enough defending a foreign place or cause, but there is nothing to compare with the man desperate to protect his own. I would gladly let you go, except that I fear the leadership you have shown will be so missed that the efficiency and discipline of the troop will disintegrate the next time it is tested."

"Do not fear, sir," replied Tom reassuringly. "Lieutenants Hanson and Wheeler are capable officers and Cornet Brown is showing promise. All three know my methods as well as I do by now. None of them flinched in the last engagement. Rest assured they will hold the troop together."

"Sir," he went on, detecting a change in Faulkner's expression which seemed to indicate a willingness to comply with his request, "it would be my wish to return to you as soon as possible after the Irish army has been defeated—if God grants us a happy outcome. Should it please you to persuade Lord Manchester to release me and Sir Thomas Fairfax to accept my services, I believe that if he penetrates into

Cheshire, I may do some good with my local knowledge and thereby serve Parliament better, as well as satisfying my own desire to play a part in ridding my native county of these invaders."

Sir Ralph was impressed by this last argument. Doubtless Tom could aid Fairfax with his local knowledge. Sometimes such advice could be crucial in a campaign. He had to consider, too, his own likely feelings had he heard that Royston was being approached by a powerful and ruthless enemy.

"Go!" he said at last, "with my blessing—and remember your promise, Tom Ley. God grant that you bring forth a glorious work against this Irish army for the happiness of the kingdom and the security of the Protestant religion. Go! And may the Lord keep your person safe until we are reunited."

Fairfax's march started with no definite goal declared, and it was also a recruiting campaign. Sir Thomas was glad to have Tom and gave him charge of a cavalry troop, which though it did not match the efficiency of the one he had trained on the Hertfordshire heath, was composed of tough, forthright Yorkshiremen who had fought well with Sir Thomas and Lord Ferdinando from the beginning of the war. There had been defeats and successes. These men had not been discouraged by the one, nor had they been made overconfident by the other. They respected Tom's authority and his popularity grew each day. The fact that he had risen from a lowly position himself, gave him the facility to talk to his men with understanding of their inclinations and resolutions, but he also had the ability by persuasion and command, when necessary, to form them to his own model. At the same time, after years in a higher social position as a successful merchant, he was able to meet and mix with officers of equal or superior rank without any embarrassment or lack of respect on either side. The clarity of his mind and quickness of his decisions won him the admiration of them all. He measured his every action against what he knew of his old model, Gustavus, and his newer hero, Cromwell, and judged their success or failure by how well they matched up to, or fell below, the achievements of these leaders.

The army crossed over into Staffordshire and tried recruiting at the county town and around Newcastle-under-Lyme. At the latter place they were surprised by Byron's men and some of them were captured. They were not strong enough yet to oppose the invaders; the Lancashire men would be needed to swell the army, so Fairfax, and Brereton who had now joined him, marched to Manchester. The march over Pennine country was a dismal affair. The already bitter winter weather was worsening. It was a route unknown to Tom. The desolate hills and miserable hamlets, the small towns hanging on the hillsides, close to streams swollen by winter downpours, had little charm seen through driving rain or patchy mist. Manchester, with its neighbour Bolton, was a bastion of Puritanism in a sharply divided county. As they approached the town, the rain ceased but the sky was leaden; the temperature was dropping and the next showers were likely to be of snow.

A busy place with about five thousand inhabitants, divided from its neighbour, Salford, by the River Irwell, Manchester, close to the foothills of the Pennines, was a town of many manufactures. It was especially known for its spinning and weaving of wool, linen, cotton, and silken goods, and as a commercial centre it had received new ideas and skills from foreigners. A collegiate church stood on a rise close to the connecting bridge, and there were a few notable residences, but the streets were narrow and muddy, the buildings, in general, untidy and unimpressive, the appearance of the place made worse by the construction of defensive walls of clay, posts and chains.

Still, it was a Puritan town, famed for one of the very first actions of the war—its defiance of Lord Strange, who was soon to become Lord Derby—when, in 1642, he came to claim the arms and stores laid up there. He had asked for money, he had requested muskets, he had demanded surrender, but all in vain. The valiant men of Manchester had told him brusquely that they would not give him as much as a rusty dagger.

The promised January snow began to fall. What weather for campaigning! These men had never heard of winter quarters! The Scots were struggling through blizzards to join the Northern Parliamentary Army; the Royalists in Yorkshire were drawing off to meet them. There was less danger to Lancashire, so Fairfax could easily slip away to face Byron and take the local contingents with him. Snow or not, the march was ordered for the twenty-first. An army was preparing to do battle in the worst of winter weather. Byron's reputation for bloodiness had assumed alarming proportions and had demoralized Roundhead soldiers so much that one who was acquainted with the ravages of his army, wrote of this 'Turkish commander':

"The Lord Byron, the King's General, hath been so terrible unto us and showeth so little mercy on those he overcometh or taketh prisoner, that some of our forces were unwilling to venture on any design where Byron was."

Much of this reputation rested on one gruesome incident at Barthomley, near Crewe Hall, when twenty villagers took refuge in a church tower and were smoked out by a Royalist officer, Major Connaught. Stumbling out with smoke-blackened faces, coughing and spluttering, they were set upon by Connaught's men. Their clothes were ripped off and the throats of twelve of them were cut. The schoolmaster son of the Rector was murdered by the major, and all were left for dead on the blood-soaked ground. Byron was not present in person, but he wrote a letter to the Marquess of Newcastle, mentioned the atrocious murders and ended with the callous words:

"They put them all to the sword, which I find to be the best way to deal with their kind of people, for mercy to them is cruelty."

Byron did not strike Thomas Ley and his troopers with terror, and many of those who had fled from him, now that they saw their strength growing under Fairfax, were ready to return and take their revenge; but it was a mixed army which would certainly prove difficult to manage.

On the day before the move started, Captain Ley had a surprise order. At first, after having been posted to Fairfax's army, Tom had expected the general to call him for special duties, but when no summons came, he assumed that the possible usefulness of his local knowledge had been overlooked. It was evening when a soldier knocked on the door of his billet, bringing the message that the general wished to see Captain Ley in his own quarters.

The house where Fairfax lodged was an old dwelling, standing close to the Collegiate Church, its beams so low that Tom had to stoop on entering the room to avoid knocking his head on the particularly low one over the door. He saluted Sir Thomas and another officer who was sitting beside him. The two commanders were poring over a large map which was spread out on the table. Sir Thomas looked up. Tom thought his dark countenance was more melancholy than usual. He stammered slightly as he spoke.

"Captain Ley, I have heard you are a native of Wich Malbank, the Cheshire town which is to be the objective of our march."

"That is true," replied Tom. "We more commonly call the place Nantwich."

"Indeed, yes," said Fairfax, slightly irritated. "This is Colonel Brereton, defender of the town against all comers for almost a year, until a superior force from Ireland compelled him to withdraw. He has given me a general view of the situation at your Nantwich—as far as he can judge it."

Sir William looked up and nodded.

"I am told you served under Gustavus in the German war," continued Fairfax. That is good. I never had the privilege, though I fought with the Hollanders—neither did the colonel—but we have both studied his campaigns and hope to emulate them in our own actions."

Fairfax was making a thorough appraisal of Tom's appearance; it seemed that he had passed the test.

"I trust you know the ways around this town of Nantwich well," said the general. "Colonel Brereton has local men among the remnants of his former army, which he has now reinforced, but you have been recommended to me by Lord Manchester as a man of parts and keen perception. Your former military experience and local knowledge make you the one man I would have as my scoutmaster in this service and you will be responsible to me personally for the duration of the campaign."

"I lived in Nantwich for thirty one years," replied Tom, "and what is more I travelled widely beyond its confines in Cheshire and the neighbouring counties. For the last twelve years I have served as a soldier or worked as a merchant abroad, but there is nothing about my native town and its surroundings which is not impressed on my memory," he added, eager to confirm the general's supposition.

192

"You will find some changes now, I have no doubt," said Brereton with a faint smile. "The place is a fortress. I fortified it myself and I believe it will hold out against Byron until we arrive."

"Fortified?" echoed Tom.

"Aye—with mud walls. Your experience will have taught you the value of these defences, I am sure. Last January I drove away Sir Thomas Aston who would have taken the place and held it for the king, when its only fortifications were a few barricades. At once I set soldiers and civilians to work constructing these walls—not miserable breast high earthworks, but a circumvallation of massive stakes and puddled clay, ten feet thick and over twelve feet high with a parapet walk and sconces guarding the street ends. Cannon balls ploughing into my walls will not shatter them as they would the stone, nor will they go through, except on rare occasions, but only serve to strengthen them, the clay having been well tempered with water to make it exceedingly solid. But I am not so foolish as to believe that it is beyond the power of Byron's strong, determined army to take Nantwich. Suffice it to say that the town is well-stocked with arms, powder and provisions. Let us hope and pray that these delays will not mean that our enemies will conquer it by force before our arrival. The final irony would be that my strong mud walls would stand and defy the one who ordered them to be constructed."

"And the people?" asked Tom, his heart pounding as he heard about the siege.

"All safe as yet, but our spies confirmed a few days ago that the Cavaliers were preparing a big attack. They took the castle of Beeston by stealth, climbing the mighty rock face in the night. This was achieved by an intrepid fellow called Sandford and eight firelocks— with a little help from inside, it is supposed. This man's boasts and threats exceed even those of his general, Lord Byron, but without them his deeds speak loudly enough. All the great halls are under their control, and the reputation for audacity and cruelty they have gained, has spread throughout the county. Now they have concentrated their undoubted power against Nantwich, and as you must realize, that is the key to the whole of the Northwest."

Tom looked hard at Brereton, whom he had not seen prior to this meeting. He had a serious but sympathetic aspect, not flamboyant—more open than Fairfax, not as vigorous as Cromwell.

Sir Thomas indicated a small area of the map with his dagger which he was using as a pointer.

"The reports I have received from Sir William tell me much about the state of the country around Nantwich and the likeliest places where we can expect resistance, but I shall rely on you, Captain Ley, for further advice as we proceed. You will hand over the troop to your lieutenant and ride with me. I understand that it was entirely on your own initiative that you came to me to assist in the relief of your town. Rest assured, Captain, I will make good use of you and your local knowledge. I also know that your own colonel and general expressed a wish that you should return to them when this present campaign is over. They made it a condition of their approval, and I give you my word that I will look favourably on such a request."

Tom was grateful to Fairfax for his favours. Everything was working out exactly as he had planned. He was aware of the fact that the general was a worried man, displeased with the composition of his army. He had his own men from Yorkshire and Lincolnshire, Cheshire men from Brereton's army with additions from Staffordshire and Derbyshire, and the Lancashire contingents under Colonel Assheton. He had complained that the troops were ill clothed and badly fed, that there were large arrears of pay due to them, and that even arms and ammunition were lacking, but he had received no response from Parliament. As a result, he had had to make good these deficiencies from his own resources. The divisions among his commanders were equally troublesome. Fairfax was an honourable man, with a conscience which made him unsparing in his efforts to achieve victory, but the work and worry of commanding this new army was such that it was impairing his health.

"Thank you, Sir Thomas," said Tom, saluting as he took his leave. "May God smile on us and grant us success."

"Amen to that," said the general crisply, and returned to examining his map.

17.   A SPRIG OF HOLLY

The march to Nantwich began in a blizzard and ended in a rapid thaw. Progress from Manchester through Delamere Forest was very slow and it took four full days to cover a distance of about forty miles. An average of ten miles a day was hardly surprising, first in deep snow, then in slush and mud, but it exasperated Fairfax who, like Brereton, was haunted by the prospect of having to lay siege to Nantwich instead of fighting a battle outside the walls.

As they struggled on through snow and along waterlogged roads Tom felt elated, despite the discomforts of the march, for he knew that after so many years he would see his old home again. He rode on contentedly never doubting that Sir Thomas and Sir William would force their way through Byron's blockade. His appointment as Scoutmaster pleased him too. He collated the reports brought in, gave Fairfax advice on the likeliest places for an ambush, and found the safest, though not necessarily the shortest route suitable for an army of over four thousand men. He knew exactly what was ahead, for during the years as his father-in-law's partner, he had travelled this way many times. Even with its cover of speedily melting snow, the countryside looked familiar. Fairfax spoke little to him, except to receive his reports courteously and to ask for information when he considered it necessary, but Tom was able to exchange friendly words with Colonel Brereton on more than one occasion, and he learned something of the resistance in Cheshire to the likes of Sir Thomas Ashton and Lord Capel, whose futile expeditions against Nantwich had only led to disappointment and ridicule. Brereton's year as master of the field in Cheshire was all the more remarkable as it had been achieved at a time when the King's forces had gained ground almost everywhere else. To restore that mastery would be a hard task. This Lord Byron, so reviled by the writers of Parliamentary journals for the misdeeds of his troops and his own boasting, was nonetheless a doughty fighter, and he had some good subordinates, but Tom had become infected with the enthusiasm of men like Cromwell and Brereton and he never doubted that with God for them, as he surely was, nothing could stand against them. He had rarely been the loser. Kate had been taken away, but he had gained Amalia. Even at Nördlingen good had come out of defeat and suffering. It had led him to Salzburg and a prosperous future. At the drawn battle of Edgehill he had come to know Oliver Cromwell—surely the rising star of the rebellion. God would not desert him this time. Yet his joy was mingled with fear. How would he find his home and people? All could not be the same as when he went away.

The first sight of the enemy came a few miles from Nantwich. Lord Byron had pushed an advance party forward to try to hold up Fairfax until he could move up his whole army and engage him away from the town where the garrison could not easily sally out to support him. He had besieged Nantwich closely, confident that no news of the approach of Fairfax had reached them. The country here was not so thickly wooded and there was a stream, once little more than a trickle, now swollen by the melting snow. Just beyond the bridge the King's men had bivouacked on the previous night; in the morning two hundred of them advanced to secure the crossing and challenge Fairfax. Apprised of the attempt by Captain Ley's intelligence, Sir Thomas took out a body of foot and dragoons who, charging the men at the bridge, swept them aside and took some prisoners. More welcome news now came in. It was reported that Lord Byron's army was divided. The thaw had caused the river to overflow and break down the only bridge in their hands. The water was too high to be safely forded, so the men besieging the town on the other side of the river were unable to join their comrades without a long detour, which Tom estimated as six or seven miles. A forced march would bring Fairfax to the Cavaliers in time to destroy their army piecemeal.

They moved on in a high state of expectancy, but the going was terrible and the rear-guard and carriages were slow in coming up. Reaching the top of a rise, they could see below them Lord Byron's army, drawn up across the road and into the fields before the village of Acton, its banners and variously coloured uniforms making a vivid splash of colour on that grey winter's day. Far away to the left, the high church tower of Nantwich stood out as a vantage point from which the commander of the garrison, with the aid of a telescope could sum up the position on the battlefield. Fairfax was ready to attack; he drew up within cannon shot. There was a sudden 'thump, thump' of ordnance from across the valley; a few inaccurate shots flew over, leaving holes in the mud and splashing water on the Roundheads, but though Fairfax was not alarmed by this fiery display, he feared he would soon be outnumbered. Behind the lines of Cavaliers which matched their own muster in strength, reserves were assembling, and it was clear that before long the divided army would be reunited. A council of war was held, and the resolution was that Fairfax's forces should be joined with those of the townsmen before an attack was made. Byron was blocking his way into Nantwich; the only solution was to bypass him. But how? Was there another road which would take them in? There was indeed one, but the bridge which carried it over the river had been torn down to hamper the Cavaliers and the "platt"—a low bridge which replaced it during the siege—had been swept away by the torrent of water.

The general stood on a rise and surveyed the countryside which could hardly have been more unsuitable for a cavalry battle. He called Tom to his side.

"A way into Wich Malbank without having to meet Byron at a disadvantage. Give me the benefit of your knowledge, captain."

"There is an old salt-road," replied Tom. "'Welshman's Lane' they call it—used for centuries by trains of packhorses from Wales. It should be passable—that is if we can reach it. The problem is to cross the fields."

Fairfax turned his glass on the hedges which, in these parts, marked the boundaries of each small field.

"These enclosures are a sore hindrance to our passage," he said, "but Byron's cavalry will be hampered too. If we can prevent him from coming upon our flank until we reach your Welshman's Lane, nothing can stop us effecting a juncture with the troops of Sir George Booth. With a thousand townsmen to reinforce us, we should have a glorious day tomorrow". He turned to his adjutant. "Bring up the pioneers and slash down the hedges. Give us a gap wide enough to pass through in column and bring on our guns and carriages unimpeded."

He indicated the numerous holly bushes.

"Take your field signs," he said. "Let each man wear a sprig of winter greenery that he might know and be known to his comrades! March on to Malbank!"

The attempt to bypass Byron was a laborious manoeuvre. The Cavaliers, seeing their enemies in difficulty, split their force, part of which, turning to meet the Roundheads threw itself on the rear of the marching column. While the Royalists were struggling in the sodden, enclosed fields to draw up in proper formation, Fairfax faced his rear regiments about and struck back. He held the attack, but the rest of the Cavaliers came on and fighting broke out all along the line. The cavalry was of little use in the mire, but Fairfax, having completely abandoned the idea of reaching Nantwich, sent in his infantry with levelled pikes. Byron's men were beginning to break, when a great shout went up from the Parliamentarian lines. In the rear of the King's army, the beating of drums the crack of muskets, the clash of swords, the cries of men, heralded the arrival of a third force. The defenders of the town had made the sally which was to decide the issue. When light was fading and the issue of the battle still hung in the balance, close on a thousand musketeers swept aside a feeble force near the bridge, advanced up the hill, and struck the decisive blow. The reserve regiments were smashed, the cannon captured, and a great hole was punched in the Cavaliers lines. The Roundheads poured through, encircled the wings, and forced the enemy to surrender in their hundreds. The final count of prisoners numbered over a thousand and a half, and though Byron escaped, many officers of note were taken. There had been no great carnage—only about three hundred had been killed—but this Army from Ireland had been eliminated as a threat to the Northwest.

The ancient stones of a village church, turned into a centre of last-ditch resistance by the Cavaliers, withstood the onslaught of the Roundheads; but the battle had already been won; the victors could wait for these beaten men to realize that their position was hopeless. All around stood waggons full of plunder, carriages, officers, strident whores decked out in stolen finery, the servants of the commanders, sutlers, and other camp followers. The women were herded together; the soldiers gained a victory over them by relieving them of their long knives with which, it was said, they used to "play the barbarous cutthroats"; then the unfortunate females were driven into the town and further relieved of their fancy clothes by the women of Nantwich. Some of the plunder disappeared into the knapsacks or pockets of individual men before there was time to collect it and organise its removal, but Colonel Brereton took charge and assembled a convoy of twenty seven waggons and twenty carriages, all laden with loot from the surrounding countryside.

Fairfax collected his prisoners and the part of his army he was taking into the town; the rest he left on the battlefield to contain the defenders of the church, and guard against any possible return by upwards of a thousand Cavaliers who had escaped with Byron.

Tom went with Fairfax. He wished it had been daylight, for he could only discern the outlines of houses in Welsh Row as they descended the hill towards the river. By the bridge he saw an amazing sight. Everything looked so different. Great bastions of earth and stakes stretched across the fields, picked out for him in the semi-darkness by points of light all along the ramparts, as men and women appeared with torches. Ditches extended on either side of the road, away and away into the gloom of the winter evening. The massive gates were open, and as he entered the town the scene became more familiar, though the debris and confusion behind the walls reminded Tom that this place too, had been the scene of a recent battle. There stood the old well known salt-houses, the brine pit where he had once worked, the Crown Inn where he had avidly read the newspaper reports of the war in Germany. The streets were swarming with people most of them carrying torches, and cheering broke out as the great column of soldiers marched past. Tom sat proudly on his horse, like most of his comrades still wearing a sprig of holly in his hat. The faces of men, women and children swam by as he ascended the slope to the High Town. Suddenly a shock of terror ran through him. Yet it was a feeling of joy. How could it be described? A girl, wearing a dark cloak, her face illuminated by the flickering light of a torch, looked out from a crowd—the only one in that sea of faces which caught Tom's eye.

"Kate!" he called out instinctively, but the girl showed no sign of recognition. Of course she would not—how could it be Kate? It was difficult to move quickly through the crowded streets. The column had come to a standstill. There she was again!

"Kate!" he called out for a second time, knowing full well that it was foolishness. The girl had disappeared into the crowd. Why was he calling for one he knew to be dead? Tom dismounted and handed the reins of his horse to a corporal. His mind was in a whirl as he forced his way through the thronging citizens who had poured out into the street to watch the soldiers pass by. He skirted the churchyard. There was the Grammar School where he and the real Kate—a young woman in the full bloom of her beauty—had walked and talked and laughed and loved. The crowd was thinner along Churchyard side. The doors of the great building were open; the light of many torches blazed from the interior; long files of prisoners were marching in. Drums beat an inspiring rhythm as a company of Parliament men marched past carrying the captured colours of Lord Byron's army—twenty one in all. People pressed forward to clap this captain from the victorious army on the shoulder, to greet him with a handshake or a kiss, and congratulate him on the outcome of the battle. But Tom had no time to stop, even to be acclaimed a hero of heroes. The girl had gone. Had he deceived himself? Was she just a memory, corporally created from the ether—a sweet reminder of happiness in times past, now beyond recall, except in the shape of such tantalizing visions? For a moment all the years fell away; the busy scene dissolved; he was here again with Kate:

"Please wear that dress and cloak again, Mistress Barton. It makes you look like the Holy Mother on the east window in church."

But Kate was truly dead. A horrible rattle of drums brought him back to reality. His old home was not far away. He would make his way there at once.

Then he saw the vision again—straight in front of him! Another company of red-coated soldiers, herding more prisoners towards the church, held him up for a moment. After them came a group of officers marching with more style to captivity in one of the town's hostelries. Some people stepped aside to allow this Parliamentarian officer right of way and he came face to face with the vision he had been following.

A girl—flesh and blood—a beautiful woman! The whole truth came upon him in a flash.

"Lynette!" he cried, his heart overflowing with joy. "Lynette! My dearest, dearest girl! God in his mercy preserved you. Oh, my sweet child! How could I have thought him to have been so cruel and have taken away your little life before you had tasted the sweetness of it?"

"Sir," she said. "I do not know the meaning of your strange words and your knowledge of my name is a complete mystery to me, but I see you are a man with holly in his hat. This is my home for the present. If you wish to step inside, I am sure my foster parents and my grandmother would be pleased to welcome one who has delivered us from such great danger, and offer you some refreshment."

She threw open the door and the light inside, though not really very great, was in such contrast to the gloom outside that it momentarily dazzled Tom. A wrinkled old lady sat near to the fire in a high-backed chair; a stocky man with grey hair, and a woman, greying too, approached the open door. It was the younger woman who first recognized the unexpected visitor. She shrieked, betraying an emotion not unlike that felt by Tom on seeing Lynette—joy mixed with terror.

"It's Tom!" she cried, turning to her husband. "Our dear brother has returned to us."

She went close to the old lady.

"Mother," she said rather gently, not wishing to alarm her unduly. "Tom has come back."

The old lady gave a little cry, too, and rose to embrace her son. Through all this, Lynette stood by the doorway. She had turned pale; tears of joy welled up in her eyes.

"Tom? Then you are my father!" she cried. "Dear Father, we all thought you were dead."

She burst into tears and threw her arms round Tom. He lifted her face and stroked her cheeks.

"Yes," he said. "I believed that of you too, but God kept you safe and I will thank him on my knees each day for His mercy."

Will came forward and embraced his brother-in-law. The practical Alice, after following suit, went into the kitchen to prepare some food.

Old Mrs Ley returned to her chair and from that vantage point admired the handsome Parliamentarian officer who was her own dear son.

As the others pressed round him, this homecoming reminded Tom of the one he had witnessed at Hallein, when his friend Leopold had returned from the German war. This was an even more moving scene—the reunion of a father with a long-lost daughter, the sudden appearance of a missing son when hope had faded that he would ever return, but the similarity remained. He thought of Amalia and Lynette. That former homecoming had presented him with a wife; this one had given him an almost grown-up daughter.

There were tales to tell on both sides, but most of them were postponed until the morrow, as Tom had to make a report to General Fairfax. When at last they exchanged stories, nothing was left out— Lützen, Nördlingen, Gustavus, Cromwell, Fairfax, Tom's meeting with George, his work as a merchant, his home in Salzburg, and of course Amalia. Lynette, in particular, was interested in this stepparent who was not old enough to be her real mother.

The family had their own adventures to relate, beginning with the story of Lynette's discovery at the cottage of Meg Broomhall. Without moving from their native county, they had been in the thick of the fray. Having been plundered and threatened by the Cavaliers in 1642, they had been forced to seek refuge behind the mud walls of Nantwich when this new invasion from Ireland was imminent. Will's school was almost at a standstill. Many of his pupils came from a distance and were afraid to travel in such dangerous times; his house had been ransacked once, but his family had been spared. However, this "Irish" army was more menacing and they might not be so lucky a second time; so Will thought it prudent to return to Nantwich, where Mrs Ley offered them shelter until the town should be relieved. If it fell, then that must be God's will and he would have to accept it, but the schoolmaster of Walbury trusted in the power of his prayers, the stout walls of Wich Malbank, and the stouter hearts of the brave garrison and old Sir George Booth their octogenarian governor.

There was a day when Will's trust was tested—January 16th, which began as a black day, when the Cavaliers almost broke into the town, and ended in glory as they drew off in disorder to their camp at Acton, having suffered a bloody defeat. At some distance from the town the Cavaliers had dug their trenches, from which they launched an assault just as day dawned. The walls were but slenderly defended, when a cannon shot gave the signal to advance. A boy of fifteen, seeing the oncoming line of musketeers in the half-light, sounded the alarm and seizing a weapon, shot dead the redoubtable Captain Sandford, conqueror of Beeston Castle. The trumpets blared out, the defenders who were off duty or taking refreshment rushed to the walls to hold back the onslaught of the Cavaliers. First came the firelocks with scaling ladders and faggots to fill in the ditches. Dragoons with snaphances fell on the defences near the river. They were seconded by musketeers coming on like a swarm of bees, and a strong body of pikes. Muskets cracked and swords flashed in the early light; cries of "God and a good cause!"—the Cavaliers' word—rang out as fighting spread all along the walls from the five points of attack. Many Royalists failed even to plant their ladders against the walls; others reached the top only to be clubbed down or pushed off on to their ascending comrades.

Tom's sister had had her hour of glory too. Passing through the churchyard on the previous afternoon, she heard a group of women being harangued by one she knew as Mary Brett. Alice related the tale with relish.

"Let not the men think that we women are naught but useless ornaments," cried Amazon Brett. "In forty-two when the King's troops reached Brentford and threatened London town, women boiled cauldrons of water ready to pour down from their windows on Prince Robber's men, as the warriors of old did from castle walls. Not far from here, at Wem, that cowstealer Lord Capel and all his Cavaliers were put to flight by a company of women and a few musketeers. Why should we not emulate our sisters in London and Shropshire? In peaceful times we boil the brine to grab the salt from it. Boil it up again for the King's men. Let them come and we will pour it on these insolent Cavaliers who would have us yield our town and use us at their pleasure!"

Alice stepped forward to join the group, but some younger women who did not know her, laughed at what they thought was a genteel person wishing to become a boiler of brine. The offended Alice rolled up her sleeve and pointed to the place where she had once been scalded in her walling days.

"I was a salter before most of you were born," she said indignantly. "It is many long years since I entered a wich house, but I will wall again for Lord Byron; if he comes, we will make it hotter for him than he yet imagines."

So the brine was kept ready on the boil and Amazon Brett's foresight had proved admirable. Soon after the attack began, the women were at their stations, ready to support their menfolk in the defence of their native town.

Tom could hardly visualize Alice as a woman warrior pouring hot liquid down on the enemy; but the story was undoubtedly true, and she even claimed one kill. A Cavalier in the forefront of the attack, firmly set his scaling ladder against the wall, and ascending to the parapet, turned to his fellows and cried out:

"The town is our own!" only to receive a full pan of Alice's boiling brine in the face, which caused the screaming man to fall from the wall and break his neck.

Lynette, too, wished to help and she reported for duty to tend the wounded, but there were not many casualties inside the town. A few of the defenders and some Cavaliers who had been dragged over the parapet or killed when they broke in at one sconce, were laid out behind the walls and later removed to the church, but the Royalists managed to take off many of their wounded and the townsmen secure behind their bastions of earth and stakes, suffered less.

Will, believing that the influence of his words on the outcome of the battle would be greater than that which he could exert if he took a musket in his hands, strode up and down behind the fortifications, using fiery speeches to encourage the defenders to do the work of the Lord. When the din of battle became so great that his words were lost in the confusion, he took to ladling out powder and loading weapons.

Despite the ferocity of this surprise attack, Byron was unable to make a breach in the walls. A small number of Cavaliers forced their way into Pillory Street, but after a bloody fight they were thrown out again, having suffered severe casualties. Dead lay piled around the walls and sconces; as usual some had been thrown into the river; wounded had been carried back to the Royalist trenches for treatment. In the full light of morning, the signal was given to abandon the attack on the town; the Royalists withdrew; the battle had lasted for one hour; a hundred men still lay on the field. At least three hundred had been killed or wounded. Will described how he stood on the walls and rejoiced after the Cavaliers had retreated:

"The townsfolk had played their parts valiantly," he said. "God had sent them his encouragements—he who is God of blessings. Without them, man is nothing; armed with divine favours he becomes a terrible instrument of the Lord's power. How we awaited our valiant general, Sir William Brereton, who guided by God, would bring us help to lay this Irish army low. We knew that he had been seeking assistance around Manchester, but we had no idea whether he was already approaching the enemy's camp or still struggling through the snow in Delamere Forest. But we had faith and we were delivered."

There were many other things to tell. Tom admired his daughter now almost a fully developed woman—the mirror image of Kate who had filled his youth with happiness. He was not surprised when Will told him that he had found a husband for her, though the betrothal had been postponed until the man's return from service in Ireland.

Tom enquired as to the prospective bridegroom's name.

"Chaplain Blackshaw," replied Will, "a godly and temperate man. I could not think of a more worthy choice."

"Blackshaw?" said Tom surprised. "He is here—captured at Acton. Having gone over in a government army to quell a rising of Irish Papists, he found himself trapped in the forces of the King in opposition to the party wherein his sympathies lie. He declared himself at once for King and Parliament, and I believe he marches with us back into Lancashire in a few days' time. I doubt if he realizes that you are lodging here in Nantwich. I will apprise him of your presence as soon as I can. He is quartered either in the Crown House or with the officers at Mr Wilbraham's."

Tom noticed that Lynette showed no signs of enthusiasm during their conversation, and at the mention of Blackshaw's name, she had rather a dejected look. He had to go back to Headquarters at the Lamb Inn, so Lynette walked along with him.

"Tell me, my little linnet," he said, taking his daughter's arm. "Do you not love this Mr Blackshaw?"

"No, Father," replied Lynette honestly. "I find him stiff and dull, quoting from the bible nearly every time he speaks and frowning on my little pleasures. I love the Lord, Father, but must I make religion my whole life, finding scriptural texts for everything, not being able to enjoy the beautiful things I see around me without fear of censure for being frivolous? Must I marry this Mr Blackshaw?" She gave her father a tearful look.

"No, no, dear. I would not force such a thing upon you. Uncle Will means well, but he too, is completely immersed in Scripture. He sees himself as a Crusader against wickedness and misunderstanding. He watches for the hand of the Lord in everything and he would educate us to recognize each one of God's mercies. In his opinion this Mr Blackshaw is well fitted to keep you from the snares of the devil and guide you on the straight and narrow path to eternal life. There is no romance in Uncle Will, dear. I am sure you have come to realize that."

"But I do want romance, Father. Why must love be only an ethereal feeling—a longing for something spiritual which we cannot see or touch. I want warm human love too—another heart beating against mine, hands which caress me and lips which can tell me how satisfying the unity of two loving humans can be."

A little tear began to roll down her cheek. Tom gave his daughter a gentle look.

"Do not distress yourself," he said. "Nothing shall be forced upon you. I will instruct Uncle Will that no betrothal shall be entered upon until I return. But I would not reject this young man so quickly. Let him see you again and speak to you. Perhaps you have misjudged him and will learn to take him to your heart."

An expression of indescribable relief spread over Lynette's face—so obvious that Tom had to smile;

"I will try my best, dear Father," she said almost gaily. "You are so kind to me. Were we not related, I am sure I should fall madly in love with such a handsome Parliamentary captain."

They had reached Churchyardside. Tom beckoned to Lynette and they stood in front of the school.

"Listen!" he said. "On this same spot I made the very first move to win your mother. She looked so lovely then—just like a holy picture, I thought—or just like you, my dear. I was an untutored lad and she was quite a lady, but I had been given a golden sovereign by old King James, and it emboldened me to ask her to take a stroll. It was love all the way with your mother, Lynette, and with your stepmother too. I will tell you the story of that tender meeting some other time. I never thought any one could replace my Kate, that I could love again as I had loved before; and yet my passion for the girl I met in Salzburg is not one whit less than that which I felt in the days of my youth. You will love Amalia, too, and I am sure she will take her stepdaughter to her heart."

Lynette clasped her father's hand to affirm his assumption. "I will love her," she said. "Perhaps more as a dear sister than a mother."

Her changed mood pleased Tom.

"Try to love this Mr Blackshaw," he said, "but if you cannot, there will be no compulsion. I will not deny you the romance and happiness I have enjoyed twice myself."

"Must you go so soon, Father?" asked Lynette. "We have scarcely been able to taste the sweetness of reunion before a time of further parting has come. It is this hateful war. I loathe it Father. It parts me from you."

"But it brought us together," objected Tom. "Had I not come to fight for King and Parliament, who knows how long I would have been away? Most likely, I would never have returned at all."

"That was a blessing, but I still hate it Father, for what it does to men."

"It is a just war, child. We must check a king who would play the tyrant."

Lynette's expression was very serious.

"War is a tyrant too. It tyrannizes the hearts and minds of men. When the attack on our town had ended and I looked out over the walls, the full horror of it came upon me. There, in the mire, lay the scaling ladders, the bundles of faggots and all the wreckage left behind by the enemy—and the bodies of many men, broken, shot and slashed—most of them stripped naked by the searchers for weapons and warm clothing. Then I thought how futile and dreadful it all must be."

"But do you not believe that God goes with us in this war, leading us to inevitable victory?"

"When General Fairfax won at Acton, his men marched grandly into our town with sprigs of holly in their hats—my own dear, lost father among them. Then I rejoiced, but when faced with the brutal reality I cannot supress my feelings of horror at it."

Tom remembered his own experiences in the German war and the disillusionment it had caused. At the beginning of this conflict he had feared that, if it could not be ended quickly, it would go the same way. Then his ceaseless activity had subdued these feelings; his ardour had been fuelled by those around him—Fairfax was a man of religion, but he did not flaunt his beliefs; many said it was hard to tell whether he favoured the Presbyterians or the Independents. Tom had been influenced more by Sir Ralph and other officers of the Ironsides, but most of all by Oliver. He knew where he was going; it was not only his duty to fight for a righteous cause, but to play his part in ensuring that Englishmen did not descend to the viciousness and obscenity shown in the German conflict. Now his daughter was calling even that noble aim in question. It was a natural womanly sentiment. He could not censure her for that, On the contrary it made him admire her more.

"You are full of pity and tenderness, my linnet. I am sure that you will find a part to play if the war comes to you again; there will always be the wounded to tend, whereby you can ease the horror of the conflict."

They were nearing the Lamb Inn.

"I must leave you now, dearest," he said as they reached headquarters. "Remember my words. I will never allow anyone to deny you happiness and fulfilment."

Tom had no desire to turn Lynette against her uncle and aunt, and offend the ones who had cared for her for so many years at their own expense while he had been away. Though he had taken every reasonable step to find his little daughter before leaving for the war in what seemed to some to be an unnecessary hurry, and had been led on a false trail which had ended with almost complete certainty that she was dead, he still had an irrational feeling of guilt about Lynette. He had left without having actually looked upon the body of a dead daughter, or having received some irrefutable proof of her death, as in the case of Kate. Yet he could detect no resentment on the part of Lynette. She had accepted him immediately as her father, and had showed no reticence before him, confiding her secret feelings in him as if she had always been together with a well-beloved and trusted parent. But Will and Alice would have to bow to his ultimate authority. He could not see the daughter with whom he had just been reunited, in whose love and society he hoped to find a rich addition to his happiness, be thrown into a marriage with one who, however upright and pious he might be, could not awaken the warm, human feelings within her which strove for expression in romantic love.

The severe ascetic looks of Blackshaw confirmed his doubt. The young man was surprised to find that this officer was Lynette's real father. Tom noticed a slight coolness towards him, as if Blackshaw detected some reservations about the coming match on the part of this new parent. Nevertheless, he readily accepted the invitation to visit the Mastersons. Tom said nothing about his conversation with Lynette to her prospective husband, and decided to leave the matter as it stood until his return.

The battlefield had been cleared of most of the debris by the time Tom rode out on his return to Lancashire. In the Lady Field, close to Acton Church, lines of newly dug graves were an immediate reminder of the recent struggle. The church walls were pockmarked, the fields churned into a quagmire where the hottest parts of the combat had taken place; great gaps had been torn in the hedges; heaps of brushwood lay about; the bright winter sunshine shone on the dark, muddy patches which marked the former camping ground of the vanquished.

Brief though his visit to his hometown had been, Tom rode out of Nantwich with a feeling of great satisfaction. The events, both military and personal, which had taken place there, had been momentous. He had played a significant part in one of the few important defeats suffered thus far by the Cavaliers; he had received the blessing of a mother beside herself with joy at the sight of a son whose memory she had cherished, never daring to hope that he would return to her.

All that remained was to unite his old family with the new one waiting at Royston. Alice and Will were returning to Walbury now that the acute danger was over, and Lynette could remain with them until the question of her marriage had been settled. Margery Ley had shown great interest in this new daughter-in-law from a foreign land and the little ones of Tom's second family. Lynette, led on by her father's description of his young wife, rejoiced in the acquisition of an "elder sister". Everyone agreed that Amalia and the children should come, as soon as conditions allowed, to Cheshire, thus fulfilling the wish for the unity of the two families. Before he went away, Tom had taken steps to assure Margery Ley's continued tenancy of her house, with provision for her in his absence. He could not countenance the dreadful possibility of his mother being destitute. Will and Alice would, of course, look after her in their lifetime, but there was always the chance that she would survive them. In that case, if she could not meet the demands of her landlord, she would at the best have to seek admittance to an alms house, which for Tom, was quite unthinkable. It was thus to his old home that he proposed to send Amalia and the children.

The continuous thud of horse's hooves and the jogging of his mount, the tramp of feet and the monotonous roll of drums behind him dulled his perception of his surroundings. Will and his fellows had tried to instruct him in the past, but he had always found it hard to understand the ways of God in handing out blessings and disasters. Yet there was surely a pattern—events seemingly catastrophic for him had led to benefits which had enriched his life; decisions, hard to make, had brought him unimagined rewards. Threads, apparently disconnected, had become interwoven as if their union were part of a grand plan. Only when he reached the end of the road, would he fully comprehend God's purpose. As time ran on, he would have to accept that the plan existed and enjoy the blessings.

A sudden call brought him out of his reverie.

"Captain Ley! The general would receive your report."

Tom spurred forward, brushing these speculations from his mind. He was a cavalry officer once more—the trusted Scoutmaster—attending on his general.

18.   THE SINS OF THE FLESH

For Luke Blackshaw January 1644 seemed like the beginning of a new life. His enforced stay in Ireland had given him little satisfaction. Over the water, likeminded men were fighting for freedom of worship and a share in government, while he actually marched and sailed amongst their very enemies. The Battle at Nantwich was a golden opportunity for him, and he rejoiced that at last he could go forward under the banner of Parliament with men who bravely proclaimed the true reformed religion and the rights of the people.

On the day following Tom's visit to Mr Wilbraham's house where Blackshaw was lodged, the chaplain had an important duty to perform. He had taken up the invitation to visit the Masterson's, but first it behoved him to see that as many as possible of these misguided prisoners, most of them already Protestants, came over to the favoured side on which God had visited such a signal blessing at the recent battle. The great doors of the church were tightly shut; musketeers were stationed round the building; but there was little danger from inside, for most of the captured troops were disaffected. They had suffered demoralizing hardships in the cold winter days and nights of the siege; some were wounded; there were many whose allegiance to King Charles had never been very strong. It would not take much persuasion to make them turn their coats.

The guards at the south porch greeted Blackshaw respectfully and opened the door to reveal a scene of obnoxious degradation.

The whole nave and the transept were full of men, lying on piles of straw or mats, leaning against the walls, squatting on the floor or reclining on benches. Some had already been released; the others were crowded together in revolting filth, wrapped up in ragged blankets against the chilly atmosphere of the unheated church.

Blackshaw strode through the nave. The stench of excreta and unwashed bodies appalled him; they had only been imprisoned for a few days; he dreaded to think what the atmosphere would be like by the time of their release. But he had a duty to perform. He mounted the steps leading into the stone pulpit whence he had a commanding view of the depressing scene. He began to speak, at first in an uninspiring and not very loud voice. Only a few prisoners gathered round the chancel steps, but Luke with his sweeping hand and pointing finger drew more of them towards him. As he spoke, his inspiration increased in proportion to the number of his listeners and potential converts. His voice grew clearer and steadier, his expression more powerful, his phrases incisive, his pauses telling, his gestures more dramatic. God had shown, first by the failure of the grand attack on Nantwich, then the defeat at Acton, that he was not with them. By the mercies granted to the townsmen of Booth and the soldiers of Fairfax, he had punished them sorely for taking up a bad cause. Once they had marched against Catholic rebels in Ireland, now they were defending a king who was in league with Papists who would deny them their liberties in church and state, and would curtail the powers of that august body, the Parliament. It would be no disgrace to change sides now—he had done so without hesitation.

"We may be termed traitors and hypocrites, yet we hope—nay we are confident—that God will in his due time make it known to the world that we study only his glory and the liberty of Parliament, for which we fight without seeking our own interests. The Lord is our strength and in him are all our expectations."

Blackshaw and his fellows had great success with the prisoners in the church. The officers were a vastly different proposition. The conditions under which they were kept were infinitely better, they had a greater sense of honour and loyalty, and being able to reason better than the men, they could pick holes in Luke's arguments. Among these officers captured at Acton, one of the most notable was Colonel George Monck who had once refused to take a special oath of loyalty to the king, and then after a personal interview with Charles, had undertaken to serve him. Refusing to change sides after Nantwich, he preferred to let them send him to the Tower of London, until in his own good time he would decide whether or not he wished to take up arms for Parliament.

213

Blackshaw, having preached to the officers, was stopped by this colonel with ironical words which he considered undeserved and wounding.

"Excellent, Mr Blackshaw,—a sermon well digested to serve a certain purpose, meriting, if I may say so, a little more substance and less excess of gesture. Admirable, chaplain—for converting common soldiers."

Having reached the peroration of his sermon to the large congregation which now crowded the east end of the nave and stood on the chancel steps, Luke said a short prayer and strode out of the noisome church, leaving the Parliamentarian guards to marshal those who wished to change sides and form them into companies. He made his way to Mrs Ley's house with more desire to meet his old schoolmaster again and exchange views than to pay court to Lynette. He did not, however, anticipate any further difficulties in that respect. By now, the girl's foolish notions would have been banished by the careful instruction of Will, and her own increasing maturity. If for no other reason than her own reading of Holy Scripture, she must have come to a realization of her true place in God's scheme of things—especially her subjection to the will of a man. He believed in his conceit, that after reflection on her part, his own merits would have found favour with the girl and she would come willingly to him.

It was Lynette herself who met him at the door.

"Mr Blackshaw," she said, greeting him sweetly, doing her best to please her father and not displease her uncle. "My foster parents are out, but Grandmother is busy in the kitchen."

"It is you whom I have come to see," replied Blackshaw. "Your father whom God spared to return among our deliverers, indicated your willingness—nay your desire—to see me, and he gave his blessing to a matter close to both our hearts."

Lynette did not believe that her father had spoken thus, but she said nothing except to offer Luke a seat. He made a move towards the old oak bench—the courting settle.

"No not there, Mr Blackshaw," said the girl hurriedly. To see him on that seat would be to picture an unpleasant possibility which she did not care to contemplate—a view of herself sitting beside him while he pecked at her with his lips between longwinded pious homilies and an outpouring of biblical quotations.

Luke meekly took another seat and continued his introductory address to the girl.

"Last time I was with you we spoke on trivial subjects—vanities which I expect your increased wisdom has banished from your mind. You are now sixteen years old. Guided by your uncle, you will have reached an understanding of the word of God, which, though far from perfect, must be sufficient to drive such fancies from your mind, *'But I say unto you that every idle word that men shall speak, they shall give account thereof on the Day of Judgement.'*"

"Mr Blackshaw," she said severely. "I pray you refrain from quoting Scripture at me every time you speak. At our last meeting I spoke of flowers and beautiful poetry. You censured me then because I admire lovely things. Surely it is the will of our Lord that we should rejoice in his creation and the fruits of the talents he has given to us."

Luke was taken aback, but he did not counter Lynette's rebuke at once. He looked steadily at the girl and felt a throb of pleasure in doing so. She had certainly grown into a beautiful creature—a sinful thought—he must concentrate on bringing her to an understanding of God's purpose.

"You must rejoice in the beauty of holiness," he said at last, somewhat less condescendingly. "Beauty is to be found in Heaven, not among the dross on earth."

"No, Mr Blackshaw," replied Lynette. "This beauty I admire is a foretaste of Heaven—glimpses we receive from God of what is in store for us in his mansions. May we not enjoy these promises of Heaven even before we are admitted to the kingdom?"

Luke found it most distasteful to have his opinions challenged, especially by a mere girl whose standard of education was so inferior to his. But, strangely enough, he felt no desire to slap her down with some caustic remark or stinging quotation from his bottomless store of texts.

"You will understand better as you grow older," he said, trying to sound comforting. "I promised before I left for Ireland that I would guide and counsel you. I understood then from your uncle that a formal agreement was to be made on my return. I have now accepted another period of service and am to march with Sir Thomas Fairfax into Lancashire, but I am willing to enter upon an immediate betrothal. I expect to receive a comfortable living. I have influential friends, and ministers of good credit and reputation are required to replace those who have been ejected."

Lynette paled, but answered him firmly.

"Mr Blackshaw, I have to inform you that the situation has changed since you first spoke about me to Uncle Will. My father has left instructions that no betrothal is to be announced until his return, and Uncle Will has, of course, agreed to this. My father also expressed a wish that I should entertain you and be civil to you. As a dutiful daughter, I shall of course obey him, but, in any case, you are one of my uncle's most honoured guests. I would not deny you the respect which you undoubtedly deserve. I am sure, sir, if you chafe at the delay imposed by my father, you will find someone else who will not place such obstacles in your path."

Blackshaw was encouraged by the politeness of Lynette's speech. It was formal, to be sure; but might it not mean a weakening of her position?

His eyes were fixed on the girl in a stare which made her feel uncomfortable—that luxuriant hair, those bright eyes, the parting of her lips, the smooth skin and the flush upon her cheeks. But no, he could not allow thoughts like that to take over. He rebuked the devil for tempting him with these desires, but replied to Lynette as if no such imaginings had been troubling him.

"Your father is a man of religion," he said in an unusually low and persuasive voice. "I am sure that one who has consistently fought for the reformed faith would not deny you the opportunity to experience life on a higher plane—to find Christ in the image of a husband."

Lynette laughed—a sound which made Blackshaw feel a tingling sensation he had never experienced before.

216

He lowered his eyes.

"No, Mr Blackshaw, I cannot see Christ in you. I will admit that our Lord was often strict and censorious with wrongdoers, but I like to see him sitting with the little children, relaxing at the home of Martha and Mary, enjoying the company of his disciples, taking part in wedding festivities. There is surely much about him which was not written down or was lost in later ages. I am certain that if we knew all that he did and said, it would confirm my disbelief in a Christ who frowns on every pleasure we enjoy, and calls it downright wickedness."

Blackshaw's reply, whatever it might have been, was never voiced, for at that moment Will and Alice arrived home. Mrs Ley, assisted by her daughter, brought in cans of ale, newly baked bread, a pigeon pie, and various confections. Will monopolized the conversation. He wanted to hear all about Luke's stay in Ireland and his personal view of the King's defeat at Acton. No mention was made of Lynette, until Alice, capitalising on one of Will's pauses for breath, mentioned that their foster child had found a stepmother as well as her lost father.

Luke glanced at Will. Was this yet another complication?

"A lady from South Germany, I believe," said Masterson, without waiting for Luke to ask the inevitable question. "The exact name of the place escapes me, but I know it is in the lands of the Archbishop of Salzburg. By strange chance, it is a salt-town like our Nantwich, but Amalia's father has no part in the trade. He is established there as an apothecary surgeon."

Luke's face darkened.

"Salzburg?" he said. "Then may we assume that having lived under the nose of the Prince Archbishop all those years, she is a Papist?"

"As far as I know, she is a good Protestant," replied Will, feeling that he was on shaky ground. "Tom told us little about her religion except to say that she professes our faith. I take it she must be a convert or an old Protestant who has reverted to her original beliefs."

Chaplain Blackshaw was certain that this was going to be a more difficult task than he had ever imagined. A wayward girl who disputed theology with him, a father with dubious religious views who suddenly turned up after many years of absence and started to exercise his parental authority, and a stepmother who had once professed the Catholic faith—who perhaps still had leanings towards Papism. A challenge indeed, but one he would have to accept! The glory would be all that much greater if he could bring the family which he was to join into complete harmony with God and one another. He would resign himself to a further delay before the announcement of a betrothal. There was a need for some good gospellers in Fairfax's army. A short period of service and he could expect his comfortable living. Will had assured him that Mr Malbon would endeavour to find him a place. Then his destiny would be fixed—with Lynette.

Blackshaw saw the girl once more before he left. The blockade having been lifted, a market was held again and the country folk were glad to bring in the provisions which they had been unable to move during the siege. Luke was ashamed to feel a sudden flush of pleasure on discerning her form among eager buyers in the market place. From a distance he could see only her white cap and the brown cloak wrapped round her slender form as she bent over to examine the produce on one of the stalls, but he knew it was Lynette by the presence of Aunt Alice at her side. The movement of her body as she came across to greet him, those laughing eyes again, the small white hands—these were thoughts which he dared not foster in his mind—not he a preacher dedicated to finding satisfaction in loving holiness. Yet he loved her—yes, he desired her in a way unseemly for a true Christian!

That evening he wrestled with these feelings in prayer and meditation, but he found it hard to subdue them. All his talk about loving only things spiritual! It was plain hypocrisy. How could he who had always striven to live on the highest plane, have fallen victim to that temptation? God sends us trials in forms which are often so desirable that they make us lose our senses. It is easy to hate and shun ugly, grim wickedness; to combat the beauteous needs all our strength and all the power of our prayers. He was accustomed to protracted devotional exercises, but this one was exceptional. He was on his knees soon after the midnight hour was called, but his candle had long burned out and morning was approaching when he arose. There seemed to be a light by the door. He thought he saw a figure—undefined at first—a mere shape, pointing an accusing finger at him.

"Luke Blackshaw!" a voice seemed to say.

"Luke Blackshaw! I say unto you that whosoever looketh on a woman to lust after her, hath committed adultery with her already in his heart."

"No, no, Lord!" cried the frenzied man. "Save me from these sins of the flesh. The fair form of this maiden has dazzled me—miserable sinner that I am. It is a trap set by the devil. Only by the great strength of your Word can I escape from this temptation. I must love her spiritually and rejoice that we may be united in Christian marriage, where we will come together in a calm, holy and respectable way. But never should I lust to possess her carnally as I have done to my eternal shame. This passion smells of brimstone. Save me from these evil, impure thoughts, my Lord and Maker!"

The room was dark again. Luke remained motionless. Suddenly he felt that he had gained the strength he required, and he called out in strong, clear tones—the voice he used when warming to his subject in the pulpit:

"Get thee behind me Satan!"

Next day as the army was assembling to leave Nantwich, Luke found himself in a much more composed frame of mind. He believed he had mastered the carnal desires which Lynette had aroused in him. He would hold Will Masterson to his promise—it was his task to wring agreement from the troublesome returned father. With Lynette as his wife, he would begin the task of improving her mind and fitting her to take her place as mistress of a Christian household.

But Luke deceived himself. Those "wicked desires" were still dormant within him—sleeping lions, only temporarily subdued. The bars of their cage were not as strong as Chaplain Blackshaw thought. Soon, they would awaken, ready to spring out, sully the purity of his thoughts, and batter down the defences he had erected for the security of his soul.

Luke's last duty in Nantwich was an unhappy one. From the town's lockup, a short procession marched through High Town and down Churchyardside to the open ground behind the church, known locally as Tinker's Crofts. An officer, degraded from his rank, his hands bound behind him, strode along in a file of musketeers. Behind him came a lieutenant of the Parliamentarian army and Chaplain Blackshaw, his face grim, book in hand, mentally rehearsing the last words of comfort he would speak to the condemned man. At the rear, two common soldiers carried a long black box of plain wood covered with pitch. Captain Thomas Steele, once a cheese factor and more recently Governor of Beeston Castle, had been sentenced to death by the Council of War for treachery in yielding up his former charge. If he was not a traitor then he must be a coward, they said, for though there were five thousand men driving through the county, the force to which he actually surrendered his garrison of eighty consisted of only nine soldiers, but they were bold firelocks who had scaled the mighty rock to reach him. He had to surrender for Byron would never let Beeston stand unconquered in his rear. But his judges refused to accept his pleas. Either it was a traitor or coward who gave up the castle to Captain Sandford and the only fitting punishment for such a one was death.

The guard halted. The prisoner was led to the Cross Wall. The lieutenant in charge of the detail stepped forward and offered him a blindfold. Steele waved him aside and stood up straight to receive his punishment. These people should know that a Captain of the Trained Band had his dignity too. Even a cheese factor could die like a soldier.

Blackshaw opened his book, but before he could read the comforting words he had chosen, the condemned man began a speech protesting his innocence of any disloyalty to the Parliament of England whose honour he prized above everything. He expressed his gratitude to those who had saved him from the angry mob when he marched his men back to Nantwich; he admitted that it had been a fair trial, but still protested that his judges had reached the wrong conclusion; he confessed to this and that sin, but continued to deny the one of treachery.

There was a pause, Luke exhorted him to admit that too, and not go from this world with such a weight of black sin upon his soul.

"Truly, Preacher," replied Steele, "as God is my judge, I was no traitor, but I had not the courage to withstand that Sandford and try it out with him."

The man's evident honesty made Luke accept his protestations, but he could not help thinking that despite all Steele's attempts to look proud and dignified, he was a pathetic figure. He could feel no anger against the former captain—only compassion for him. A simple man, a peaceful merchant, happy with his family, enjoying good cheer with his friends, worshipping each Sunday in the Parish Church, proud of his ability to satisfy even the most exacting demands of his customers, had been swept out of his depth by the tide of war. Did they expect to make a hero out of a cheese factor? Luke gladly pronounced a blessing; two shots rang out; Steele crumpled up and slid to the ground, struck in the belly and the throat. The Lieutenant stepped forward and declared the traitor dead; the soldiers bundled him into the coffin which stood on the ground at the place of execution, and they resumed their silent march to a grave by the north wall where Steele was laid to rest—a victim of circumstances which were too large for him.

Human weakness! Steele's fate was a lesson to be heeded. But a cheese merchant could not be compared with a minister of the Lord. Blackshaw believed himself to be better armed for the struggle. There would be no lowering of the defence he had built up by prayer—no loophole to admit those insidious temptations. God's strength had cancelled out human weakness. There would be no submission to the sins of the flesh.

19. AMALIA

Tom had decided that his wife should be brought to Nantwich to stay with his mother, but he had left it to others to carry the plan into effect. None of the nearer relations were able to undertake such a long journey and make arrangements to bring a young woman and two children through war-torn England, but Mr Barton stepped into the breach. Sixty five years old, hale and hearty, with a thriving family of his own by his second wife, he was pleased that his former son-in-law had at last taken his advice and found himself another mate. His knowledge of country roads, wayside inns, and better class hostelries, was legendary; no one in the town could have been more suitable to escort Tom's family, and it was natural that Will and Alice should turn to him. Apart from demonstrating his continuing ability to jog along over the worst roads, scorning the discomforts of the weather, the threat of meeting robbers or even becoming embroiled in the war which was going on all across the country, Mr Barton was curious to meet the young woman who had replaced his Kate. He was anxious to find out just how much or how little she resembled his daughter in temperament and character. He would pride himself on being the first to bring this young German woman home to Nantwich.

It was the middle of March when he was approached by the Mastersons, but Barton insisted that it was an absolute necessity to wait until the roads were firm. Then came the passages of Prince Rupert through the county, the whole area became insecure and Barton regrettably put off his expedition. The defeat at Marston Moor changed the balance of power in the North completely. Now Parliament was not only in firm control of London and the East of England, but the King's dominance had been broken in the North. So at last, in. mid July, he decided that the time was opportune.

The journey to Royston was uneventful. The servants Barton had chosen to accompany him had been long in his service. They were both of reliable, calm temperaments, men with a steady hand on the trigger and reins. He was careful, too, in choosing moderate horses, unsuitable for cavalry charges and therefore unlikely to be requisitioned, but hardy enough to stand a long journey over rough roads. In any case, it was his intention to obtain fresh mounts for the return. Although Ashley Hall was only a few miles from Royston, Mr Barton spent the last night at the *Bull Inn* to sample its delights, and after placing it high on his list of comfortable hostelries, he drove over to Sir Ralph Faulkner's residence early on the following morning.

Amalia had received news from Tom several times in the past weeks, either directly or through Lady Faulkner. She had heard about the Battle of Nantwich, the discovery of Lynette, and Tom's intention for her and the children. Of this she thoroughly approved, for although life with Lady Faulkner was comfortable enough, she had no wish to enjoy this hospitality indefinitely, however freely it was given. Amalia had proved a good companion for Sir Ralph's wife; in the absence of their husbands on active service, the two became firm friends. Amalia was also able to exercise some of her talents by playing a part in the education of both her own and Sir Ralph's children. Her command of English, which she had begun to learn from Tom, steadily improved, and she was able to give valued instruction in music and Italian. Her popularity with the five Faulkner children meant that she would be sadly missed when the inevitable day for her departure arrived.

She was in a part of the country blessed with comparative peace, but she had no roots there. She had been used to having to be without Tom for quite long periods during his business journeys on the Continent, but of course she had had her own family around her then. Though every member of the household, from the lady down to the humblest servant, was kind to her, she longed to be with her own people—not to return to Salzburg, for that would mean leaving Tom— but to be with her new family, especially Lynette, for whom she already had a strong sisterly feeling.

More alarming news came when it was reported that a great battle—the greatest in fact of the war—had been fought in the North of England.

Marston Moor had resulted in an overwhelming victory for Tom's party, and by far the larger number of dead and wounded had been on the king's side, but even if Parliament had suffered only one casualty, it could have been Tom. Four thousand Cavaliers had died and three hundred Roundheads. Could Tom be among them—or had he been one of the wounded, lying on the field, horribly maimed and piteously crying out for water? That night she did something which would have shocked Luke and Will, but she knew that Tom would not disapprove so long as her heart was in her prayer. A deep seated feeling, thrust into the background by her recent acceptance of Protestantism, had been awakened in this hour of extreme anguish.

Sir Ralph Faulkner had a little chapel—a simple room with no gaudy ornaments—just a plain table, a reading desk, kneeling mats, and clear glass. Amalia knelt and looked up at the light shining, through one of these windows. She folded her hands and prayed to the Virgin Mary. She had no picture or image of the Mother of God, so she looked at the bright opening and fixed her mind on the beautiful, painted statues she had seen at her home in Salzburg. Later in the day she repeated these devotions; on rising, she was met by Lady Faulkner.

"A message for you in the hall, my dear," said the mistress of the house, kindly, noticing Amalia's confusion. "It is good news," whispered Lady Faulkner—but Amalia had no time to ask her to explain. She rushed out of the room to the hall to meet this bringer of glad tidings. It must be news of her dear Tom. Surely her prayer to the Virgin had been answered. It had indeed been answered, though not quite as Amalia had expected.

Tom had not been present at the Battle of Marston Moor. Having returned to his own regiment after Nantwich, he had been struck down by a malarial type of fever, but once more in the expert hands of his friend George, he had pulled through. Left behind for a few weeks convalescence when the army moved on, he was entrusted to the care of Annie White, a charitable woman and well-wisher, whose conscientious nursing brought him back to health. His old wound and his age were beginning to tell on him and Tom feared that his days as an active serviceman were numbered. True there were others equalling or exceeding him in age; he was no older for instance, than his Lieutenant General, Oliver Cromwell, the greatest man of the war. But Cromwell was an exceptional person; few could aspire to match his genius. No doubt many of the others of his age were feeling the weight of years too.

He longed for his dear Amalia. At the age of forty-five, at least ten more years of life would be normal, fifteen not unnatural, and twenty generous. His wish was to spend them all with her. And now there was Lynette! He hardly knew his pretty, young daughter yet. How much joy was owing to him for all the time he had missed! By the mercy of God an end would soon come to the war—one more battle like Marston Moor and the king's power would be forced to come to terms.

These hopes and the suggestion that she should join his relations in Cheshire, which he expressed to Amalia in his letter, strengthened her determination to brave all the hardships of the road to be united with those he loved and to await her husband's return in his own home. Tom had instructed his wife to await news from Nantwich, and it was about two weeks after the reports of Marston Moor had been received, that Mr Barton's servant arrived with the forewarning that his master was now lodged in Royston, and should be expected at Ashley on the morrow.

Preparations for the journey were brief, for Amalia had always been ready for some such summons. As soon as he had rested, Mr Barton was anxious to be on his way. The children were excited at the prospect of a new adventure; Mariana had almost forgotten the former taste of it on the journey from Salzburg; Karl, though younger, remembered sighting the pirate ship, and constantly talked about the possibility of another such encounter on the journey. Amalia had a strong feeling of dread at the thought of these men—land-pirates in this case, instead of water-pirates—but the journey proved less eventful than she had dared to hope; until they reached Peterborough they saw nothing of the war. Then, still within the sight of the squat towers of that cathedral, a great cloud of dust and the steady beat of drums heralded the approach of a column of marching soldiers.

Barton led the little party into a side lane, from which they saw line upon line of redcoats and greencoats passing with pikes and muskets shouldered, breastplates glinting, the officers riding high on their horses. A train of artillery followed, the heavy guns, pulled by oxen, moving slowly and laboriously along the dusty, stony surface of the road.

"A regiment of Lord Manchester's men, going out bravely arrayed. A different sight they'll be coming back, win or lose—battle-stained, bloody, and torn. Some folk care for causes and will suffer any kind of horror, even death, to promote them. For me life is to be lived in happiness, and I cannot see the enjoyment of material comforts as wickedness. If the King has his way, I must needs fall in with him; if Parliament wins, they will rule me better or maybe worse. I cannot feel strongly about this quarrel. Do not call me hard on those who do battle; it is the way I am made. And think now! If each and every person agreed like I do to live and let live, would not the world be a happier place? Come dear," he said, thinking he might have aroused fears in her for Tom's safety. "God will be with your man and bring him through."

During the journey, Barton drew quite close to Amalia; the two were really of very similar temperaments. He talked incessantly, telling her about Nantwich and her new family, digressing on many subjects—even giving her a lecture on salt-making.

His travels, particularly in the North of England, were however his favourite topic and he prided himself on showing Tom's young wife how expertly he had managed to arrange a long journey such as this. Amalia listened avidly to his talk. She thought him a lively and interesting old man, and his fund of information about her new home had already answered many of the questions she had been preparing to ask. The children, too, liked this new "uncle"—or was it "grandfather"? For, by the journey's end, he had with some presumption encouraged them to call him "Grandfather Barton" and to Amalia he had become plain "Matthew".

The freedom, of the travellers from molestation by highwaymen was maintained.

"I expect they are all in one or other of the armies where they can do their robbing and murdering and be paid for it, instead of swinging on the gallows; or maybe they have gone to join the clubmen."

The children overheard this remark, and it left them wondering what these strange clubmen should be.

"You'll see, you'll see," said Mr Barton to Karl's question; and see they did while passing through Leicestershire. Unlike the disciplined, even ranks of the marching soldiers, a great horde of men swarmed across the fields and assembled on the road. Some had swords and old muskets, but the majority carried only clubs, billhooks or pitchforks. The travellers watched them as they marched away—no stepping out to drumbeats this time, just a crowd of country folk following their leaders, who by their dress and deportment appeared to belong to a higher class—probably minor gentry. Among them, Amalia espied a clergyman and one who stood out from the rough countrymen by his standard buff coat and feathered hat. It could almost have been Tom—but not leading a rabble like this.

"They are banding together against both parties," said Barton. "Plagued by the exactions of the armies, the foraging and billeting of troops, they are telling them plainly that they want to be left in peace. Sometimes their support can be gained for a time if a commander is very persuasive, but they are demanding no less than a return to normality. This war will be the ruin of our country; the armies will find nothing to spare if the people cannot farm their land, tend their livestock and sell their produce. These people are telling the King and his Parliament what to do about it before it is too late."

"Can they do much with their primitive weapons against well-armed trained soldiers?" asked Amalia.

"Alone, I suppose very little; they would soon be mown down by a salvo of musket fire; but to face a determined enemy in front, while men with a purpose are hampering you in the rear, is no light matter."

There was no cheering or shouting as the grim procession passed. The children shrank back, but on seeing them, many of the clubmen waved in a friendly fashion, and the travellers went on their way reassured.

At Lichfield Barton learned that the way to Nantwich was completely open. Prince Rupert was still in Chester, but after his defeat at Marston Moor, much of the terror had gone out of his name. His scattered units had been defeated near Liverpool and in Wales; the Welsh forces and the remainder of the troops from Ireland were being harassed. The way had been prepared for Sir William Brereton to achieve his greatest aim—the capture of Chester.

The weather was fine, the going was good enough, so, God willing, they should complete the journey in two days. To Amalia and the children these last forty miles were the most tedious they had ever travelled. Not that the countryside lacked interest, but the mental picture of the place where Tom had lived throughout his early life, had aroused such expectancy within them that they chafed at the slow passing of each of the last miles which separated them from their goal. Thus the last hours seemed to stretch into eternity.

The actual arrival was an anti-climax, for, delayed by a short thunderstorm, it was growing dark when they reached the town walls. The children were weary, and even Amalia could not take her usual lively interest in the surroundings as they passed through Hospital Street gate into the town. The mud walls, scene of such fierce fighting in January, looked especially dismal in the gathering gloom. At first they seemed deserted, but then Amalia noticed the sentries patrolling the parapet. Then a change of guard commenced; the harsh sound of marching feet and barked orders sounded through the night air. She shuddered. It was a sharp reminder that the war was still on. Acute danger had passed now, but the town was still a garrison—the main headquarters of Parliament in Cheshire—so vigilance had to be maintained. Preparations for the reduction of Royalist Chester were being made from Nantwich, and it was still not known whether a fresh reversal of fortune would bring a new Cavalier army northwards to attack the Roundhead base.

A few people in the High Town stared at the travellers who had obviously come from afar; then recognizing Mr Barton, one of them greeted him respectfully and the others followed suit. There were some whisperings among them as the horses passed; they had heard of Barton's mission to the south and were anxious to see this strange lady and her children. Waving them brusquely aside, Barton turned his horse into a side street. He had decided to lodge them, for one night at his own house down by the water's edge. Amalia was glad of this; it would give her time to prepare herself and the children, to meet these new relations.

On the following morning, Matthew Barton, who had risen early and had been about his business for nearly two hours, returned home to accompany Amalia and the children to Mrs Ley's house. He was startled on seeing her dress, not because he disapproved of her appearance, but because he knew the effect it would have on others.

She was wearing a beautiful gown of green with a lace collar. The silken dress was cut away to show an embroidered yellow underskirt and she carried white gloves. A string of what Barton deemed to be semiprecious stones set off her white neck; her long ringlets, falling to her shoulders, were impeccably groomed; her face shone with pleasure and the expectation of a compliment.

"Beautiful!" said Mr Barton, clapping his hands. "But sadly not very suitable for the Mastersons—I doubt that even Mrs Ley would approve. You know, of course, that Tom is no lover of strict Puritan dress, but I am afraid your appearance as a Cavalier lady would shock your new relations and set tongues wagging in the town. Have you nothing simpler?"

Amalia went pale. She did not want to offend these people's sensibilities on the very first day.

"Nothing fit to wear," she replied. "I did not think that this would offend. Lady Faulkner complimented me whenever I wore it."

But Amalia was susceptible to the feelings of others even if she thought them wrong. She listened patiently as Barton explained;

"There is much division on this issue," he said. "We have the Cavalier lovelocks and the shornsheep Roundheads; there are the satins and velvets in gay colours of the court party on the one hand; on the other side we see coarse material of sombre hue—the men with their plain cloth suits and steeple-crowned hats, the women with their broad, white aprons and kerchiefs. One would think to hear them talk, that God made the world in black and white and brown, when we know he created it in many beautiful colours."

"Of course," he added, "there are many who believe, like I do, that we need not subscribe to the extremes of either party."

Amalia had, of course, already seen the plainly dressed Puritans during her stay in the south, but living on the estate of a knight and his lady who were not strict in such matters, she had given the propriety or impropriety of her costume little thought. Whenever she had gone beyond the confines of Sir Ralph's property she had been in the company of Lady Faulkner, and she had dressed as her friend did. Looking back, she could now see why neither of them had ever gone out attired extravagantly. She had not thought it of much importance, as during her whole stay at Ashley, she had never come into close contact with anyone of narrow Puritan views. Without due consideration, she had endeavoured to make herself as attractive as possible to impress her new relatives. She did not wish to appear inferior to Tom's former wife, Kate, in beauty or personality, and while hoping to be a credit to her husband and create a good impression on his family, she would unwittingly have had them to believe that she was a woman full of vanity who was mocking their beliefs.

Besides, she was anxious to please her new friend, so she removed her necklace and gloves and laid them on the table.

"I am sorry Matthew," she said. "I could not present myself like that even to make the right impression on my relatives, but I have the plain cloak I wore for riding and for my head that grey bonnet. Perhaps they will make me less conspicuous on the way to the house. Will Mr Masterson be present?" she asked nervously.

His reputation having gone before him, Amalia feared Will's disapproval more than that of any of the others.

"I have been informed that he is, indeed, here in Nantwich with Lynette, though your meeting with Alice will have to be postponed, an indisposition having forced her to remain at home in Walbury. Cheer up, young lady!" said Barton, playfully pinching her cheek. "They are not so grim, except for that fellow Blackshaw—a ranting Puritan, stiff as a ramrod, not a breath of humour in him. They want to offer Lynette up to him, but I am sure Tom will have something to say about that when he returns."

Amalia looked surprised. She had not heard of Lynette's proposed marriage.

"What does my little sister think of him?" she asked. "Is she very devout?"

"She's a good, dutiful girl but I take my granddaughter for one of my people, who would enjoy their all too short lives to the full and rejoice in all the favours of God—very like you my dear. You and Lynette will get along happily together."

The appearance of Amalia and her children in the street caused less interest than she had expected. It was late for the townsfolk, who had been up and about their daily tasks long before Amalia, weary from her long journey, had even risen. Some soldiers were drilling on the open land behind the church, trailing pikes, shouldering pikes, advancing in line, marching in file. Behind them, close to the wall, some artillery was parked and a number of horses presumably used to draw the baggage waggons or cannon, were grazing peacefully. The earthworks were a dreadful eyesore; many of the gardens, especially near the fortifications, had been trampled down; several houses, burned out in the siege, were mere shells; others had been taken over for the use as sentry posts or guardhouses. Shabby as it was, the whole place had an air of home about it for Amalia. The timbered houses, the old church, the brine pit where Tom had once worked, the clutter of salt-houses by the river, all spoke of her beloved husband. Something of his spirit seemed to be in the very wood and stones, welcoming her to his birthplace. It was thus with confidence that she followed Matthew down Hospital Street towards Mrs Ley's home. If the town itself could inspire such feelings in her, surely Tom's own flesh and blood would grant her and his own little children a warm and friendly reception to match it.

Mrs Ley's first impression of Tom's family was very favourable. As Matthew Barton had predicted, she considered Amalia overdressed, but she put it down to foreign ignorance of English ways, even though she knew that her daughter-in-law had been in the country for close on two years. Tom was, of course, a mature man when he chose her, but she knew he was a person of strong passions and she had feared he might have taken a German peasant girl as his wife if she had had sufficient physical charm to recommend herself. But perhaps that was a harsh judgement on her son. His choices had always been women of both beauty and intelligence. He was only a lad when he married Kate and that union had been a success; his love for her had not cooled as time went on, and there was no reason why this Amalia should not grant him the same happiness. Margery's own marriage to Roger Ley had been a conventional one—arranged with little reference to her. She had accepted it as natural; in his time her father had married at the bidding of his own father, and without great passion, he had had "much happiness with a handsome wife". But Tom, who was capable of feeling great surges of love, had never failed to find the right woman for himself. In both cases he had aimed high—yes, it was unjust to think of the German peasant woman.

Both his wives were from families of some standing, who had brought him good dowries, so it appeared that his choice had been limited to some extent by common sense. Both marriages had helped him to establish himself, first as an English man of business and then as a continental merchant. Yet, setting these considerations apart, Tom's romantic notions which she had so often heard ridiculed, had proved themselves to Margery. There was more than one road to happiness. Alice and Will represented one way; Tom, Kate and Amalia the other. In the days of Tom's first marriage, Margery had not seen matters clearly; now she could rejoice that she had Amalia—the kind of girl she would have chosen for her son.

Luke Blackshaw's service as chaplain with the Parliamentary forces in Lancashire had been short but eventful. Mighty Lathom House was his first stop. There Fairfax and later Colonel Rigby were defied by a woman—a wellborn French Countess, wife of the Earl of Derby—but nonetheless a woman. Luke's invective against this Amazon, had been lurid, his writing vivid and full of details of a great siege for the Parliamentary annals. It had been a series of humiliations—insults from the Countess, the initial ineffectiveness of the bombardment, the lack of success in mining, and then the capture of the great mortar which could have won the day for Parliament. Finally the coming of Rupert—the Prince Robber of Luke's chronicle—put an end to immediate hopes of victory. "God in his wisdom had seen fit to chastise the party of His cause with the failure of an enterprise", and they drew off to Bolton.

Worse was yet to come. Rupert and Lord Derby took the town by storm. Luke escaped with his life but many were put to the sword. Feelings that God had deserted his cause, his prodigious labour to suppress his unchaste desire for Lynette, brought on an enthusiasm for army life waning, but at the same time his religious fervour increased. The judgements the Lord had sent his party were due to insufficient zeal, and it would require redoubled efforts to make themselves worthy of his favours again. Luke preached fiery sermons to the soldiers, denouncing the Book of Common Prayer—that idol such as a cross or gilded image—that refuge of the lazy and ignorant clergy— and he filled out his chronicle with more denunciations of Papism and high churchmanship. Then two events raised his spirits and made these efforts seem worthwhile. The victory of Parliament at Marston Moor showed that God had not deserted His people. Furthermore Blackshaw had a call. In its concrete form it was a letter from Mr Malbon, Vicar of Walbury, informing him that the living of Marton, near Nantwich, was his for the taking. What a challenge! All idolatrous ornaments would be removed, all sinful forms of worship banished. He would make the church fit for prayer and praise and the people worthy of the Most High who would see their perfection and dwell among them.

A few days after Amalia's visit to her mother-in-law, Luke paid a call on his friend and former schoolmaster, William Masterson.

"It must be decided once and for all—this very day," he said to himself as he rose on that fair August morning.

It was nearly three years since he had been promised Lynette. He would tolerate no more delay in announcing a betrothal. All this pandering to the girl's whims and fancies was quite unseemly—unChristian in fact. She had no idea of her proper obligation to those who had brought her up; and her father's views on social responsibility and the relationship between men and women were highly suspect, if not downright dangerous. But there was his dear friend, Will, and his spouse, the faithful Alice. It would be worth suffering these irritations from Lynette and her unconventional parents to be united with such a pious family—a shining example of a truly Christian home.

In this frame of mind he rode over to Walbury; he was light of heart, quite cheered by the thought that he would soon be Will's son-in-law and would have a wife who, once her stupid immature resistance had been broken, would grace his vicarage at Marton. He believed his sinful lust to be under control, for he had been less troubled by fantasies of the girl of late—but it was a constant battle. Marriage would relieve him of this strain. *"Better to marry than to burn"*—who can burn in wedlock? He had, however, to admit that though he disapproved strongly of Lynette's attitude, it was a fact of the case, and to win her he would have to change his tactics. He would have to use stratagems instead of a frontal assault. He was also curious to see this woman that Ley had brought home with him. The first reports he had received had been most disturbing. Rumour had it that she had appeared dressed like a Cavalier lady on her first day in Nantwich, had crossed herself in church, and had said prayers in Latin instead of plain English. He had not met Will once since Amalia's arrival, and though Masterson had not denounced Ley's wife, the cool way in which he had spoken of her, suggested that he did not fully approve of her behaviour.

On approaching the Mastersons' house, Luke could see the slight figure of Lynette moving around the garden. He had a thrill of pleasure which gave the lie to his belief that he had subdued his unchaste desires. Rather than go into the house and present himself to Will and Alice, he decided to approach the young lady directly, so preparing a little speech and putting on the least severe expression he could manage, he entered the garden. Lynette was now sitting on the stone seat at the far end with a basket by her side, and she did not appear to have made any progress in gardening. In fact she was reading a book which she laid aside on Blackshaw's approach.

"Pardon me for disturbing your studies, Mistress Lynette," he apologized, hoping that it was an improving book she had been reading.

She did not offer to show him the title and in turn he did not question her about it.

"Lynette," he said surprisingly tenderly. "There must soon be an understanding between us. This present uncertainty cannot continue."

"Must there, Mr Blackshaw?" replied Lynette turning her large, beautiful eyes on the preacher; then removing the basket she indicated the seat.

"Sit down, please. I feel uncomfortable while you remain standing."

"There was talk of marriage once," he said, seating himself beside her. "It is time to fulfil that promise."

"No, Mr Blackshaw, I was not formally promised, as you well know, and there is no need to go over old ground again. I am sure you must realize by now that we are quite unlike in temperament and would make anything but a perfect match—a fact which Uncle Will is coming to accept and which my father knew from the start."

A strange, uncomfortable feeling came over the girl as she spoke. The man was staring at her in an unaccountable way. His eyes were fixed on her—searching, penetrating; his face had reddened. She saw sweat starting on his brow.

It was not rage. She had feared Luke would boil over and pour out biblically founded reproaches at her, reminding her of her position as a woman—her duty to God, her duty to her uncle, some fantasies about her father, and all the rest. Instead he just kept on staring at her. It was as if he were stripping her of her clothes, revealing her nakedness to his searching eye, delighting in his lustful thoughts—for now she could see that they were there behind the facade of his pious speeches.

Blackshaw spoke so suddenly that he startled her.

"Lynette," he said hoarsely, "I love you. I want you to be mine. Tell Uncle Will and your father that you will marry me."

The girl's immediate reaction was to burst into a peal of laughter. These words coming from the mouth of the solemn minister changed a highly unpleasant situation into one of   comedy.

"Mr Blackshaw!" she said. "You surprise me. I never expected to hear such words from you."

She rose, from her seat, but Luke slid down on his knees and stretching up, he tried to grasp her hands.

"God forgive me for it. I have battled against it, but I am doomed. God forgive me, Lynette, but I love you. The beauty of your face and form has tormented me constantly in these weeks past."

Lynette's colour rose.

"Stand up, Mr Blackshaw," she cried angrily. "You have surely no idea how comical you look down there. I say you do not love me if you have to battle so valiantly against it. Why is it wickedness to love a girl and enjoy happiness with her? Must you lash yourself with whips and scorpions for such a natural thing?"

Blackshaw began to open his mouth but no words came out as Lynette rattled on.

"Oh yes, I know—the Fall of Man—Eve the Temptress—the lure of the flesh—the place of woman in society. I have heard it all; but, Mr Blackshaw, I assure you I do not want a man who takes me as a burden on his soul."

"Stand up at once!" she repeated, stamping her foot. "Your proposal is sheer hypocrisy. It is not love you feel for me. I judge it to be carnal lust which you have tried so hard to supress. You have done nothing but put me down with Bible quotations and talk of improving my mind or leading me by the hand to heavenly bliss. Now you come to me and speak of love when you mean lust, which I daresay you hope to satisfy before returning to your holy speeches and reproaches. Go away sir! I have a quotation which you can take with you— Matthew 23 verse 27, if you care to recall it: *'You are like a whited sepulchre which appears beautiful outward, but is within full of dead men's bones and all uncleanness'*. Do you not see, sir, that it is not enough to appear righteous unto men and be full of hypocrisy?"

Blackshaw was staggered by this outburst. That a woman—a mere girl—should rail at him like that! It was the supreme humiliation for him to have chosen the only one in the whole district who would have dared. It was a streak of bad blood in her, inherited from that irreligious father, to be so rebellious against one who offered her a position of standing as a minister's wife and a chance to be educated by her husband until she came to a full realization of God's purpose. Such ingratitude! Such unmaidenly arrogance! He rose to his feet; his hat had fallen off his head; he stooped to pick it up without a word. Lynette noticed that his face had turned from crimson to grey. Luke knew in his heart that the girl had spoken the truth, but he would not admit her right to tell him so. Her darts had struck home; he had been guilty of hypocrisy; he was not offering love from his heart. This struggle between desire and discipline within him had made his offer to her appear as a sacrifice of his integrity.

But why should he offer love from his heart? Need love be closely related to marriage? It has been said that affection is false—we cannot trust it to stay firm. Blackshaw was not the man to see the other side of the coin for long. His pride had been hurt, not only by the refusal, but by the way in which it had been made.

"Your uncle will have something to say about this," he stammered as if Lynette's speech had knocked the breath out of him. The girl now felt completed confident. She had the minister at her mercy.

"Mr Blackshaw," she said with emphasis, "as far as I am concerned the matter is closed. If you wish to marry me, you will have

236

to win my true father's permission, and that, I fear, will prove as difficult as taking a jewel from King Charles's crown."

Luke pushed his hat down firmly on his head and dusted his knees after his unseemly contact with the gravel path.

"Well," he said," in that case I have nothing to say."

He turned on his heel and would have quitted the garden immediately. Mounting his horse, which was tethered outside the wall, he would have ridden away without another word, had not Will who had just become aware of his visit, stopped him by the gate.

"Luke!" he called, giving him a questioning glance. "Surely you are not leaving without a word for your old friend. Come inside and take a little wine with me. I am sure you would wish to refresh yourself before your dusty journey back to Marton."

He darted a reproving look at Lynette who had come up towards the house and was standing behind Luke, her confused expression clearly betraying the fact that she had given the clergyman serious offence by her attitude and speech.

The two disappeared inside the house; Lynette walked slowly round the garden, her head bent, deep in thought. She partly regretted having been so forthright with Blackshaw, not because she had put a wearisome, self-righteous man, for whom she had lost all respect, in his place, but because she feared she might have hurt Uncle Will and Aunt Alice whom she loved—a sentiment which even the coming of her father and stepmother had not diminished. Lynette was a feeling girl. Her heart was large enough to accommodate two fathers, a mother and a "sister".

She began cutting the autumn flowers, laying them in her basket and tidying up the bed; but she had no mind for gardening, so she returned to the stone seat. She picked up her book and turned over the pages, but she had no real desire to read either. The opening and closing of the garden gate and a horse's steps outside the wall announced the departure of Blackshaw. Lynette did not raise her eyes until the familiar footsteps on the gravel path warned her of Will's approach. Her heart beat faster as she feared his displeasure, but her uncle's look was of pity and tenderness, not anger. He seated himself beside Lynette and she turned her face towards him.

"The Lord has guided me in this matter," he said. "I have told Mr Blackshaw that he must look elsewhere for a bride. There will be no betrothal."

Will had expected that Lynette would show pleasure and gratitude at the announcement; but instead, she burst into a flood of tears.

"Why, child," he said softly. "Surely that does not make you unhappy."

"No, Father," sobbed the girl. "I am not unhappy. You have lifted such a weight from my heart."

"My dear!" exclaimed Will, surprised at this depth of feeling. "I had no idea that you would find marriage with Mr Blackshaw so distressing. I still believe he is a good man—a little pompous, perhaps, but a true Christian to whom the Word is more than the World; but I love you dearly and I would not see you miserable. You are only seventeen. God is just, and in due time he will send you someone to whom you can cleave and in whom you can combine your love of Christ with the love of a husband. Come!" he said, briskly, as he rose and endeavoured to cheer her up. "Wipe your eyes and take your flowers. Aunt Alice will welcome them to bring some colour to the house."

Lynette threw her arms round Will.

"Thank you, Father," she said, brightening up. "There is a man I would marry."

Will looked quizzically at her.

"No," she said. "I have not seen him yet; but I am sure that he is coming and when he does, I will recognize him at once."

Luke Blackshaw's humiliation at the hands of Lynette was only a temporary chastisement. Soon he recovered his old fire and was preaching with as much vigour as before. Among his congregation was a girl somewhat older than Lynette, by the name of Margaret Whitworth. The third surviving daughter of a yeoman farmer, she was a hefty country girl and could make no pretence to being a beauty, but her family aspired to some social standing. The parents were by no means as devout as Luke would have wished, but he noticed that they showed him more than the usual deference and he detected a much more amenable disposition in the girl. He had already learned that fair women could turn even the holiest head, and he accepted Margaret's inferior physical charms as a blessing, since they did not arouse him as Lynette had done. As they walked together across the glebe land behind the church, Margaret listening patiently to his holy words, Luke was sure that this time he had captured beauty beneath the surface. God had directed him to the one who would not reject his word and dispute his judgement.

" *'All that glisters is not gold'*. Well said poet! Here is the way to bliss!"

More serious than his loss of Lynette was the break with Will. Although there had been no hard words at their last meeting, Will's tame acceptance of his foster daughter's wilful rejection of him as a suitor, rankled with him. He had never forgotten how his old tutor strictly but kindly had set him on the right path in life. It would be sheer ingratitude to attack him. Thomas Ley was away on service, and even Blackshaw would hardly dare to tackle the major in open combat. Lynette was out of his reach too, so he turned his attention on Amalia who was slowly but steadily advancing her position with the people of Nantwich.

Fighting was going on along the Welsh border, around Chester, and in the neighbourhood of Nantwich. Parliament had been generally victorious, but there had been casualties who had been brought to the town. Prince Rupert had gone down the border of Wales—his destination Bristol—but other commanders had taken up the cudgels with Sir William Brereton. Amalia, coming from a family of apothecary surgeons, had picked up considerable knowledge and skill which put her ahead of most of those who were rendering assistance to the sick and wounded. So the "young German lady" was in great demand whenever casualties were brought in.

Margery Ley took to Tom's wife from the first, more in fact than she had ever done to Kate; and the children, were a constant delight for her. Amalia's unruffled nature and lack of condescension endeared her to the old lady; and her pleasant words, often quaintly pronounced but accompanied by cheerful smiles, won over most of the others with whom she came into contact. Even the Mastersons were disarmed by the young woman's easy-going manner and Will's circle of friends heard nothing but praise for his German sister-in-law. In the matter of dress Amalia felt that she could not comfortably wear the full Puritan attire, but she agreed to avoid the brightest materials and contrasting colours, and she never displayed anything more than her simplest rings or necklaces when she appeared in public—especially in church. Nevertheless, she still stood out in a crowd as a well-dressed lady, the people of the town accepting this slight reformation as sufficient to show her willingness to conform—and nobody demanded more of her.

On November 4th 1644, a general thanksgiving was held to mark a number of important Parliamentarian victories in the Northwest. The castles of Powis and Ruthin in Wales had been taken with gold to the value of five thousand pounds and other rich spoils. Liverpool had fallen and Parliament was in the ascendancy again. It was an intriguing prospect for Amalia when she heard that Luke Blackshaw would preach at this service. She knew that the match between him and Lynette was no longer under consideration, but she had never been told the full story of her stepdaughter's spirited rejection of her unwanted suitor. As soon as she heard that he would be in the pulpit, she was curious to see this Luke Blackshaw and judge the man for herself. What was to follow, she certainly did not expect.

Blackshaw, in his turn, was anxious to see the German woman who had so insidiously wormed her way into the hearts of people who did not usually take readily to foreigners. His initial prejudice against her for having been a Roman Catholic had in no way lessened; the rumours which had come to his ears had confirmed it; his wrath engendered by the rebuff from Lynette urged him on to hurt someone else, so poor Amalia became the target of one of his most vitriolic attacks.

As he stood up in the pulpit, even though he began in his usual indifferent way before his quickening enthusiasm for the subject brought fire into his words, Amalia felt oppressed by his presence. She was close to the wooden pulpit which stood on the north side of the nave—a carved oak three-decker from a previous reign, chosen by Blackshaw in preference to the mediaeval stone pulpit he used on the

240

occasion of his sermon to the Royalist prisoners. His theme was, of course, the mercy of the Lord in delivering his people from the clutches of their sworn enemies, and his text from the eighth chapter of Romans, was predictable: *"If God be for us, who can be against us?"*

He dwelt on the elements which had made them worthy to receive this mercy from the Almighty. His eyes darted shafts of fire; his gestures assumed theatrical extravagance, just as on all other occasions when he reached the climax of his sermon.

"We are the elect. To us God will ever show his favours if we hold to the purity of our worship—suffer no canker in our bosoms—no tempting corruption in our midst... vanities... worldliness... immodest dress... lascivious movements... Romish practices..." The words poured steadily out of Blackshaw's mouth.

Amalia began, to feel faint:

"The Day of Judgement! Dies irae!"

She had heard that said before. Those coals of fire glared at her. The sweeping hand of the preacher sawed the air and pointed her out to the whole assembly. He was holding her up as Jezebel, like to the one who had brought corruption to Israel and had caused the wrath of God to fall upon His people. He believed—or wished to believe—that it was she who had seduced Tom and the Mastersons and had caused Lynette to defy him.

"There is one among us—"

He was telling the people that her presence in their midst was offensive and would cause God to withdraw his favours. What had she done to deserve this calumny? She had tried to understand their prejudices and do nothing to shock them. She had moderated her style of dress and had strictly avoided doing anything which could be described as Romish—a difficult task for one who had venerated saints, told her beads, and attended Latin Mass for many years. She had made friends among the townsfolk and had attended to their wounded. This man Blackshaw was so hard—so full of hatred for a fellow Christian. She looked up at his menacing figure—black-robed in the dark oaken pulpit like a spirit of the night still breathing fire against her. As she looked, the shadows seemed to be closing upon him. His shape was hard to define in the dark mist. She felt she was going to faint.

"Sweet Jesus!" murmured the distressed woman. "Sweet Jesus, have mercy upon me!"

The preacher stopped. There was a dead silence. Though she had spoken, only softly, he had heard her words. But though the Lord was ready to show mercy to Tom's unfortunate wife, Blackshaw was not. As he returned to the attack, Amalia rose from her seat. Mr Barton who was in the pew opposite, saw her first unsteady steps in the aisle, and taking her hand, he led her out into the porch. Blackshaw thought his triumph over the young woman was complete, but the sermon was by no means over. There were heads turned as Amalia and Barton walked out, and sensing approval for them among the congregation, the preacher judged that it would take at least another twenty minutes of his most inspiring words to rally his forces.

Matthew Barton comforted Amalia in a fatherly fashion.

"Do not take on so, dear," he said. "It was cruel, but that is Blackshaw's way. You will now see how relieved I am that there is to be no betrothal to Lynette. He sees our Lord crying *'Woe unto you, scribes and Pharisees'*, but cannot picture him saying: *'Come unto me all ye that are heavyladen. Do not weep or let your heart be troubled'*. Blackshaw thinks he has won a famous victory—cast out a devil and made the body whole. Go back and face him out. Show him that you love the Lord no less than he does, with the feeling of a true, compassionate Christian, which is strange to him. Go, my dear! Remember we all love you."

Amalia was a happy person, not given to weeping, but she found it hard to suppress her emotion. With a grateful look at Mr Barton, she pressed his hand and returned with a dignified step into the church. Blackshaw had not finished speaking, but he stopped, as on reaching her pew, Amalia fell on her knees and folded her hands, the preacher towering above her. In a moment she raised her head and looked straight up at him, challenging him to renew his attack. He returned her stare before turning over the pages of his bible on the desk. He raised his hand preparatory to denouncing his Jezebel again, then instead of exploding into a new outburst of wrath, he repeated the text of his sermon, closed his bible, and descended the steps of the pulpit.

20. GOD IS OUR STRENGTH

May the twenty-second, 1645 was a day of alarm in Nantwich. Bells were rung backwards, a public fast was held and prayers for help were offered up, as the town was in great danger. For days now, work had been going on to strengthen the walls and lay in provisions in readiness for another siege. The King was coming with a great army, reported to number twelve thousand men led by himself and Prince Rupert, and moreover it had reached Market Drayton, a mere dozen miles from the town. Sir William Brereton was ordered not to oppose him but to withdraw and unite with other units. Parliament hoped to crush the King's forces with the large army—the New Model which had been formed early in the year.

The old generals had been found wanting and by a Self Denying Ordinance, which forced MP's to lay down their commissions, they had been excluded. But there was no law against reappointment and Cromwell was the obvious choice for Lieutenant General of Horse in the new force. Fairfax was Captain General, Skippon, a professional soldier, Commander of the Infantry. Bright in their red coats, disciplined on the lines of Cromwell's Ironsides, the twenty one thousand men of this New Model Army would be liable for service anywhere in the country.

This reorganisation meant a fresh parting for Thomas Ley and George Waldheim. As a major under Cromwell, Tom had a strong sense of fulfilment. The work he was doing in the cause was important, but he was finding that though his will was strong, it became increasingly hard to sustain it. The prospect of fighting on his home ground again would have given him added inspiration, but it was not to be. Charles declined to be "trapped in the angle of Cheshire" and turned away towards the eastern Midlands, through Stone, Uttoxeter and finally Leicester; the sack of which, like that of Bolton, remained a blot on the reputation of the King's army.

The armies were moving steadily together, and as dawn broke on June 14th parties of the New Model sighted the Cavaliers. By eight o' clock they were facing one another on the grassy ridges of the open Leicestershire countryside—the last great army that the King could muster and the new instrument of Parliament's power. It made a brave show and even Cromwell, to whom it was no new spectacle, was moved by the banners, flashing breastplates, cloaks and scarves, streaming in the morning light—"the things which were", coming to oppose the "things which were not". But the "things which were not", could claim superiority in numbers by as much as two to one and their predominance in cavalry was even more telling.

As Major Ley drew up his squadrons to meet the cavalry of Sir Marmaduke Langdale, he had a prescient feeling that this would be his last battle. As he rode up and down along his sector, the major's mind went back to those other occasions at Lützen, Nördlingen, Edgehill, Winceby and Nantwich. He had never had this feeling before; then he had always been confident that matters would turn out well for him. He thought of the word for the day that the general had given them: "God is our Strength"; the Cavaliers had the more mundane call of "Queen Mary". As his horse pawed the ground and waited for Cromwell's order to advance, Tom's head sank on his breast. The awful certainty that, win or lose, this battle would mean the end for him, weighed heavily on his mind. Fighting was already in progress on the other flank. Rupert's men had broken General Ireton's ranks; the Parliamentary infantry was giving ground.

The din from the far side of the field did not break Tom's train of thought. God's hand had always been upon him in his hour of need. This time would be no exception. He felt sure there was more work for him to do, more happiness to bring to his dear wife and children. As he waited the depression began to lift. He murmured the words "God is our Strength" as he had done many times before on other fields. Then he repeated it with more emphasis and half-aloud. The fury of battle was exploding in the centre of the Parliamentary lines. "God is our Strength," he declared firmly, as if dictating orders to his second-in-command. Certainty that God was with him flowed through his mind and he lifted up his head high. "God is our Strength!" he cried out in a voice which had recovered all its old quality; then as the General called out, "March!" Tom raised his sword and his battle cry rang out, full of assurance and determination, across the serried ranks of horsemen—a shout which was taken up by line after line of riders—

the triumphant declaration of faith which was to be their word for the day: "God is our Strength!"

Tom's expectation that God would see him through the day was justified, but so was his foreknowledge that it would be his last fight. Gravely wounded in the thick of the battle with sword cuts and a pistol shot, at the moment when Sir Marmaduke's Northern horse was breaking, he was carried to a dressing station at the rear of the army near the village of Naseby. The wounds in his right arm were severe and for some time it seemed likely that they would take it off, but the surgeon had more ability than the common run of medical men and he was able to save it, though the injuries left it paralysed and his skill did not extend to restoring its power. The thrust in his body was less dangerous and the shot had grazed his head, wounding him without becoming embedded in his flesh. From Naseby the stricken major was taken in a coach to Northampton where many of the wounded had been collected to form a local hospital. As he lay on his bed of pain, his mind went back to the time when he had received his last serious wounds at Nördlingen and the conditions under which he had suffered. He thought of the enigmatic Leopold Brunner and the busy George Waldheim who had acted so resolutely to save him. Now he was in more comfortable surroundings and others were giving him their best attention. He thanked God that twice in his lifetime he had been snatched from the jaws of death by such friends and comrades.

The first news that a great victory had been won at Naseby meant little to Tom as he struggled for life. He had taken part in the charge of Cromwell's horse until with a cry of "Queen Mary!" Sir Marmaduke's men engaged his front line. Then all he had seen was a flying mass of horses' legs, falling men, dust and smoke, until dragged from the whirlpool of riders and beasts by rescuing hands, he had been carried away to the dressing station. Only gradually, as the fierce fever abated, did Tom become sufficiently well to realize the importance of the victory—a thousand Royalists slain, four thousand prisoners captured, all their guns, waggons and coaches, and the King's entire correspondence taken.

This last find was extremely important, for it revealed Charles's attempts to get men and money from the King of Denmark, the King of France, the Prince of Orange, and the Duke of Lorraine, and to bring an Irish Confederate Army over to England. Charles's last great army had been defeated; the papers published under the title of *"The*

King's Cabinet Opened" destroyed goodwill and deepened distrust at a time when the harassed monarch needed more help.

Major Ley's hospital was a rectory on the outskirts of Northampton where he was tended by the minister's lady and some of the soldiers' wives who had been enrolled as nurses. At first his case was very demanding. Not many months had passed since he had recovered from his sickness at the time of Marston Moor and this new fever was just as deadly. For a time he hovered between life and death but the thread was not broken. Once or twice the nurses thought he had gone, but the dark spectre of death gave way to the light of life and hope. Lying in his room with a glimpse of the blue August sky, he began for the first time in many months to ponder over the future. For two years now, military life had once again mapped out his days for him and it was many years since he had had to make a fresh start. The war would not last for ever—after this latest victory probably not more than a few months; the end to his army service would be as he had prophesied—on the field of Naseby. What would he do afterwards?

It was the minister's wife who first put the idea into his head—a little, kindly woman of middle age, plainly dressed as befitted her station. Tom thought she must have once been very attractive and he admitted that she still was, in a matronly way.

One evening she had brought her patient some warm broth, and she sat beside him as usual. He was telling her about his early life in the salt works. He never tried to conceal his humble origin and found it a source of genuine pride that he should have risen from being a common briner to become a successful merchant and a major in Cromwell's cavalry. But there was no element of vainglory in his words. He admitted that he had constantly striven to advance himself and his cause, but God had been with him and that had assured his success.

"Will you return to salt making when you leave the army?" the little lady asked. "You know the industry from the bottom upwards. Could you not become master of your own salt works or a purveyor of the product?"

Tom explained the difficulties involved in trying to make salt by private enterprise—the restrictive laws of walling which as far as he knew still operated in Nantwich.

"Is there not somewhere else, close by, but outside their jurisdiction, where you could find a spring and have a salt works built? You could install the latest equipment—pumps and those iron pans you described to me. And use coal instead of wood for fuel. Surely, major, the idea appeals to you?"

Tom started with a violence which made his wounds twitch. The excitement caused by this sudden idea caused his conscientious nurse some concern.

"I hope I have said nothing to cause you pain," she said apologetically. "Lie back and take some rest. These matters need not concern you yet. I will bring you a warm posset later."

He broke off considering his plans for the future on the arrival of Mr Hill, who prompted by his wife, had come at this moment to say some prayers over Tom. Like Mrs Hill, the minister took his duties towards the patients very seriously and earnestly prayed with them at night and in the morning. So many an officer in the torments of pain or fever, was thankful for the soothing hands of the lady and the comforting words of her husband. This man was no ranting preacher. Tom liked his calm Christian message, not tarnished with Papism or High Churchmanship, but reasoned and sincere. When the minister had gone, Tom's mind returned to Mrs Hill's suggestion. She was right; he had the experience and ability to carry out such a plan if the right opportunities came his way. Why did he not think of it before? There was precedent for it. Sir Robert Needham had established works a few miles outside Nantwich at Baddington. Salt was made, too, in the lands of Sir Thomas Smith on the other side of the river. When his mind became clearer he would be able to think out the way he should go about it. Hatherton, Baddington, Dirtwich; there were several minor wiches along the winding river.

He lay back. As Mistress Hill had said there was no urgency. When the time came God would be with him to guide him.

The New Model Army had wheeled round to the west after Naseby, achieving victories at Langport, Bridgwater and Sherborne, followed by the capture of Bristol and Rupert's eventual dismissal by the King. The scene of action had moved away from Tom. Sometimes, as he recovered his strength, he felt a momentary urge to be in the thick of the action once more, but these moods passed with the realization that a soldier of forty six, weakened by two severe bouts of fever in less than a year, with an arm practically useless to wield a sword, a man who for a long time would scarcely be able to sit astride a horse, would be of little service to the cause of Parliament.

The Rectory garden was a pleasant place for recuperation. When he had sufficiently recovered, Tom, while enjoying a leisurely stroll along its shady paths, worked out his plans for the future. He was now realigned to a less active role in the struggle, and it was with few misgivings that he applied to be released on the grounds of unfitness for further service. The reply he received pleased him even more than a simple affirmative. He would be permitted to return home and join the garrison at Nantwich in a staff post supervising the war effort in his own county.

There were officers, civilians and ex-officers on these shire committees. At first they had been composed mainly of minor parliamentary gentry, but later expansion had brought in men of industry and administrative ability from lower social orders. Apart from overall control of operations against the King, they were responsible for collecting voluntary subscriptions, the levying of the bimonthly tax or assessments, and the sequestration of the estates of delinquents. As the war moved away from Nantwich, the town became too remote to be a convenient base for some of the work and Forward Headquarters were established for the Parliamentary committees a few miles from where the action was around Chester.

Supplied with newssheets, Tom kept in touch with the progress of the war and speculated on the possibility of a march northwards by the King in hope of linking up with the Marquess of Montrose who still managed to win victories for him in Scotland. This would mean an inevitable intensification of the struggle in his native county. He wrote a letter to his wife over which he shed both tears of joy and sadness; a reply came back full of sunshine and hope. He rejoiced in the goodness of God who had linked his destiny with that of his dear Amalia. Peace was just around the corner. The final phase in his life would be the best of all.

At length the day came for Tom Ley's departure. He took a last look tinged with regret, at the Rectory where he had been granted a new lease of life, and his leave of the minister's wife who had afforded him such excellent treatment. Amid all the excitement and joy of being able to return to Amalia, he suffered a pang of sorrow when he remembered that he was not likely to see the good lady again. The influence some people have on one's life is out of all proportion to the time in which they pass through it. Mrs Hill had not only saved him from death by her careful nursing, but she had set him on the road to a new career with an inspired suggestion. In the full length of his life these few weeks could only be the briefest of interludes between the end of an active military career and the resumption of civilian life, yet their importance to him could not be overestimated. He had been healed, uplifted spiritually, and was leaving with a new aim in life.

Tom embraced Mrs Hill and the minister sent him on his way with a blessing:

"*We know that we are of God*," he said earnestly. "*Hereby know we too that we dwell in him and he in us, because he has given us of his pirit.*"

On September 24th, ten days after Major Ley's arrival in Nantwich from his convalescence at Northampton, King Charles's final attempt to link up with the loyal forces of Montrose ended with the destruction of his last sizeable army before the walls of Chester.

After a lull during the summer months, pressure on Chester had increased, culminating in a big attack in September. Five hundred horsemen, two hundred dragoons and seven hundred foot soldiers advanced during the night of the nineteenth. They penetrated the city defences and occupied the eastern suburbs, but the besieged rammed up the Eastgate with earth and dung and issued out from a sally port upon them. They were driven back, but managed to fire houses in the suburbs to deny their enemies cover. Then, on the twenty second of the month, two pieces of Roundhead ordnance made a gaping hole in the wall. The defenders rushed to this breach with beds and woolpacks to block up the hole. The Parliamentarian soldiers, fortified with alcohol and gunpowder, entered the gap, but were thrown back leaving their dead lying thick upon the ground.

The breach had been closed, but the position was precarious; without outside help it seemed likely that the city would soon fall. Such was the need to hold on to it, that King Charles decided to lead an army in person to the relief of this loyal place. Exultation prevailed in Chester. Everyone expected a speedy defeat of the enemy now that the King was near.

"Hold out for another twenty four hours," said Charles's messenger to Lord Byron. "Grant His Majesty that and he will not fail you."

In Nantwich events had come full circle. The king was only twenty miles away again. Mr Bostock, Tom's clerk at the Committee of Sequestrations brought him the news that Charles had reached Chester.

"He slipped in by the back door from Wales," observed Bostock with a worried look. "It will stiffen the courage of Byron's men. Should Sir William's siege be broken, they will be free to set out on a re-conquest of Cheshire. Imagine the sight of hordes of avenging Cavaliers pouring out of Chester. The "Turkish Lord" will avenge his humiliation before our town. Remember Barthomley, Major, and how poor Protestants were barbarously used there. "

"I do remember it," countered Tom, "although I was not there myself . But I remember Naseby, too,—and Marston Moor and Holly Day here at Nantwich. They may cheer their supposed saviour as much as they like in Chester, but I do believe their power is broken. Be of good cheer, Master Bostock. We cried "God is our Strength!" at Naseby and it was not mere vanity. Do not fear the king or bloody Byron. The Lord will continue to preserve us from ruin as he has done unto this day."

Bostock was silent. He was not fully convinced. In general he believed that God was on his side, but His mysterious ways puzzled a mere clerk to the War Council. Even those who firmly believed suffered periodic setbacks. Testing? Yes, but testing could be full of unpleasantness.

Tom could not help wondering how George was faring. It was sad that their paths had divided, but his friend had joined the Northern Army, so he would be coming up with General Poyntz if that commander were chosen to oppose King Charles at Chester. Wherever George was, his faith would sustain him. Just before they parted, the young man had used the phrase which later became the field word at Naseby:

"Der Herrgott ist unsere Stärke." That was the truth, the comfort and the inspiration—in German or in English.

Meanwhile Colonel General Sydenham Poyntz, commander of the Northern Army, originally a runaway apprentice who had risen in the world and had served on both sides in the Thirty Years War, had been watching Charles's movements. Taking another route, he came upon the royal troops just outside the walls of Chester. There was a hot fight on Rowton Moor and the Roundheads were repulsed. But the king, who was now in the city, failed to take advantage of this opportunity, even though he was informed of it by an intrepid officer who paddled across the Dee in a tub.

"God with us!" cried the Roundheads as they counterattacked. Hacking and slashing in a terrible storm, firing in each other's faces, the armies locked in combat, until a fierce charge by Poyntz's men, sure that the Lord would bless their efforts to reverse the defeat of the morning, drove the Cavaliers right back to the walls of Chester. Back to the walls, tumbling against the besieging forces! The royal army faced utter ruin. King Charles witnessed the rout from the vantage point of the Phoenix tower. All was confusion around Chester; the lanes were crowded; the ground was unfit for cavalry. The Royalists were captured in their hundreds or driven away and left to the mercy of the country folk. Three hundred Cavaliers had been killed and a thousand prisoners taken.

Next day the king left Chester for Wales, accompanied by five hundred horsemen. Screens were erected by the unguarded bridge and Charles easily passed over. Before he departed he gave instructions to Lord Byron that if help did not come in ten days he had his permission to surrender the city. He was deeply afflicted by the defeat he had suffered and a personal loss had moved him too,—the death of his cousin Lord Bernard Stuart. As he left the city with head bent and his face full of sadness, he was heard continuously to speak; these words of lamentation:

"Oh Lord, Lord, what have I done that should cause my people to deal thus with me?"

It was no mystery; but then this Charles was never one for acknowledging his own faults. His enemies had the answer. It was clear enough. The All-knowing One was displeased with a tyrant king, had seen the evils of his reign and had duly taken them into account.

21. APOTHECARY SURGEON

Among the troops of Colonel General Poyntz, who rode through the Midlands to victory at Rowton Moor, was a young apothecary surgeon whose competency earned him respect of all, from the general downwards. Poyntz's long experience of campaigning on the continent and the fact that he had married a German wife, made him especially interested in George Waldheim's antecedents. He admired the young man's knowledge of the doctrines of Paracelsus and praised the skill of their practical application. As a regimental surgeon, George had served under Lord Manchester until Marston Moor after which he had remained in the Northern Army. In the late summer of 1645, he had been chosen as the most suitable surgeon to join Poyntz in his thrust against Chester. Even more than his obvious skill, the natural cheerfulness of the man set his patients at ease, and his quiet efficiency endeared him to his staff. He was allotted two mates to assist in performing the often difficult, frequently thankless, and mostly unpleasant tasks to which they were called in the hectic hours during and after a battle. He prided himself on his knowledge of the magic of herbs and even of chemical medicines; his ability to produce excellent balsams and plasters to ease the pain of wounds was unrivalled. So this apothecary surgeon, handsome and flaxen haired—"the young German sawbones", "the man with the medicine chest", was a popular figure in camp or without, wearing the baldric which was his charter in the field.

On more than one occasion, this passport of the non-combatant allowed him to enter a hostile camp to treat men of his own party where his sincerity and firmness of purpose earned him respect and praise even from his enemies. Among the army surgeons of the day George Waldheim was a gem, for many of them were quite incompetent. Above the regimental surgeons and assistants were the general officers controlling the medical services—the Physician General, the Apothecary General, and the Surgeon General to the Army. The choice of regimental doctors was limited as not many men of standing chose to enter army service. Pay for the surgeon was low, but George's sense of dedication to the profession, permitted him no wavering. It was his calling, and that was the end of it. As he rode about making arrangements for the billeting of his patients, performing the inevitable amputations as skilfully as the knowledge of his day permitted—but saving as many limbs as he cut off—or lifting the lid of his famed medicine chest for just the right prescription, he was universally blessed.

This was not the case with some of the surgeons in the army. A certain Mr Fish was declared by his commander to be inefficient and one who was "never bound prentice to the profession"—a criticism never levelled at George. Another surgeon, Edward Cooke, accused of incompetence in that he let his patients die, complained that "the physician or surgeon is but Nature's handmaid; the Great God of heaven has ordained and appointed several diseases which are incident to men and they have to attend them one Death, who does and will prevail, notwithstanding the most excellent means which the gravest and wisest physician or surgeon can use in the world."

Of course George's patients sometimes died, but then it was accepted that everything within the competence of a conscientious surgeon had been accomplished.

After the battle of Rowton Heath, close on a thousand captured Cavaliers were removed to Nantwich so once again the great church became a prison. . There were a number of wounded among those marched away, and General Poyntz put Surgeon Waldheim in charge of their medical needs. As the great columns of dejected, defeated men wound their way along the road from Chester, followed by walking wounded and then the more serious cases in carts, George rode alongside, pleased at the thought of being able to visit the town which was the home of the Leys, and the probability of meeting some of his family. He did not yet know that Tom had been discharged. News had come through of the grievous wounds his friend had suffered, but he had been cheered by indications that recovery was on the way.

As they approached Acton, the edge of the forest coming up almost to the village, the old church and the few houses around it reminded him of his own home in Germany. He had not thought much about those days for a long time. George was not the man to dwell on the past. He was content to serve God and his fellow men in the present. His religion was of the practical type, not complicated with deep theological concepts; it encouraged him to carry on with his work when others would have given way to desperation—when he stood, sweat coursing down, his cheeks spattered with blood, his arms aching from the physical exertion of performing operation after operation, his heart and mind assailed by the piteous cries of the wounded—of those he could not save. The Lord's strength was his and so he carried on. Strength from such a source was limitless; it flowed into him and through him—he could impart it to those who aided him—his assistants, the wives of soldiers nursing his patients, the well-wishers who took them into their homes and to the victims themselves. Familiarity did not make him less aware of the pity of war. This suffering was unnecessary—avoidable if only men's minds could be changed; but George Waldheim's ability did not lie in that direction. That monumental task must be left to the divines, though he could not see them making much progress towards a more peaceful state; often they did quite the contrary.

Trust in the Lord makes one's passage through this life that much easier. Though there was nothing flamboyant about George's religious beliefs, the reward was surely waiting for one who had loved God and his neighbours.

Only the crowds in the streets of Nantwich surprised George. The buildings were like old friends—Tom's description had been so exact. The place was still a Parliamentary garrison; the citizens had turned out in force to see their enemies marched into captivity, so it was Holly Day all over again.

Until late in the evening the surgeon was fully occupied with his patients, but on the following morning he paid a visit to Mrs Ley's house where, so he had been informed, her daughter-in-law, the German lady, and her two children were residing. Amalia was overjoyed to see her husband's old friend again. Karl and Mariana scarcely remembered the man who had doctored them on the journey by sea, and they stood back overawed when a tall Parliamentary officer with a bronzed face, a high-crowned hat, and an important-looking sash across his chest, entered the room. But George soon had their confidence; taking them on his knee, he told them they must find room for yet another "uncle" on their growing list of real or adopted relations. His eyes lit up with joy when Amalia told him of Tom's return, but a sadder mood took over when she related the circumstances of her husband's release.

"He has been out of Nantwich on Parliamentary business and is visiting his brother-in-law at Walbury, so he is not expected back for a couple of days. We have a servant who could take you over if you wish."

George declined the offer with thanks.

"No need for that, Amalia. Just give me some directions. Remember George Waldheim is an old hand at finding his way."

Amalia smiled, recollecting how he and her brother Leopold had brought Tom from Nördlingen to Salzburg—and, best of all, to her home at Hallein.

The day was fine—a little misty perhaps, when he set out—but the sun soon broke through. These days, before the fall set in and gaunt branches replaced the russet and gold, while hedgerows were heavily laden with the tokens of munificent nature, had always a special appeal for George. The bustle of Nantwich behind him, he enjoyed the keen fresh air of this stretch of countryside. His ability to shut off scenes of woe and enjoy the English beauties of nature just beyond the battlefield was an admirable characteristic of the young German.

He turned into a narrow lane where a stream flowed across his path. Instead of fording it, he stopped to water his horse. On each side of the road were hedgerows, and there was only a partial view down to the village which was very close. He sat down on the grass for a moment, humming an old German song he had learned in Salzburg and took off his hat. He broke off in the middle of the melody, lay back and looked up at the sky which was uniformly blue—"Summer's last fling," he thought, "before autumn proper takes hold."

He was about to remount, when he noticed the figure of a girl coming along the lane from the direction of the village. A large dog, which had been walking by her side, bounded up to George in a friendly fashion and he ruffled the animal's hair. He put his hat on his head solely in order to remove it again, for when the girl came closer he took it off with a flourish and greeted her with a smile.

"Pardon, me, young lady," he said. "Am I right in believing that the home of Schoolmaster William Masterson is just ahead?"

Lynette, for she it was, looked in surprise at this Parliamentary soldier with twinkling eyes; she had never seen him before, yet strangely enough there was something familiar about meeting him—a kind of "I know I have been here before" feeling.

"You are quite right, sir. Down in the hollow, just across the river. But who are you who seeks my uncle?" she asked rather nervously. "Your speech is not of this country or even of this nation, yet I see that you are in the service of Parliament."

"Surgeon Waldheim, serving under General Poyntz; and if you are the schoolmaster's niece, then you must be the daughter of my good friend, Tom Ley, with whom I have seen service in many a passage of arms both here and in Germany."

"I have heard my father speak of you," said Lynette, surprised at this chance meeting with yet another Parliamentary officer—first her own father, now his closest friend. "But I had not thought to see you here. I will walk down with you sir; the dog can be exercised on the way back."

She slipped a leash on the long-legged, rough-haired animal. George led his horse and walked alongside the girl. Neither spoke much—they were sizing each other up. Though Lynette had heard about George from her father, she had somehow imagined him to be an older person. This man could not be above twenty five. She looked shyly up at him—certainly he was handsome, taller than average, with such a pleasant expression as if he were about to burst into song at any moment. George had for some time, been aware of Lynette's existence. Tom had described how he first espied his daughter among the crowds welcoming Fairfax's troops after the battle of Nantwich—but this young lady! He had naturally assumed the daughter of his dear friend to be a pleasant person, but this charming girl exceeded his expectations—little like Tom, it was true—but had he not heard that she was the very image of her mother?

As they reached the wooden bridge close to the church, he stopped. "What shall I call you? Your father told me that you have no commonplace name—Lynee is it not?" he asked, stressing the first syllable.

"Do call me Lynette," replied the girl, "and I know you are George."

Surgeon Waldheim nodded confirmation.

"Lynette!" he repeated, regarding her in a way which made her feel slightly embarrassed. "That is a beautiful name. What does it mean? I am George, the husbandman. Now tell me the meaning of yours."

Lynette looked at him in surprise. She had not imagined that such a matter would concern the young man.

"Firstly, a linnet is a little bird," she replied; "and then in our neighbouring land of Wales there is a "llyn" which is a deep pool. You may take your choice."

"Linnet?" said George, baffled. "I do not know this bird. Tell me more about him."

"His plumage is a warm brown with crimson on his forehead and his breast. He feeds on seeds and likes linseed best—hence his name. A pleasant songster, he is among my favourite birds."

"Yes, I know him—"der Hänfling; but he is just a common finch."

"No sir; really I think he is quite an uncommon finch."

"Perhaps; but not uncommon enough for you, my dear. No, I choose the pools. See, there they are, my little llyns—those deep, brown eyes. What lies below those dark pools—that is worthy to be explored."

"Sir, you flatter me," said Lynette, protesting faintly, though she was encouraged by George's pretty speech.

"Honour, not flattery, maiden," replied George with a smile. "Tell me how did you come by the name?"

"They say my father chose it because mother liked to read the story of Gareth and Lynette—but truly she was a haughty lady and taunted poor Sir Gareth while she thought he was of humble birth. Her sister, Lady Lyonora, was milder mannered. Had my father turned over another page he would have chosen that name for me."

"Ah well," remarked George, consolingly, "now you have much more to strive for. You must redeem the reputation of all young ladies called Lynette."

They had reached the house and Lynette ran in to announce the visitor. George was shocked at the appearance of his friend whose recovery was still by no means complete. Tom was cheered mightily by the visit. Will and Alice, unused to welcoming complete strangers, were rather stiff in their attitudes, but Lynette had no doubt whatsoever about the charm of this man. Soon she was bringing out her treasured books to show him and inviting him to let her act as a guide through the garden. They strolled together down the path where she had walked with Blackshaw. What a contrast between these two men! Luke with his hands folded and his head in the air, looking up to catch a glimpse of the plains of Heaven; George Waldheim wandering enthusiastically along the narrow gravel paths, admiring God's creation on earth, telling her something interesting to remember, diverting her with descriptions of his apothecary's garden down in the south of the Empire—and all in such a cheerful voice which penetrated Lynette's breast and found her heart.

"Do you speak the language of flowers?" asked the young man as they sat on the stone seat at the end of the garden.

"I have read in old books that each bloom has a meaning, but I am not encouraged to think on these things. I have been told to cast my mind aloft, not to dwell on earthly dross."

"But God's creation is not dross," said George, a little shocked. He picked an autumn rose and held it up for Lynette to inspect.

"Look at the care he lavished on this little plant. Think of that third day when the earth, brown and barren, was clothed in verdure by God's hand—a glorious green mantle, speckled with red, gold and all the other wondrous colours—plants in profusion to bring joy and healing to mankind. No, no, maiden; do not let them speak of dross."

"It must interest you to see an old book of mine," remarked Lynette. "I keep it in my room and if you care to peruse it, I will bring it down."

As she hurried away to fetch the precious volume, George walked round the garden thinking how he would reorganise the little plot of ground if he had it for his own, peering at a plant, shaking his head, examining a small handful of soil, and looking up at the sky to determine the sunny and shady parts of the garden. Then the door opened and Lynette came towards him, a heavy volume under her arm. George returned to the stone seat where he took the tome on his knee. He turned to the title page.

"A Herbal or General History of Plants, gathered by John Gerard of London, Master in Chirugie" Imprinted in London by John Morton 1597. He glanced through the book, turning the pages carefully, lingering over some of the profuse woodcuts which appeared on nearly every one of the fourteen hundred pages.

"A great work," he said. "I have heard of Master Gerard, but until now I have never seen a copy of his book. I believe that the illustrations come from the Dutch herbal of Tabernaemontanus with which I am familiar."

"And did you know that this worthy man was born here in Cheshire?" said Lynette. "It is believed he came from Nantwich and went to school in Wistaston, two miles away. This was confirmed when he wrote of our Wich as *'the place where I had my beginning'*. He knew all the fields and flowers growing in the neighbourhood and described them in his book. Did you know, too, that he made many journeys to uttermost foreign parts before he settled in London as Superintendent of Lord Burleigh's garden and then Surgeon and Herbalist to the King and Queen?"

George's finger was indicating a passage in the book and when Lynette had finished speaking he read it out:

"Flowers through their beauty and variety of colour and exquisite form, do bring to the liberal and gentle mind the remembrance of honesty, comeliness and all kinds of virtues."

But George was forgetting something. Lynette's reminder came naturally after this little speech about the beauty and variety of blooms.

"Sir, you asked me if I speak the language of flowers. I know but little of it. Tell me more."

"Maiden," replied George in a gentle, teasing tone, as he closed the book. "My mother called me George, but neither King nor Emperor added 'sir'".

Lynette blushed. "Tell me then, George," she said softly. The young man looked around him.

"Autumn is not the best time for your garden. A man should behold a goodly show of summer beauty and spring flowers in abundance, when abroad scarcely a leaf is to be seen. In autumn too, when yellow leaves wither and fall, such splashes of colour brighten our lives. Even dull winter can give quite generously with berry-bearing bushes and hardy plants."

"Now had I this little garden," he continued in an excited voice, "I would strive to obtain from foreign parts all the variety of herbs and plants I might in any way obtain. I would labour with the soil to make it fit for the plants, and with the plants to make them to delight in the soil, so that they might live and prosper in this climate, as in their native and proper country. But to the language of flowers! I will satisfy you," he assured the eager girl. "The meanings are so interesting:—one could write a letter with a bunch of flowers. Take the rose in three colours. Yellow: *"I love another"*; white: *"I love you not"*; but red: *"I love you"*. Then there is the lily, once the favourite flower, now close behind the rose. In purple it signifies: *"You are my fond sweetheart"*; in white it is an emblem of your purity. Among the others there are some I would not choose for you. Snapdragon: *"You mean nothing to me"*; sunflower: *"outward show does not impress me"*; dianthus: *"flirtation"*; gladiolas: *"pain"*. Nor should we forget the wild flowers. Not only those we cultivate in our gardens have their meanings. When I return we will see what your beautiful countryside has to offer."

George rose and straightened his uniform. He took the girl's hand.

"I regret that my stay must be short, dear Lynette, but duty calls."

He raised her hand to his lips and kissed it, making a slight bow. Tom, who had come out, embraced his friend; Will and Alice followed behind. The schoolmaster darted a glance at his niece. A strange look in her eyes betrayed more than a normal interest in this Parliamentarian surgeon. When George disappeared from sight, Lynette went straight up to her bedroom, ostensibly to replace the book. She sat down on a chair facing the window and looked out across the garden to the stone seat where she and George had talked half an hour before. She remained there watching, until the sun had gone down and the seat was scarcely visible in the gloom. The voice of her aunt calling from below roused her from her reverie. Lynette opened a drawer and took out a small book. A pen lay on the table; an inkhorn stood close to it. After dipping the quill she paused for a moment, then in bold, decisive handwriting, she wrote across a blank page:

"September 20th 1645: Today my life begins anew. I love George Waldheim."

22. CAPTAIN MYNTON

Stephen Mynton, brought to Nantwich as a prisoner after the Battle of Rowton Heath, hailed from the neighbourhood of Blackburn in that hotbed of malignancy—Central and West Lancashire. He had served under Sir Marmaduke Langdale, an avowed Catholic, as a cavalry captain, but the young officer strenuously denied being a Papist.

Nevertheless, he classed himself among those who loved High Church rites despising the sectaries who would vilify the Prayer Book and show less respect than was due to the holy mysteries. His father was of the minor gentry; his estates on the hilly slopes overlooked by grim, old Pendle were not extensive, but he was attached to the soil and the traditions of his fathers. Even as a youth these principles had taken hold of Stephen's mind and were never replaced by a desire for significant change. He did not subscribe to all the pretensions of the King; like his father he grumbled about Ship Money and the other exactions laid upon the people; but nevertheless, he saw in this office of kingship, stretching back through the ages, a line of stability and accepted authority which, if broken, could only lead to the dissension of rival factions striving for supreme power. He revered the King too, as one who upheld the faith which he had been taught to believe was the true concept of God's purpose. Without a King, who would prevent the Presbyterians, the Independents, the Anabaptists, and who knows what else, from destroying the ordered, reformed system of worship he knew and loved?

In appearance Mynton was every man's idea of a Royalist gentleman. In dress he was extravagant, earning his father's disapproval on more than one occasion for his slavish desire to catch the latest styles. There were of course Parliamentarian gentlemen, who dressed far closer to the court fashion than to the strict simplicity of Puritan extremists, but if Mynton knew any he strove to outshine them. He wore his hair and beard in direct imitation of the king whom he

263

resembled facially. To his friends he seemed light hearted, full of Cavalier oaths and jests, his merry eyes sparkling wickedly as he spoke of his amorous adventures and daring deeds. But in battle he was a resolute fighter. They said he had the skill of a Tartar horseman, the sword-arm of a knight of Camelot, and the ability to extract himself from a difficult position. Nevertheless gunpowder had its way; a pistol shot felled the daring captain, but using his own weapon from the ground, he brought down the Roundhead who wounded him.

Mynton was well schooled and his knowledge of the classics, of Erasmus, More and Grotius, was surprisingly keen. But study of the works of these worthies was not his life; it was on the field of action that his destiny lay.

The captain's hurt was not very serious and soon he recovered his usual spirits. George found him a difficult patient. He had the impression that the man resented him more for being a foreigner than a Parliamentarian. This was illogical, for Mynton himself had served in a foreign army. Before the start of the Civil War he had fought in Flanders on the Dutch side against the Spaniards. He had some knowledge of the German and Dutch languages; his common greetings and simple everyday phrases were impeccably pronounced, but when he tried anything further, George found his conversation almost unintelligible and soon reverted to English.

"Why do you serve with these roundheaded rogues?" he said cheekily to George as the surgeon was inspecting his wound.

"I would not speak so disparagingly of your adversaries," retorted George, offended by the man's bluntness. "The 'roundheaded rogues' could have left you to die on the battlefield. Your treatment here is as good if not better than that afforded to any officer in the continental wars, as you should well know. And I am inclined to think that no arrogant Cavalier has received more consideration than you in this present conflict. "

"Damn it, man, I do not speak of that. I mean loyalty. Did you not have a king, a duke, or one of your elector princes in your part of the German backwoods?

"My birthplace lies in Baden where we were ruled by a margrave, but more recently I lived in Salzburg, in the lands of the Prince Archbishop."

"By my faith—a margrave and a Prince Archbishop! Had you no loyal feelings towards this count who had given you his protection? Or was his Eminence not deserving enough? Where did you say? In Salzburg? But I expect too much. How could a sawbones have the sense of honour of a gentleman?"

"Protection!" echoed George sarcastically. "My father killed, my mother ravished and murdered, my sister taken away as a camp-whore. The count, as you call him, gave me no protection. But I will say a word for his Eminence of Salzburg; he kept us out of the war and for that I give him thanks. No, Captain, my loyalty was towards my master, now my friend, who saved me—a man who has served the cause of freedom under Gustav Adolf and Cromwell."

"Under warty, copper-nosed Noll!" said the Cavalier with a sneer. Gustavus I'll honour, but not that canting hypocrite. "

George gave him a severe look.

"It would be wise to keep such opinions to yourself in this place. I am a tolerant man, but there are others around with less patience. In any case, Cavalier, what am I doing to give you offence? See, I am treating you as I do my own party. I am not injuring your king, nor have I made any assertions as to the rights and wrongs of the struggle. "

"Nevertheless, you put these wounded right and send them back to fight in rebellion, against his sacred majesty. When you have patched me up you will keep me as a prisoner unless I agree to turn my coat. "

George, whose patience with the man was exhausted, called over a young woman who was acting as a nurse.

"Finish bandaging this man," he said curtly. "I have other patients to tend."

Mynton, realizing that he had been too outspoken, called across to the retreating surgeon.

265

"No hard feelings, Master Waldheim. Your honour is different from mine. You say a bond of loyalty binds you to your friend—well and good! Your devotion to the sick and wounded is not in doubt. Perhaps when we talk again we can find some subject on which we can agree."

George was recalled to Chester soon after this conversation and he went through the fury of the siege. No further meeting occurred, but Mynton remained in Nantwich, neither free nor closely confined, his fighting spirit suppressed, but his enthusiasm for his cause unshaken.

"Who is that damned attractive young woman who flits in. and out like an angel of mercy?" he asked his friend Lieutenant Jones who was a local man. "She's as comely a daughter of Eve as I have ever clapped my eyes on. It's refreshing to see her among all this Puritan glumness—not overripe, just developed nicely to delight a Captain Mynton."

"Have a care friend," warned Jones. "She's a married lady, the wife of Major Thomas Ley, a member of the local committee of Sequestrations and other councils of the rebels."

"By my faith, Major Thomas Ley! I have heard of that sham gentleman—risen from the salt pit, to the dizzy heights of one of Cromwell's lieutenants! Is he not the friend of that German sawbones I put in his place the other day?"

"The very man—the highest in Friend Waldheim's estimation."

"So! Then he is the one to whom the mountebank owes more loyalty than to his count or king."

Jones was displeased at Mynton's disparaging remarks about the surgeon who had treated him well, but he had a suggestion which cheered his comrade.

"But there is one good thing about our Master Ley. He has a pretty—nay, I should say a beautiful daughter. She is a real milk and roses, sweet and simple country girl; if my judgement is correct, she will suit you admirably."

"Aha!" cried Mynton. "A beautiful daughter! Unmarried, I presume. Now that is better. Joy without danger there!"

"As far as I know she is neither wed nor promised, but seduction of this maiden will be no easy task. Her upbringing has been strictly Puritan."

"Oh this Puritan rigmarole and hypocrisy! At heart they are just the same as we are. Look now at a girl, her curves concealed in their homespun garb, fed on porridge and scriptural texts. What more could she wish for than to break away and have a little fling with a handsome Cavalier? Deuce, man, if she is as beautiful as you say, I will show this Puritan maiden that there is something more in life than callousing her knees on the hard floor and turning over the yellowing pages of an old bible. How do they call this little paragon?"

"Lynette."

"Lynette," said Mynton, savouring the pronunciation of her name. "Not Jane or Mary, but Lynette."

The captain had been granted parole to move freely within the walls. He feared that unless he took desperate steps he would not have much chance to meet the girl, especially when he learned that she lived in Walbury, so he waited until it was reported that she was visiting Nantwich and decided to attend church—which, considering his contempt for the Puritan clergy, was certainly a desperate step. The minister, John Saring, had been ejected by Parliament, a new man having been appointed in his place. Though a Puritan, his preaching had not the virulence of Blackshaw's, and Mynton thought he could endure sixty minutes of misery, listening to the man's rambling theology, for the sake of a sweet hour in the company of Tom Ley's daughter. Therefore, instead of attending the service held for the Cavalier gentlemen by their own chaplain, he walked to the church and took a seat close to the west door. He could see Amalia a few rows nearer the front and he strove to catch a glimpse of Lynette while the parson droned on. His friend had spoken the truth. Even in her dull clothes she outshone all around her.

"The pearl of Nantwich," he said; then in a burst of enthusiasm, he promoted her to "the comliest maid in Cheshire". Before the service was over Lynette had advanced to the top rank of all the young ladies he had known, and he was ready to award her the crown.

It was in the churchyard that he first came up close to her. Amalia smiled on seeing Mynton, whom she recognized as one of George's patients.

"I see your wound has healed well, Captain," she said. "I trust you found our minister's words as good a physic for your mind and spirit as that prescribed by the surgeon for your body."

"Ich danke Euch, gnädige Frau. Mir geht es besser."

"You speak my language," said Amalia in surprise.

"But little. I served among the Low Germans and the High Germans in their never ending wars, and learned enough to satisfy my daily needs. Nevertheless, honoured lady, I must say "vielen Dank" for the very special care you lavished on the enemies of your cause."

"But I hardly saw you, captain. Your debt must surely be to Surgeon Waldheim who pulled you through."

"Mynton," declared the captain, sweeping a bow, first to Amalia and then Lynette. "Stephen Mynton! But, lady, your very presence was an elixir which gave me new life."

"Your sister, I presume," he continued, pretending he knew nothing of Lynette and hoping to please Amalia by placing her in the same generation as her stepdaughter.

"My husband's child; but to me she is indeed a little sister—mein Schwesterchen—rather than a daughter. Lynette had not yet spoken.

"Do you expect to be kept here long, Captain Mynton?" she asked suddenly.

"Very probably they will wish to move me to Manchester in the next few days. They dare not risk their fortunes by having bright sparks like Mynton near their front line for long. But I must tell you now that it is my firm intention to change the colour of my sash and offer my services to your party. Tell me, Mistress Ley, do you not usually reside with your schoolmaster-uncle at Walbury?"

"Indeed I do, captain," replied Lynette, "and I shall be returning home shortly."

"You greatly surprise me that you should have decided to join the forces of Parliament," said Amalia. "What has His Majesty done to make you desert his cause now? I take you for a typical king's man."

"I do not desert his cause, gnädige Frau," replied Mynton, loyally. "Do you not all say you are for 'King and Parliament?' I desert only those who are leading His Majesty to ruin. Yet there are many principles held by your party which I do not understand. I would fain have someone with whom I could discuss these matters. Perchance you will be calling at my billet again."

"No, my duties are finished," declared Amalia, and Mynton thought he detected a tone of regret in her voice.

"But you may call on us if you wish," she added, appearing to be pleased that she could do something to assist the man's conversion.

Opportunity had been afforded but progress was slow. Mynton did meet the Leys again, but he had no chance to catch Lynette alone. The ladies found him highly entertaining with his tales of exploits in the wars. He was always the hero and was never worsted—not even when the Roundheads captured him—such was his ability to turn the story to his own advantage. His light-hearted talk and obvious boasts made Amalia and Lynette laugh, but they found him shallow. The serious purpose of his visit was forgotten, and it was not until Tom arrived home that he came out with it.

Mynton left the house knowing that he would either have to join the army of Parliament or leave for Manchester in a few days' time. His object was to postpone making an agreement he could not possibly keep until he had had a chance to seduce Lynette.

On the following day he had more luck than he had dared to expect. A market had been held and the captain caught sight of Lynette returning with her purchase. He suggested that they should walk a little way and she accepted his offer to carry her baskets although they were not heavy. Mynton amused her by pretending that they were indeed so, straining himself as if lifting great weights. When they reached her house, the captain suggested that since the afternoon was fine, they should walk a little further. Lynette saw no harm in agreeing—he was certainly diverting company; so leaving the baskets in the house, she walked with him across the open land between the Leys' house and the mud walls of Nantwich.

"There is little space for me to stretch my limbs," complained Mynton as they crossed the path leading towards the church. "My parole extends only within the walls and I have to be content with Tinkers' Crofts and Wallers' Lane instead of the open countryside. But with you, my dear, this dismal scene is changed to one of sparkling streams and fresh green fields instead of dull streets and a dirty river."

Lynette laughed at her companion's words.

"Oh, Captain Mynton. A pretty speech, but insincere! We hardly know each other and I cannot see myself walking through Arcady with you. Are you really serious about wishing to change sides?"

"By thunder girl, I'd change to the devil's side if you were on it."

"There you go again, sir," remonstrated Lynette. "It is a wicked thing to speak familiarly of the devil. You are just as I have been warned a Cavalier officer would be—all oaths and fire, and pretty but shallow speeches. I doubt that you even mean to change sides. It is just a ruse to trap me."

"No, never, my pretty doe; why should you think that I would trap you?"

"I see it in your eyes, Master Cavalier. There is no honesty in you."

Lynette had stopped and she leaned against a little fence.

"You wound me," he said with affectation, "when you do not take me for an honest man. I say that you are beautiful Mistress Lynette. Why should you deny the truth of that? Glance into the looking glass, I pray you. You will doubt the veracity of Mynton's judgement no longer. Have none of your Puritan boys ever told you so, or did they not look up from their bibles long enough to notice it?"

"You flatter yourself, Captain, if you believe that you are the only one to think of me in that way. In fact there is one that I love."

"Ha!" said Mynton. "Let me see; it must be some psalm-singing shopkeeper turned cavalryman—or perhaps a glum-faced preacher full of pious pompousness. I know!" he said triumphantly, reaching the truth with surprising accuracy; "it's that German quack who patched me up—about as romantic, I should think, as the bones he saws."

Lynette flushed angrily at the mention of George, and Mynton laughed.

"So I have struck home! It is the German with his black bag who has trapped our little Lynnie. Come along, dear, you can't be serious! See, I have a private room in my billet now. Nobody will disturb us—a little supper together, some good red wine, and it will be an evening to remember. What do you say, Lynnie, to a kiss on account?"

He put his arm across Lynette's shoulders, but the girl wriggled away.

"Sir!" she said. "Have you no respect for a lady? It is ungallant of you to take advantage of my youth and treat me in this way. I can tell you now that I am not one of your Cavalier misses. I will not come with you and you need say no more about changing sides. You are as malignant as ever you were. Goodbye sir. I have no desire that we should meet again."

Lynnie!" began Mynton, but she turned on her heel. He said no more but was not used to such a rebuff and could hardly believe that she meant what she said.

"It is just her maidenly pride," he declared, consoling himself. "She will come round in the end, and I will have my way with her."

The bumptious captain did not, however, find the opportunity to prove his point, for on the following day she returned to Walbury thus sparing him a further refusal. He was also due to depart from Nantwich for Manchester, having given up all pretence of wishing to change sides. This could not be allowed to happen—these roundpated traitors would not confine Stephen Mynton like a caged beast any longer. It would by no means be his first successful escape. During fighting in Flanders in 1641, he had successfully gone through the Spanish lines near Genepp, disguised as a peasant. He would try again.

If he could outwit the foxy Spaniards he would certainly prove too much for these boneheads.

It was simple enough to bribe a townsman to obtain plain clothes, and he passed out of Nantwich with a packtrain bound for Chester quite unnoticed. Once clear of the walls he left the train and struck out across the fields. But walking was not the way of a cavalry officer— even an escapee. There would have to be some means of obtaining a horse.

The day started fine, but during the afternoon clouds built up. At first only a few spots of rain fell and there were brief pauses during which Mynton believed that the weather god was perhaps being kinder to him than he deserved; but then, to his dismay, the showers became a downpour from the leaden heavens, which showed no signs at all of abating. His intention was fixed on escape to Wales, but he kept close to the river bank for fear of losing his way. At last he saw a farmyard and he crept into an outhouse to seek shelter. A low whinney from a neighbouring shed tempted him. It did not prove difficult to break into the primitive stable where some poor nags were tethered. Choosing the least wretched of the beasts, he untied it and looked out of the shed. A light showed in the house; he heard bolts being drawn back and a shout, but there was no time for explanations or haggling over the animal. Jumping on the horse and crouching down over its head, he rode it bareback across the field. Though past its prime, his mount responded to the expert hand of Captain Mynton, and streaked away from the railing peasant until it reached the highway. Stephen had been given rudimentary instructions by his friend Jones as to the route he should attempt to follow. It bypassed Walbury and Mynton was tempted. Walbury! A magic name! A village graced by the presence of the fair Lynette! But no, he would have to forego that pleasure, much as he would have loved to tame the little vixen and feel her pressing her soft body against his. No matter! In Denbigh there was a house with "Welcome" for Stephen Mynton on the threshold—the humble but inviting dwelling of a buxom maid, Myfanwy, who needed no taming and chattered away incessantly in Welsh while he pleasured her.

These fond thoughts were disturbed by a sudden cry. Turning, he saw a Parliamentary patrol splashing along the muddy lane behind him. Whether the soldiers were searching for him, or they were just amazed at the sight of a peasant riding like a Mongol, or they wished to make an innocent enquiry, he never knew, for urging on his horse, he made for a small wood in which he could find cover. Suspicions now fully aroused, the soldiers galloped after him. Mynton realized that his inferior animal would have no chance in the chase, so on turning a bend, he hurriedly dismounted and fled on foot into the wood. The undergrowth was dense, but the thicket was only small and he soon passed through. Nevertheless, he was rid of his pursuers, who instead of following him, rode off in the direction of Nantwich, suggesting that rather than being a party out to search for him, it was a patrol with the duty of investigating all suspicious characters in the neighbourhood.

A long slope led down to the little village below, which he knew to be Walbury. The rain had stopped but he was soaked to the skin, weary and scratched by brambles; his recovery from the wounds he had received at Rowton Heath scarcely completed.

A dog set up a vicious barking as he entered the village. Lynette had told him that the schoolmaster's house was near the church—but which one was it? The lane was deserted and, in any case, he would hardly have dared to ask his way. Ah, that must be the Rectory, close to God's acre; on the other side within the shadow of the old, grey building, stood the schoolroom, then a little over a hundred yards away, just across the river, was a house which matched Lynette's description of her home.

The clouds had broken at last; pale moonlight shone on the village. Mynton took a determined step forward over the narrow bridge to the place where he hoped to find some shelter and refreshment—dry clothes too, he hoped. A chill breeze blew through his soaked garments and left him shivering like a leaf. Although he had been brushed off so decidedly by Lynette, he had no compunction about approaching her again—if he could catch her alone. That was essential; he could hope for no assistance from the sanctimonious schoolmaster or his prim wife, but a sentimental maiden seeing him in such distress, would surely succumb to his charm. It had worked well at Genepp. There was a Dutch girl Magda; and a German—he never really knew how Klärchen came to be there. Both had helped him in different ways. She was a pretty catch that Klärchen—but what a slippery fish to land! Such a tale of "Oh, Captain, you are too bold! A maiden has her pride!"—and all other kinds of "brimborium"—but she came to him in the end; and by thunder, her performance was among the best!

Lynette was certain that there was someone in the garden. Her room overlooked it and on mild evenings she liked to open her window and watch the sunset or sit looking out into the inky sky, lit only by stars or a pale moon. She had not done so this evening due to the inclement weather, but she threw open the casement on hearing an ominous rustle within the bushes. Springer, her longhaired canine friend who slept at the foot of the bed, pricked up his ears and gave a low growl.

"Come on, boy!" said his mistress encouragingly. "Chase him off!"

Lynette descended the stairs and unbolted the door. Before she had time to let Springer loose, a dark shape rose from the bushes and came towards her. He was in peasant clothes, but he knew her name and advanced in a friendly fashion.

"Lynette!" he called "Hold your dog! I mean no harm."

"Discover yourself, sir," said Lynette, checking the animal. "Who knows my name and hides in my garden at this time of night?"

"Captain Mynton," replied the man. "Believe that I am he. I took on these hateful rags to hide my true identity; but see me now dear Lynette! You must surely know the features of a man to whom you so recently showed your favours."

"You deceive yourself, Captain," replied the girl. "I walked with you and talked with you, but as you quite well know, that is all. Your insolence in expecting kisses and other 'favours', as you put it, drove me to tell you that I did not wish to see your face again. Yet you appear in my garden. Why are you here?"

"I have come to see my little Lynnie. I broke my parole and placed my life in jeopardy for another glimpse of your bright eyes."

"Captain Mynton, you never give up," said Lynette, exasperated. "Do you really think that I believe your protestations? Furthermore I should be obliged if you would desist from calling me Lynnie. It is familiarity which I have not granted you. It is plain to me that you are escaping to join the King's army in Chester, Wales or somewhere else. Surely you would not expect me to look on while a prisoner under the law of war returns to his own party—to the camp of my enemies?"

Mynton tried another tactic.

"I fear you are much too perspicacious for me. But I am soaked, scratched and bleeding. Surely you would not deny an enemy a bite of food and a few moments in front of the fire before he returns to give himself up. I humbly beg your pardon for my presumption when I called you Lynnie. It is a sweet name—honey on my tongue."

Lynette hesitated.

"Wait a moment," she said. "First I must ensure that both my uncle and aunt are abed."

She closed the door and hustled Springer upstairs, but it was some time before she reappeared, and Mynton was afraid that she would not come. He was preparing to leave, when at last the door was unbolted and Lynette, a candle in her hand, called gently into the darkness. "Captain Mynton!"

Once inside, Stephen gave up his contrite pleading and recovered something of his confident, gay manner.

"You err too, Captain, when you think that I would trust any assurances that you would return to Nantwich after 'seeing my bright eyes'," declared Lynette as she brought a can of ale, a piece of meat and some bread and cheese to the hungry man.

She stoked the fire. Seeing the amount she threw on, Mynton felt confident that she was weakening and preparing for a long stay by a perhaps not so unwelcome visitor. There were still a few ploys he had not yet used. One of them would surely work. But Lynette, though she had fed him and was attending to his hurts, would not let him off lightly.

"Does it not seem dishonourable to you to break the parole given, to captors who could have kept you in close confinement had they been severe and not men of honour themselves?"

"Breaking parole given to a cropped poll! Fie, chide me not for that!" said Mynton, grimacing at the thought of those whose rebellion against the King had put them beyond the pale.

"But sir, it was on your honour that you gave your word not on theirs. You degrade yourself by breaking it more than you injure them. A gentleman should keep his word to whomsoever it was given. If you despised your captors so, then you should have refrained from giving it."

"Then I would have been closely confined and any chances of escape would have been lessened. I feel I gain more credit by striving to join my monarch's forces once more, than I lose by breaking my word to this band of rebels."

"Then you admit that you intend to try for Wales. Let me tell you now that your cause is hopeless. Sir William Brereton is pressing hard on Chester. Your men in Wales have been scattered. It is likely that you will be captured and will end up in a Parliamentarian prison with sore feet and a wounded honour. You took what those men gave you readily enough—a limited liberty it is true—but freedom enough to allow you to walk round the town, to make advances to me, to enjoy my favours if I had been willing to give them. Now do something in return. Go back to Nantwich and give yourself up."

"Your castigations hurt me, Lynette," said the captain more humbly. Have you not a little corner of your heart left vacant for Stephen Mynton?"

"I pity you only because you are cold and hungry. I hate to see a chase; the pursuit of animals does not thrill me. If a fox sought shelter in my barn, then I would do my very best to save him. That is as much as I will grant you. Have you any more wounds and scratches for my attention? I am confident that none of them will be beyond the limits of my skill."

Mynton's hurts were not at all serious, and Lynette soon had him sitting in a chair wrapped in a blanket, his boots, cloak and jacket drying before the fire. He had fallen silent. This girl was the kind one marries not a wench to play with like a toy.

"Mynton! Mynton!" he reproached himself. "How you have misjudged her!" But there was another plan to win her over; it had worked very well in the past. Once a girl felt his embrace and kiss her defences had almost always melted. In particular he remembered a Yorkshire lass, Bessie Harrison; his short affair had allayed the bitterness of defeat for him after Marston Moor. She was nearly as firm as this Lynette until her lips met his, when she almost swooned in his arms. It was his last throw but certainly worth a try.

"Then I must go," he said, reaching for his jacket.

"You may stay here longer," said Lynette, surprised, "at least until your clothes are dry."

"No," insisted Stephen. "I must go."

He began to draw on his boots. Lynette eyed him. Did she really suspect his purpose?

"One last favour, dear Lynette—no, let me call you Lynnie for the last time and henceforth you will be troubled by my familiarity no more. Please Lynnie, give a parting traveller a chaste kiss."

He had planned to begin with a formal embrace and let it develop into a burst of passion. Such a beautiful girl! That kiss would be a memorable moment even if he went no further.

"If I believed that you would peck me on the cheek and depart, then perhaps I would allow it," replied Lynette; "but Captain Mynton, you are not honest. I see within you desire supported by the vanity of a Cavalier gentleman who believes that every maid must accommodate him because he has a straighter nose, a trimmer beard, a firmer chin, and a brighter eye than any of his rivals. No, sir, my kisses are reserved for another. You will not win me by such a ruse."

"Tell me," said the captain wonderingly as Lynette rearranged his drying garments, "whence do you draw all the confidence to say these things to me?"

"The Lord supports me," replied the girl proudly. "We know that God is with us. Manifold mercies have been showered upon us. Our armies have done wonders everywhere. Soon, the King will have to make peace with Parliament. And I have been personally blessed, Captain Mynton. The Lord has given me all his beauties to enjoy and has filled me with the capacity to study and I hope finally to understand, the purpose of his creation. He has shown me the man I wish to marry and by his mercy we will be united—honourably I mean, not in the wretched, unholy way you desire."

"God's bones! You people bore me!" burst out Mynton petulantly. "Why do you always imagine that God favours only you? God with us! Gott mit uns! Thus you cry and cry again in battle. Was God with the Protestants at Breitenfeld and Lützen, only to turn his coat like a Scottish mercenary and desert them at Nördlingen?

"Could the Lord not decide which way to go at Edgehill, then after following in the train of the Cavaliers for half a dozen battles, did he throw in his lot with the Roundheads at Marston Moor and Naseby? Did he go north to favour bold Montrose with a string of victories, only to say in the end: 'Enough, James Graham, your cause is not mine,' and let him down at Philiphaugh? I cannot accept this as the end for us, either here or in Scotland. As you see, fortunes change in war as the wind blows. If God intervened actively in these conflicts then your party would have been damned from the start for your rebellion against his anointed one. We can draw strength from God to carry us on to victory, but we must rely too on our powder and shot and our strong right arms. Our enemies have plenty of both. We must plan and strive to surpass them before we can reverse these humiliations."

"I do not believe that God is fickle and acts so unpredictably," protested Lynette. "It is blasphemous to say so. I am not surprised that he has withdrawn his blessings from those who have so little understanding of his ways."

Mynton was not chastened by Lynette's rebuke. "Do you think you have a monopoly of enjoying good things and living a clean life?" he asked scathingly. "Many a King's man and good Protestant has spent more time on his knees in church than in the stews and alehouses. No, Mistress, do not give me the 'holier than thou art' treatment."

"Now Master Cavalier," retorted Lynette. "I would not dispute that many of your adherents are good people and that God often tries us by withdrawing his favours. But look at your own conduct, sir! You have lowered yourself by making improper suggestions to a maiden, by breaking parole, blasphemy, and I judge, by whoring and drinking too. If your faction contains such honourable men as you declare, then I suggest that you have disgraced their cause and should make amends. I will not betray you. That would make it too easy. It is up to you to redeem yourself by returning to your captors in Nantwich and by repenting on your knees for the other sins you have committed."

Mynton's bowstring was slack and there were no more arrows in his quiver. This girl had proved too much for him—his most dismal failure since he had first looked on the fair sex with an urge to prove his manhood. He remained huddled by the fire for a while after Lynette had left him to return to bed, then rising, he drew on his partially dried boots and donned his jacket and cloak.

The clouds had cleared after the downpour; the stars shone with unaccustomed brightness. A pale crescent moon was struggling to assert its authority as Queen of the night sky. Somewhere up above the vault of Heaven the Lord himself looked down on a world full of woe and sin. There was enough misery for him to see in this little corner of creation. Would a certain Captain Mynton escape the notice of God among the multitude of mankind? Of course this was foolish. Nobody can escape from the eye of the Lord—not even Jonah who fled to Tarshish. For all his brave words, which Lynette had considered blasphemous, Stephen Mynton was, in his way, a religious man; in moments like these, stripped of his outward levity, the strong conviction remained that God would give him strength to carry on the struggle and that his party would triumph in the end. He was defending the right of an anointed king to rule untrammelled by a petty Parliament. Not even Lynette's principles had shaken that belief. The other faults with which she had taxed him? He was a whoremonger? That was untrue. He never took a girl unless it was for love—at least while he was having her. His drinking and swearing? He admitted no excesses. His blasphemous words? Her own people need say nothing about that. They were notorious for their attacks on sacred relics and even the holy Prayer Book. He had disgraced himself by breaking his parole? These rebels had defied God's Vice-regent and in their desecrated churches worshipped God in a heathenish fashion, using lengthy, extempore prayers instead of the beautiful, ordered service laid out for them in that book they reviled. The king would reward, not blame him, for using the pretence of an agreement to gain his end. He

279

felt sure that Charles himself would do the same if it were to his advantage.

He sat on the stile munching the apples which Lynette had invited him to take. What was his choice? A romp in bed with Myfanwy at Denbigh and a pat on the head from King Charles? Or close confinement in Nantwich humbling himself to these traitorous villains?

"The devil take them all!" he cried aloud. As far as he was concerned his honour was untarnished, and a few hours listening to Myfanwy's Cymric ramblings, which at least he could silence with kisses, was a whole world better than the censures of that saucy, puritanical, Lynette.

On the following morning, Will and Alice both detected a change in their foster daughter. She was up early, and after breakfast which she ate quietly, instead of commencing her household duties, she sat a long time by the window seat—not even reading as she was wont to do. Rising suddenly, she called her dog and walked out across the fields to the stile at the top of the rise, her cloak worn loosely around her shoulders, the wind tossing her curls.

After a few moments, silhouetted statuesquely against the sky, Lynette returned down the hill and passed through the churchyard. Mr Malbon was surprised at the curtness of her greeting—so unlike the cheerful affable girl he knew. It was Alice who first approached her. Lynette had come in silently, had removed her cloak, and was turning the pages of the bible which always stood on a table by the window for the instruction of the family. Will used it only when reading to his wife and foster daughter in the mornings and evenings. For his studies he preferred his own bible kept in the inner sanctum.

"What is it, dear?" asked Alice kindly. Have you some heavy weight on your mind?"

"Mother," said Lynette with a troubled look and the suggestion of a tear. "I am afraid I have acted wrongly, yet at the time it seemed wrong to do otherwise."

"Tell me, child, what have you done? It is unlike you to be so downcast."

"A maiden prizes her honour too. It is not just the privilege of a gentleman and a soldier."

"Come, come, Lynette," said Alice. "You speak in riddles. What is this about honour and not knowing right from wrong?"

"I let him go, Mother. I lied when I told you there was nothing amiss. I rose early this morning to think over the events of last night. I have studied the bible and can find justification enough for my action, but there is censure too. It was certainly wrong to lie."

Alice remembered Lynette's words as she came up with her candle and answered Will's enquiry about the noise below.

"For that you will be forgiven if you are truly sorry," she assured her niece. "But who was here whom you let go? A fugitive? A criminal? Tell me, Lynette."

The girl remained silent for a moment to collect her thoughts, but Alice took it to be reluctance to confide in her.

"Then tell your uncle," she suggested. "He is the one to advise you on a matter like this. I am sure he will be ready to forgive any fault freely confessed and he will guide you to a clear interpretation of your bible texts. There is no need to be alarmed, Lynette. Your uncle is a just man and has always treated you fairly. Surely you know that."

Will looked up from a Latin poem he was perusing, to find his foster daughter standing before him with downcast eyes. She raised them slowly to his and said in a low voice:

"Father, I must tell you that I lied to you last night. Captain Mynton was here and I let him go."

"Did you?" said Will, without showing undue surprise. "The Cavalier officer who expressed a willingness to change sides?"

"That was over even before it started," replied Lynette. "He never had any intention of serving Parliament."

"His reason for the pretence was offensive and dishonourable," she added, blushing at the memory of his suggestion. "He had escaped from Nantwich to join the King. He was cold, wet and hungry. I bandaged his cuts and scratches and gave him some food. Then I let him go for I pitied him, Father, as I would have felt for a wounded animal."

Will stroked his beard as he listened. He rarely heard a confession like this from Lynette. "Go on," he said. "Is there more to tell?"

"This morning I searched the Bible to justify my action. I read how King David spared his enemy, Saul. I found the story of the good man—the Samaritan—who cared for the enemy of his nation when a Jew had fallen among thieves. Now, Father, I respect your wisdom. Did I do right? I upbraided the captain for breaking his parole and I told him that the only honourable course was to return to Nantwich. I said that to hand him over would be to relieve him of a decision which would do him credit. Was it my privilege to test this man in my own way instead of reporting his whereabouts to the authorities? I hope that I am forgiven, Father. It would be hurtful to think that I had given offence to two good persons who have always loved and cherished me."

Will rose from his chair and comforted Lynette. "There is no need to upset yourself, dear girl. Your confession is laudable. God will forgive your lie; I know it, for I see you are truly sorry. You were right to send the captain on his way. But what was the offensive and dishonourable reason for his pretence of wishing to change sides? Why did he choose to seek shelter here?"

"Because he thought me fair game for his amorous intentions," replied Lynette. "He would have bedded me as he has done to wives and maidens from the Rhine to the Dee. But at the Weaver he was stopped, I would have none of him."

Will could not help smiling at Lynette's colourful words, but he was quite serious when he said.

"This man will get his deserts. Go now, dear, and speak to Aunt Alice. Tell her what has passed between us or she will fear the worst."

Lynette was at the door when Will, who had resumed his seat, called her back.

"You said not long ago that you would recognise at once the man you wish to marry. Have you seen him yet?"

"Yes, Father," replied Lynette. "The Lord showed him to me once and will bring him back again, of that I am certain. When this man comes, I will place my hand in his if he will ask for it. I am sure that God will guide our hearts and give us his blessing. The will of the Lord cannot be evil, for as you have often told me: 'God is Love'."

Will was surprised at the frankness and confidence of Lynette's speech, but he preferred not to question her further. "Your sentiments do you credit," he said, kindly. "Rejoice in the Lord and give thanks. He will never fail you."

23. SEALS OF LOVE

Just as Lynette had prophesied to her uncle, George came back to her. It did not require very remarkable clairvoyance on her part to make this assertion, for the man she loved was already her father's best friend, but God had preserved him through the dark days of a siege and he returned to Nantwich, though not quite as soon as she had expected.

The siege of Chester! Though he should have been ministering to the attacking party, George found himself trapped in the city witnessing the horrors and suffering the privations of that dreadful time. The shattering bombardment which opened the attack! The valiant storming of the breach which filled the streets and gardens in the suburbs with dead and dying! George worked at all hours in his makeshift hospital while around him the roar of guns shook the crowded house and reverberated across the city like the claps and rumbles of a perpetual thunderstorm. Diurnal and nocturnal labour was the lot of a surgeon at that time and it left him with almost no pause for reflection, yet in a few brief moments young George was transported from the dreadful present scene to the serenity of that garden in Walbury where his love for Lynette first sprang to life. There he had enjoyed the blessings of Nature's harmony; here he suffered from the pain of man's discord.

Right from the start he had been captivated by Lynette and the pretty speeches he made were not practised or artful. Her beauty was undeniable. Even in her plain Puritan clothes, she shone as brightly as the morning star—such rich dark curls, bright eyes and rosy apple cheeks—the little white hand he raised to kiss—and, above all, her gentleness and innocence, her interest in the things he loved, the sincere faith free from bigotry which endeared her to him! It had been a happy interlude.

Imprisoned in the city! He entered with a trumpeter to succour wounded prisoners and was denied the right to leave. It was a criminal act—a violation of the rules of warfare by the severe, arrogant Lord Byron who revoked the pass and refused to be lectured on correct military procedure by a mere sawbones. Such an insult! A man who wore the baldric of a surgeon not allowed to pass freely—accused of being a potential spy! It was exactly what he refused to do. Though the Cavalier commander had acted illegally, George's sense of honour forbade him to retaliate and he rebuffed the Parliamentary agent who attempted to recruit him as a spy.

For nearly five months the siege continued. "Messengers of mortality" came steadily over; attack was followed by counter attack. The constant rain of bursting shells, crashing stones and balls of iron was terrifying, but it was not the bombardment which forced the garrison into submission. Relief failed to come and hunger took its toll. The people railed against the stubborn Lord. Rats and domestic animals were eaten first; nettles, weeds, boiled wheat and spring water was all that remained. Terms had to be made at last, but they were honourable. Lord Byron and his men marched out leaving a miserable city, its suburbs in ruins, its walls defaced, its lands mortgaged, its plate melted, its funds exhausted. George watched them go. The King's War was almost over and he longed for home. That meant Nantwich to him now—Tom, Amalia and his dear Lynette.

The loyal city had fallen, the besieging forces divided; some to the south where they won the last pitched battle of the war, others into Wales to reduce the last bastions of Royalist resistance.

It was agreed that Nantwich was in need of a garrison surgeon and George Waldheim fitted the post admirably. His first visit to Lynette at the home of her stepmother was only brief, but the few words which they were able to exchange assured her that he still thought fondly of her and more significantly the young man promised that he would pay a visit to Walbury as soon as an opportunity arose.

It was Whitsuntide and the sun was warm like the young man's heart as he jogged along the road to Walbury. Peace had arrived—but would it last? Hatred and bitterness still abounded and that did not auger well. No, it was not yet peace, just a lack of war. The soldiers no longer stood in serried ranks awaiting the trumpeters signal. No longer were they asked to redden the soil with their blood. They had withdrawn into their garrisons with no enemy to menace them. Their generals had led them to a great victory. Now they would have to strive to win the peace.

George had another purpose in making this journey besides paying a visit to Lynette. He had been called to attend to a patient at Beeston Castle and Walbury was on his way. His hope was that if Fortune smiled on him, he would be able to persuade Lynette's guardian to allow her to accompany him.

This might have proved difficult, as Will, who knew now that this man meant more to his foster daughter than he had imagined, was not very keen on the idea of a union between her and a German apothecary surgeon. When she had revealed her love for George he had taken it lightly. There had been enough emotional strain over Captain Mynton, but he thought much about George and Lynette in the following months and searched his Bible for texts to guide him. Time went by and Waldheim did not reappear. Will imagined he had been posted away to some distant part of the kingdom, and the importance of the matter diminished. In fact George had gone over into Wales and had been present at the sieges of Chirk and Ruthin Castles. After the surrender of the latter place in April, he was ordered back to Chester where his commission to take charge of the medical services in Nantwich was handed to him.

Now the reappearance of the surgeon in South Cheshire and his meeting with Lynette in Nantwich, indicated that perhaps guidance from the greatest source of all wisdom would be required once more. He was not inclined to leave this fatherly duty to Tom—for he mistrusted the unconventional attitudes of his brother-in-law. Avuncular advice could be just as good if not better. It had been agreed that Lynette should continue to live with her uncle and aunt until her marriage, which undeniably gave him some authority over her. Tom could see his daughter whenever he wished and he had not yet purchased a suitable dwelling house for his family, so he agreed to this arrangement. So far no serious problem had arisen and consequently there had been no clash of authority. Will could not see this Waldheim as a candidate, but while ruling out the possibility of using a heavy hand on the sensitive girl he had found his foster daughter to be, there were ways of discouraging this man's suit without issuing crude, forbidding orders.

George was right in believing that he was Fortune's favourite child when, on his arrival in the Masterson household, consent was readily given by Tom, followed by grudging approval from Will and Alice who grumbled at the strange standards of behaviour her brother had brought back from foreign parts. So Lynette, her heart pounding like a carpenter's hammer, changed into riding clothes and led her horse, Dapple, from the stable. George was already mounted. Lynette thought he looked like one of those great equestrian statues which adorn the main squares of important cities. She had not seen any herself but had heard about such from her grandfather, Mr Barton, whom she considered to be almost another Marco Polo, and she had studied the drawings in one of his illustrated books. She was sure that none could be as handsome as George. He was immaculately turned out, for the young man was always very fastidious about his appearance. He had not yet covered his hair; the sun shining on it seemed to crown him with gold. Lynette liked his small moustache and his clean-shaven chin, but most of all his eyes—at times thoughtful, then twinkling with humour. George placed his hat on his head and waved to Tom who had just come out. Lynette blew her father a kiss and the pair rode off up the slope towards the Wrexham road.

It was a pleasant journey on a balmy spring day; for both of them the company was the best their hearts could desire, and the miles melted away as they rode through the lush, green pasture land and along the wooded slopes of a low hill range towards the mighty rock on which the castle stood.

Built in 1220 by the sixth earl of Chester after he had returned from the Holy Land, it was of irregular form having round and square towers. It occupied a commanding position, for it stood on a high sandstone crag detached from the neighbouring hills. The castle was always intended to be a military strong hold and was never turned into a dwelling house. On the death of the seventh earl it passed to the king, was repaired, strengthened, and linked to the royal castles in Wales as a second line of defence against incursions from that country. Then, after the War of the Roses, when Henry VII subjected the nobles to royal power, it had been sold to a private person. Deserted and neglected it stood for decade after decade, its sole occupant a caretaker. Only in this war of King and Parliament did it come once more to the fore, when its capture by Captain Sandford had been one of the most remarkable episodes in the local campaigns.

The first glimpse George and Lynette had of the castle was from the side of the easy ascent. A great swarm of men covered the hillside like an army of ants, hacking away with picks, loosening the stones with crowbars, battering down the greater part of the walls and towers, loading the stones on carts drawn by big boned oxen which lumbered away with the rubble along the narrow lanes. The castle had been taken by Parliament during the siege of Chester, but not until food supplies were down to the remnants of a turkey pie, an emaciated peacock, a peahen and two biscuits, did the garrison of fifty six soldiers surrender. Men and horses alike were found in an extremely languishing state when the castle was taken—the Governor's own mount was so weak that it was scarcely able to stagger out of the gate. The fortress had to be denied to a future enemy, so warrants were sent out in the spring of 1646 to parishes in the neighbourhood for help in carrying out the ordinance of Parliament that Beeston Castle should be slighted. Thus the ancient building was defaced—towers were shattered, walls were levelled, and the former stronghold was left an abject ruin, its military history ended.

The officer in charge of the demolition was surprised to see George accompanied by a woman. Smiling, the surgeon explained that as he thought the presence of a nurse might be necessary, he had brought this experienced young lady along with him. The patients, with the exception of one, did not prove to be seriously injured. The workman, whose foot had been crushed during his efforts to dislodge one of the unyielding stones, was sent to Nantwich in a cart after George had attended to his injury—and the men in charge were instructed to report to Surgeon Waldheim's capable assistants at the Lamb Hotel. Another man who was sick George bled, dosed with medicine and cheered with a few words of comfort, the latter being perhaps more effective than the rest of the cure.

These duties performed, he suggested that he should return via Walbury to Nantwich, but Lynette asked to see the castle, and as his medical tasks had been carried out in a shorter time than he had expected, the sun being still high in the sky, George saw no reason for undue haste.

They walked up the slope towards the upper Ward which was now in a deplorable condition. A fearsome moat divided them from the top part of the fortress, but the drawbridge was still standing and they crossed into the courtyard. Even in its present state, Lynette thought the castle romantic. She peered down the well over three hundred feet deep.

"They say that treasure was hidden down there in the days of the second King Richard," she told George who was watching men dislodging stones from a wall which was already half defaced. "He loved his trusty Cheshire men—his best archers—and when Bolingbroke rose against him he hid his jewels down this well—so the story goes. What a hiding place! They would have had to climb right down into the bowels of the earth if ever they were to reach it. Think of all that gold, that silver and those shining stones out of the enemy's grasp!"

A sudden, sharp explosion, followed by a long rumble like thunder, startled Lynette and she ran to George for protection. He put his arm round her, pressing her hard to his chest. She looked up at him.

"Do not be alarmed, dear. They are blowing up some of the most defiant parts of the walls. Oh, my Lynette," he said gently, "you run like a frightened sparrow."

The girl began to apologize. George stopped her.

"You need not be ashamed. I do not want to make a warrior out of you. Believe me, the cannon's roar alarmed me at first, but now I hardly hear its cough."

Lynette was still gazing at him, her wide, brown eyes shining with admiration.

"Dear sweetheart," he said, tenderly, stroking back her hair. Lynette's lips parted as if she were about to say something. The words were never uttered, for George silenced her with a kiss.

The great precipitous rock at the rear of the castle was a source of utmost wonder to Lynette. How Captain Sandford and his men could possibly have climbed it in the night, was hard to imagine. George could hardly tear her away from the awesome sight.

"Have you ever seen anything like it?" she asked.

He had to admit that it was formidable, though during his stay in Salzburg he had seen much greater precipices. Lynette listened eagerly to his descriptions of the Hohensalzburg Castle, the salt mine at Hallein, the Durrenberg, and the greater snow-capped ranges beyond.

The return ride to Walbury was even happier than the outward journey. Both the young people felt sure that they were destined for each other—now and for ever—a perfect match.

They rode on at a leisurely pace. There was no need to be in Nantwich or Walbury before nightfall. The sun was sinking but still warm; the wild flowers tossed their heads in a light breeze. Now and again a small animal—a hare or a rabbit—scampered across their path, or some tiny shape whose exact identity they did not discover, scurried along through the undergrowth. Close to Marton, the last village before Walbury, the couple stopped to rest. Dusk was approaching and the sun seemed to be taking his ease on the church tower. Even before she met George, Lynette had always felt herself to be in close communion with nature; but then she had been alone in a scheme of pairs. Now he had filled that gap and she could take her place in this scheme just as God had intended.

She leaned back looking at the darkening blue of the sky immediately above her and thanked the Lord for his mercy. George, who had been gazing from above at the reclining girl, smoothed out the folds of her dress. Lynette opened her eyes which had now fully closed. His manly face was close to hers; all was quiet around them; the twittering of birds had ceased; only a slight rustle in the wood behind them, the very distant call of a deer, and the wind softly sighing through the leaves, broke the stillness.

"These are my Seals of Love, darling girl. I place them on your lips as witness to the trueness of my heart" said George as he kissed her.

The girl had never felt such bliss. Could such a sensation last, or would she tumble from ecstasy into sadness and despondency? Never while he was with her! She felt she could not bear a parting. George must have had the same dread prospect in his mind, for when he spoke it was as if to reassure her.

"Believe me, my pretty one, God will be with us and give us comfort even if we have to part. I love you, dear girl. I offer you myself and all I have. That is my bond. I seal it with a kiss."

The sudden tolling of a bell from the church in Marton village aroused Lynette from this heavenly relaxation. She remembered too, who the incumbent was—Blackshaw, the man whose offer of marriage had plagued her for so long.

"Let us make a detour, dear George," she said. I fear to meet the minister on the way."

"So that is Blackshaw's church!" said George, looking down at the old building half hidden in the valley, with its square, battlemented tower projecting just above the tops of the trees which lined the confines of the village. Through a gap there was a glimpse of the porch and south door. George joked and Lynette laughed at his mockery of Blackshaw.

"I see now the portal through which the leader of the elect marches to do the work of the Lord," he said. "A painful and pious preacher—it is reported; a magician too, who can change an old oaken door into the pearly gates, for when he stands in the pulpit all is Heaven around."

Lynette felt relieved when they reached the road leading to Walbury. George was talking as one animal lover to another, praising the swift-footed Springer and telling her about his little dog in Germany.

"He's as red as a fox my Rolf, a hound with legs so short that his belly almost touches the earth, but he's just perfect for going down holes in search of badgers, rabbits, or what ever else goes to earth. I did not hunt, but as a pet he was ideal," went on George. "He has a ringing bark, a friendly nature, a hardy constitution, and is altogether a capital little fellow."

"Perhaps we will see some of them in this country soon," suggested Lynette, "and—" she broke off.

The familiar figure of Luke Blackshaw appeared riding towards them. Despite the mild weather he was wrapped in a dark grey cloak. Lynette shuddered. George drew close to her and gave his sweetheart a reassuring look.

What misfortune! They had made a detour to avoid meeting this man, and had now run into him coming away from Lynette's own house.

"Good evening, minister," said the young man, removing his hat. "God has blessed us with a fine day to be sure."

Blackshaw darted an accusing glance at Lynette and stared stonily at George.

"Indeed he has," he said stiffly. "Good evening to you, Mistress Ley; and to you, surgeon."

"So that is the famous Preacher Blackshaw, who publicly castigated our Amalia and would have run off with my little Lynette. Fancy having to suffer his sour look and pious homilies from breakfast until supper time! My dear, you have escaped a fate worse than death."

Lynette laughed in spite of her fear. She felt sure that somehow Blackshaw was planning another stroke against her. Long after George had taken his leave, she sat thinking of this chance encounter. She could not drive the look of scorn and bitterness Blackshaw had given her from her mind, nor the unfeeling stare he had reserved for George. She should not care what kind of looks the minister had given them, but she feared that he could and would undermine the happiness she had now achieved. He had married his Margaret and could no longer ask for her hand, but he was not likely to forget the humiliation she had made him suffer, or the boldness of Amalia who had not been crushed by his violent denunciations.

Two days passed before the thunderbolt struck. Will was surprised to see Luke again. For some time after he had forbidden a betrothal, the relations between the schoolmaster and his former pupil had been cool. But they were like souls, though the fire of Will's Puritanism burned lower than in the flaming days of his youth. Blackshaw thought his friend was becoming too moderate; his zeal, assailed by the evil influences around him was slackening dangerously.

The complaint he brought was, of course, the behaviour of Lynette. He was surprised that his old master should so far forget himself as to allow this girl such freedom. Riding out with a German mercenary soldier! Returning home late at night! Treating a man of the cloth with scant respect and a contemptuous look when caught in a disgraceful act! What else had taken place he shuddered to think.

He started to quote Ephesians:

"For it is a shame to speak of these things which are done in secret," but Will interrupted him.

"Pray do not preach to me, friend. You are not in the pulpit now. It is not for you to teach me my duty or reprove me with Bible texts. If you will know, I was not in favour of Lynette making this journey with the surgeon, but her father overruled me."

"He may be her father," said Blackshaw testily, "but he deserted her for many years and her upbringing was left to you. Surely that gives you some right to control her wayward conduct and to choose a suitable partner for her. You pandered to her fancies when she refused me. You have now given way again to a father whose unorthodox behaviour can be nothing but a bad influence on her."

"That is enough, sir," said Will, angry at being lectured like a schoolboy by a man half his age. "I do not see that Lynette's behaviour is your concern. You are no longer a candidate for her hand; she is not one of your parishioners and your interference can only breed bad blood. I will trouble you not to speak in such a way again."

Blackshaw did not try to counter this outburst. He had no wish for a permanent breach with Will.

"I am sorry, Friend," he said in a milder tone. "I believe I went too far."

Apparently he had been defeated, but before the minister left the house he had reason to believe that he had triumphed. The look in Will's eyes showed that he had not brushed aside all his friend's censure as lightly as he had made it appear.

Another reason for the continuing friendship of the two men was their collaboration in producing a chronicle of the war. Blackshaw's experience as Chaplain Historian in Ireland and Lancashire had stimulated his interest in such accounts. Will's diary had now reached monumental proportions. No less than five volumes had been filled with his firm, neat handwriting, and he was well on into the sixth. Blackshaw had ceased to write himself, but he collected news reports and incidents which he believed were evidences of the special intervention of Divine Providence, thereby making the book a lantern to illuminate God's purpose as well as a history of those stirring times. On this occasion Luke had brought broadsheets for Will to peruse and some happenings of local interest from his own and neighbouring parishes.

The disagreement was forgotten and the two men sat discussing the latest news until a light tap on the door announced the appearance of Lynette, enquiring if Mr Blackshaw would care to take some refreshment. Though uncomfortable at the sight of the girl he had slandered, Luke accepted the cakes and ale and returned to serious discourse. The king, besieged in Oxford, his capital throughout the war, had escaped through enemy lines disguised as a serving-man. First he had made for London and then in the direction of Market Harborough, where he hoped to hear news of the demands of the Scots. Finally he turned towards King's Lynn, hoping to be able to escape and join his friends in Scotland, Ireland or abroad. News was brought to him that the Scots would receive their king with honour at Newark and would not wrong his conscience. So, having ordered the governor of the town to surrender, he gave himself up to the Scots and terms were signed on the following day. Three days later they departed for Newcastle-on-Tyne and took Charles with them.

Will's pen scratched away as he entered the news and some of the local items. He laid his quill on the inkstand and looked across at Blackshaw who was thumbing over the pages of one of the earlier volumes.

"The work of the Lord is done," he said. "This closes one more chapter of our history."

He drew a line under the last sentence.

"Yet I fear another turbulent passage is beginning. Our king will not accept God's condemnation of him. His belief in a divine right is ingrained in him. Rarely is one so unshakeable. As I see it the problems remaining for settlement are threefold—control of the Church, control of the Army, the treatment of delinquents. Will there be a united stand against him? I doubt it. The Scots might be won over to support the king if he would agree to establish Presbyterianism in both countries and remove the barriers to free trade between them. Many of our brethren in Parliament would be willing to set up a Presbyterian system, but others, with myself among them, stand out for the religious freedom of all Puritan sects and the establishment of independent congregations; a few would even tolerate episcopacy and stop short only of Papists. Our King is a clever politician—he will not depart from his blind belief in divine right which gives him the power to control the armed forces and choose the religion of his subjects—'cujus regio, ejus religio' as in Germany. Nor will he hesitate to play off one party against another and claim that any concessions he might have made, were wrung from him under duress."

"Come Luke," he said rising from his chair. "Pay your respects to Alice. She looks forward to your visits. Like any artist she likes to show off her skill, and she is an artist in the kitchen."

He closed the book which still lay open on the table. His expression was one of relief and satisfaction as he spoke. "By God's mercy we have been spared to see the end of this unnatural struggle. Let us pray that Parliament and Army will unite against the common enemy of freedom. If they do not, they will have won the war and wrecked the peace."

24. A NEW SON FOR THOMAS

The summer of 1646 was full of trouble for Tom. In June he suffered a loss, sad but not unexpected. His mother, in her seventy second year, succumbed to a fever. Stubbornly she refused to take to her bed claiming it was but a little indisposition. When at last the old lady agreed, it was found that the sickness was far more serious than she had admitted. George, who was called in preference to any civilian physician or apothecary, found neither his leeches nor his medicine effective and old Mrs Ley died quite peacefully in the presence of her son and daughter-in-law. Amalia put her arm round Tom as he bent over his mother to kiss her forehead.

"There lies one who never rose from obscurity," he said, "who harboured no great ambitions, but whose goodness of heart and simple faith were a model for all around her. Multiply this artless soul by thousands and tens of thousands and make thereby a happy nation. She was the veriest Christian."

Soon after this bitter blow, Tom suffered another loss—not one so close to him, but a person he liked and respected. Mr Barton followed Mrs Ley to the grave within a month, but the circumstances of his death were quite different. He was accustomed to taking his luncheon with friends after Divine Service on Sundays. The fare served up at the Crown Inn was, as usual, excellent. The landlord boasted that he had been able to keep his staff almost intact throughout the war. Barton lingered over each course, but for once he carped about the wine.

"This bottle is not much to my taste," he said suddenly to the same Mr Clutton who had spoken so eloquently against Lord Grandison in 1642.

"Let us hope now that this war is over, to receive some better vintages."

He stopped short. Clutton noticed a sudden change in his friend's face. A physician was called, but in an hour Matthew was dead—struck by an apoplexy—gone as he would have wished in the company of his friends enjoying to the last the pleasures of the little life God had given him.

The war in Cheshire had ended, as was the case almost everywhere in England and Wales, only a few Welsh castles still holding out. Tom's work was much concerned with sequestration, and though he did not find this much to his liking, it was nevertheless his duty. Parliament had made the Committee of Sequestrators responsible for fining all those who retained their Royalist opinions or refused to agree to the Covenant. Estates of the wealthier delinquents were seized and their rents were regularly collected. Poorer people were imprisoned and their goods were confiscated. It became possible to compound for sequestration by paying a fixed sum of money and this was frequently done. Lord Cholmondeley for instance, was assessed for the payment of £7,742; others had fines levied, some in thousands and some in hundreds. The minister of Nantwich, Mr Saring, was one of the less wealthy delinquents, from whom goods were seized to the value of five pounds, comprising, in addition to beds, cupboards, and tables, such items as a pair of old bellows, an old frying pan, a close stool and a chamber pot. Monies from these sequestrations, taken for public use, were used for many different purposes, including the payment of officials, repair of sentry houses, the guarding of prisoners, and making good the damage done by the Cavaliers or the garrison of Nantwich.

Considering that the town had been occupied for four years, soldiers of Parliament, civilians and prisoners, rubbing shoulders within the compass of the walls, the population swelled at times to unnatural proportions by the influx of refugees from the surrounding countryside, there had been comparatively little trouble. Drunken brawls outside alehouses were the most common disturbances. Occasionally a soldier was court-martialled and hanged. The gibbet also played its part when deserters were brought back to Nantwich, but most regrettable was the hanging of Irish prisoners taken in battle, when the others had been granted quarter. Tom was saddened by this blot on Parliament's record of justice, but he was only a soldier under orders. The directive had come down from London, so he had to stand by and see injustice done.

Then, in July 1646 matters came to a head. The discontented soldiery mutinied over pay and for a time even held their officers and some gentlemen, including Tom, in the town gaol as hostages. The authorities were compelled to surrender to their demands, but thereafter they decided that the town should be disgarrisoned.

The warm summer days were giving way to the mellowness of autumn when George Waldheim came to his friend Tom with a not unexpected, but uplifting request.

"It is my desire to change my role once more," he said. "At first I was a trusty servant and you my honoured master. Then you accepted me as your friend. Now I would take on another part, closer even than that. I would be your son."

A son for Thomas! How could he have guessed in war-torn Mühlbach that the boy he set upon his horse would become a second son?

The two men were sitting by the chimney corner in the Ley's old house. Tom had taken the place occupied for so long by Grandfer Wyche. His hands were resting lightly on the arms of the chair. He looked straight in front of him considering his answer. George searched his face for a sign that his proposal had been accepted. A smile spread over Tom's rugged features. He leaned back in his chair the way Grandfer used to do.

"Nothing would please me more, George, than to see you and my angel married. For the last two years I have cherished a secret hope that you and Lynette would come together. It was a blow to find her destined for Blackshaw, whom she plainly could not stomach, and it was a joy when that obstacle was removed. Does Lynette love you? I would not have her marry without love."

"I believe she does—I am sure of it," replied George, hastily correcting himself. "I beg your permission to ask her formally to be my bride."

"Gladly, gladly, son," said Tom proudly taking the young man's hand in his. "There is however the possibility of objections from one quarter which we cannot ignore."

George looked at his friend in surprise.

"Will Masterson, I take it. But you are her father. Surely your word must be final."

"It is indeed—but I would be very loth to override my brother's objections, if there are any. He has cared for her throughout the years while she grew from a mere child of six into a young woman. I cannot dismiss all that long care, and treat him as a person of no importance in the matter. Yet I will not let him give my Lynette to another Blackshaw, nor will I miss the opportunity of promoting you to be my son. I will speak to my brother-in-law. No doubt there will be some text that he can find in his bible to justify my demands. Go to Lynette and speak the necessary words to her. Cheer up, mein lieber Sohn," he concluded, feeling that the glum mood which had settled on George needed banishing with a few bright words. "All will be well. You have both God and Thomas Ley on your side."

George's feeling for making place and time appropriate to the occasion, led him to suggest to Lynette, one fine September evening, that they should seek wild flowers in the wide fields bordering on the river. The worthy Master Gerard had written of the variety of plants he had seen in his native place—of the quakers and shakers, known to the learned as phalaris pratensis, the pashions and snakeweed, the wild horseradish, the ladies bedstraw, the wallflowers and navelwort. Trees and bushes including whortleberries and the wild ash or quicken tree had been noticed and recorded by the ever-observant herbalist.

George's particular interest in these fields beyond the mill had been aroused by something Tom had told him. While walking along the bank with the young man who aspired to be his son, he had pointed to a patch of grass close to a crooked willow tree and sighing, he had mentioned that the place brought back memories of days past. It was the grassy bank where for the very first time as a young, inexperienced lad, he had declared his love for his first wife, Kate. So George chose this spot to make his own proposal to her daughter and gently steered Lynette towards it. This was not without difficulty, for the girl darted here and there, finding some new, noteworthy flower to take home, press and preserve in a volume of interesting plants she had collected.

"This seems a pleasant place to rest," he said brightly as he reached his chosen spot just by the crooked willow and spread his cloak on the grass. He seated himself and looked around just as if he had never seen the place before. The girl placed her basket on the ground and sat beside him. The area of the cloak was not very large, so the two lovers were very close together.

"Dear Lynette," said the young man, "no garb could hide your beauty, but I should dearly love to see you dressed in some clothes of fashion—not gaudy like the Cavalier ladies and some of our party who ape them, but in the elegant style of our Amalia; she combines beauty with modesty outshining all the rest—except you, my dear," he added quickly.

Lynette smiled.

"You need not fear that I shall be jealous of my stepmother, George. But you are right. I hardly remember my own mother and for me Amalia is an ideal of womanhood. My earnest wish is to be as she is and thereby resemble my own mother too. I know she was dark and Amalia has light hair and a fair complexion; but I am sure Father would not have chosen as his wives ladies whose virtues were very dissimilar. However, I fear I must be content. My uncle and aunt consider that these garments, because they lack outward show, are best to demonstrate the virtue of a maid or a wife. I would not wish to wound them by defiance and I am sure that you, dear George will not love me less on account of my plain clothes."

"My darling how could you believe otherwise? But maybe I will gild the lily yet. That virtue of which you spoke would shine forth just as well from a Lynette dressed in the latest fashion, as from a plainly attired Puritan maiden. Sweet girl," continued George, coming gently to the great matter he had in his mind. "Your mother must have been a very beautiful lady. I can imagine her, twenty five or thirty years ago with your father, walking along this river bank in the cool of the evening, sitting perhaps on this very spot, by our friend the willow tree, then a mere sapling. Think of those days—no war or rumour of war in this land—just two young people talking of the future generation which would spring from their own love. Can you imagine it, my dear?"

"Oh George!" she exclaimed. "You thought I did not know why you brought me here. Father has told me that old story too how he and mother sat on this same bank, how they talked about courtly romances and he declared his love for her. George, your little plans are so naive, but I love you for them. She threw her arms round his neck, and he drew her to him. I love you so, my dearest man and I am sure I could desire nothing more than to be with you always."

"Then you will marry me," said George ecstatically. "As God is my witness I love you Lynette, more than life itself. By this match I am doubly blessed, for I have found a wife to adore and a father whom I can not only honour and respect, but love as if he were the one who begat me. All my life has been leading up to this moment. It was your father who found me and not a Swedish or Imperial soldier; this war brought him back to England with me as his companion; it was arranged that I should serve in the Northern Army and be here in Nantwich to see you before some Blackshaw, or his like, carried you off. It was a kind power that ordered these affairs and brought me to Lynette, who when I was a little boy of eight in far-off Germany, came on this earthly scene and waited for St. George to ride in and claim her."

"And Blackshaw was the dragon!" said Lynette.

George thought of the preacher as a scaly monster breathing fire from the pulpit and joined Lynette, who was shaking with laughter at her former suitor's expense.

"One difficulty and one only," said George suddenly, the laughter wiped in a moment from his face. "Of your father's approval I am assured, but what of Uncle Will?"

Lynette ceased laughing as suddenly as George had done.

"Ah yes," she said, "but even there I am confident. If God approves this match, as I am sure he does, Uncle Will can never oppose us."

It did not take much shrewdness on Will's part to realize that from the first encounter in the lane at Walbury, Lynette was in love with

George. It was confirmed by her remarks when she confessed her part in Captain Mynton's escape, but Will did not care to question his niece about it. He found George clever and pleasant enough, but when it came to choosing a suitable candidate for his foster daughter's hand, this young German would certainly not head the list. His objections were based on such flimsy grounds that the schoolmaster hoped he would never have to declare them. As a military surgeon he would be called away and Lynette would only see him rarely. The immature feeling she had conceived for this young man would die a natural death; then he would be spared the embarrassment of having to put his objections into words. Boiling affection seldom lasts; its very nature dooms it to die. Therefore it displeased him greatly when Tom came to him with the news of Lynette's proposed betrothal to George and forced him to come out into the open and oppose his brother-in-law.

"Believe me," he said kindly, "I have nothing against this young, man, but I know so little of him. He is a stranger not only in this district, but to our country. Is he a godly person?"

"You will have to take my word and be content," replied Tom. "I have known him since he was a lad of thirteen. He served me, saved me in battle, led me to safety, and kept me company in times of peace and war. And much more than all that, he sincerely loves Lynette. What more could a father want? As to his godliness, he is a true Protestant, a man who grasps the kind of religion I profess."

Will was not much impressed by this last remark. He thought his brother-in-law's religious views unorthodox and had hoped to step between him and the girl by marrying her to someone sound.

"He is not the man I would have chosen," he said candidly. "Nor do I think his conduct in this courtship has been entirely proper. You allowed him to ride with her against my advice and have encouraged private meetings and walks together unchaperoned."

"Allow me to judge what is proper for my daughter," said Tom stiffly. "I am grateful to you for your care during the years of my absence, but I will not be forced into the position of your deputy."

"It was God's will that the care of Lynette should be left to us. I prayed for a child when Alice could not bear one. God did not allow her to conceive, but he sent yours to me—that little child—lost—

302

abandoned—has been our joy for twelve years, I will not lightly surrender all the parental rights I exercised during that formative time, and see her led into less godly ways."

"Abandoned!" cried Tom shocked and angry. "I will not have you impute that to me. You know full well the circumstances of my departure; you expressed your approval and rejoiced in the fact I was going to fight for the Protestant Cause in Germany. You did not anticipate the return of Lynette any more than I did. Less godly ways? You say the Lord intervened and occasioned matters so that by my departure you gained a child. Think, however, that he also granted me a mercy. He preserved my Lynette throughout the days of the plague and brought me safely back to her. I know the Lord has been at my side. Brother, you would know it too had you been in battle! There is no mistaking that feeling—the certain knowledge that God is with you. We proclaimed it loudly. Some shouted and only half believed. I cried it out and I knew it. Do not speak to me of godliness! Are your ways the only ones to please Him? Have you ever considered that you might be deceived? It was surely better to expect my daughter and my friend to behave honourably, than to look on them with the eye of suspicion. The Lord watched over them, they needed no human guardian."

Will accepted Tom's rebuke, but to dispute his opinions was not to make him change them. He was sorry that he had offended one so close to him and his tone was conciliatory.

"I had wished for better prospects to offer Lynette," he said. "Blackshaw, a respectable clergyman, was not good enough for her and yet she will give herself to this German surgeon. His profession affords him little social standing, and while these troubles continue, his employment with the military is likely to take him on his travels as soon as Nantwich is disgarrisoned."

Tom sprang to George's defence.

"Do not disparage his calling, Will. Those who have suffered in the wars know the value of a good chirugion. The uplifting words of the minister, whilst they elevate the soul, can do nothing to close a wound or remove a musket ball. George served under a noted Paracelsian in Salzburg, and apart from his skill in surgery, he has a knowledge of medicines equal to that of any grave physician. To me the social standing of my son-in-law is of less importance than you

303

think, brother. Lynette will never starve. If necessary, I will see to that. The fact which strikes me most of all, is how much the young ones care for each other. Can a marriage not thrive on mutual love, with the essential purity in life and worship?"

"Has my marriage with Alice suffered from what you call lack of love?" asked Will.

"Perhaps it has not, but your nature and mine are different. A smoothly running contentment satisfies you. I demand stronger stuff—more robust happenings, romance, and great bursts of ecstasy. Lynette shares that desire with me and therefore she must have her George to experience the supreme happiness I have felt, first with her mother, Kate, and now with Amalia. I hear views similar to yours voiced all around me, but I must protest that they are false. Love need not boil away like an unattended pot of water."

"Despite all this, I cannot feel that he is one of us," protested Will. "Her understanding of higher matters is fragile. The imperfection of her conception of God troubles me. She needs one who can guide her, be her master and tutor, and share with her the love of Christ."

"I would not presume to quote Scripture to you, my friend and brother, but I say: 'Search your bible and your heart.' There you will find justification for granting these two young people your blessing."

"What if I refuse? Will you then overrule me?"

"I must, though it would be a blow to me that such divisions in our family should arise."

Will rose from his chair and paced the room.

"The decision is not mine," he said. "I must commune with the Lord."

His communion was interrupted by the sudden appearance of Lynette.

"George has arrived," she said, rather timidly, seeing as she spoke that there had been some heat in the argument between the two men. "He would like to see you, Uncle Will, as soon as he may."

"Where is he now?" asked Tom, expecting to see George appear from behind Lynette.

"In the kitchen with my aunt, chopping up the herbs he gathered, and preparing what he calls a 'schnitzel'"

Will found the idea that his wife needed instruction in the kitchen highly amusing. Tom joined in the laughter.

"Teaching his granny to suck eggs," said the schoolmaster, not unkindly. "But, *'Qui docet, discit'*. Truly, a remarkable man! Skilled with the cook's as well as the surgeon's knife! You are in luck, brother. Your son-in-law will never lack employment. He turned to Lynette whose face betrayed disapproval of what she considered mild mockery.

"Bring the lad here that we may offer him some refreshment."

Pleased at the apparent friendliness of Will's last words, Lynette disappeared, but several minutes passed before George entered.

At their first meeting, Will had not paid much attention to the young man's appearance, nor had he tried to judge his character. He was Tom's friend but it went no further. Later, he found him to be an intelligent man and apparently a good Protestant. Now he was to become part of the family. Should he receive him with open arms? Not to do so would mean a break with Tom, for he could see that his brother-in-law was as determined as his dearly loved foster daughter.

There was no longer any real justification for objecting to the young man who approached him in such a disarming manner. It was clear that the Lord could not wish him to cause dissension in his family. *"A brother offended is harder to be won than a strong city: and their contentions are like the bars of a castle."* Will stretched out his hand to George.

"Welcome, nephew," he said. "Come and take some wine with me."

Disgarrisoning! The word meant parting for George and Lynette. Political events were moving fast, too. The king was playing for time, hoping that the other parties would be so torn by dissension that he could divide and rule. He surrendered to those *'Men of the North'*, but they sold their *'precious blood—yea their own blood'* to the English Parliament who in turn lost Charles to the army. A web of intrigue was woven—intrigue with Scots and English, aimed at restoring royal power—woven by Charles at Hampton Court or Carisbrooke Castle whence the king had fled. Thus with the scene set for a renewal of war there would be fresh battle casualties to succour.

George Waldheim would be needed again and he was duty bound to heed the call, but in his new great happiness with Lynette his fervent prayer was that the mercy of God and the genius of Cromwell would make the conflict short.

25. DARWEN STREAM

In a cottage close to the bridge which spanned the river Darwen, a tributary of the Ribble, close to the strategically placed town of Preston, George Waldheim rested his weary limbs. It had been a hectic day—one of the most eventful of a momentous month. Oliver Cromwell who on July 15th had taken the surrender of Pembroke, had, a mere month later, come within three miles of the Scottish flank, and a bitter battle had been fought on that August morning. Fourteen days earlier, the invasion of the Scots in favour of King Charles had begun when the Duke of Hamilton crossed the border. His army was strong on paper, having over twenty thousand men, but it was drawn out in a long, straggling column like a caravan in Tartary, risking the chance of being cut asunder in the mistaken belief that Cromwell was nowhere in the vicinity. But Oliver and his nine thousand men were close at hand ready to strike. Only a flanking force of three thousand, commanded by Sir Marmaduke Langdale, could do anything to hold him off.

George had come all the way with Cromwell through the Midlands and South Yorkshire, for the risings in Wales had preceded the coming of the Scots. After reducing the Welsh fortresses, Oliver had produced his masterstroke. A march of thirty four days, much of the way in worn out boots, had brought his men through the backbone of England almost to the Irish Sea. "Hamilton beware!" said the reports of the scouts. "Cromwell is near!"

George remembered the battle at Ribbleton beyond the river as a confused mass of shooting, slashing men in front of him, of the pitiable wounded brought to him on rough stretchers, of the smell of powder, the clouds of smoke and the splashing mud. They had stopped in a narrow lane before the town of Preston—very deep and ill, they said it was, with enclosed fields on either side. There in that mud and water the Roundheads charged. Even after the fighting had begun, reports were discounted that Cromwell was present with his whole army, and though the main force of the Scots drew up on Preston

Moor, it took no part in the battle. The English Cavaliers fought bravely while Hamilton's men held aloof, but at length Langdale's ranks broke and he was driven into the town. It was even suspected that the Duke had burst out on hearing of Sir Marmaduke's plight:

"Let them fight! The English dogs are but killing one another."

Later, however, he denied having made this uncharitable speech. Many casualties had fallen that morning and there was a dire lack of surgeons, George and his two mates having been worked to the point of exhaustion. Then the signal was given to move up through the town to new positions. Driving the Cavaliers on before him, Cromwell secured a narrow five arched bridge which crossed the Ribble at Walton, though not without another furious battle, coming to push of pike by the broad Ribble and the little Darwen, the enemy retreating in pulses, until at last they were driven into and beyond the village at the foot of a steep bank which guarded the river crossing. The streets had been scoured by the time George rode through Preston. The Cavaliers and Scots had either reached the river or lay dead in the gutters. The civilians had disappeared into their houses; there was debris at the end of Church Street where Hamilton had rallied a small body of his men, trying by personal courage to rectify the mistakes of his generalship. If only he could check Cromwell's advance until his main force had passed over the river.

"Charge once more for King Charles!" Hamilton had cried, beating a man with the flat of his sword, but it had all been in vain, for with Cromwell at the bridge, the Duke had been forced to retreat from the town and swim across a river which, swollen by the heavy rains, could not be forded.

Atrocious as the previous encounters had been, the scene of carnage at the bridge was much more terrible. The dead had been thrown aside to clear a passage for the troops. Among them were some wounded which George caused to be carried to a substantial cottage by the bridge which spanned Darwen Stream. The Scots were just ahead—within a musket shot—and Cromwell's soldiers were posted round the houses, on the bridge itself, and in the muddy fields. The lights of many lanterns, like so many fireflies showed where the enemy lay around Walton Hall, but as the night wore on they were gradually extinguished and a blanket of darkness covered the defeated army. George could not sleep; his body ached with weariness yet he was unable to enjoy this period of rest. The intense activity of the last few days had wound him up so that he found it almost impossible to relax. Richard Lowe, one of his assistants, looked at his chief in surprise.

"Cheer up, surgeon," he said. "Today we gained a notable victory. Hamilton is doomed. They say he only escaped capture by a hair's breadth, but though his bones have been saved, his treasure has not. At Walton Hall his gold plate spilled out of an overthrown wagon, and though they longed to lay their hands on it again, the enemy had no mind to come and rescue it."

George, who had been sitting resting his head on his hands, looked up.

"How much longer will these wars last?" he asked rhetorically. "Even in my own country they are coming to an end. Ever since the French crushed the Spaniards at Rocroi in 1643, there have been negotiations for peace. Only now does it seem that a happy conclusion is at last in sight. Thirty years of strife! God forbid that, outdoing the German, our English peace should be so long in coming."

"The truth is, my friend," continued George after a long pause, "that my love of this life as an army surgeon is fast disappearing. Once I thought how charitable it would be to help the sick and suffering in war, now my only thought is: 'Stop the fighting and then there will be no casualties to cry out for me'. Let me return to my peaceful, green woods and meadows, my herbal garden, the countryfolk who need me, and my own dear wife. Lowe did not disagree but his interpretation was different.

"It is this king who has renewed the war by his duplicity. Can he not see that arbitrary rule is a thing of the past? In these modern times he cannot rule like an Eastern despot. He must be brought to a realization of his defeat and submit himself to the pleasure of the victors."

"Truly he must," agreed George; "but how I do not know."

"Hush!" said Lowe, putting his hand on his chief's arm. "Do you not hear a stir in the Scottish camp? If I am not mistaken they are on the move."

It was true. The Scots were forming up for a drumless and matchless march southwards. The rain which had been falling steadily for some time was slackening and the infantry was moving off. They were making for Wigan, there to join the cavalry at the head of their giant snake of an army, eighteen miles long.

In the grey light of morning, George rode through the deserted Scottish camp. Rain dripped from the wretched, improvised huts in which for a few brief hours Hamilton's men had sheltered; the still smouldering ashes of camp fires hissed as the drops fell on them. Around the Darwen there were signs of battle, for in the night General Middleton, returning from the van, had met a hot reception. He had taken a different road from Wigan, and after passing his own advancing army at some distance, had found himself in Cromwell's den instead of Hamilton's fold as he had expected. Corpses lay by the roadside everywhere and prisoners kept coming in. The road itself was a wretched track.

"Beyond belief," said George.

Even on his journeys in the loneliest parts of Baden or Bavaria he had never seen a worse road. The weather, too, in this August of 1648—the wettest month of a dismal summer—was unmerciful and conspired with the muddy ground to make the journey a nightmarish experience. George was mounted, but the poor infantry found it even worse—a case of one foot went forward while the other back did slip. Very dirty and weary was the army which quartered in the fields near Wigan as the Scots, after plundering the countryfolk almost to their skins, skirmished in the market place, yet dared not turn and face Cromwell in a pitched battle.

So they drew off, ever further towards Warrington and the Mersey Bridge to make their last stand. At Winwick church, barely three miles from the river, they drew up for this final battle, a strong body of pikes facing the Roundheads while musketeers lined the hedges. Powder was short and much of it had been left behind in the magazine at Walton and some of the flasks had been spoiled by the rain, but cold steel can be deadly, too, and the last stand was a brave fight.

By the time George came up, the Royalist had been driven off and bodies lay thick in a deep lane. Against the church wall, one man was leaning grotesquely, his head on his breast just as if he had been propped up there. In fact he had been killed standing by the wall, as a long, bloody mark bore witness. His helmet lay by his side: his sword was still in his hand, but a great stain on his breast from which blood oozed, and a total lack of movement, showed that he was dead. George raised the man's head; a slash across the forehead which had hardly bled, was the only wound on his face. Instead of giving the usual cursory glance at one for whom he knew he could do nothing, George stared hard at him trying to recall the place and time of their last meeting. Then it came to him in a flash. "Captain Mynton!" It was almost as if King Charles himself were propped up against this old church wall, so closely had the devoted Cavalier modelled his appearance on that of his hero. But now the smile of scorn as he spoke those mocking words while George was attending to the hurts, which had not tamed his spirit, had been replaced by the stare of death. He knew of the man's insulting behaviour towards Lynette, for she had told him the whole story of her meetings with the captain and his flight.

George had been interested to see this Mynton again—not to reproach him for his insolence and the advances he made to her, which were past history, but merely as a student of human nature to judge the man's mixture of fierce loyalty and recklessness, hollow compliments and careless morals—a combination which was strange to George. Now that he had gone who would weep for him?

Not King Charles for whom he had given his all. It would be of no great import to the monarch that in his service fell a Captain Mynton. He had never spoken of a wife, but there must be a girl somewhere who had taken him seriously enough and would shed a tear on his behalf, while a father, mother, or sister mourned the passing of a son and brother. Meanwhile, a short prayer from a "German sawbones" would have to suffice.

While George remained with his charges, Cromwell was meeting General Baillie on Warrington Bridge where he granted quarter for life to those who had surrendered. Four thousand prisoners were in his hands, besides a similar number taken at Preston and others by the way—ten thousand men in all, many killed and wounded on the flight and the rest of the Scottish army scattered.

"Surely," wrote Cromwell that evening, "this is nothing but the hand of God. He only is worthy to be feared and trusted and his appearances patiently to be waited for. He will not fail his people."

So Surgeon Waldheim returned northwards, back to Wigan, then by a different route thus avoiding the dreadful direct road to Preston, he came to the town of Chorley. The depression he had felt at Walton had begun to lift. The reason for it had been plain to see. In the last conflict a carefree and hopeful young bachelor had gone out to do his duty in the field. Now he had a wife and thought daily of the anxious moments she must suffer as she heard of the sieges and battles he had seen, for even a surgeon could become a casualty.

At Chorley an event occurred which raised George's spirits right up from the low point they had reached after the battle at Preston. The army camped for the night round the little market town, and scarcely had the young surgeon settled into his billet by the church of St. Laurence, when he received a summons. It was one he had to answer promptly—a signal honour in fact—for he was called to attend upon the Lieutenant General. Mounting his horse, George rode up the long drive towards the Elizabethan Astley Hall, the home of the Charnock family.

An unspectacular but pleasant seat, it stood among green fields and woods at the foot of the windswept moorland heights, by a small lake known as the dam which drove a water mill. It had stood for seventy years though it had seen some alteration,—a nest of Papists or a citadel of the old faith, for the owner, Robert Charnock, was a noted Roman Catholic. Both this man and his father-in-law had taken part in the siege of Lathom House under the Countess of Derby. Captain Charnock had suffered at the hands of Parliament, having lost an eye as well as his estates. To get the latter back, he had been forced to compound for £266 in 1646. Now his home had been taken over by one of these archrebels, and the soldiers of Parliament were camped around his park.

At the end of the Great Hall was a screen with a minstrels' gallery above it. This was reached by a small stair which also led to the upper floors. It was up here that George was taken to a fine, panelled room overlooking the courtyard. A number of senior officers were present when the surgeon entered. He assumed that a council of war had just broken up, for though they were standing taking pipes of tobacco,

312

papers were spread out on the table at the places where each officer had sat.

Cromwell received George cordially, despite the surgeon's humble rank, and spoke in a tone usually reserved by high ranking officers for their fellow generals and colonels.

"I have work for you here, surgeon," he said. "Three wounded gentlemen are in these quarters, one of whom is a senior colonel of the enemy forces—but no matter. I would have him afforded equal treatment with the others. I was impressed by your diligent care of the Duke of Hamilton's kinsman, left behind at Wigan, which was brought to my notice by the gentleman himself. I assured his Lordship by letter that his cousin would be granted civil usage and the best attention to his wounds. I am pleased to say that I was not disappointed by your attendance on him. When you have seen these gentlemen, have bandaged them and dosed them with physic as you think necessary, wait on me again. I would speak with you further concerning your service in this army. The orderly will show you the way."

A soldier lit a candle and opened the door.

"This way, surgeon," he said. "The gentlemen are quartered at the back of the house."

It was some time before George had dressed the wounds of all three men, though only the Royalist colonel had suffered seriously. At least it was more reassuring than the task he had been called upon to do at Chester. Flattered by the praise Cromwell had given him, he was determined to prove by his efficiency that the Lieutenant General's trust in him had not been misplaced.

The Royalist was the most difficult patient, but George made excuses for him, fearing that the severity of the man's wound would mean that he would soon have to return to perform an amputation of the foot. Having made each officer comfortable with clean linen bandages and soothing potions, he returned to Cromwell's room. The sentry at the door moved deferentially aside; George knocked and heard the general's distinctive voice—sharp but not unpleasant— bidding him enter. The colonels had gone and Cromwell was alone except for an orderly who was serving his supper. The soldier turned to put some fuel on a fire which had been lit to drive the dampness of the wet summer's day from the chill air. Cromwell dismissed the man.

"Leave it," he said. "I will attend to it myself if necessary. Come closer, surgeon."

George approached, still doubtful as to the purpose of this summons.

"I take it you are quartered to your satisfaction, Master Waldheim," he began in a friendly fashion.

George assured the general that his billet was as good as any that he had had on this campaign.

Cromwell spoke musingly as if hardly aware of George's presence.

"They entertain me well these malignant Charnocks. Methinks they fear their friends more than their foes. They have offered me their best bed—a very king in its class, though my weary bones would rest just as well on a truckle. But to business! I have need of a good physician on my staff and I understand you are as skilled in medicine as in surgery. How long have you served with this army?"

"Since Edgehill, General, when I and my father-in-law came from Germany to support the cause of Parliament. I am sure you remember Major Ley, sir. Wounded at Naseby, he returned to Nantwich to serve on the Council of War."

"Thomas Ley! Indeed I do. A man of great valour and resolution unsurpassed in this service. So he brought you with him from the German wars! His son-in-law, you say! Your father was one of our company. The best of us are poor, weak saints—yet saints; if not sheep, lambs and must be fed. We have the encouragement of merciful Providence from day to day. We shall have it in spite of all enemies."

George marvelled at Cromwell's enthusiasm. He had never seen him at such close quarters. Much had been written and spoken of his sanguine complexion, warts, and prominent nose, but to George these physical defects did not detract from the grandeur of his countenance and the impelling power of his speech.

"Know you, surgeon," went on Cromwell, "that wherever anything in this world is exalted or exalts itself, God will pull it down. His people are as the apple of his eye for whom even kings shall be reproved if they will not leave troubling the land. These have been glorious days, Master Waldheim. God help England to answer the Lord's mercies. There are those among us who anticipate these mercies. I say anticipate them, surgeon. A poor, godly man in Preston who died on the day of the fight, before his death, desired the woman that cooked for him to fetch him a handful of grass. She did so, and when he had received it he asked whether it would wither or not, now that it was cut. The woman said 'Yea' and he replied that the army of the Scots should do likewise and come to nothing so soon as ours should appear."

"A son-in-law for Major Ley!" he said going off at a tangent. "I did not even know he had a daughter of marriageable age."

"Neither did he, General Cromwell, until Nantwich fight. There, marching with Sir Thomas Fairfax, he found the little child, Lynette, he had long thought dead, grown into a beautiful, young woman."

"Congratulations, surgeon," said Cromwell, clapping him on the shoulder. "A moving story! May the Lord bless your union and make it fruitful. Love and rejoice in one another, but let it not cool your ardour for Christ. Go now. I will send when I require you."

As George rode back to his quarters he felt uplifted by his interview with Cromwell. It had only been short—some words of encouragement and advice, but in those few minutes he had felt that he was in the presence, not only of the greatest general in the conflict, but of one fit to be king. This aura of greatness which Cromwell possessed, and the fact that his own services were so highly regarded, had banished the depression which had assailed him after Preston. Though he would still long to see his wife and their expected family, he felt a new enthusiasm to go forward in his role of staff physician and follow this new Alexander as he went from success to success. Some of the things Cromwell had said surprised him a little.

"Kings shall be reproved if they will not leave troubling the land."

315

"Anything which exalts itself God will pull down." It was no longer a case of *"leading the poor, beloved monarch from those who had clouded his fine understanding, back to his people"*, but of humbling one who had infamously renewed the war. Would they actually go as far as to depose him? Were there even more drastic penalties they could impose upon a king?

George had never held royalty in any special awe. He came from a land with a multitude of petty princes presided over by an elected king. Whether he was blessed by the Pope with the title of Emperor, or took it upon himself as a matter of course, his name and person had no oriental magic for the young man. He did not despise kings, but he would rather see one elevated to that position on his merits and not by mere accident of birth. If God appointed kings, why should some be weak men unfit to rule—even imbeciles—and others tyrants who oppressed the people? It seemed to him that their power rested on a tradition based on the strong right arms of their ancestors rather than any divine appointment. Should not a king, hereditary or elected, be accountable to a higher power? If it were solely to God, as this Charles would have it, then should not the monarch rule according to the Word of the Lord? God could not wish him to oppress His people whom Cromwell had called "the apple of His eye". But what of those people? Was there no divine right for them? Lowe, who was more politically minded than George, spoke of those "fundamental laws of England" to which even kings were answerable. Was that a valid legal concept?

The route of the fleeing Scots was not towards Nantwich as Cromwell had supposed, for they marched to Malpas some distance from that Parliamentary town. There, six Scottish lords left them and surrendered to the Sheriff of Shropshire. They included Lord Traquaire, but Hamilton refused the offer of terms and decided to continue his march to Uttoxeter. Lord Traquaire and above fifty officers and persons of quality as well as a thousand common soldiers, were sent to Nantwich. Once more the church became a prison, until on the fifth of September the noblemen were removed to Warwick Castle and the common soldiers were sent to the parishes around Nantwich, only the captains, chaplains, and other officers remaining in the town.

Meanwhile, Hamilton, the Earl of Callander and Marmaduke Langdale were marching through the midlands. Hamilton offered his Garter Star to his captors and asked for quarter; Callander evaded them and Langdale, though taken near Nottingham, managed to escape in disguise from the castle.

Cromwell pushed up into Scotland against only weak resistance and was entertained and feasted in Edinburgh. Oliver believed he had impressed them with the witness he had shown them, for after their conversations about government and religion, he said:

"There is that conviction upon them that will undoubtedly bear its fruit in due time."

In the middle of October Cromwell returned to England, arriving in London on the very day when Colonel Pride stood by the door of Parliament and prevented the members who would have treated with the King from entering the chamber. The generals had pacified the country. Now the momentous events began which would end on the thirtieth of January with the execution of the King. Cromwell was to be the moving spirit.

26. THAT MAN OF BLOOD

While Colonel Pride was turning away members from the House of Commons and Oliver Cromwell was entering London with his victorious army, George Waldheim enjoyed a break from his duties in Nantwich. The General had permitted him to visit his home and he was to rejoin Parliament's forces in London by the Feast of the Epiphany. The late autumn days passed quickly; the Puritan Christmas—just another day—robbed of its own special appeal as a feast of jollity to brighten the dark winter months, was celebrated with some of the old gaiety in the house of Thomas Ley, but much more simply at the Mastersons. George rejoiced in the company of Lynette, the knowledge that the next year would bring the first addition to his family, the fellowship of Tom and the many friends he had made in Nantwich, and the rest from labour. He felt a growing sympathy towards the Mastersons, who were beginning to succumb to the charm of their new relative. Will, who had rejected George's bid for his foster daughter's hand, was puzzled as to why he had misinterpreted God's purpose on this occasion, and he found the young man's ideas closer to his own than he had imagined. Besides, he was anxious to say and do nothing which would cause a break with Lynette now that she was no longer in his care. Thus it was easy for him to recognise the serious side of George's character which lay beneath that happy-go-lucky exterior.

George's views were puritanical but not intolerant. Will had imagined him to be shallow and worldly, but in his thoughtful discussions George surprised the schoolmaster. He had underrated the education of a man who had attended the University of Salzburg and he could not find any taint of Catholicism remaining in his discourses. Will did not realize that his niece's husband had modelled himself so closely on the Lieutenant General, for he had not had the honour of meeting him, but George's attitude was becoming increasingly Cromwellian and this was close enough to Masterson's heart to win his sympathy. Even the young physician's speech bore the typical turn of phrase of the Parliamentarian leader.

The news from London was of a steady march towards the denouement of the Second Civil War. The army was embittered; the events of 1648 had forced the generals into the belief that Charles would never hesitate to plunge the country into yet another conflict if he imagined that he could regain his lost royal prerogatives—supposing that an agreement were made by which they were curtailed. They had lost confidence in Parliament too—hence the purging of that body—and they suspected it of wishing to throw away the fruits of hard won victory by making an accord with the King. Only Will among the three men who came together in Tom's parlour one evening in early January to discuss the latest news, was surprised by the report that a Commission of Parliament was to be set up to try the King.

George had noted Cromwell's hints at Chorley and there had been mutterings in the army even before he left, that this Charles Stuart should be brought to account for his tyranny before a court constituted by Parliament to try him. Tom thought of the sacrifices in the cause made by comrades who had paid with their blood. He remembered, too, his own partial disablement, the destruction and waste of treasure, and the passing of years in combat instead of more peaceful pursuits. All this to allow a king to restore his powers by political juggling! Will feared that the legal case was too weak—no court could try a king. But he had to admire the courage and resolution of those who would carry out such a bold plan.

"I doubt that any judge will be found to preside over such a tribunal which dares to arraign a king. There is no precedent and the personal risk is great—unless our Mr Bradshaw—"

"Now there is a possibility," interrupted Tom. "The Chief Justice of Chester. Perhaps he will be invited to take the office."

"He would accept, I am sure he would," added Will. "And he would do his duty without flinching."

"This discussion reminds me of something which happened long ago—before you came to England, George,—but perhaps you can recall the time, Will," observed Tom, his face betraying an effort to remember all the details.

"It was in "Seventeen" or "Eighteen"—I do not remember exactly. I and my father of that time, Mr Barton, went to visit Matthew's brother at Over, and while we were enjoying Uncle Henry's hospitality, the discussion came round to the sayings of a certain prophet by the name of Nixon which were currently a common topic of conversation in those parts. The lad, apparently an idiot, spoke words of wisdom when in trances. He said something like this:

"If a steward shall be slain, the master's neck shall be cleft in twain."

Now at that time we did not know of any Fairfax or Cromwell; Charles had not even come to the throne; old King James was still browbeating Parliament and letting them have their way by turns, while trying to avoid a breach with his subjects. First I thought the murder of Buckingham had been prophesied then came the death of Strafford which was more to the mark, for Charles was responsible in that he gave way and signed the death warrant. I remember the debate we had at that time on the impossibility of bringing a king to justice. Then there was more:

"'The men from the north shall sell their own blood and a man from the east shall bring his lord to the tribunal.' Do you not see the Scots who sold their king to the English Parliament, and Cromwell, the East Anglian squire, in these sentences?"

There was a pause.

"Surely I told you of this before, Will," said Tom, looking searchingly at his brother-in-law.

Will shook his head.

"No, never," he said firmly.

"Ah well, probably I had too much respect for the opinions of my tutor in those days to risk a scolding for consulting prophets. I wish I had written down all that he said. There was something about a great man's soul, a river, and a yellow fruit. Matthew is no longer with us and neither is his brother."

"They seem foolish to me," declared Will rather scornfully. The babblings of an imbecile—which you admit that he was. A river and a yellow fruit! Look rather into the Bible for your guidance."

"Much of what he said came true," insisted Tom. "He told me of the war in Germany before it began and prophesied the loss I suffered in my family and said I should find no peace until I came to a great mountain."

"Indeed?" said Will, displeased that Tom was producing all this evidence to support the prophet.

George had heard that part of the story before and appreciated its fulfilment when Tom met Amalia, but he was not aware that the death of King Charles had been foretold.

"It is a necessity," he pronounced decisively. "Cruel or not it is a necessity. Those who would treat with the King believe that he can be bent by their persistence, but they are mistaken. He thinks out his plans based on the assumption that our men will baulk at a capital sentence, but I do not think that even the certainty of that fate would deter him. His stiff-necked obstinacy will lead him on to make himself a martyr if no other course is left to him. He is clever enough to win popular sympathy for himself when facing your Judge Bradshaw."

"I wonder what happened to our prophet," said Tom who was only half listening to George's assertions.

"I have a mind to ride across to Over and find out."

"Do it then," said Will, not particularly interested in Tom's proposition.

"And do you think that General Cromwell will have the firmness of purpose to see this great work carried out?" he asked, turning to George.

"Cromwell has the resolution for anything," said George firmly and proudly of his commander.

"I heard him say that this second war was a more prodigious treason than any that had been perfected before, because the former quarrel was that Englishmen might rule over one another, this to vassalize us to a foreign nation. He will not exclude the King, the chief architect of the second war from retribution. Once he recommended me to read the eighth book of Isaiah, verses ten to twelve. I am sure you know the text," he said; then he added: "Read all the chapter! Cromwell has no doubts, for he knows that God is with us. However difficult our course may seem to be, I am convinced that he is right."

On the following day George departed for London and Tom made a much shorter journey of his own. The Swan Inn had long been under different management, Bessie Barton having followed her husband to the grave before the beginning of the war. The fare was, however, still as good as Tom remembered, although it was so many years since he had visited the place. The welcome was friendly enough, but the landlord could give Tom little information about Nixon, except to say that he was dead. However, he suggested that Tom should visit a certain Master Palin who dwelt away over the heath. This onetime steward of Mr Cholmondeley's had been present at the time when Nixon appeared before the squire and had, according to other retainers, taken down the words spoken by the idiot-boy in his trances. Thomas Palin was proud of his book of prophecies and would not show them to just anyone who came asking, but the landlord was sure that he would be impressed by Major Ley's standing and his personal experience of Nixon's surprising words of wisdom.

This proved to be true. Palin was pleased to speak about the prophecies, and to Tom's delight, he delved down into the depths of an old oak chest and produced a bundle of sheets of fading paper, unbound, but bearing all the sayings of Nixon which Mr Cholmondeley had ordered to be written down. There they were—the sentences Tom remembered and many others—prophecies about plagues, a great fire in the capital, local sayings concerning the Cholmondeleys, strange predictions of falling walls and the bones of a British king. Tom read these over and shook his head. Some were very hard to understand. Yet what of deputies falling from a great height and suffering no hurt? That had seemed fantasy enough at the time, but that infamous defenestration in Prague had proved that the prophet had an insight into the future.

"I hear he prophesied his own death," said Tom. "How did he in fact meet his end?"

"As he predicted, so 'tis generally believed," replied the old man. "The exact truth was hard to find, but we know that he died at the Court in London to which King James had summoned him. They mocked him unmercifully in the King's absence and locked him up for stealing in the kitchen. There they let him starve in a place of plenty."

"I remember that he ran about shouting: 'I'll be clemmed' and everyone laughed because it seemed so impossible at the King's court. And he died locked in a cupboard!"

"I cannot vouch for the truth of it, for I saw it not," declared Mr Palin, "but so it was told to me and it fits in with the prophet's own view of his destiny."

Tom's eye alighted on one paragraph just below the prophecy of King Charles's death.

"He who is a king but not a king shall rule us for a season. Though his issue shall fail us, his worth shall be seen by generations to come."

"When an oak tree shall be softer than men's hearts, then look for better times, but they be just beginning."

Mr Palin willingly allowed Tom to write down these and other predictions before lovingly wrapping his copy in a large sheet of parchment, tying it carefully, and laying the bundle in the chest. Enough truth had come from this prophet for the remainder of his sayings to be accepted. His curiosity satisfied, Tom returned to Nantwich. All the way those words came back to him:

"He who is king but not a king—his issue shall fail us—many generations shall see his worth."

It was a tantalizing "history" of times to come. The prophet must surely be referring to Cromwell. Did he mean that this man was a new Machiavelli, a schemer aiming to bring down the king of his land, an ambitious striver for supreme power for himself? Yet Nixon denied him kingship. A regent for another prince? The president or chief magistrate of a Roman—or Venetian—style republic? Only time could tell. It was all ordained by Heaven. Tom did not believe Oliver to be a dissembler. All his impressions of the general had been good, and what he had heard from George had confirmed them. Oliver sought the Lord's will daily and all his actions were guided by a study of the Scriptures. This strange man's prophecy was a glimpse of what God had in store for Cromwell and England—supreme power below that of a king, no continuance in the ruler's line, but influence and precedent for generations to come. Thomas Ley was content to watch and wait for the rise of Oliver.

On his return to the Army, George found London in a state of high excitement. The King had to pay for causing conquered enemies to take up arms again, old comrades to apostasise from their principles, and a foreign enemy to invade England. Before they had parted for the campaign of 1648, the soldiers of the Parliamentary Army had declared at a great prayer meeting in Windsor that if the Lord ever brought them back again in peace, Charles Stuart, that Man of Blood, should be called to account for the blood he had shed and the mischief he had done.

Now the Man of Blood had been brought to London to answer for his crimes. Charles Stuart was to be tried by a High Court of Parliament. One hundred and thirty five commissioners were appointed, but some, including Fairfax, did not act. As Will had suggested, Judge Bradshaw took the office of President of the Court, but he failed to persuade the King to plead, as Charles persistently refused to acknowledge its authority.

London was a vast army camp. On the first day of December the Saints had marched into Westminster and occupied Convent Garden, Durham House, St. James's and Whitehall. Soldiers were everywhere, riding in troops, appearing in the streets, filling the alehouses, and gathering on the greens and in the churchyards. The great Gothic cathedral of St. Paul and its environs swarmed with soldiers, vagabonds and those seeking inspiration or spiritual refreshment. Ministers fulminated against the King at the Cross; even in the wintry weather listeners were drawn to this and other open-air preaching places.

George sought out an old friend in London—the same Richard Lowe who had assisted him in many battles. After Preston he had been discharged and resided now in Fleet Street, close to the house of a leatherseller, Praise-God Barebone, whose name combined Puritanism with comedy. George was anxious to meet this Praise-God with whom Richard maintained a close friendship.

Picking his way with difficulty through the crowded streets, he was held up by a column of marching soldiers. Their smart red coats and good discipline did not impress some of the folk who were standing by. There were scuffles in the watching crowd and rough voices called out: "A king! A king!" Believing he could silence them with mockery, one of the soldiers seized an old sack and stuck it on a pike.

"There is your king! Look at him good people! A king of rag! Behold your Golden Calf, ignorant Israelites! Fall down and worship this your sacred monarch!"

The laughter of the soldiers and the tramp of marching feet drowned the indignation of the London rabble. Though he staunchly supported the cause of Parliament, George found this display crude and distasteful. He pushed his way through the mob and hurried on towards Lowe's house with as much haste as he could make.

Lowe was steadfastly in favour of justice for the King—not stopping short of a capital sentence. On December 22nd he had attended a public sermon given by Army Chaplain Hugh Peters in the courtyard at Whitehall where he preached to the troops.

"Standing in the pulpit he appeared to be fast asleep. Then he woke as if startled by a voice from Heaven and revealed that the Army in the role of an avenging angel was to lay the monarchy low. As he spoke I saw clearly the divine inspiration in his argument—*'All the kings of the nations lie in glory, everyone in his own house, but thou art cast out of thy grave like an abominable branch, as the raiment of those that are slain, thrust through with a sword. Thou shalt not be joined with them in burial, because thou hast destroyed thy land and slain thy people.'* As I stumbled away from the place, all doubt had left me. The king would have to die. No fear of outraging the sanctity of his person would hold me back if I were called upon to take part."

"Can it be done within the framework of the law?" asked George, studying Lowe's face which shone with messianic fervour.

"Law?" said his friend, dismissing any possible objection by George in a tone which bordered on scorn.

"Parliament will make the law by the direction of Divine Will. It is God's purpose; the law of men must be subordinate to his word. Other kings have been deposed and secretly murdered for reasons of state—Edward II, Richard II, the sixth Henry, the young King Edward. The Queen of Scots was privately executed on the orders of our Elizabeth, but this grandson must be openly arraigned and suffer his just punishment before the people he has wronged. God wills it. We must be his instruments."

"Maybe you discount it, but many will flinch from laying violent hands on one they believe sacred as the Lord's anointed. Cromwell spoke of rebuking kings, but he is merciful and astute. He would neither wish to exact unjust revenge on this Stuart, nor would he make him a martyr and let his son, as a second Charles, raise enemies against Parliament."

"I had my doubts concerning Cromwell," replied Lowe, weighing his words carefully. It did seem once that he would be too lenient with the King. But when Charles refused all further offers to compromise, when it became clear that he would keep no promises made to his captors, then Noll saw that the King's heart was hardened no less than that of Pharaoh of old, and it was as by an act of God that he turned away from this man and took the path of no accommodation with him. 'We will cut off his head with the crown upon it,' he said—and so he will."

"Then Charles will go," declared George, swayed by Lowe's enthusiasm. "But we will have a king. I fear that in this age men are still too closely bound to the idea of majesty. For me the rites and robes do not make a man a true king. It is the value of the one who holds it which sanctifies the office. This act of necessity will be a lesson to all those who would encroach on the liberties of the people. Tyrants beware! Ye are but men beneath those kingly garments. Armed with God's commission we will throw you down if you oppress his people."

"Well spoken, Friend," cried Lowe, clasping George's hand as if entering into some kind of bond, "But yet I would have no king."

326

Charles refused to plead—they always knew that he would. In law there could be no trial without a plea. He challenged the legality of a court which had been constituted by the Rump of the Commons. It was an irregular tribunal, but even the most traditional and honourable court could not try a king. He maintained that he stood for the freedom of his people against a usurped power which would betray their liberties.

"The king," he said, "cannot be tried by any superior jurisdiction on earth. It is not my cause alone; it is the freedom and liberty of the people of England."

But the judges bypassed these objections and sentenced him to death by the severing of his head from his body.

"Remove the prisoner," said Bradshaw when Charles strove to make some protests.

"Expect what justice other people will have," returned the King.

But sentence had been passed. The Man of Blood would have to pay for his folly.

George Waldheim accompanied Lowe to witness the execution in Whitehall and they stood near the Holbein Gate which crossed King Street. It was cold with bitter frost; the wait was long. Was the spectacle of a king suffering the supreme penalty worth it? They had tried their monarch in Westminster Hall where by long tradition traitors had stood before their accusers. They had brought him into the open street before his banqueting house where he should die. Verily it was not a thing being done in a corner, but in the full light of day. Drums began to roll in the distance; the sound of marching feet could be heard. A column of infantry crossed the park from St. James's Palace to Whitehall, the King between the files. They disappeared into the banqueting house and from his vantage point George could see very little. The word went round the crowd: "The King is here."

The rattle of drums went on; tension mounted among the spectators. In front, over the heads of some rows of expectant men and women, the black-draped scaffold presented a grim sight. They had built it up to the level of an upper window so that the King could step straight out. The block was there waiting for the one who would lay down his head upon it, but no one appeared. The mounted troops were drawn up tightly, hemming in the closely packed crowd. There was no chance of coming or going, only the long wait.

The minutes Charles had expected lengthened into hours.

Rumours flew around amongst the crowd:

"The warrant has been cancelled."

"No executioner can be found."

"The Dutch or Scots have intervened to save him."

"The Commons are in session forbidding the proclamation of a successor."

The person who started that last rumour had guessed correctly. There was not time to arrange the declaration of a republic, but at least the rallying point provided by the accession of another Stuart could be avoided.

At last the solemn procession began to come out on to the stage where the final scene of the drama would be acted—the executioner, masked and bewigged, wearing a false beard, his assistants similarly attired—Bishop Juxon, Charles's trusted counsellor,—and the King. Anyone who expected to hear words of contrition or even defiance from Charles, was disappointed, for as he spoke he could not be heard except by the very few who were close to him. George looked for some drama in these last moments, but the King was still speaking to those around him as if he were acting in an intimate drama away from the great stage on which he was the central figure. He was behaving with dignity, but George had not expected a king to cringe and whine. Lesser men had done the same in similar circumstances. He looked much older than George had expected. The cares of state, the hard campaigns of war had taken their toll. If only some of Charles's words could be heard. Doubtless his faithful friends would record them all. It would be surprising to hear that even the approach of death had changed his inflexible opinions.

Then the moment came which was the climax of the drama—a moment of horror for some—of sadness and of terror, yet one of triumph for those who saw in an act unparalleled in modern times, the judgement of the Lord on a bad king.

Charles knelt down in prayer—he slipped off his cloak—he placed his head on the block—he stretched out his hands. The axe fell.

"Behold the head of a traitor!" cried the executioner, but from the crowd went up a penetrating groan of wordless condemnation.

A woman close by started sobbing. Lowe reproved her.

"Silence!" he cried. "Do not weep for him. This was but another traitor."

"He was the King," said a man, presumably her husband. "Cursed be those who lay bloody hands on sacred majesty."

"Blind fool!" retorted Lowe. "He was no god but just another man like you or I—a man rightly punished for a grievous fault."

Another bystander was more forthright:

"Curses on thee and the pains of hell, thou Cavalier dog!" he shouted.

There were some shouts of disapproval at this speech and a scuffle broke out in which Lowe and George were jostled until they were forced to join in to protect themselves. Others were pressing forward from the rear as relic hunters strove to dip their handkerchiefs in the King's blood, scrape up the earth from beneath the scaffold or tear strips from the bloody pall.

George found his breath squeezed out of his body as, jammed against the scaffold, he struggled to free himself while the multitude clamoured for their relics. Then the thunder of horses' hooves from both the north and the south, swept up Whitehall like a double storm and the crowds scattered. In double quick time George dodged into a side alley, pulling Lowe who was less fleet of foot along with him. They ran on though they knew not why, for no one was pursuing them, until at length, their breath all spent, they realized the folly of this flight and after slackening their pace to a walk, finally came to a stop.

They were close to the river bank. Over to the right was Parliament House, a cluster of buildings around it and the venerable Abbey of St. Peter. The Thames was flowing on as quietly as before. No power had caused it to rise up and avenge the wicked deed done by this parliament. No torrents were rushing in to drown the members in their own house.

No thunderbolt had struck; no fire and brimstone had come down as in Sodom's day. In short there were no signs to show Heaven's disapproval. But neither were there any signs and portents from above to herald the new era which should follow the death of a wicked monarch.

If the Lord seemed indifferent, Richard Lowe was fulsome in his praise for those who had carried out this great work. Cromwell he hailed as a new Joshua who had brought many of the waverers into line. His sword would smite the last of these Canaanites and establish the rule of the Saints, making England a place as goodly as that ancient land promised to the Chosen of the Lord.

The two men walked towards the city. George was silent; he feared that the men who had done this king to death had miscalculated—they were living before their time. The old, superstitious feeling of awe before anointed majesty was still very much alive in the popular mind. He had no qualms himself about the deed though he could not rejoice in it, but he was apprehensive that this public execution would only serve to turn Charles, the wicked disturber of the peace, into a royal martyr, and it troubled him.

When the news reached Cheshire that the deed had been done, Blackshaw exulted in a Peterish fashion; Tom, well prepared by a prescience derived from Nixon's sayings, took it calmly as the inevitable solution. The indefatigable Will duly entered it in his diary:

"King Charles beheaded near the Banqueting House at Whitehall, London, on Tuesday xxxth of January 1648."

Then he added:

"A strange act and the like never seen or known of in England before."

A few days after the execution of the King, a newssheet brought over by a German merchant, came into George's hand. It had been published in the previous October, and although he had heard the news it contained before, he had not yet been able to read any such account of the momentous events in Germany in his own language.

The war in Germany, which had begun even before he was born and had dragged on for three decades, continuing even during the peace negotiations, was finally over. This coranto heralded peace in a highly dramatic way. There, the angel resting on a cloud, sounded the trumpet "Fama", and waved the flag and olive branch, while the god, Mercury, bore the proclamation of blessed peace which had now descended on war-ravaged Germany.

"Pax: Frieden: Peace: La Paix:"—this was the message of a picture full of symbolism, showing broken arms, flags hanging out in Vienna, Stockholm, and a much more distant Paris; while underneath in doggerel verse, the long awaited news appeared.

For thirty years they had fought and reduced the land almost to a desert. Now at last life could begin again—so the newssheet said. The rosy picture of the happiness which would follow, now that peace had been declared, amused George by its naiveté. It was true that German soil would no longer be soaked with the blood of thousands, that the streets would cease to echo to the tramp of marching feet, that the peaceful occupations of the people would begin to flourish again, but many years—even decades—would have to pass before the longsuffering land would reach the blissful state depicted on this newssheet. For twenty five years they had fought before there was even a will to make a lasting peace. It had taken five more years to conclude it. The terms of these Westphalian treaties were less important to the common folk than the mere fact that the fighting had ceased. The agreements concluded by the Emperor with the Protestant powers at Osnabrück and the Catholics at Münster, provided that Calvinists should share in the privileges of the Lutherans, and that church lands were to be secured in the possession of those who had held them in January 1624. There were territorial changes in favour of

331

Bavaria, Sweden and France, and the independence of Switzerland and Holland was finally recognised. Now it was over! Poor, blighted country! Though he had readily adopted England as his homeland, George had never lost a deep affection for his native soil. There were tears of joy in his eyes that day—tears of joy for Germany.

Was it worth such turmoil and destruction? Could not these terms of toleration have been reached before? Need it have taken thirty years for passions to cool? Men will do much to gain their ends, to enforce their wills on others. Naked aggression, the ambition of princes and religious fanaticism, had all played a part in this struggle. Whatever it had solved, the war would leave enough problems to fuel another conflict in some year to come. For a time, however, there would be peace and a period of reconstruction.

The bells of Osnabrück and Münster had pealed out their joyful news that the German war had ended. George put aside the newssheet with a heartfelt prayer that the bells of London and Oxford, of York and Canterbury, should join in and greet with their acclamations a new era of peace at home.

27. DUNBAR FIELD

Sunday September 1st in the year 1650 was a day of humiliating retreat for the English forces in Scotland. A poor, shattered, hungry, discouraged army withdrew from the environs of Dunbar. This small port was no stranger to the dramas of Scottish history. Edward I had gained a victory near the town in 1296 and had captured the castle which stood sentinel on a headland projecting from the broken, red, rocky North Sea coastline. In a notable siege of 1338, the bold Countess Black Agnes had stoutly defended it, and within living memory, the Queen of Scots and her lover Bothwell had taken refuge behind its grim wails.

The English army under its new Lord General, Oliver Cromwell, had been battering at the gates of Edinburgh and skirmishing around Musselburgh, but sickness stalked through the camp and the Scottish winter weather was approaching. It was politic to retreat to Dunbar, where the harbour was good and where their lifeline, the English fleet, could fill the stomachs and the powder flasks of the Army.

George's hope for a rapid return to peace after the execution of the King had not been fulfilled. In Ireland the war had continued; the Scots had received Charles Stuart as their king and he had pledged himself to their Covenant. This second Charles had been proclaimed in defiance of the English Parliament.

Fairfax, nominated to supreme command, had been unwilling to march against his coreligionists, so Cromwell was in his place. On the hills above the town, an army outnumbering them by two to one brooded over the English force. Why did they not come down and fight?

"Bring down your army," said a doughty one-armed soldier captured by the Scots, to General Leslie himself, "and you will find both men and great guns too."

George Waldheim was at Broxmouth House on the evening of the second. Behind the General's headquarters, tents and huts covered the peninsular. Rough grass swayed; the ubiquitous pools of water were ruffled in the strong wind which drove rain on to the camp and defied the rude tents to stand its battering.

The church of Dunbar stood just outside the town. There on rising ground the cannon were lodged, but now a more threatening and advantageous position had been found; Dunbar itself straggled down the slope to the harbour and looked out across the North Sea, its ruffled water dotted with rocks and islets, where the English fleet guarded the left flank of the Lord General's army.

As usual on the eve of battle tension mounted, but in these latter years George had learned to relax. He had just finished writing a report. He laid it aside and took another sheet of paper preparing to write to Lynette. His dear wife! How he longed to see her face—and young Thomas, now a year old, who had been born in his absence, for on his return from Ireland necessity had sent him hurrying here to the North with Cromwell's forces to discipline the Scots.

Ireland was a dismal memory—the wicked weather, the mounting sickness, the fearful slaughter. Drogheda was the greatest nightmare of them all. It still haunted him.

"If upon refusing this offer of mercy that which you like not befalls you, you will know whom to blame," wrote Cromwell to garrisons he summoned—and they liked it not, for the storm was terrible. The batteries were planted, the breaches were made assailable, but the town, strongly fortified, would not easily be taken. The dispute was hot; the order "No quarter!" was given.

Cromwell was transformed that day. George had never seen him so. His fury burst out as fiery as the storm itself. In the heat of the action he forbade them to spare anyone in arms in the town, and over two thousand were slain. George knew it was the rule of war. Cromwell had justified it as the judgement of God on the bloody Irish. The sharpness of this thrust made the terror of Cromwell's name so great that no such signal lesson was necessary again. Surgeon Waldheim knew well that a deep and painful cut was often necessary to effect a cure. Yet it was a dreadful day for which there was no rejoicing. The screams of the dying, hacked down in cold blood; the

334

man who cried, "God damn me, God confound me, I burn, I burn!" in the flaming church; the miserable prisoners marched off to servitude in Barbados! He could justify them perhaps on grounds of legality, example, or necessity, but not forget them. Now it was Scotland's turn. There was no such bitterness here as in Ireland. Cromwell was eager to convert the misguided Scots.

"God hath a people here fearing his name, though deceived," he said of them.

But war cannot be taken lightly; many would have to die before these quarrels were settled. None of these broodings should reach Lynette. To her he would be the same happy-go-lucky George she had always known.

He broke off from his writing. An orderly entered and called him to one of his charges. The weather had become wild in the extreme.

"Our men are drawing up and manoeuvring for position," said the man, anticipating a similar speech by his Lord General. "The Scots are coming down to challenge us here below. It will be a great mercy that the Lord has vouchsafed, if they are delivered to us thus."

"That surprises me little," replied George casually. "There is no shelter up there unless they huddle under the sheaves of corn and scattered bushes."

He pulled on his cloak as he had to cross over to a farmhouse which stood some distance away on the headland. The sound of the wind and the waves beating on the rocks drowned the noise of preparations for battle in the English Army. Cromwell was drawing up his men by torchlight in front of the burn which ran past Broxmouth House, until the moon added its pale beams to brighten the scene. George could see very little of the preparations, but movement all around him showed that he would soon be in the very thick of the fight. He returned to his writing—another sheet to enclose for Tom. The night wore on; he nodded and slumbered; the gusty wind still moaned around the house but George noticed nothing.

Then, suddenly, a louder roar of cannon shook the building. It was light and the battle was on. George consulted his timepiece and found it was six o'clock. The planned dawn attack had been delayed. He thrust the papers in his wallet and called his staff together. Trumpets were sounding. Cries of "The Lord of Hosts" and "The Covenant" rose above the wind. The resistance of the Scots was fierce and Cromwell's men retired, but a determined charge by the English horsemen dislodged them from their gains. Louder and louder mounted the din of battle, overtopping the wind and surf, as the men of Cromwell, Lambert, Fleetwood, Monck and Pride charged with flashing swords or levelled pikes.

"The Lord of Hosts!"

Those who called upon their God would carry the day! Like a whirlwind the English stormed through the Scottish ranks.

"They run! I profess, they run!" cried Oliver. All was confusion as the sun came up across the sea and flooded the grisly scene with heavenly light. Ah sun, what grim and deadly deeds have men done in thy absence!

To Oliver this red orbed sun rising from the dark waters of the ocean at the crucial moment of the battle was a timely sign.

"Now let God arise; let His enemies be scattered!" called the Lord General, as the ruined Scottish army rushed to destruction helter-skelter over sodden ground with the victorious English close behind them. Then the chase stopped.

George stood and listened as another mighty sound swelled up from the battlefield—not the roar of wind or waves, not the clash of steel or the bellowing of the cannons, but the voices of men—of thousands of men—uplifting their praises to God. Cromwell had made a halt and there he led them in a song of praise to that Lord of Hosts whose name they had invoked in the thick of the fight.

"O give ye praise unto the Lord,
All nations that be,
Likewise ye people all, accord
His name to magnify."

It was a short psalm, this one hundred and seventeenth of the book, but the singing of it confirmed their faith and gave their horsemen time to rally.

"For great tousward ever are
His loving kindnessess;
His truth endures for evermore
The Lord, 0 do ye bless!"

The last words rolled aloft, and the moment of praise to the Lord gave way to the secular work of driving those they saw as His enemies before them. And so the Scots fled; the English whose losses had been very light, pursuing them like demons, killing all the way. Three thousand of General Leslie's men had fallen, ten thousand were prisoners. In little over an hour the battle had been won and the way to Edinburgh was open. The casualties among the English were totally disproportionate to the slaughter in the Scottish army.

So Cromwell's medical services were not overtaxed. On the day following the battle a Proclamation was issued allowing the countryfolk to remove "in carts or by any other peaceable manner" the wounded enemy soldiers still lying on the field.

Cromwell had gained his greatest victory, but the war was not yet over. He would pursue it with words at Edinburgh, and force of arms elsewhere until this misguided Scottish people saw the light.

Edinburgh! George had good reason to remember his stay. The ancient castle, sitting atop its rocky perch; continued to be held by the Royalists for many weeks after Cromwell's entry; there were skirmishes but no more great battles; the Scots had retreated to Stirling and the Borders, leaving the men on the crown of Edinburgh rock in a state of siege.

Cromwell had his quarters at Moray House, George at the 'Globe' not far distant, just off the Lawnmarket. The landlord of the hostelry, Master William Douglas, was in appearance a typical Scots landlord. A sturdy man with reddish hair, he showed no animosity towards the English, but there were hints that it was more a matter of policy than genuine feeling. He had two presentable daughters—Jeannie aged sixteen and Barbara a little over twenty. The elder girl mingled with the guests in a very forward way and was much in demand for service. George did not think her very pretty, a view shared by most observers, but she was an extremely vivacious girl and men were easily captivated by her flashing smile and coquettish manners.

One evening when the inn was not very crowded, a trooper sitting at a table close to George, made a remark to the girl as she passed, which caused an angry look to replace the usual pleasant smile. She tossed her head and turned away, but the soldier drew her towards him. Barbara, whose manner was usually theatrical, tried to escape from him with a kind of "Unhand me, sir!", but the man taking this to be just a coy refusal which really meant acceptance, pulled the girl across his knee to kiss her. George had not heard the man's remark sufficiently well to understand it, but from the sniggers of the onlookers he thought it to have been something obscene. From his corner he observed the changing moods of Mistress Douglas and judged her protest more correctly. He rose from his seat.

"Let the young lady be, Trooper," he said calmly, as he stood over the man, looking down on him with displeasure.

"Young lady!" repeated the solder with a loud guffaw. "Young whore, more likely," and he pushed the girl off his knee to the floor where she landed in a heap.

"Now Master of Physic," said the trooper, confronting George and recognising him for the first time in the dim light of the inn parlour. "From whence comes your authority to order me?"

"I do not order you, my man," replied George, stressing the first person. "I tell you only what is decent, godly and fitting for one of Cromwell's soldiers."

"So now our potion peddler would play the minister and tell us what is godly! The devil take you! I do not care a tinker's damn for you or your preaching," cried the man scornfully, and picking up his tankard of ale he dashed the contents into George's face.

"From which regiment do you come?" asked the physician severely, ignoring this offensive act. "I would have your colonel's name. You insult the lady, you revile me, you use ungodly oaths. There are severe penalties for such behaviour."

"My regiment?" replied the man mockingly. "Carry my words to the colonel would you? If you were a man instead of a bag of wind and penny powders, you would stand up and fight."

George declined this offer firmly.

"I will not fight with you, Trooper, and add brawling to your offences. You are of the meanest kind of men who disgrace a fine army. But I have the ear of General Cromwell, and unless you make your peace with the lady and leave this inn to better company, my complaint will go even beyond your own colonel."

The man's temper had abated. The fear of the consequences if he resisted the physician any further, wrung a grudging apology out of him.

"Now leave!" commanded George in a stern voice. "Presently!"

The landlord, who had been out when the quarrel began, had returned to find George completely in charge of the situation. He thanked the young man warmly and went off to search his cellars for something special to offer him. Barbara's look of indignation at the rough treatment she had received, had changed to one of admiration for George, and her face glowed as she seated herself beside him uninvited, smiling in a way which implied that she was giving him a very real reward for his defence of her.

"You are gallant, Master Physician," said the girl, placing her hand on the table, palm upwards, as if she expected George to take it. "You made that man slink away like a whipped dog."

"It was not just gallantry, mistress, though I do not like to see a lady injured. It is my hope that it has helped to preserve the reputation of our army."

"You are no Sassenach," said Barbara, looking him up and down with obvious pride at being close to him. "Father says your name is Wallhame. How do you come to be in this Cromwell's army?"

"Waldheim!" corrected George. "German by birth, but English by adoption. I came over in forty-two and I have served the Parliament ever since."

"Under Cromwell?" asked the girl. "You made that trooper turn as white as a winding sheet when you said you have his ear. Is he so terrible when he's aroused?"

"He can be terrible," admitted George, "but his great passion subsides as quickly as it flares. When he is in a quiet temper he is the sweetest man to know. He shows great compassion; I have seen him shed a tear for some object of his pity. He can laugh too and share a joke. Once he bellowed and guffawed like an apprentice lad with merriment when a soldier jammed his head in a Scottish butter churn whilst trying to drink the cream. He can be generous too. At Dunbar he gave a man who complained that he had been plundered by the enemy, twice the amount he had lost, out of his own pocket. Yet in battle you would scarcely recognise him; he is all fire and inspiration; the English Cavaliers and the Irish learned that to their cost. But Dunbar was his greatest day. That will be written in the history books. This man does the work of the Lord, Mistress. We must fear God's wrath and bow to his punishments, but we receive his love and mercies too. So it is with Oliver."

"Enough of your Cromwell," said the girl impatiently. "Tell me more about yourself."

George felt that he had said sufficient, and did not wish to appear to be gloating over the Scottish defeat. He was about to comply with Barbara's request, when he was interrupted by the landlord who returned with a bottle of wine which he had hidden somewhere in the cellar to save it from plundering. To Barbara's annoyance he seated himself at the table and monopolized the conversation with her new acquaintance, which was uninspiring, since he agreed with everything George said and stimulated no discussion. There was more about Cromwell, Dunbar Field, and Charles Stuart now called King of Scots. George had not expected any radical talk from this innkeeper, but his constant agreement and praise for Cromwell and all his works seemed insincere.

Barbara rose from the table to go about her work. At the first available opportunity, George thanked the landlord for the wine and returned to his room. It was a small and barely furnished chamber but well-scrubbed and comfortable enough for a man accustomed to the hardships of soldiering. He had heard tales of the primitive nature of Scots life—the warren of narrow streets in the old grey stone city, the high lands or tenements of six or seven storeys, the unpleasantness of the lodgings which necessitated the carrying of sweet smelling herbs, and the stink of privies which offended the whole house. He had been warned, too, of the 'sluttish, nasty and slothful people', but if it was all true and this was the face of Edinburgh, then he could call it more than common luck to be quartered at the '*Globe*'. His first impressions of Scotland had been mixed; he had observed the lack of pretty gardens, though he was in the most fertile district, extensively farmed with fields of wheat, oats, and barley. The only part he knew—the coastal strip—was not lacking in industry. All along the way from the town of Dunbar through Prestonpans, he had seen the familiar houses where salt was gained from the briny waters of the Firth of Forth. But George could not imagine how the Highlands must be—all wild and barren with a devilish climate—no fit habitation for a civilized man, he had heard.

He lit a candle. On a small table were two books—Luther's bible and a copy of a recently published work by John Milton, with the title '*Eikonoklastes*'. This was a reply to '*The King's Book—Eikon Basilike—a Portraiture of his Sacred Majesty in his solicitudes and sufferings*'. Purporting to be the king's own account of his trials, it had in fact been written by his chaplain Doctor Gauden. Milton, who had already written a pamphlet pointing out many historical examples of tyrannicide from Greek, Roman and English history, referred to the divine right of a people and praised the removal of a man who had betrayed his trust.

"It is lawful and has been held so through all the ages," ran the subtitle of '*The Tenure of Kings and Magistrates*', "for any who have power to call to account a tyrant or a wicked king, and after due conviction, to depose and put him to death."

'*Eikonklastes*' followed this tract as a counterblast to '*Eikon Basilike*' which was turning the "Man of Blood" into the "Martyred King". Royalists took comfort from this pity-provoking book; the undecided or indifferent were touched by a wave of sentimental feeling for Charles as a meek and mild monarch suffering unspeakably at the hands of the wicked rebels. That he denied his people any right in government was ignored or forgotten—that he had said on the scaffold:

"It is not having a share in government; that is nothing pertaining to them; a subject and a sovereign are clear different things."

This unrepentant statement had appalled George and it justified the removal of a man who was so unshakeable in his belief in his own divine right. Milton's words confirmed his stern opinion of this king, when he complained of people with a "besotted and degenerate baseness of spirit who would fall down flat and give adoration to the image and memory of this man who hath offered at more cunning fetches to undermine our liberties and put tyranny into an art."

But though George appreciated Milton's attempts to pull down the idol of the "inconstant, irrational and image-doting rabble", he could see that his arguments—strongly worded and reasoned though they were—appealed more to the intellect of scholars than the sentiments of the common folk. Thus *'The King's Book'* scored over *'Eikonoklastes'*—though certainly not with George. His head bent over the book and his mind on the substance, he did not notice first a gentle knock on the door, then the creaking of its hinges as it was pushed slowly open. When he looked up, Barbara was standing in the entrance holding a tray in her hands.

"Pardon me, Master Waldheim for opening the door. I thought I heard you say, 'Come in!'"

"No," replied George "I never spoke—but perhaps I was murmuring the words of this book while reading. 'Tis a habit I do not seem to be able to cure."

"Strange," replied the girl, "but then perhaps it is a custom of your country. Will you no have a wee bite to eat, Master Waldheim?"

George looked surprised at this invitation to a second evening meal, as he had already supped below, but he felt he could not refuse. He noticed on the tray two glasses and a bottle of wine similar to the one which the landlord had opened for him. Barbara saw him glancing at the glasses and misread his thoughts.

"Is it ale you are wanting?" she asked. "Our brew is good and strong, but I brought you this wine. Many young gentlemen prefer it".

"Do not trouble yourself—I am content with wine," replied George, though he did not particularly relish the idea of taking any more, having drunk sufficient of the landlord's special vintage downstairs.

He indicated a chair.

"Sit with me," he said graciously, feeling compelled to accept the company imposed on him.

"Your fare is excellent," he continued, considering a compliment to be in order after the girl's kind attention to him. "I am lucky to be here. Most of my comrades are short of victuals."

"Good, plain food," said the girl, pleased at his praise, "and none of your foreign kickshaws." Her face changed and she looked embarrassed. "But then I should not say that, and you a stranger in this country."

"Hm," said Georg "foreign kickshaws—" trying to fathom out the exact meaning of the last word. But Barbara did not enlighten him. She had noticed a sheet of paper lying on the table, across which George had written the headings:

Edinburgh,

October 7th, 1650.

"My dearest Lynette,"

There was still magic for George in pronouncing or spelling her name. Sometimes he substituted the German for the French diminutive when writing or speaking of her, and then she became his Lynchen.

"A lady you know?" asked Barbara, archly.

George nodded. He should have said: "She is my wife", but somehow he refrained. A desire he had not admitted to himself to enjoy the company of this girl for a little while longer blocked his words and prompted him to conceal his marital status.

"Tell me about her," said Barbara, coyly, "is she prettier than I am?"

George had never believed anyone to be prettier than his wife. He was sure that the fabled Helen or Mark Antony's Egyptian Queen would have stood on a lower step. Yet he hesitated to say so.

"You are different," he replied evasively. In fact he was beginning to find this Barbara prettier than he had at first judged her to be. The wine may have contributed in part to the formation of this opinion, but the friendliness and vivacity of this girl added charm to her none too striking features.

"To say 'different' means little, Master Waldheim!" said Barbara, laughing. "Cromwell is different from Charles Stuart. You told me where that contrast lies; now tell me how I compare with your Lynette."

"Call me George," he said in reply, hoping that she would not press him further about his wife. To his relief she did not insist on an answer and abruptly changed the subject.

"Our city, George," said the young lady, relishing the pronunciation of his name. "How do you like our Auld Reekie?"

George had to admit that he had seen little of the sights of the Scottish capital since his entry, and this was Barbara's cue. She proposed that on the following day she should show him something of it and he found himself accepting. He did not know exactly why, except that the girl's personality was compelling and he found it painful to refuse.

When she had gone he thought little about it, but when he saw Barbara again he had the feeling that perhaps it would be unwise to make a public appearance with her. Yet would it really be such a wicked act to let a young lady show him some of the sights of her city? He could not go as she had proposed on the following day, but he resolved that at the first opportunity he would keep his promise.

"Fama nihil est celerius". Oh George! Nothing travels faster than scandal.

28. TEMPTATION

It was three days before George was free to take his planned walk round Edinburgh in the company of Mistress Douglas. When he came down to meet her he thought she looked quite charming in a better gown than he had expected from the daughter of an innkeeper—not of a gaudy colour but a tasteful silvery grey. The radiance of her smile compensated for her indifferent complexion, improved to some extent by cosmetic arts, but her hair of a squirrel colour and a rather coarse texture, lacked the lustre of Lynette's tresses. He had to admit, however, that she was pleasant company, and he was looking forward to a stroll in the environs of the city with a knowledgeable guide. It would be a welcome break from the routine of his medical duties, a cheerful episode in his enforced stay in Edinburgh.

Babbie—as he was instructed to call his companion—was full of enthusiasm, and to the uninitiated George she seemed very well versed in Scottish history, though a student of the subject would have noticed many inaccuracies in time and place. At least she could show him the kirkyard of Greyfriars where in 1638 noblemen, gentleman, burgesses and commons signed that defiant document the New Covenant, declaring that without any worldly respect or inducement they would resist all those contrary errors and corruptions in religion to the utmost power God had given them. Barbara's description was vivid and George could well imagine the congregation of noblemen and ministers lining up to set their hands to it while the crowds of Edinburgh citizens flocked in to sign their names or make their marks on the historic document. He saw, too, the High Kirk which these Covenanters had striven to keep undefiled. He laughed at the way Babbie told the already familiar story of Jenny Geddes throwing a stool at the dean when he opened the hated Prayer Book to read the collect.

"De'il colic the wame of thee!" cried Barbara in her broadest Scots accent. "Thou foul thief! Wilt thou say the mass at my lug?"

More sobering was the sight of the severed head of James Graham, the Great Marquis of Montrose and King's General in those parts, who had been hanged and dismembered by the Covenanters. His limbs were severally displayed in Glasgow, Aberdeen, Stirling and Perth, but here was his head spiked high above the Tolbooth, supposedly as a warning to traitors, but more truly a reminder of the fate of the vanquished at the hands of a pitiless enemy.

At the bottom of the Royal Mile the old dark walls of Holyrood revealed their secrets through the medium of Mistress Douglas, who, in a lighthearted way, related the escapades of the Queen of Scots with Bothwell, Rizzio and Darnley. Even the murders of the two latter gentlemen were not treated as respectfully by Barbara as one might have wished.

Above the town, the castle on its rock glowered down at them. Sir Walter Dundas, the governor, had still not decided that the time was ripe to submit to Cromwell. An occasional puff of smoke heralded a foretaste of the bombardment to come. Mortars were being brought up to the supposedly impregnable fortress; miners from eastern Scotland and even from Derbyshire, burrowed into the rock like moles.

George and Barbara struck out into the open fields which led up to Edinburgh's own mountain—Arthur's Seat, an extinct volcano shaped like a great couchant lion. Barbara, almost out of breath as well as stories, took her companion's arm. He felt rather embarrassed, but he did not shake her off.

"You are a good listener, George," she said. "It is seldom that I ken a man who hears me out like you do."

"Necessity," replied George. "I ken—as you say—but little of your country's history."

That was of course true, but in any case he liked the sound of Barbara's voice, her pleasant Scottish accent. It was a cheerful one which made him feel at ease. She spoke the English she thought he would understand, avoiding Scottish expressions whenever possible. George was pleased at this consideration, for once or twice on hearing

Scots converse apart from him, he had imagined for a while that they had been speaking in Gaelic. He was less pleased, however, when she began begging for compliments, asking how he liked her dress, hoping he would praise her hair or eyes, but avoiding for a time the awkward demand that he should compare her charms with those of Lynette.

From this high ground there was an excellent view over the city, which was mainly one long street from the castle to the Palace of Holyrood. George counted the spires he could see projecting above the rooftops and Barbara named each kirk in turn. The air was clear and the view across the city and the fields beyond extended right down to the sea at Leith. George pointed out ships and specks on a far horizon.

"Now tell me how you like our Scottish capital, Georgie," said Barbara. "Have you seen enough to give a judgment?"

"Aye," said George, "I'll admit it's a fair place, especially when viewed from a distance."

His reference to the infamous smells made Barbara smile, but George assured her that he would always be pleased to return to Edinburgh.

"In many ways it resembles the fair city in Germany which I made my home. Near there I lived with a well-known apothecary surgeon and attended the University. Besides the knowledge I gained in that newly founded but respectable seat of learning, I acquired many skills in medicine and surgery under the tutelage of Herr Brunner who modelled his practices on the teachings of a learned Swiss doctor. Yes, there was a castle up on a towering rock, mountains all around, salt works in the neighbourhood; but there, alas, the likeness ends; no ocean comes close to the confines of that city, only lakes—or should I call them lochs? Many lakes; magical, beautiful ones with snowcapped mountains backing them."

"How do they call this place you speak of?"

"Salzburg," said George. "The realm of a Prince Archbishop."

"Salzburg," repeated Barbara. "So far away and like our Edinburgh? You speak the English language well," she said admiringly."

"Thank you, but I had a friend with whom I served in the German war. He taught me English first but now I hear it all around me. It is not very difficult for a German or a Hollander."

"Wait a while, George Waldheim, and we will have you speak it like a Scot."

"Perhaps," said George. "There are words you say which sound more like the German than the English. 'Wir kennen' as you 'ken' and 'gehen in die Kirche' as you 'go to the kirk'. But no, Babbie, I am a good Englishman now. I cannot think that I would ever make a Scot."

They came to a little burn tumbling down through heather and bracken. Barbara sat down and took off her shoes. "Aah!" she shrieked as she dipped her feet in the cold water, but still she invited her new friend to come and take the same kind of punishment .

He reluctantly complied for a few moments, then finding no pleasure in it, soon withdrew his toes from the sparkling stream. Barbara stretched herself out on the grass. George thought she looked quite seductive lying there.

She began to laugh and his puzzled expression only stimulated more merriment. At last she explained.

"I was just a-thinking how ye'd look dressed up as a kilted Highlander."

She began to laugh again; George who could not imagine why he should cut an undignified figure in a kilt any more than a brawny Scotsman, only smiled at the improbability of a German surgeon in Cromwell's army ever appearing in such a costume.

"You are a very serious laddie, Master Waldheim," said Barbara. "It's all those Latin names of plants and cures you carry round in that scholar's head of yours."

"Oh no, Babbie, I am no great scholar," replied George modestly, seating himself besides her, "though I hope to be admitted to a doctorate when I leave my army service. It is the practice of my calling, rather than the study of physic, which gives me the greatest satisfaction."

"Then tell me; what do you care to do when free from duty apart from walking with young ladies?"

George blushed.

"I read of course, and when at home I like my garden. That will soon be a sight to see. I have planned it out anew with every kind of herb I need, and flowers to line the borders—some of which have scarce been seen before in England."

"Still serious, Master of Physic," declared Barbara. "Do you not confess to something wicked? A vice that would shock your Cromwell—dancing perhaps, the players, or perhaps some hardy sport? I do know you like to take a wee drop of something stranger than our ale. Did you never offend the staid burghers of your Salzburg with your wild behaviour?"

"Salzburg no longer," replied George. "When I came to England I made my home in Nantwich, a pretty town in Cheshire. But you are wrong Babbie. Cromwell would not censure me for taking pleasure, unless I did it to excess. Music is a solace. My father's second wife, Amalia, is an excellent musician—I do not call her mother for she is a mere three years older than I am. I have little skill myself, but it is always a great delight to hear her sing and play."

He felt a pang of shame that he had used the word 'father' instead of 'father-in-law.' Was he deliberately concealing the fact that he had a wife, or was it just a common figure of speech? No, he would tell her if she asked him. Babbie did not; she noticed nothing and chattered on.

"And how are you as a man of sports, my gentle physician? See, I will race you to yon bush."

Jumping up and still barefooted, Barbara began to run across the rough grass and heather of the open land to the stunted bush which she had indicated as the winning post. George was slow in deciding whether or not he should join in the fun, but the laughing girl turned and beckoned to him.

"Come on, Master Huntsman," she called. "Catch your prey!"

In fact he was quite a swift runner and began to gain on the girl who made for a patch of bracken beyond the bush. She turned again. To George she seemed an elemental spirit sent to tempt him as she ran down the hillside, the wind billowing her skirt, her hair streaming behind her, her laugh ringing out across the empty heathland.

"Come on my soldier laddie!" she cried. "Am I not a fair quarry? See, here I am, you have won."

She stopped suddenly and George ran into her. He caught her round the waist and the two tumbled into the bracken. Barbara made a short pretence of trying to wriggle free, then George found himself kissing her. He knew not how it came about; for a moment it was pleasing—then bitterness. He stood up.

"No, Babbie," he said. "It should not be."

"Georgie," whispered Barbara huskily, in her most appealing way. "Georgie, could you not find it in your heart to love a lass like me?"

George felt he could no longer avoid an answer, but still he wavered. "I could," he said, "but would I?"

"Aye but you would, you would," said Barbara jumping up and throwing her arms round his neck. She kissed him with an ardour which almost took his breath away.

"I know a wee place away over the burn," she said. "A shepherd's cot it is, but there's never a body in it."

George felt himself all aquiver. What could he do to shake off this girl? What was her power over him? She looked twice as beautiful now as she had done before; her ever changing expression fascinated him; he loved the pretty way she spoke.

Near the bottom of the hill, Barbara paused and opened her arms for George to run into; then again she teasingly turned and hurried on towards the distant shepherd's cot she had chosen as a love nest.

"Let your physic work upon me, Doctor Waldheim," she said. George was blinded by her magic. To him she was the Lorelei or a siren of Odysseus. On and on he hurried drawn by Barbara's power, seeming to be heedless of the tragedy and ruin this simple act would bring.

A dark cloud brooding over Arthur's Seat brought an immediate solution to George's stark dilemma, in the form of a heavy shower which caused Barbara to reject the idea of seeking shelter in a distant shepherd's cot. Instead, she suggested another evening assignment in George's room.

"Do not come down for supper, I will bring it up at ten—then or thereabouts."

She squeezed his hand and turned her head towards him.

"Why so glum my bonnie laddie?" she said in a voice which George feared he could not resist. "You will love me yet."

He felt self-conscious as they walked up Canongate and was pleased to reach the obscurity of the side streets.

Barbara's father treated his guest as obsequiously as before, adding more discomfort by his obvious insincerity to George's already troubled mind. He strode into his room and slammed the door. He pushed the books on his table to one side and supported his chin on his hands. Staring idly at its oaken top he studied the lines of the grain and the little smudges—dark marks which testified to long service—stains of ink, a small tobacco burn, the little grooves made by a previous visitor cutting up something with a sharp knife.

"Ach George, George Waldheim," he murmured. "What have you done to your self respect? All for a girl who cannot hold a candle to your own Lynette."

He began mumbling in German, cursing his weak and foolish action, praising the coming of the shower which he took to be a sign from God—a ram in the thicket which had stopped him at the fatal moment and given him a chance to redeem himself. How could he betray Lynette—his sweet, faithful wife? How could he disappoint his best friend, her father, who had entrusted her to his care? How could he soil a reputation which his general had praised so highly? He thought of how Lynette had scorned to associate with Captain Mynton. She had shown the strength that he had lacked. He must follow her

351

example and not allow this girl to break his will. He had sat so long in such a state of remorse that he had forgotten how wet he was. He rose, removed his outer garments, pulled off his boots, and placed his timepiece on the table. He drew the books and papers he had pushed aside towards him and began to sort through them. The sheet on which he had written "My dearest Lynette" was still there. Pressure of work had not allowed him to proceed further and his guilty conscience told him he would have been more honestly employed finishing a letter to his wife than walking out with young Mistress Douglas. But now he would take it up again. What should he write?—"My dearest Lynette. Today I took the air with the daughter of this house, embraced and kissed her and tacitly invited her to my bed." Were those 'Seals of Love' which he had bestowed so tenderly on Lynette, now cheapened to a common gift to be received by any wench with a modicum of charm? Could this stroll on Arthur's Seat be more important to him than the ride to Beeston Castle with Lynette? Was the sunshine warmer? Were the beauties of nature more intense than on that day when he had proposed by the River Weaver? Had they conspired with Babbie to turn his head?

"Nein! Niemals!" he called out in his characteristic way. But what should he do? Open the door and cruelly send the girl packing? Perhaps her appealing look would renew that temptation and it would be a fearful thing if he should weaken. He was fortunate in that his room was above the kitchen, and unlike most of the others, it had the blessing of a fireplace. He threw some faggots on the small blaze he had ignited to dry his wet clothes. The flickering light shone on the crude well-worn timbers of the door. Through this the temptress would come, and he would cry: "Begone!"

But what if at the last he should succumb to temptation, accept her wine and sweetmeats, and not refuse her favours? That door would not be opened!

The agitated man hurried across the room as if it were a matter of immediacy, and slammed the bolt across. He removed the key from the lock and returned to his table. He found a place in his book, and to save a candle he read by the dim firelight until his eyes forbade it. As he laid aside the volume, he heard that same low voice speaking and a gentle knock on the door,

"Let me in," it said, "I am sorry I am late."

George took up his pen and smoothed out the sheet headed "My dearest Lynette". He paused a moment before dipping his pen in the ink, then he began to write in a bold, clear hand.

The second knock was louder:

"George, are you asleep?"

He gave no reply, but wrote on:

"Our victory at Dunbar was complete. The Scots having been totally routed we came up to Edinburgh where we are now quartered. Believe me, dearest Lynchen, I have missed you sorely in these past weeks, all the more because the hope of an end to these troubles and our separation seems to be approaching—within our sight, yet just out of our grasp. That is the pity of it."

"George!" came the voice again in exasperation. "Let me in. I know that you are there."

The words began to flow from George's pen. He found that once more he was murmuring them, aloud. A blot dropped on the paper, but he ignored it and his pen scratched away.

"The bible tells us to love our wives. I need no such injunction to adore you, dear Lynette. It is said that men should love their spouses as their own bodies. That is a poor commandment, for the man who does not value a loving woman above his own life is not worthy of her."

He laid down his pen and looked towards the door which stood between him and an act of shame. He never meant to open it, yet why could he not call out the few commanding words? "Go away and leave a married man in peace!"

Barbara's exasperation had turned to anger. The handle rattled, the door shook;

"George, you are a villain!" she called. "Say why you do not open the door."

There was no reply.

One last bang from the infuriated girl followed, then a moment's silence.

She was going; now at last he would be left in peace. Then he heard a crash and a clatter as if something had been thrown or kicked, followed by retreating footsteps. He wrote the final words: "If ever I have done anything unworthy of you, dearest, put it down to human frailty and be assured that there was no malice in it. You are dearer to me than any other—you and our little Thomas. Be assured that you always will be."

He signed his name, folded and sealed his letter, then rose from his chair and went over to the fire to light a pipe of tobacco. He had gained a famous victory against that 'other self' we have in all of us, which sometimes surfaces and leads us on to uncharacteristic and foolish actions. He paced around the room as he smoked, then suddenly he stopped and knocked out his pipe. The situation which had seemed so serious to him, had now assumed the aspect of a comedy. He opened the door and saw the wreckage of his cold supper in a pool of spilt wine, and among it the pieces of a broken jug. A solitary tankard lay at the end of the passage, a long damp trail marking its way to the wall.

George laughed at the petty temper of the girl and at his own foolishness in that even for a moment he had thought of this woman as a substitute for Lynette.

"George!" he said, "you are a marvellous beggar who would ask for penny alms when possessing the riches of a king."

Next morning he was sufficiently composed to endure Barbara's black looks and he received her sarcasm without flinching.

"You retire early and sleep soundly, Master Waldheim," she said. "I see you did not even touch your supper."

George felt that no explanation for his action was necessary. He looked straight at the girl. Somehow that bright face had lost its lustre. He wondered why he had let it overcome his common sense.

"Some words, Mistress," he replied, "are better left unsaid—and some actions undone."

The atmosphere was relieved by the appearance in the next few weeks of another soldierboy for Barbara. Much younger than George, he was a musketeer in Colonel Monck's regiment. The ever enthusiastic young lady's passion flared up again for her new love, and her affair with George passed into history—at least it seemed so for a time; the next few weeks were full of incident in other ways and there was no time to brood on the past.

On December 24th Governor Dundas surrendered the castle and offered his services to Cromwell, though such a strong point could have withstood a much longer siege. The Scottish weather was wicked and many succumbed including Oliver himself, who after a short campaign in Fife, fell ill. The general had long been plagued by malarial agues—a hazard of life in his East Anglian fenland; in Ireland his health had broken down; now he suffered a relapse.

Though he only played a minor part in this crisis—for Oliver had his own physician, Doctor Goddard—George felt an awful weight of responsibility even when only asked for advice. But as the raw climate took its further toll, he was more and more involved in doctoring other members of Cromwell's staff. At last the Lord General, nursed by his faithful French valet, Jean Duret, who fell sick and died while tending his master, recovered sufficiently to give the lie to the constant rumours that he had died. Once more Oliver took upon himself the great burden of the campaign, only to be struck down a second time. The stone and a raging ague brought him—now a man of fifty two—to the very point of death. Notable physicians were sent from London to reinforce the team, but the Lord had plucked Oliver out of the grave and when Doctors Wright and Bate arrived, the general had recovered. George felt immense satisfaction, not simply because he knew that the Commonwealth needed Cromwell more than any other, but because his own efforts had contributed in some measure to saving the life of a great man.

He had not seen Mistress Douglas for many weeks. During Cromwell's first illness he had moved from the *'Globe'* inn to quarters close by Moray House. He did not find it such a sweet place, but he had perforce to accommodate himself to it—this being made easier by the fact that he spent much of his time out of his room.

Once or twice he passed Barbara in the street as she went laughing by with her handsome Englishman and George assumed that she had married him. This was occurring with great frequency; the bagpipes were skirling at the weddings of all sorts and qualities of persons, including the daughters of lairds or knights and the maidservants of the great burgesses of Edinburgh who were absent from the city.

He was surprised, therefore, when one evening the lady of the house announced Mistress Douglas would see him on a matter of urgency. She looked askance at Barbara as she showed her in. The girl's reputation had preceded her, and the good wife wondered why a seemingly upright young man like George should have business with a person of this class.

The fact that Mistress Douglas was pregnant was very obvious. She was ashamed to see George looking at the tell-tale protuberance.

"He's left me," she said simply.

"Your soldierfriend?" asked George

"Harry Garnett, He was wounded at Linlithgow and he still lies there."

"That should be no problem," said George optimistically. "Will he not send for you?"

"He denies responsibility for the bairn. He says it happened on that day we went to Arthur's Seat. All the world saw us go down Canongate. He says there are many who would testify that some physician-fellow from Cromwell's headquarters got me with child."

"But you know that it is not true," said George. "You would have had it so, but my sense of honour forbade it."

"Your sense of honour!" said Barbara harshly. "You led me to believe you loved me; then, you played that dastardly trick on me. You meddled with fire, George Waldheim. Believe me," she threatened, "it is dangerous to scorn a woman. At first I thought of many ways in which I could take my revenge, but I could never bring myself to the point of hurting you. Time tamed me and now here I am humbling myself and seeking help."

George was not visibly affected by this confession. "You err, Barbara. I did not love you then, nor do I now. If you loved me, I must beg your pardon for not having recognised that feeling in you. I took it for common desire, lightly felt and easily forgotten."

He rose from his chair and walked over to the window. For a few moments the clatter of a troop of horse passing on the cobbles outside prohibited further conversation. When they had gone by, he pronounced the words he had failed to say before, which would have saved them both much pain and misunderstanding.

"I did not say, Barbara, and for me it is a matter of deepest regret—I must tell you—"

He stumbled in his speech, even yet unable to bring out those fatal words as easily as he would have wished. "I must tell you now that I am married."

"Lynette?" she asked.

"Lynette," replied George, "and I have a son too—my little Thomas. Had you asked me, then I would doubtless have told you so, but something always held me back from spoiling the enjoyment of your company."

Barbara was shaking with anger. She rose and faced George.

"You are a deceiver, Master Waldheim," she said. "That was not common honesty. You mocked me when you locked me out of your room. You deceived your wife when you were with me on the mountain."

"A kiss was all I gave," said George offended at the not unjustified accusation of impropriety.

"One mere kiss! Is that not more than a small sound of the mouth—more than a sharp intake of breath? Does a kiss really mean naught to you?"

George paled, as once again he remembered his talk of 'seals of love' to Lynette, but he found new confidence.

"Why do you come to me now? What do you want?"

"I had hoped you still loved me a little, but I see I was in error. Now shameful as it seems, I can only invoke your pity. My father swears he will have no bastard in the house. With a bairn to feed, I will be without means or a roof over my head. What will I do? I dread to think that like many others I have known, I will end up as a common whore."

"God forbid, dear girl," said George sympathetically, as big tears rolled down her cheeks. "I will help you for the sake of your bairn and in memory of the few joyful hours spent in your company. This man will be found. There are articles in the ordinances of war to punish adultery, fornication and other dissolute behaviour at the War Council's discretion. I will speak to the General myself tomorrow and see that justice is done."

"You will speak to Cromwell?" said the girl nervously. "Will Harry not suffer? It will profit me nothing if he is shot or imprisoned."

"Never worry," replied George confidently. "Trust me Barbara— me and the Lord General."

She put her arms impetuously round his neck.

"Oh George, if only you had not married! Then, you can be assured, I would not have turned you over so easily to your Lynette."

She would have kissed him, but George placed two fingers on her lips.

"No, no, Barbara," he said quietly. "Let us not renew those temptations. The Lord has shown the way and I will hold to that. Go now! Do not be disappointed if there is no word immediately. Rest assured I shall not forget you."

Cromwell was sympathetic. His stern expression relaxed when George made the voluntary confession that he had been accused of improper behaviour for examining the sights of the city in the company of a young lady.

"Ha! So they say that of you, Physician. My enemies accuse me too of many things."

George was embarrassed. He had heard that the Royalists had spread a story that Cromwell pleasured a lady of the town and gave her twenty shillings a time for her services, but he dared not laugh, much as he was amused at the idea of a dissolute Cromwell.

The Lord General scanned the paper which bore the details of Barbara's complaint and tossed it on the table. George detected an expression of mixed anger and disgust.

"Mistress Barbara Douglas of the *'Globe'* Inn, where you were formerly quartered! Daughter of the house! Are you certain of this man's guilt?"

"I am satisfied, General, that the lady speaks the truth. It remains to be seen whether Garnett will admit his fault when confronted by authority."

"Tell me of this woman's family. Are they good Protestants?"

"Yes, I judge them to be so," declared George. "Her father was among the first to sign the Covenant."

"Hm," said Oliver, "Presbyterian. I would give no support to marriage with a Papist. It would be a great hazard to the cause and work we are engaged in, and displeasing to the Lord. I disapproved of such in Ireland and I can see necessity coming for an order banning marriages here without express consent—even with Presbyterians. We cannot have a nest of Royalism in our midst. But I will see to this case, Physician. Though it does not come within the normal duties of a Captain General, for your sake and for the maintenance of good order in the army, it will be done. He will admit his fault and marry the girl or he can expect the worst from me. When men can hang for theft or robbery of a few pence, will I allow fornicators and adulterers to suffer less?"

Cromwell was as good as his word and Private Garnett had to answer for his folly. No claim that George was responsible could be substantiated and his voluntary confession to Cromwell had taken the wind out of a potential accuser's sails. The girl was not proved to have had any other lover within the period of her pregnancy and Garnett was known as an adventurer, having been involved on other occasions with local girls in England and Ireland. To avoid arraignment by the Advocate General before a Council of War, he privately confessed his guilt and seemed to be fully repentant. He apologised to George, accepted the child as his own, and was ordered by the express command of the General to marry the girl promptly. Barbara, fearing the hostility of her father, whom even this solution did not satisfy, found an aunt in Dunbar who would take her in and went there to have her baby. George had hoped to hear some happy news, but then the storm burst upon, them.

The Scottish summer with its long and light days was smiling on the Army at last. A new campaign took Cromwell up to Perth, leaving the road to England open if Charles chose to take it. He thought it worth the risk. The Royalists would rally round the son's flag as they had done for the father. The Scots were with him this time, better led and under the rightful king of both countries. Cromwell, their greatest threat, was well away from the road to England, almost in the Highlands. Those were his expectation, so Charles, now proclaimed king of England, led his army southwards down the western side of the country, well-trodden by Scottish armies in these campaigns.

The Scots believed that they had out-generalled Cromwell—but had they? Or had he allowed them to march into England to trap them, in country less favourable to men of the North, where he could pounce on them and destroy them?

On his return to Leith, George quickly rode over to the *'Globe'* inn to find out what he could about Barbara. The landlord greeted him sullenly, his deference and affability had gone. He affected to know little of his daughter. She had married her Sassenach and had had a bairn. He believed the brat had died. Was she now in Edinburgh? He had no idea. For aught he knew or cared she was still biding in Dunbar. There was no time to find out more about her, so George wrote a short letter which her father grudgingly accepted to pass on to her. In it he expressed regret at the loss she had suffered, wished her happiness as Mrs Garnett, and hoped she would be reunited with her husband as soon as the present campaign was over. He did not mention his own relationship with her, except in the last few words.

360

"Our friendship was a thing which sprang up and died on an autumn day. It was brief and had no deep meaning, for my heart was elsewhere, but even though I believe that your affection for me was light and unstable, I will always think kindly of you. Think too, sometimes, just a little of that day on Arthur's Seat."

29. A BROKEN ARMY

The chase was on; Nantwich was seething with excitement as report after report came through:

"August 5th: The Scots are in Carlisle."

"August 15th: They have passed Preston and reached Wigan without a battle to deplete them."

"August 17th: They have reached Warrington and the bridge over the River Mersey."

Now they were less than thirty miles away and would arrive in Nantwich, if it were on their route, in less than two days. Warning bells were rung; criers read out proclamations; the reputation of the Scots as marauders made the prospect of their coming fearful. This was "forty eight" all over again and now they were approaching as a fighting force under the effective leadership of the experienced General Leslie, not as dispirited fugitives fleeing from the might of Cromwell.

But more cheerful news came through as well—the Lord General was in hot pursuit. The hare had a good start, but the hounds were swifter. Major General Lambert was hard on the heels of this pretended king and racing to Warrington, even overtook his quarry in an attempt to break the bridge and prevent the passage of the Scots over the Mersey.

All this was dangerously near Nantwich, which no longer had a permanent garrison. Gone too were the old mud walls which had held off the Cavaliers in 1644. Surely it would be on the line of advance—a place for a moment's rest and the replenishment of stocks by plundering.

Lynette's feelings were ambivalent. On the one hand she feared the entry of hordes of wild Scots, but on the other hand this renewal of war would probably mean the homecoming of George. Cromwell would crush these invaders and then her husband could return to civilian life. Her calculations did not include the possibility of a defeat. A complete victory would mean the close of hostilities—and that was what Lynette expected from Oliver. For her, as for her husband, this man could scarcely do wrong, so much had George's hero-worship of Cromwell infected Lynette. She and little Thomas with a solitary servant were living in the Leys' old home. Tom had moved out to Walbury with Amalia and the younger children, but his eldest daughter found pleasure in their frequent visits and those of Will and Alice, this compensating her to some extent for her separation from George.

On the evening of the sixteenth, Tom rode over to Nantwich. His face was serious when his daughter greeted him. There had been news both good and bad, but the scales had tipped on the grimmer side. He suggested to Lynette that she should leave:

"I would rather stay, Father," said the young woman decisively. "Many of the townsfolk are going, I know, but I should not like to leave my home to the mercy of strangers and wander off into the country. I know I could come to you at Walbury—but would I be any better off there?"

"Then I will remain here to protect you," replied Tom, rather proud of his courageous daughter. "Amalia and the children are close enough to Will if any danger should threaten them."

He was able to give Lynette the latest news.

"There have been arrests today," he said. "Two gentlemen accused of favouring the cause of the Stuarts were taken in my sight. Others are being collected from all over the county, and it is reported that they will be taken to Chester Castle. As you know, the local levies have left to join Cromwell, so we must rely on the Army returning from the north to ward off our enemies. General Lambert failed to stop them at Warrington; he drew up on Knutsford Heath and after skirmishing would have given battle; only the Scots refused to fight. Charles Stuart would not accept a duel with John Lambert, but passed on to take up cudgels with a greater enemy, Oliver Cromwell. I fear there is insufficient power to stop them here, though more local forces are being raised and I expect them to arrive among us by midday tomorrow."

Lynette called in the servant for help in preparing her father's bed and supper. Tom went to see to his horse and for a moment she was left alone. A sudden knock startled her. It was not her father's. If he knocked at all, he always gave a light tap before entering. This was a loud, imperious summons to the front door. An irrational feeling of anxiety, as if she expected a fierce Highlander to be standing on the step, assailed Lynette as she opened the door. A youth saluted her respectfully.

"A message for Major Thomas Ley."

He handed her the paper he was holding in his hand, just as her father returned from the stable. Tom hastily scanned it.

"More news. The Earl of Derby has been routed at Wigan. He came from the Isle of Man and helped to raise the county where he is Lord. But many had more sense. They would not support one who brings in a foreign army to regain his crown. An army of Scots! The very name is abhorred in those parts. There is a deep-seated enmity which goes back to the days of Robert Bruce who harried their land— and earlier. Then they remembered 'forty eight' and the time when our Oliver fell on them at Preston and Warrington. Those who did rally to him—the malcontents, the Papists, of which many live in those parts, the King's men who would regain what they have lost, not scrupling to use the claymores and lances of the Scot to set their Charles up again—they had the worst of it at Wigan Lane. Colonel Lilburne drubbed them in a bloody fray and many are believed killed. It is reported that the Lancashire Cavalier, Tyldesley, fell in the fight, but if my informant is to be believed, Derby has escaped to join Charles Stuart."

"I am pleased at the victory," said Lynette, but she displayed no great emotion. She was thinking of George.

The morning haze lifted early on the eighteenth and the sun climbed up a cloudless sky. This was true campaigning weather. The first few hours, spent in nervous anticipation, passed slowly for Tom and Lynette. Once or twice a false alarm was sounded and the two watchers hoped against hope that they would be bypassed. Then, about

364

midday, the thudding of hooves dashed any such expectations in them. Lynette looked out to see a party of Scottish horsemen, well mounted, carrying long, deadly lances with iron pegs on the side, coming along the lane which led across the heath to the townend.

"It is their forlorn hope," said Tom "—an advance party. The main body will not be far behind. Come inside, Lynette, but do not lock the door. It will only encourage them to break in."

However, the horsemen rode past and there was no more sound from outside except for distant voices. Hearing nothing, for some time other than this indistinct babble, Tom decided to walk to the High Town to investigate. It seemed certain that the Scots had come down several streets and had occupied the town centre. Lynette promised to go to a neighbour's for safety until her father's return.

It was true—the square, churchyard, and streets down to the river, were full of Scotsmen—lancers, Lowland musketeers and kilted Highlanders. More were arriving in columns, six abreast, preceded by their officers, marching to the sound of bagpipes, fifes and drums. There were few citizens on the streets: most of those who were, looked on sullenly. A number of them tried to raise a cheer when some important-looking officer went by, but the black looks of the majority strangled their applause at birth.

A whisper went round: "Charles Stuart comes!" Nobody dared to say "King". Tom pushed his way through the crowd as a swarthy young man, towering above the others in height and significance, rode by. Tom looked up and regarded his dark countenance. Charles's gaze swept past him and through the onlookers, searching for some sign of rejoicing. A few of those previously suppressed, emboldened by the royal presence, tried again to raise a cheer. Charles, grateful for a small mercy, reined his horse and faced the crowd. He smiled and waved his hat. Tom had a chance to study him for a few minutes. It was only a brief encounter, but he had become a good judge of men, and saw nothing in that Stuart face to convince him of its owner's worth and sincerity.

Roger Wilbraham, whose father, Thomas, had entertained that other king in 1617 at Townsend House, rode close by him, and some others in his train Tom knew as English gentlemen. It was a dangerous game; in a week or two they could be in the Tower for underestimating the boldness and power of Cromwell. Charles having passed, Tom entered the Crown Inn to find his friend Mr Clutton. This gentleman, as always in the forefront on these occasions, had all the latest news about the entry of the Scots. A demand had been sent requiring the inhabitants of Nantwich to pay three thousand pounds before five o'clock on the following morning to furnish the Royalists with shoes and other necessities. Mr Wilbraham had promised to make all possible efforts to save the town from plundering. Arms and cheese had already been loaded into waggons, but there were no reports as yet that their enemies had begun indiscriminate stealing.

"At least we are sure that they will be on their way again tomorrow," said Clutton comfortingly. They are not likely to hang around long enough to start systematic plundering with John Lambert on their tail. Did you see their king?"

"I saw him who would be our king," replied Tom, "but I myself would have no king at all unless it be a Cromwell."

"A Cromwell?" queried Clutton, who was republican in sympathy.

"You have fought, and would have us fight again, to change the House of Stuart into the House of Cromwell?"

"Let him who is fittest wear the crown," replied Tom. "It is a law of nature."

Lynette was relieved that the danger from the Scots was not as great as she had imagined, but she slept badly that night as her excitement mounted. Tom had to explain what exactly he imagined Cromwell's plan to be; much of it was, however, pure speculation for reports were very sketchy and rumours abounded.

On the following day the town was quiet once again. God had smiled on Nantwich; the citizens had been let off lightly. Mr Wilbraham made it known that he had been chiefly instrumental in saving the town from plundering and no one chose to disagree with him. This claim he duly recorded in his journal so that not only his contemporaries but posterity should be informed.

The danger over, Tom rode back to Walbury and Lynette's state of high excitement turned to impatience at the lack of news. George must be somewhere in the south. If only Cromwell's army had come through Nantwich instead of these Scots, then she would perhaps have seen her dear husband. Even a glimpse of his handsome figure riding by, his cloak folded dashingly over his shoulder, his hat on at a slightly rakish angle—just a glimpse—a blown kiss—would have satisfied her. Or perhaps a word would have been possible; even that glance which needs no words—which says "I love you Lynette"—would have ensured that she should suffer no disappointment.

Young Thomas was a comfort to her. The little man toddled around now and would run up to mammy, putting his baby arms around her as if to compensate for her missing George. He could hardly know that he had a father, yet it was as if instinct told him that he had to play the man and say by this simple act: "I will love you and comfort you, dear mother, while my daddy is away." All this was fancy, but such imaginings were a solace to Lynette.

The golden days of summer went on though broken by occasional thunderstorms. News arrived that Charles Stuart had entered Worcester, while Cromwell with an army twice as large, was threatening him from Warwick.

"He beat them with half their numbers at Dunbar and made them run like rabbits," said Lynette. "What will he do now when he has double their force?"

On September the first, weary of waiting and speculating, she joined her father and stepmother at Walbury, leaving her servant, Edward, to look after the house. It was nearly two weeks since the Scots had ridden on and no clear picture of the situation in the South had emerged. Worcester was a strong place, a faithful city to its king like Cheshire's own county town, graced too with a fine cathedral. Here it was that the first engagement of these civil wars took place. Would it be the scene of the last? Charles had it well garrisoned. The bridges would have been blown up and cannon mounted. Would there be a long siege and many casualties?

The next few days passed quietly. Lynette spent much of her time in her father's garden which surpassed that of her uncle both in its situation, the neatness of layout and the variety of plants. Amalia had spent a long time in earnest discussion with George on the occasion of his last visit and the newly-planned garden was the result of these conferences.

There was not much to do—stroll by the river, watch the little fishes darting hither and thither in the clear water, gather an armful of wild flowers, sit on the bank and look out for a heron or water vole. She had little Thomas for company; his needs had to be catered for, but otherwise she had few household duties, and time crept at a snail's pace. She began to think of returning to Nantwich and her responsibilities there, as hour after hour passed and one day succeeded another.

Friday began as just one more day. The warm sun of the morning glowed down on sleepy, little Walbury. The weariness of constant expectancy had overcome Lynette's youthful senses; she had slept more soundly than for many nights. The fresh air and exercise had contributed. Thursday afternoon had been glorious; she and little Thomas had walked along the bank of the river and through the woods. He was beginning to talk and at first he ran by her side excitedly pointing out something which to Lynette was a common sight, but which in the innocence and enthusiasm of his boyhood, seemed to him like the start of an adventure. Then he had tired and she had carried him home. That fresh air and exercise had worked its magic on Thomas too. The child still slept as Lynette opened the shutters to let the sun stream in. A distant sound, scarcely audible at first but growing gradually louder, was coming from the direction of the town. She threw open the window.

It was an even, constant noise, not like a faraway explosion or a clap of thunder, nor like trumpets, drums, or martial music, but melodious and sweet—a sound befitting a bringer of joyful news.

"Bells!" cried Lynette, leaning out of the casement to hear their message better. "Bells! A victory has been won!"

Suddenly a clamour ten times louder than that which came from the distant steeple, broke out in silent Walbury.

"Father! Amalia!" cried Lynette throwing on her cloak over her nightgown and rushing to the door.

"Listen to the bells! They are ringing for victory. Cromwell has defeated the Scots!"

The battle fought on September 3rd, the Day of Dunbar, was as complete a triumph as the former one had been, but the people of Nantwich had not seen the last of the Scots. Driven from Worcester by Cromwell's hurricane, they were racing northwards to gain the safety of their homeland, but their anxiety to escape would not necessarily forbid plundering. The local levies which had united with the forces of Cromwell now joined in the pursuit of the fleeing Scotsmen and armed bands were formed to round up the stragglers. Tom rode with one of these parties. In the years of comparative inactivity since Naseby, he had recovered most of the use of his right arm. He suffered sometimes from severe headaches and twinges of pain in his back and shoulder from wounds received both in the German and English wars, though in Amalia's care his general health had improved since his return to civilian life.

The first of these expeditions was the most dramatic, the others were only a matter of taking individual fugitives. A strong body of Scots, reported to be about a thousand in number, were making their way across Cheshire, hoping that they would outdistance their pursuers, avoid the local forces and reach their homeland. Tom's troop had gathered in a few tired cavalrymen, footslogging after having abandoned their equally weary horses. They became aware of this larger party of the enemy close to them, noted their position and line of advance, but were unable to oppose or capture them. Consequently Tom decided that they would not come out into the open, only shadow them until the pursuing English came up or they reached a town where they could reinforce their own company.

The market town of Sandbach stood in front of them—the very place to which, long before, Will and his devoted Puritans had marched to vent their wrath on the ancient crosses. The approach to the place was open; the view was not obscured by trees. Tom's troop stood off as a straggling column of horsemen kicked up the dust along the straight road which led into Sandbach. When the Scots had passed, Major Ley motioned to his men to move up closer, and as they approached, it became plain that something was going on inside the town or just beyond it. Tom spurred on his horse and a scene of great confusion and devastation met his eyes as he came out on to the common where a fair had been held that morning. As the Scots had ridden through, the townsmen had fallen upon them armed with clubs, billhooks, staves, and even poles from the booths and stalls, belabouring their enemies with these primitive but nonetheless effective weapons, and dragging them from their horses as they tried to defend themselves with swords and lances. Some of the Scots had ridden on, others tumbled from their horses by the blows of the rustics, had drawn up at the end of the common.

"They fire! They fire!" went up a shout and the townsmen ran helter-skelter towards the houses. Tom and his men dashed forward, but the Scots had no mind to stand and fight.

"I wonder if they really have any powder left," remarked Tom to Richard Clutton who was riding by his side.

Whether it had been a dangerous posture or just a bluff, the Scots lowered their weapons, seized horses and galloped away, apart from two bright sparks who demonstrated that at least they had the capability to fire by loosing off a couple of shots at the flying Cheshire men; then after a defiant shout at Tom and his troopers which sounded something like a war cry, they charged off after their comrades. Others were coming in and the townsfolk, more confident since these new fugitives made no show of firing at them, returned to the attack. The horses they had turned loose trotted across the fields or had taken to grazing on the neighbouring pastures. The mounted Nantwich men cornered many of their foes after pursuing them over the common or through the town.

In the square Tom stopped; a Scottish soldier was sprawled across the steps of the former fine Saxon cross, now a mere stump. He stirred and raised his head as Major Ley approached him over the cobbles. To Tom it was sixteen eighteen all over again; he remembered how he had surveyed the damage done by Will's zealous Puritans. Then it was broken crosses, now it was a broken army.

"You are my prisoner," he said quietly. The man rose unsteadily with a weary, dazed look on his face.

"Aye," he replied with complete resignation. "Aye, there's no disputing that."

Returning to the fairground, Tom found that the fight was over. Thirty had fallen in this skirmish; more than a hundred had been captured. Plans were being made to attack the remaining Scots on a hill not far distant, to which they had retreated to rest and reform. One of the leaders, fancying himself as a second Cromwell, was working out the details of a dawn attack. He approached Tom for some expert advice, but the major declined to cooperate.

"Leave their fate in the hands of others," he said. "We have done enough and there is no point in risking more lives. Worn out and dispirited as they are, I doubt that they will ever reach Scotland in safety."

The prisoner he had taken personally in the square, was an officer—a lieutenant, who once the shock of his capture had worn off, became friendly and very talkative. Tom had no animosity towards the Scots as a nation, and he found the company of this lieutenant on the road back to Nantwich, both entertaining and informative.

It seemed that the Cheshire volunteers had missed a great prize. In the party which had retreated through Sandbach there had been two generals. The officer would not name them, but Tom took him to mean Lieutenant General Middleton and General Leslie. If that were true and he had been able to take one of these men, it would have been a feather in the cap of an ageing, retired major. But Fate had not allowed him that luxury.

The lieutenant was confident that Charles Stuart—he too was careful not to say 'king'—was still at large. He had seen him in the thick of the battle as he came out of the Sudbury Gate in Worcester at the head of his troops. He had admired him then for his bravery, but this feeling had turned to disillusionment when Charles had ridden off to the protection of the oak trees in the nearby forest and had left his army to its fate. He was full of admiration for Cromwell, though it was awe inspired by fear, not by love. He detailed the move by Oliver across a bridge of boats to attack the Royalists holding the city, and drew a picture of the Lord General leading his own men on, riding up and down and exposing himself recklessly to the fire of the enemy. The grim struggle when the Royalists had been pushed into Worcester, the streets blocked by dead men and horses, the withering fire of their own artillery turned on the Scots by Cromwell's men, were described in vivid detail by the talkative prisoner. Two thousand killed, nine

371

thousand prisoners and a mere four thousand escapees, among them this John Mackenzie, lieutenant in the regiment of General Middleton—and still proud of it.

"The Scots had to fight Cromwell," he said. "Against the devil we would have had a chance, against Oliver—never!"

Leaving Mackenzie in Nantwich, Tom parted from his companions and rode slowly back to Walbury. He was unaccustomed to such exertions after his years of retirement from soldiering. As he came close to the house, he thought he saw Lynette waving from the window in a more excited way than that usually occasioned by her bubbling, youthful spirits. Then another figure appeared by her side— a young man with light hair and a trim, pointed beard—unmistakeably his old friend, George—his son-in-law. The door opened and the two of them came out to meet their father. Tom dismounted and embraced George. Not to be left out, although their parting had only lasted eight hours, Lynette threw her arms round her father.

"A great victory," said Tom as they walked back to the house. "It has set the seal on Oliver's distinguished career as a general. He regarded George.

"I am surprised to see you so soon," he said. "When do you return to the Army?"

"Oh Father, dear Father," cried Lynette, her happiness frothing over as she clung to her husband's arm:

"He is not returning to the Army. He is to be Doctor Waldheim."

30. SWORDS INTO PLOUGHSHARES

There were two things which George brought back with him from the wars of which he was especially proud. The first was the Dunbar medal. To celebrate the great victory it was decided to strike a commemorative medal to be issued to both officers and men, the first time such a one had been awarded in this way. The medallist, Thomas Simon, journeyed to Edinburgh, and despite Cromwell's protests that he did not want his effigy on it, he produced a portrait of the Lord General. The medal showed a profile of Cromwell with a scene from the battle and the inscription *"The Lord of Hosts"* (the Word at Dunbar) above his head, the obverse depicting the Parliament of England in session.

Young Thomas, who was allowed to hold it in his hands and admire the memento of a great victory, took it for a piece of money.

"That is the king," he said in a prophetic fashion. George smiled at Lynette.

"No, little man," he replied. "We have no king, but if ever one is crowned again, this man is my choice."

The second thing he produced from his voluminous wallet was no less interesting and much more important for George. It was a letter from the Lord General himself, recommending Army Physician Waldheim for the reception of a doctorate at Oxford University. Cromwell, recently appointed Chancellor, titular Head of that august institution, wrote to the Vice-chancellor, "his very worthy friend, Doctor Greenwood," in glowing terms of his physician.

> *"I have had much experience of this gentleman's fidelity, diligence and abilities,"* he wrote. *"Master Waldheim attended a well-known German University and has served as surgeon and physician in the army in England, Ireland and Scotland,*

having done much good to the officers and soldiers by his skill and industry. He has desired me to recommend him for the obtaining of a degree of doctor in the science of medicine. Wherefore I earnestly desire you to give him your best assistance for the obtaining of the same degree when he shall repair to you. By doing whereof, as you will encourage one who is willing and ready to serve the Public, so you will lay a very great obligation upon,

Sir, your affectionate friend,

Oliver Cromwell."

It was a great moment for George. He had determined that upon receiving this degree he would become a London physician. The Lord had guided him throughout his rise in the world. Yes, He had been very gracious to him through the intervention in his life of three men— Thomas Ley, Leopold Brunner and Oliver Cromwell, as he progressed from being an orphaned peasant boy in war-ravaged Baden to the status of a respected and learned physician, Doctor of one of the premier universities in Europe. He said all this to Lynette and she concurred.

"Do not forget your own efforts, George," she added loyally. "God helps those who help themselves."

Charles Stuart had been luckier than the faithful Earl of Derby in avoiding capture by Cromwell's soldiers and escaping to the Continent. The spreading branches of the oak tree had screened the royal person. It had indeed proved *"softer than men's hearts"* for the Cavaliers. But the Earl was reviled for more than mere loyalty to the Crown. He was charged with responsibility for the massacre at Bolton and was returned to that town for execution. Blackshaw, who had been present on that fateful day, rode over to see the hated Earl beheaded. Derby had been the enemy of everything which Luke held dear, but though he admitted no actual pity, he admired the Earl's demeanour on the scaffold and came to the conclusion that the execution was unnecessary. For his part, Oliver Cromwell was sure of God's hand in the triumph.

"It is for aught I know a crowning mercy," he had said after the battle. It was certainly a fitting end to a great man's military career. It was a watershed of the time, dividing the victories of war from the necessary, "no less renowned" victories of peace which should follow to achieve a settlement of the nation. The sole authority, the Rump of the Long Parliament, needed reformation; the kind of church suitable for the newly-awakened nation was to be decided. In foreign affairs, with whom should the Protestant Commonwealth throw in its lot? With Catholic Spain or with Catholic France, Spain's rival and England's ancient enemy? The Netherlands too! Here was an even thornier problem, for though they were Protestants, the commercial policy of the Dutch was a strong threat to English trade.

As usual the wars had left their toll of misery. Beggars roamed the countryside and invaded the towns; the prisons were full of debtors; the large standing army and navy were a drain on the country's economy. It was said at the time that it was a good world for nobody except the lawyers.

Cromwell urged the government to relieve the oppressed, to hear the groans of the poor prisoners and to reform the abuses of all professions.

"If there is anyone who makes many poor to make a few rich," he wrote, "that suits not a Commonwealth"; and he prayed that "justice and righteousness, mercy and truth should flow from the Parliament as a thankful return for the great victory at Worcester to our gracious God."

For Thomas Ley the actual division between war and peace had come earlier, discounting the minor skirmishes after Worcester and the part he had played in them. Nevertheless, he too felt this to be the dividing line for him as for others. Even after his withdrawal from active service, the fact that the war was continuing—or could be renewed—had always given him a sense of uncertainty. Now it seemed that for the foreseeable future the settlement of the nation was to be a peaceful one in the hands of the Parliament and Lord General.

Will's life had hardly changed since he became a schoolmaster except in a brief period when war had flashed upon him in 1644. Yet he noticed this dividing line just as strongly as the others. His battles had been fought in the mind and on the pages of his diary but they were as real to him as those fought out on a bloody field.

For Lynette it meant the greatest change of all. The country girl had hardly ever strayed beyond the boundaries of Cheshire. The prospect of being at the centre of things in London filled her with anticipation and excitement. Like her mother, Kate, she was not content to leave all matters of religion and politics to the men. The return of her father, who encouraged her enquiries, had quickened her interest in the happenings of the day. She was immensely attracted by the prospect of being mistress of a London household. Lynette found it easy to combine her feminine responsibilities with her more masculine concerns. She was a whole woman and her happiness with her husband was complete. The harmonic blend in her character of these differing traits appealed strongly to George; his aberration in Scotland and his struggle against temptation were soon forgotten in the domestic bliss which followed. On his return he had told Lynette the story of his short friendship with Barbara Douglas. He had flinched from mentioning it in a letter to his 'Lynchen,' for he feared that in writing the story, it would appear cold and perhaps deadly. He believed that when he could face Lynette, it would be warmed and altered by the charm of his person, the sincerity of his regret that it had ever started, and the pride he would show that he had allowed it to go no further.

"Is that all?" she asked when he had finished. "Who shall be free from the wiles of the devil, when Our Lord himself suffered temptation? Our love went through a testing time and I rejoice that it proved to be so firm, that not only did it survive but it was even strengthened. Satan chose to tempt you—a man far away from his loved ones with no one to lean on for support—but you shocked him. I am sure he will not approach you in that guise again. So we must not bewail events which confirmed our love."

"My heart and mind are barred against him," said George. "It was a little thing in Edinburgh—a little thing which could have been a greater one."

"Without the strength of our love," rejoined Lynette.

George embraced her.

"The strength of our love," he repeated, and these were the last words ever spoken about the incident.

Since her marriage, Lynette had adopted an Amalia style in dress and her attitude towards strict Puritanism remained unchanged. To her it was essential that young Thomas should grow up in a religious but not bigoted household. She was lucky in that all her nearest and dearest, with the exception of Uncle Will, whose influence had now diminished, agreed with her outlook on life.

Notwithstanding all these bright hopes for the future, the day of parting was a sad one. On the previous Sunday the whole family assembled in church—Tom, Amalia and their three children, Will, Alice, George, Lynette and little Thomas—to hear an inspiring sermon from Mr Malbon.

The minister showed pride in the achievements of the Commonwealth, but expected it to be ruled by godly men and the present body in no way matched up to expectations. There were honest men in it, but many were corrupt, enriching themselves with bribes, pluralities and monopolies—fortune seekers not public servants. Malbon charged his listeners to play their parts in the new era to the full. Unlike Tom and George who would set a crown on Oliver's head, he bid them act only as agents of the Lord without any pretension to personal greatness, for as he observed at regular intervals during his sermon: "Christ not man is King."

He spoke of the parting and assured them that God would continue to bless both those who were leaving and those who remained in Walbury. The Lord's promise to His people was a true comfort—the greatest gift which could be offered to them. He had assured His disciples of it before His ascension into Heaven, and those who were leaving could be certain that true believers would be united in Christ with the ones they loved when earthly distance separated them. Thus their Saviour had spoken:

"Lo! I am with you always, even unto the end of the world."

The wheel has turned, Reader! Judge for yourself their proud claim:

"GOD WITH US."

Lightning Source UK Ltd.
Milton Keynes UK
UKOW040135011212

203021UK00001B/53/P

9 781781 766798